THE LOST RING OF DESTINY

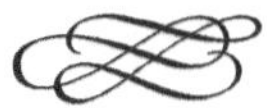

ANDREA H ROME

ISBN 979-8-9898225-2-2 [paperback]

ISBN 979-8-9898225-3-9 [ebook]

Library of Congress Control Number: 2025907066

Printed in the United States of America.

10 9 8 7 6 5 4 3 2 1

Cover design and artwork by Michael Perry

❀ Created with Vellum

WORKS BY ANDREA H ROME

The Standard Book of Anything (2024)

The Lost Ring of Destiny (2025)

*For Bev and Jim Huckaba,
the ideal grandparents for a girl who loves books, math, and the Marx Brothers.*

PRUTIAN TRIBAL LANDS
(DISPUTED TERRITORY)
LUVITT
YARVULE
BONWHITE
NORTHERN COLONIES
HEMNISVILLE
FRIDERA
ESNANIA
The Silver Nightingale
THE HIGH PLAINS
ZANIT
FUGEA
ANTILLEI MOUNTAINS
FARROW
BROOKERBY
EPERILA
DRECOVIA
EXETON
KAROKI
EVEDERELL
ARRENMORE
THE SUN CORRIDOR
ABINGDON
GILLAMOR
BRILDONIA
FRIENDSHIP SEA
TO AGLEN

The Silver Nightingale
Nomadic Camp
Quarantine
Rocky Sea
Smugglers Cave
Mining Town, Abandoned
Antillei Mountains

PROLOGUE

Sam Monterey couldn't feel his face anymore. The icy wind pounded his exposed skin without mercy, and he ducked his chin into his collar, seeking respite. He had been trudging through the snow for what felt like hours, scanning the blurry horizon for signs of civilization. The sky was growing darker, and he wouldn't survive the long, cold night.

"Where did that bitch send me?" he muttered for the umpteenth time, rubbing his hands together to warm them. His dark hair, normally neatly combed and waved, was crusted in ice.

Earlier today he had been in Arrenmore. In the Gray Horse resort and spa. *His* resort and spa. The weather there had been balmy, and he wore only a thin collared shirt and linen trousers. His designer clothing provided little protection from the ice pellets pummeling him now. With a simple flick of a map, Emaline Strider had sent him to a frozen wasteland.

Sam growled. Em Strider. The source of his misfortune. Her thieving parents had reduced Arrenmore to ruin, and Em had continued the trend. Keeping secrets. Destroying his livelihood. Sending him here. But she would pay. If he ever got out of this hellhole, she was target number one. And then Anne and Farrigan Strider. And then the boy with the dog.

The thought of revenge warmed Sam as he continued to crush the powdery snow beneath his Brildonian leather boots. His feet were like bricks, so deeply frozen that they felt like they were no longer a part of him.

His mind cast back to the moment of his banishment. Em had bested him. He hung helplessly in a net, fallen off a step she had purposely designed to collapse. She had double-tapped his finger on a map. Then the world spun, the colors around him swirling into a vortex, and he was deposited in a snowdrift.

"Think Sam. What was on the map?" He pushed his exhausted brain to remember, if only to forget the stabbing numbness of cold.

He remembered Esnania in the center of the map. He had been hanging upside down, but the Antillei Mountains were clear enough. Em had guided his finger to the periphery. So, he was north. Sam rolled his eyes. Obviously, he was north. Did this look like bleeding Aglen? So Fridera, then. Or the Northern territories. He furrowed his brow, trying to concentrate. Did Em guide him to the corner or center top of the map? He thought the corner. But what did it matter his longitude? The latitude was killing him either way.

He stopped on a crest to scan the horizon again, squinting against the wind. In the distance, he spotted flickering light—signs of life. Perhaps he would survive, after all. He could get back home. Rebuild the Gray Horse, which Em had likely burned to the ground in his absence. Destroy the Striders using their own warehouse of plundered magical items. Make Em wish she had never been born.

Feeling hope spark within him, he stumbled toward the lights in the distance.

CHAPTER 1

In fairy stories and legends, everything happens in threes. Three brothers. Three monumental tasks. Three choices for the hero. This scholar allows that, if these stories hold a modicum of truth, the rule of threes does not hold. Real life is more complicated.

"An Analysis of Legends and Folk Tales"
The Standard Book of Anything

Two Months Later

Most successful people find that after a victory, there is a lull. A breath. A return to normal that is comforting to all but the victor. For worse than danger and strife is the feeling that one is not needed anymore. And what a person does with that pause determines how they will get on with the business of living.

Em Strider was not handling the lull well.

She had saved her town. She had traveled into the unknown and brought back a magical healing herb and chopped down the warding tree of protection, which saved Brookerby from the ugly magical influence it had wrought. But now, rest felt like sloth, and the fear that she had done the most important thing she would ever do rushed through her at unexpected moments, leaving her breathless. So instead of appreciating the return to normalcy, she found herself on the bustling streets of Drecovia looking for someone she didn't know.

It was market day, and the whole town seemed to be out shopping at the same time. Em was not accustomed to navigating large crowds, and more than once she had to apologize for bumping a woman carrying a loaf or jostling a man toting a crate. She even apologized when someone bumped into her; the woman gave her such a look of disgust that the words tumbled out before Em could stop them. It was foolish—she was apologizing for existing. But that's how things had gone the past few months.

Her client in Drecovia was a Northern man who wished to remove his unbreakable oath. She continued to scan the crowd for him as she ducked and dodged. Since "Northern" was her only descriptor, she assumed dark hair with swarthy skin. Black hair should be easy to spot in the countryside of Esnania.

She had discovered a few months ago how to remove her own unbreakable oath—a painful affliction that caused pounding headaches and sharp stabbing sensations throughout the body when thoughts drifted toward the oath topic. It was the worst kind of censorship, administered by the empress of the realm. Em's own oath was related to her town's warding tree. She had helped Liam get rid of his oath too—also tree related. Then, by chance, she helped another person remove theirs, and word spread: "Meriwell gave me your name," they would tell her. Or, "I heard you cured Dremmel."

Her expanding reach meant no afflicted person had ever contacted her without a reference. They all had ties to previous clients and the warding trees. Until now. The person she was meeting had no connection. The note had come to the *Brookerby Leaflet* office with no return address and no signature. Minimal communication and lack of context felt dangerous.

Gram warned her not to go. Her dearest friend, former guardian, and roommate had called her foolish. Reckless. She had been quite forceful about it, in a way that made Em stiffen at the memory of this morning's fight. Although she didn't have the right to dictate how Em spent her time, the woman was skilled at making Em feel the wrongness of her choices.

But Em had gone anyway. If someone needed to be released from the pain of an oath, she would take the risk.

A group of children shoved by her, pushing Em to the side of the road. As she regained her balance, she eyed a ribboned blue dress in the nearest storefront. "Mendel's," she murmured as she drifted over to the brick building. She was woefully inept when it came to fashion, but any dress that expertly crafted had to belong to her tailor. She tilted her head back, and indeed, Mendel's name was on the sign. This must be his flagship store. The one he had built his fashion empire on.

Em felt a warmth in her chest. The man was like a second father to her, but she had only recently discovered the larger enterprises of Brookerby's tailor, and she was enormously proud of her friend for all he had accomplished in the fashion world. Not that she was equally excited about any of his ongoing frilly presents. Lace and satin snagged and dirtied when she climbed ladders or crawled under staircases. They were highly impractical.

She studied the ribboned dress on the mannequin, wondering if she could pull it off. The medium blue would highlight her blue-gray eyes. It had some interesting weaving on the bodice, and it wasn't too cupcake-esque. Maybe she should order one, to surprise Liam. But— she reminded herself—Mendel had gifted her a dress last month. She hadn't worn it yet. It still lay wrapped in paper on the floor of her bureau.

But she couldn't linger. She had a job. Turning away from the storefront, she scanned the crowd and moved toward the wide plaza in the center of town. There. Across the square. On a bench near the fountain was a black-haired man. He sat far enough away from the crowd that she wouldn't have to suggest relocation. She ducked through the throng and approached him, and he watched her, warily. She sat on the far end of the bench, turned, and nodded.

"Emaline Strider?"

She nodded again. "Call me Em."

She tried to study the man unobtrusively. He was slender with a paunchy gut, and his black hair was thinning on top. Like most Northerners, his skin was light brown, almost an olive shade. He wore laborer's clothes, freshly laundered. One hand was buried in his jacket pocket. Em was ready to dash away into the crowd when she realized the pocket was much too small for a weapon. Maybe he was just nervous. But she remained on guard. "What's your name, friend?"

"Randall. I wondered if you'd come."

"How did you get my name?"

"I heard rumors."

Em didn't like this. Not a referral. Just whispers. How long before the empress caught wind and put her neck in a noose? A problem for future Em to ruminate on. She turned to face Randall on the bench and spoke, drawing from her standard script. "Could you please repeat the words of your oath for me? Exactly as you swore it?"

The man nodded. "I will not write or speak any Prutian history. Nor will I distribute any documents to spread Tribal Prutian history."

Em started. This was new—his oath wasn't related to the warding trees at all. The Prutians were a tribal culture native to the Northern colonies, but they also existed in Fridera, and the northern parts of Esnania proper. Why was the empress suppressing their history?

She had so many questions, but she didn't want to trigger the painful side effects for Randall. Or did she? It would be the one way to prove he was telling the truth. "Do you have any documents on Prutian history you can show me?"

Randall nodded, then immediately clutched his head, visibly trembling. Em waited while his crippling pain subsided. Unless he was a very good actor, he had taken the oath that he claimed. She felt guilty for triggering it, but safer knowing the man before her wasn't lying.

Em couldn't meet his eyes as she returned to the standard script. "I was under an oath that prevented me from replanting warding trees of protection. I permanently removed my own oath by chopping my town's tree to the ground. So, I learned that the oaths are confounded when you do the opposite of what you wish to do. In your case, if you simply avoid passing on history, the oath will remain. But if you take an action, say, destroying a historical document, you should be able to fulfill the oath and therefore break its hold."

Randall shifted. He put his hand back in his pocket. "You want me to destroy Prutian history?"

"If you want to remove your oath, yes."

It was clearly not what he expected. "Is there another option?"

"Live with it. Or petition the empress to remove it."

"That's it?"

"That's what I know. There may be other ways, but I'm not aware of them." Em stood. He was not ready to take action today. Em had seen this reluctance in a few of her other clients. Eventually, he would become so fatigued with the oath that he would take her advice and free himself. Until then . . . "That's all I can do, my friend." She moved from the bench.

"Wait!"

Em turned to see Randall clumsily following, hand still in his pocket. She waited, wondering if he was ready after all. He tripped over a protruding cobblestone, and his hands flew out to catch his fall. A small wooden box tumbled from his fingers.

"Crumb—" the man spewed, scrambling.

Em bent down to pick up the item that had landed at her feet. It was the size of a matchbox, made of walnut wood, with tiny ornate carvings spread across it. She felt a small tingle in her fingers as she held it. That tingle told her the box was no ordinary matchbox, but some kind of magical device.

She glanced up, a question on her lips, but Randall snatched back the item and sprinted off into the crowd.

Em left Drecovia after her encounter with Randall. She didn't know what to make of the man, but she hoped, rather than believed, he was sincere. He did seem to have an oath upon him, and the box could have been some kind of magical protection. After all, he took a risk as well by asking for her help. Yet the dread remained. Maybe it was

Gram's influence again, but Em felt the wrongness of the encounter as it flitted through her mind again and again.

Em found a quiet alleyway and traveled by fast-map to Arrenmore, the magical parchment transporting her with a simple double-tap on the city's location.

The Gray Horse Inn & Spa was under new management, and it showed.

Several employees greeted Em as she entered the brightly lit, bustling lobby. They had finally repaired the enormous chandelier, and the gray-clad furniture scattering the first floor had been refurbished. The walls had a fresh layer of wallpaper, and the film of dirt that covered every surface under the former proprietor, Sam Monterey, was long gone. She searched the crowded reception area and spied her father.

Farrigan Strider was holding court in the parlor, the small lobby pub. His hulking frame was squeezed into one of the wooden booths, Gray Horse waiters surrounding him. They were laughing uproariously at a shared joke. Em smiled. Farrigan was the type of man who knew how to have a good time wherever he was.

Then she hesitated. They had a standing weekly meeting for magecraft lessons, but each time she came, she felt as if she were interrupting a party. She had believed—for most of her life—that Anne and Farrigan died when she was small. Imagine her surprise two months ago when she had met them, had found them alive and thriving, with no memory of the daughter they had left behind in Brookerby. Another byproduct of the warding trees' ill-formed magic.

Now Farrigan spotted her and waved her over. The employees dispersed, a few still chuckling. One or two nodded toward Em, but most brushed by without acknowledgment. Em didn't mind. On the one hand, she had freed them from the tyrannical management of Sam Monterey. On the other hand, she had employed sleeping gas and tied up more than a few of them in her attempt to defeat Sam one-on-one. They likely hadn't forgiven her yet.

"Em!" Farrigan greeted. "Sit! Did you come from a job?"

Em slid into the other side of the booth and reached for the tankard of ale Farrigan had ordered on her behalf. "I came from Drecovia. Thanks again for letting me use the map."

Farrigan waved his hand dismissively. "We have other traveling methods, and you seem to be making good use of it. Successful trip?"

Em shrugged. It wasn't successful, and something about that little magic box had her mentally balancing on a fence rail. Randall's oath also concerned her. Why was the empress suppressing Northern tribal history? She met Farrigan's gaze. "What do you know about the Tribal Prutians' history?" she asked.

Farrigan let out blast of laughter. "What a question! Must've been a doozy of a job."

Em took a sip of her ale and waited.

"I've been up in the North a few times. Nasty business. The tribes don't consider themselves part of the empire. Some of their territory was annexed years ago, but they've never really accepted imperial rule. Every so often, there's an uprising. A demand for independence. Those are squashed quickly, and quite brutally."

Em shivered. She had seen the news headlines printed in the *Brookerby Leaflet*. There always seemed to be fighting, but it was so remote. So pointless. Maybe the empress was trying to quell the fighting by taking away their history?

Farrigan was studying her. "You aren't getting tangled up in that, are you?"

Em threw him half a smile. "Not intentionally. The oath today was related."

"Messy business. Gramalia will not be pleased."

"I know." Em stared down at her pint. This morning's fight flashed in her head again, twisting her stomach further. She had mentioned Gram's displeasure a time or two before, and Farrigan had remembered. Come to think of it, she and Gram had been at odds for months. They'd been fighting ever since the woman's voice had been healed by a magical herb.

"How is Lord Hallson? And when can I expect to have a son-in-law?"

The abrupt change in subject was welcome. Em smiled and shrugged. "No longer Lord Hallson, remember? He ceded that to his brother when he moved to Brookerby."

Farrigan's eyes glinted with good humor. "Avoiding the question?"

"He hasn't asked."

"Why the hell not? He's a good guy. He loves you. You love him."

Em took another long swig before answering. "He's wonderful. I think I do love him. It's early, though. He's . . ."

Her father tilted his head but said nothing. That was one thing Em liked about Farrigan. For all his boisterousness, he knew when to just let Em talk. "He's been so supportive. And he's fit in better than I expected. But I've been off-balance since the tree fell. I repaired everything in town, and now there's a lull. I have nothing to do, and I'm in the way all the time. Gram thinks I should expand my repairs to other towns, but it's just . . ."

"Boring?"

Em laughed. "Kinda. I went through this life-changing adventure, and now it feels like everyone in town just wants me to settle down and be normal."

"Whatever that means. You can always join the family business."

Em tried to picture herself on a magical heist with her parents, but the image was fuzzy. And likely ended with her behind bars. She shook her head. "I don't think that would solve my problems."

"That reminds me—" He reached into his pocket and pulled out a rusty padlock, which he placed in front of her. "Time for your lesson. Try this one."

Em turned it in her hands for a minute or two, happy for a change of topic. Then, concentrating that spark feeling, she directed it toward the ancient pins and tumbler.

Farrigan had started training Em in small magic a month ago. Anne, Em's mother, was better with lock-picking, so she came along that first day and explained how to direct her magic with intention. With that instruction, Em had spent an hour trying to open a diary with a small flimsy lock. After that, Farrigan had presented a new challenge every week. Once it was a strongbox. Once, a deadbolted door. It was always breaking and entering with those two.

The padlock clicked open in defeat. Em allowed herself a small smile. That was getting easier.

"Nice," Farrigan said. "You've been practicing, oh daughter of mine."

Em grinned at him. She had also learned to move silently by directing the spark into her shoes, and how to use distraction magic to misdirect a pursuer. "You're training me to be a thief. Can you teach me any skills that don't involve criminal activity?"

"I admit, those are the most utilized in my repertoire." Farrigan scratched his salt-and-pepper beard absently. "I could give you a full warehouse tour sometime. The items are more helpful than some of these parlor tricks."

The warehouse. Her parents had spent years stealing rare magical artifacts from all over Esnania, gathering them in a single warehouse in the capital city of Gillamor. As time passed, magical items in the world wore out or broke, making Farrigan and Anne's intact collection more and more valuable. This thought triggered a question Em had been meaning to ask for some time.

"Have you ever made an item?"

Farrigan shook his head. "Your mother attempted. She was tired of washing clothes, so she tried to make a pair of pants that would self-clean. The results were . . . messy." He chuckled at the memory.

"But it's probably similar, right?" Em pushed. "This lock—I can magically pick it by understanding the mechanics. Could I create a lock that would open only for me, so long as I understand how it works?"

"Possible," Farrigan responded. "But we've never done it. You might need to ask a real mage about that."

Em knew that Gram had created a magical reference book, but she was remarkably tight-lipped about how she did it. Farrigan and Anne didn't seem to have that knowledge. Not that Em had any idea what she would make, but the idea of being able to craft new items was appealing for many reasons. Not the least of which, it would give her something to do now that her town didn't seem to need her anymore.

Em handed the padlock back, and Farrigan pocketed it.

"Any other wild schemes in the works?" he asked.

Em felt remarkably blank. She defaulted to the big news. "Marcellus and Cass are getting married next week. In Gillamor. We're going. Did you meet Liam's brother?"

"That's the soldier?" Farrigan smiled. "No. Your mother and I take great pains to avoid law enforcement. Sounds like he's a nice fellow, though."

"Maybe I can drop by the warehouse while I'm in town?"

Farrigan winked, then downed his pint. "Don't bring any evil resort owners this time, and we might just let you in."

CHAPTER 2

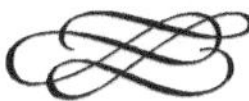

The basic rules of the sticks and stones game are universal: build a pathway on the grid that bypasses the other player's path. But rules may be added or modified to include new pieces, strange grid shapes, or side objectives. Consider your opponent before agreeing to these added rules. (See "Play the Player, Not the Game.")

"Game Theory: Sticks and Stones"
The Standard Book of Anything

*L*ater that afternoon, Em fast-traveled back to Brookerby. She emerged on Main Street and waved to Fern—the schoolteacher—who was chatting with a few of her students' parents outside the mercantile. She ducked around the corner, through the alleyway, to the bookshop. The door was a somber dark green, and the inside smelled of dust and ink, much like the owner of the shop.

Em appreciated the respite from the town and its inhabitants. After the events of the summer, everyone wanted to talk to her—not to hire her for repairs, but to share opinions about her relationship with Liam, the handsome bakery owner she had brought back from Gillamor, and ask when she was going to settle down. She couldn't handle that conversation at the moment. Not with her tools sitting idle and Gram's derision in her head.

She couldn't ask Gram (or her shape-shifting encyclopedia, *The Standard Book of Anything*) about the Northern tribes and their history without raising more shouting matches. The bookshop, in contrast, was a haven filled with answers and no nosy questions.

"Good afternoon," a soft voice greeted her. Cornelius, the bookseller, was seated in a high-backed chair with his long legs draped over the padded arm, and a stack of herbalist texts on the nearby table. He set down the tome he was reading and shifted to a proper seated position.

"Good day," Em replied. "How go the studies?" She knew Cornelius had been pursuing advanced studies through correspondence; in what, she didn't know.

"There is so much to learn. And I find myself distracted by all the other books not on the syllabus." Cornelius reddened, as he often did when holding ordinary conversations. Em used to think he was just bashful around her, but then she observed him blushing when speaking to Earl McBean and realized his reaction wasn't personal.

She spared him further chitchat. "I need your expertise. Do you know, or do you have, any histories of the Tribal Prutians? Or the Northern territories?" She didn't quite know why she needed to read them, but she had to verify that history wasn't being erased.

Cornelius stood, no longer uncertain. He was now the master of the bookshop and inquiries about references were his domain. "Right this way."

Em trailed his slender form as he wove his way through the stacks. She had built or repaired half of these shelves and had also assisted with some of the interior touches that made the store so cozy. She scanned the ceiling, looking for leaks or peeling paint, but no luck. It was pristine. Cornelius halted at the back wall shelf, labeled "Esnanian History."

"Hmm," he murmured, leaning in to read the titles. "I thought I had something. The tribal peoples are not included in standard history, but I hoped I had at least one specialty book stocked."

Em scanned the other titles as Cornelius searched. *Histories of Fridera, Silver Mining Era in the Antillei Mountains, Clavonion Dynasty.*

"Not here," he concluded. "My apologies. I could order you one?"

Em nodded, trying not to assign sinister motives to the missing histories. "I would appreciate that. If it isn't too much trouble."

"Shame about those tribes. They were there for centuries. Their own traditions and customs. They had very sophisticated religious beliefs, and their own rulers. Then the empire marched in and planted their flag. Now, they are desperately fighting for the right to exist. Can you imagine? It must feel like when our tree fell. Very sad."

Em glanced at Cornelius, surprised. It was the longest speech she had ever heard from him. Was he secretly harboring radical tendencies? She chuckled at the thought of the meek bookseller charging at imperial soldiers, waving a banner and shouting. "Well, thanks for the lead anyway. How are your shelves holding up? Any repairs needed?"

"They are solid. Thank you. No repairs right now."

Em sagged a bit. She nodded her thanks again and motioned him back to his chair and book stack. She ducked out of the bookstore, feeling a bit lost.

DOWN THE STREET, Em pushed open the bakery door and was engulfed in the smell of yeast and butter. She breathed in deeply and let out a contented sigh. No offense to the mercantile, but this was fast becoming her new favorite place in town.

Bob greeted her with a furious wagging tail. The hound dog wore a little apron, and Em smirked at the costume before patting the dog, then relenting and scratching behind his ears. He had loved living in Brookerby,—at the bakery. Em was concerned he'd been sneaking scraps because the dog was growing plump.

No patrons waited, an oddity. A midafternoon lull, perhaps?

However, the curved glass pastry case—which had been bursting with treats this morning—now appeared picked over, like the bakery had recently hosted a gaggle of ravenous geese.

Em felt a twinge of pride. Liam had been open only two months, but he was successfully living his dream. He was even attracting customers from several towns over through word of mouth.

She ducked behind the counter, eyeing a lone chocolate croissant lying haphazardly in the front of the case. She snaked her hand in to retrieve the pastry, but then heard a sharp voice behind her.

"Tongs, Em!"

She reddened but turned an impish grin on the man. Her Liam. Solid muscle, eyebrow raised, and covered in flour. He was ferrying a tray of rolls to the display basket and had stopped to frown at her.

"Sorry. I couldn't resist."

"You can have it, but for crumb's sake, don't use your hands."

Em retrieved the tongs hanging by the case and reached for the croissant again. Liam bustled by, stopping to give her a quick peck on the cheek. Em smiled at the gesture. He wasn't really cross with her, then. Bob circled their legs, as if rounding them up, before he went and flopped down in his little basket in the corner where he slept.

"Good trip?" Liam inquired as he started to arrange the fresh rolls in the display basket.

"Farrigan says hello. Also, my lock-picking is getting really good." Em sank her teeth into the croissant, and chocolate dribbled out onto her fingers.

"Happy to hear it. I'll let Marcellus know," Liam teased. He finished unloading the rolls and set the tray aside. "What about Drecovia?"

"It was . . . different." Em was focused on her pastry and forgot she had intended to conceal the strange encounter. She quickly took another bite, avoiding eye contact with Liam.

"Different?"

She stole a glance at him. He had paused his work, leaning on the counter. Waiting.

As she chewed, she gave him a shrug. Might as well tell him the highlights. "Different oath this time. Nothing to do with trees. And the guy didn't seem to want to break it after I told him what to do."

"Weird. What was the oath?"

"He wasn't allowed to share Northern history." Em studied the chocolate drip on her fingers, then nibbled on the pastry again, letting out a hum as she chewed.

"How do those compare to last week?"

"These?" Em raised what was left of the treat. "Top-notch. A bit drippy, but I don't mind." She started to lick some of the chocolate off her fingers when a towel hit her in the face.

"Use the towel, squirrel. Are they better or worse?"

"Just as good." She shoved the rest into her mouth.

"You're no help at all."

She pouted and then wiped off her hands.

"Are you headed home?"

"Not if I can help it. Gram's still . . ."

He nodded. Em had been avoiding home during daylight hours. Then she would sneak home after Gram had gone to bed. She had mostly managed to avoid the woman, but it wasn't a very mature way to handle their conflict.

He plucked the chocolatey towel away and gave her a smooch. She felt a small zip run through her body.

"I could thicken it into ganache," he commented. Then, kissing her again, said thoughtfully, "Maybe add some dark chocolate."

Em raised an eyebrow. "I'm sure that will be good too."

And then he kissed her in earnest, twining her hands in his. She smiled into the kiss. This was the one thing that was right in the world.

At that moment, the door opened, the bell tinkled, and a few patrons entered. The afternoon was waning, and soon it would be wall-to-wall customers buying bread for their supper. The arrivals tittered over the unintentional show from the town's newest couple. Bob leapt up to greet each of them, and Em pushed away from the counter. She was blushing and looked to make a quick exit.

Liam walked her to the door, not ready to let her go. "When do I see you again?"

She glanced at the waiting line. "Later. After you close for the day?"

He nodded quickly. "Upstairs?" He kept a small bachelor's apartment above the bakery. But Em didn't like the idea of sitting above the shop, waiting.

She shook her head. "The clearing?"

He nodded happily and kissed her temple. There was an audible "aw" from the crowd as Em left the bakery, her face reddening again.

A MULTILEVEL TREEHOUSE built around a large elm sat on the green across from the blacksmith. Em had intended to speak to the blacksmith about repairs, but she slowed her pace to admire her handiwork. She had constructed the treehouse as a gift for Grady, a kid in town who really needed cheering up after the warding tree fell. Now, there were nearly a dozen children squealing and climbing on the structure.

Grady had advised on the initial single story, but Em kept sneaking back in the evenings to add more. Additional levels. Rope ladders and suspension bridges. A secret code that might encourage the brainier kids to climb up and try to decipher it. The kids had started adding their own touches, and the treehouse became fully theirs.

Em searched among the leaves and wooden slats, finally spotting Grady in the crow's nest peering at Main Street through a telescope.

"Ahoy!" she shouted, waving her arms.

"Miss Strider," he grunted back in a pirate voice. Then he clambered down the rope net to where she waited on the ground.

"Miss Strider," he said in a rush, "no one has cracked the code yet, but Minnie Filbit thinks she's close. Wanna see the new things I added?"

"Sure." Em nodded. "Show me."

Grady trotted around the tree. Em followed, trying to keep up. He walked under the lowest platform, which had been built on stilts as a starting point into the rest of the treehouse. Em ducked her head slightly to fit.

"See, Miss Strider, a communication portal. Like Miss Ilna's." He tugged on a tin can attached to a wire that ran up through the platform slats. "Hello up there," he bellowed into the can. They heard a faint "Who is this?" come back from the other end.

Em laughed. "That's brilliant, Grady! Good thinking."

But the boy was already off, leading her somewhere else. He stopped at a square dirt patch a few steps from the treehouse. "Sticks and stones!" he declared.

Em immediately realized what it was. Grady had scratched a game board onto the soil. He'd also piled up shortened sticks and round white rocks to play the game with.

"You are quite an innovator, my friend. This treehouse just gets better and better."

"Wanna play?" He grinned up at her.

Em returned his smile and nodded, kneeling down to sit in the grass. Sticks and stones was a children's game, but there was enough strategy in placing the stones and connecting them that even adults had not mastered the game.

Grady plopped down opposite Em and placed the first piece. "You okay, Miss Strider?"

"Sure, Grady. Why do you ask?"

"You've been gone a lot. And your face does that sad-bird thing sometimes when you're here."

Em scowled as she placed her piece. "Sad-bird thing?"

Grady pursed his lips and darted his eyes around—in imitation of her, she supposed.

Em rolled her eyes. "I do not do that!"

"You do. Especially when there's nothing to fix. Also, my ma says you might be getting married. To the baker guy."

Em said nothing and placed another stone. She recalled the very public kiss from moments ago. Perhaps she and Liam should be more discreet.

"Ma also says you're out adventuring in other towns, but you should really just focus on setting up your home."

"Your ma sure has a lot of opinions," Em muttered, trying not to grind her teeth. Busybody, gossiping, opinionated . . .

Grady had paused his playing again and was glaring at her.

"What, Grady?"

"Miss Strider. I'm ten soon. I know when adults aren't telling me things."

Em sighed. She didn't want to explain the ebbs and flows of her repair business, and she definitely didn't want to talk about her issues with Gram with a nine-year-old. She could explain the oath removals, however. "Grady, you're right. When there aren't repairs, I feel a bit sad. Also, I've been doing something I think is important. But it's dangerous."

"Why, then?"

She thought for a moment. "What if, at school, a bunch of kids had their shoelaces tied together. And you were the only one who could help them before they tripped and got hurt. What would you do?"

"I'd help. I'd untie them," Grady said.

Em let out a breath. It was that simple, wasn't it?

Grady placed a final winning stick that connected all five of his stones. "But I'd try to find the jerk who was tying them in the first place and make them stop."

CHAPTER 3

News portals were invented by accident when an artificer mage tried to make a self-licking, self-mailing stamp. The first prototypes were quite messy.

"Inventions of the Age of Magic"
The Standard Book of Anything

Ilna towered over the printing press, making changes to the galley of letters, her inky fingers flying over the words she created. "Em!" Ilna greeted. "Take a seat. I'll be a minute."

"Any repair work? Also, I was just wondering if you had any messages for me."

"No repairs. Something over the portal less than an hour ago, though. Let me get this going, and then I'll find it." Ilna used a news portal—a magical device where anything of import was broadcast to all news portals or sent to a specific location from any other news portal. She received important updates to be included in the *Brookerby Leaflet*. She also received messages from other portals that requested Em's oath-removing expertise.

Em glanced around the newspaper office, hoping she could quickly spot a message among the disheveled stacks of papers. She finally gave up and sat in the hard wooden chair by the window.

After a few moments, the printing press was in motion and Ilna sidled over to Em. "Right. I was looking for something for you . . . what was it?" Her face suddenly fell. "Oh. The message." She started rummaging quickly through the stacks on her desk. "Aha, here it is, love." She handed over a small slip of paper. "Bad news, I'm afraid."

Em scanned the paper, reading twice.

Emaline Strider is hereby ordered to appear before Her Imperial Majesty, Empress Regina de Silviana Augusta, Ruler of Esnania and the Northern colonies, at her seat of power, the Golden Lark Palace in Gillamor. If Miss Strider fails to appear within one week of this summons, an arrest warrant will be issued. Long live Her Imperial Majesty.

She glanced up, a question on her lips, and saw that Ilna was watching her read.

"Maybe it's nothing, dear. After all, you did save Brookerby without replanting. Perhaps the empress is grateful for your efforts?"

Em was already shaking her head. "Unlikely. She wouldn't threaten to arrest me if it was good. This must be about the oaths. But I've been careful." *Except today.* "I don't know how she would've found out."

Ilna tilted her head. "You could pretend you never saw the summons? Take a long vacation?"

Em considered. If she left tonight, she could claim ignorance. Use the map and flee to Zanit, or Brildonia. But she knew it was only a matter of time, even if she did flee. Those countries had no desire to incur Esnania's wrath by harboring a fugitive. She'd rather arrive under her own power, anyway. The empress was more inclined to be merciful if she didn't have to hunt Em down.

"I'll go," she said.

It wasn't an arrest. Just a summons. She soothed herself with that thought. Maybe the empress had heard rumors, and nothing more. She would issue a warning. Maybe another oath. Em shook her head. She glanced up to see Ilna still watching her with concern, the printer's eyebrows pinched together.

"Thanks for passing this along." Em stood.

Ilna put a hand on her shoulder. "Let me know if I can help, dear."

"Can you keep this off the record?"

"Of course." The slight twinge of disappointment in Ilna's voice nearly made Em smile. Ilna would've sold a lot of papers with this news.

Em thanked her friend and pushed her way out of the *Leaflet* office. She grabbed the latest edition of the paper on her way out, if only to hide from the folks on the street the fact that she was still clutching a portal message.

EM WISHED she had worn her tattered quilted cloak to block the wind. Autumn was fully upon Esnania, and there was a crispness in the air as the sun dipped. Or maybe Em had chills that were unrelated to weather. She didn't know. But cloak or not, she couldn't wander and process this news. It was nearly dark, and she needed to meet Liam.

There was a wooded area right off the main road that led across a creek to the outer reaches of town, and to Em's cottage. At the edge of the creek sat a huge field where the sycamore, the warding tree of protection, had stood for decades, until recently. The tree's breaking had caused all manner of magical chaos that had mostly been sorted, repaired, and healed. Brookerby was better than new, and Em's repair skills were, for now, obsolete.

Em had built a bench by the creek to fill the empty glade with something positive; she headed for that seat now. She kicked off her shoes despite the chill, wanting to feel the grass between her toes, and took some deep breaths, trying to quell the anxiety rushing beneath her skin. The autumn wind toyed with her honey-brown hair. An ant crawled over her foot, ignorant of the troubled woman it stood upon and only aware of the fleshy obstacle in its way. Em watched it, softening her grip on the *Brookerby Leaflet* and the portal message that she had been clutching since she left the newspaper office.

Gram had been right. Of course she had. Gram was always right.

Em's brain—unbidden—darted to that first fight. The one that kicked off the many tense moments over the past month.

"SIT DOWN. We need to talk about this."

Gram's tone had been frosty. Her vocal cords had recently been healed, thanks to a magical herb called warfern. Em was still trying to relearn her friend's vocal patterns after years of silence, but this particular intonation was clear.

Em flopped down into one of the lumpy chairs in the living room they shared. "Talk about what?"

"Oath removal. And how you've completely lost your mind."

"Gram!"

The older woman was holding the fireplace mantel with one hand, almost casually, but her posture was rigid. "If you want to help people, expand your repair business. Offer your services at a discount. Volunteer to tutor kids for Fern at the schoolhouse. But these oaths? Do you have any common sense at all?"

"I do, in fact." It was Em's turn to be frosty. She was too old to be scolded like this.

"You don't. Or you wouldn't pursue such a stupidly rebellious thing."

"Rebellious? These people need help. I'm helping."

"By slapping the empress in the face. How do you think she'll respond?"

"She'll never know." The empress wasn't going to follow up and check on the people she had cursed. That was absurd.

"She will find out. And when she does, she'll execute you. Great deities, Em. I raised you to be smarter than that."

Em was silent. Brooding. The last time she had received such a tongue-lashing—years ago—she had tried to jump off the roof with her flying machine. This was different. She allowed that her activities were probably dangerous, but those oaths were torturous. Em wouldn't wish that on anyone. And Gram didn't know what they felt like.

Gram's tone modulated. "What's wrong with going back to repairs? You're great at those."

"I'm great at this," Em growled, pushing out of her chair.

"A great idiot."

"You're allowed to think what you want, but I'm not a child. Liam understands."

"Then he's a fool too. If he really cared about you, he'd discourage this."

"What do you know about any of it? You sit here with your dusty old stories, not learning magic and wallowing in obscurity. I want to *do* something." It wasn't fair, and she knew it as soon as the words came out of her mouth, but she was too incensed to back down now.

Gram's fist clenched. "I did not spend my life 'wallowing in obscurity' so that you could run headlong into danger. Child, check your ambition before that empress slips a noose around your neck."

Em was fuming. She was done with this whole ridiculous fight, and she marched out the door, letting it slam behind her.

THEY HAD REPEATED the fight many times over the past month. Each time Em successfully removed an oath, Gram repeated her plea to stop, growing more and more insistent. Em had started avoiding the cottage. Wandering the town. Helping Liam in the bakery. It had been fine. Nothing bad had happened. Until now.

Now, Gram's warnings seemed prophetic. She tightened her fingers on the summons. The empress had found out.

She'd kept a small chip of wood from the destroyed warding tree.

It was in her pocket, and she reached for it now, brushing the smooth wood fibers with the tips of her fingers.

It would be okay. When the tree fell, she felt this same dread, and everything had gone wrong in her quest to find a new tree. Yet somehow, things had worked out. Maybe this was just another adventure. The empress had not exactly been kind when they'd met before—she had forced her to take an oath, after all—but she didn't consider Em a threat to her rule.

Liam appeared out of the shrubbery. The sky was fully dark now. How long had she been sitting here? He looked happy, if a little tired. His light brown hair still had flour clinging to it, and he had a few days of stubble on his jaw. If Em weren't so on edge, her heart would've fluttered at the sight. Stars, he was handsome. Em gestured to the open bench seat and offered a smile.

Liam perched on the bench, knees toward her, meeting her gaze with his own. "Something wrong?"

Curse him. He could always tell. Em lifted her hand from the papers she had been clutching and handed the wrinkled summons to Liam without comment. His face was inscrutable as he read, and he finally lowered the paper and leveled a gaze at Em.

She grimaced.

He raised an eyebrow.

"Gram was right?" she offered.

He sighed heavily, not at all amused.

"Maybe it won't be so bad," she sighed. "She can't have any proof, just circumstantial evidence."

"That's true. Unless somebody talked."

Em paused at this. Did she trust everyone that she had freed?

"Ilna thought I should run."

Liam scoffed. As a former soldier, he knew how impossible it was to evade the imperial army indefinitely. "No, you'll need to go. Maybe you'll get off easy again. Another oath. A warning maybe."

Em opened her mouth to protest that an unbreakable oath was hardly "getting off easy," but under the circumstances, it was a best-case scenario. She took the summons back and shakily read it again. "When should I go?"

"Tomorrow, or the next day? Before Marcellus's wedding. We need to get this sorted. I'm coming."

"Liam—"

He met her eyes. "I don't think I could've stopped you." He paused, his meaning fully hitting Em. He hadn't been on board. Maybe Gram had gotten to him. Maybe he had started to worry, but hadn't told her. It made sense. She had treated Gram badly for voicing concerns, maybe she wouldn't have listened to him either.

As if reading her mind, he continued, softer. "You fixed nearly every place in town that needed it. You were climbing the walls. Waiting for things to break. I get that. And you found a way to help people. I get that too."

Liam had seen more than she realized. He hadn't stopped her because he knew she needed to do it. She squeezed his hand. "Thank you. You don't have to come."

"Try and stop me, squirrel." He placed an arm along the back of the bench.

She reached a hand to his cheek, turned his face to hers, and kissed him softly. She tried to put all the love and gratitude she felt into it. He responded in kind. He still loved her. After all this.

"I'm sorry," she said. "After we get through this, I'll make it up to you."

He tightened his arm around her and said nothing more. Em snuggled against his warmth, ignoring the summons paper that fluttered to the ground between them.

CHAPTER 4

Larks are expansionist birds, forever increasing their territory. Woe to the simple wren who obstructs the lark's way.

"An Overview: Birds of Esnania"
The Standard Book of Anything

The Golden Lark Palace stood in the center of the bustling city of Gillamor. The soaring white-stoned towers and domes had served as the seat of power for the Empire of Esnania for the past age, and it was impossible not to admire the structure as it glinted in the midday sun.

Em had been at the palace once before, in the dead of night and escorted through a side entrance. Now, as she stood at its front gates, she marveled at the construction of the lifted archways, the elegantly carved swirls in the stone window settings, and the enormous iron gates that must've required twenty men to lift into place. Her breath caught as the ponderous gates pivoted open. When she had been there before, an unbreakable oath was forced upon her. She could still feel the water trickling over her palm as she swore to forgo her plans to save her town. She could still feel—like a ghost—the violation of the oath in her brain, even though it had long since been removed. It was the single most miserable moment of her life. So far.

Liam squeezed her hand as they moved forward. She had been summoned, and the guards seemed to understand the visit would not be purely social; they flanked the entrance, eyes watching closely for signs of panic or escape.

As she put one foot in front of the other, Em distracted her mind with the structure of the grand hallway that opened before them. The ceilings rose taller than ancient trees. She wondered if she could design such a hall for Brookerby. She pointed out an ivory carving that spanned the hallway to Liam, in awe of the craftsmanship. He nodded appreciatively, but Em had the feeling he was less impressed by their surroundings. He had been surrounded by fine things in his former life, after all. Em's slight clearing of her throat ricocheted along the empty corridor, and Liam slipped an arm around her shoulders as they walked. Guards guided them to another large doorway at the end of the hall, flanked by more soldiers who ushered them into a massive round room.

Em's eyes widened. This was the throne room. White marble pillars were spaced evenly around the inner circle of the room, and sunlight streamed from the domed skylight to the inner circle. Behind the pillars was a shadowed perimeter.

She had read about the ancient Esnanian king Gerbralton, who had demanded a round room to avoid intrigue and dealmaking in dark corners. Eliminate the corners and the business of the empire would be conducted out in the open. Theoretically, at least.

They were led to stand in the center of the room, and Em discovered she was trembling. Only her determination to appear unworried —for Liam—was keeping her on her feet. She focused her thoughts on the floor, a wooden masterpiece of concentric circles. In the center of the floor was an inlaid mural, freshly installed. It shone with many different colors of wood, assembled to form an image of three birds: a golden lark being freed from a cage, a nightingale perched on the cage top, and a sparrow observing from a nearby branch. Exotic flowers surrounded the whole image. It was the work of a master craftsman. Em wondered if the lark represented the imperial family, evading enemies. Or was the bird Esnania itself? If so, what was the cage?

A door across the chamber thundered open, and she heard the sound of many feet crossing the threshold into the throne room. Em's head jerked up in time to see Her Imperial Majesty, Regina de Silviana Augusta, sweep into the room. Em had met the woman once before and found her sharp and clever, if somewhat unyielding. Her advancing years did not diminish her regal beauty; a braided crown of gray hair was artfully arranged on her head, and she wore a velvet-trimmed robe of peacock blue and gold on her shoulders.

The empress seated herself on the golden throne, which perched just inside the innermost circle of the room. A semicircle of advisors, richly dressed men and women wearing dull expressions and the vestments of the inner council, flanked her. One or two gave terse nods to Liam; his own prior title and military service made him worth their notice. Around the room, guards stationed themselves at regular intervals. It was an impressive display of power. The message was not lost on Em—the empress was not a woman to be trifled with.

Em had a feeling this interview would process quite differently from their previous encounter, a private garden chat. Em noticed Liam's deep bow and quickly dipped into an awkward curtsy. A breach in etiquette would only make this worse.

"Miss Emaline Strider of Brookerby," the empress began. "It has been some months since we spoke. And in that time, you have violated direct orders from your empress, skirted the terms of your oath, and used unlawful magic. Tell me, Miss Strider, is there any reason I should not execute you?"

Liam stood. "Your Majesty, wasn't her healing of Brookerby lawful? It was just a magical herb." He and Em had strategized. Their opening plea would be a play of innocence and a reminder of Em's accomplishments.

Em lifted her face in time to see the empress gesture to a guard. Another door opened, and a man was ushered in. Em's jaw dropped and she quickly closed it. It was the Randall, from Drecovia. He did not meet Em's eye as he shuffled forward and placed a small wooden box on a side table next to the dais. The very same box that Em had seen him drop that day in the square. She couldn't feel her body for three seconds, and then suddenly every part of her was shaking.

The empress motioned once more and her entourage—save one guard—exited the room. Em's shaking had given way to dizziness. If Randall was here, the sovereign knew Em had been removing oaths, a hanging offense.

Randall slid a panel on the side of the box, and suddenly Em heard her own voice, tinny and small, but undoubtedly her, coming from the device.

"The oaths are confounded when you do the opposite of what you wish to do. In your case, if you simply avoid passing on history, the oath will remain. But if you take an action, say, destroying a historical document, you should be able to fulfill the oath and therefore break its hold."

"You want me to destroy Prutian history?"

"If you want to remove your oath, yes."

Then silence. Somehow, this man had captured and replayed their conversation. Improbable, in Em's mind, yet here it was. Her own words condemning her. Randall had retreated to the edge of the room, clearly wishing to escape.

The empress broke the hush. "I have heard other reports as well. You are, how did you phrase it, *confounding* my oaths. I sent informants to verify, and there are many former oath takers who are no longer bound, thanks to your instruction. This is treason."

There was that word. Treason equaled death. Em's dizziness stilled at the certainty of it. She had known discovery was a possibility, but she hadn't expected its crushing swiftness.

Grady's small voice was drumming in her head. *I'd find the jerk and make them stop.* Em could hardly make the empress stop the oaths, but she could say something.

"Your Majesty, I beg of you. The oaths are extremely painful. I was trying to relieve suffering. I want to petition that the oaths be stopped."

The empress raised an eyebrow. "Petition? You are not in a position to ask anything of me, girl."

Liam spoke again, sounding agitated. "Your Majesty, please. Em was not intending—"

"Silence!" the empress barked. The word echoed, and a pall fell over the room. Em felt Liam twitch beside her; she felt nothing in her own body except a spreading dread, like ink in a pool of water.

The older woman steepled her hands, resting her fingertips on her lips. "Most magic users I have encountered are sorely lacking in creativity. They try to perform cantrips from ages past and learn only what has been given to them. But you. You have healed your town with a common herb from our gardens. And you have found a way to remove an unremovable, unbreakable oath. It is remarkable. Quite remarkable."

Em lifted her eyes to meet the older woman's steely gaze.

"At our last encounter, I underestimated you. Despite your name—your family—I assumed you were no threat."

Em rasped, "I am not a threat, Your Majesty. I am a loyal subject."

"And yet, you petition. You question. I cannot trust you. As I could not trust the last mage I executed," the empress declared, standing. "May the deities forgive you for your crimes." She gestured guards toward Em as she swept from the center of the room. The hearing was over. But that couldn't be it. Em couldn't let her life be snuffed out that easily.

"What can I do to prove myself?" she pleaded. The sovereign was halfway out the door, and several guards' hands gripped Em's arms, pulling her toward the opposite exit. Her legs were jelly and her heartbeat thundered in her ears. Why hadn't she said goodbye to Gram? Their fight seemed childish now.

Liam stepped forward. "I wish to invoke the boon you promised Grigory of Evederell."

The empress froze, then pivoted toward Liam, who stood defiantly in the middle of the room. "Your father received his boon. The Hallson manor and lordship were granted to him."

"He never asked for them, as you well know. He reserved his single favor for my brother and me. If we had need."

The empress's face twisted in anger. Em's heartbeat pounded in every extremity. Liam was saving her? The woman swished back to them, robes flowing around her. "You would be wiser, young Hallson, to use your boon on something less . . . complicated."

Liam stood firm. "Wise or not, I love her, and I can't lose her."

The woman's fury did not abate. She shifted her gaze to Em, then glared at Liam once more.

"Like father, like son, I suppose. Wasting your affection on the unworthy."

Liam did not flinch at this. But Em did. After a moment of silence, the empress motioned for the guards to stand down, and Em was released.

"Consider the boon granted. I owe your family nothing further," the woman spat at Liam. "However, I cannot just let her go free."

"Your Majesty?" Em asked.

"You wish to prove your loyalty and avoid the gallows? Very well. I offer you a task that will utilize your creativity. If you succeed, I will pardon you, and you are free to return home. If you fail, your punishment stands—your life is forfeit. I will give you several months to complete the task. You will report back on the last day of the twelfth month, the solstice. Are we agreed?"

Em dipped her head in assent, feeling relief. "What is the task, Majesty?"

"Bring me the Ring of Clavonion—the lost signet ring—and you may live."

A cartload of bricks had been dropped on her. The ring was a legend, a myth. Surely it wasn't real. If it was, it had been lost for centuries. And she would have to find it in just over two months? The empress might as well just execute Em now and get it over with. She began to tremble anew.

"Report back when you find the ring. If you defy or evade me, you will not get the courtesy of a meeting before I hang you. Do we understand each other?"

Em's stomach was in her throat. "Yes, Your Majesty," she croaked.

CHAPTER 5

Brildonia, Esnania's closest ally, is known for their wool industry and for their intricate hooked and woven rugs.

"Decor in the Modern RQ Style"
The Standard Book of Anything

Nine Weeks until the Solstice

They were silently escorted from the Golden Lark. When they reached the street, Liam turned and hugged Em fiercely. She clasped him back, still feeling as if everything was spinning.

"What just happened?" she murmured.

"You're not dead. That's what."

"Not yet."

"We can figure all that out. Her Majesty wants a magical legendary ring? We'll find it."

Em nodded, still feeling dazed. "That boon business. Your father?"

Liam pulled back and grasped her hand. "Came in handy, didn't it? Let's get out of here before she changes her mind."

Hallson Manor—Liam's former home—was abuzz with pre-wedding activity when they returned from the Golden Lark. After Em saved Brookerby from post-warding tree malaise, Marcellus had resigned his military commission, moved into the manor as the new Lord Hallson, and rekindled his relationship with Cass. And now, Marcellus and Cass would get their happy ending.

Liam and Em weren't acknowledged as they crossed the marble foyer and collapsed in parlor chairs. They had spoken very little during the short walk from the palace to the luxurious townhouse. Em's body felt wrung out and her mind jumbled, so Liam simply took her hand and let her be with her thoughts.

The steward entered their field of vision and started at the sight of them. "Oh, Lord Hallson—urm, forgive me, Master Liam. Still getting used to it. I did feed Sir Bobson Fuzzyton his afternoon snack." They glanced over at Bob, who was snoozing on the parlor rug, and Liam cracked a smile for the first time that day. Bob lifted his head, and at the sight of Liam, he climbed to his feet, tail wagging.

"Is there anything I can get you?"

"Don't mind us, Fisher. We're just trying to keep out of the way."

The man turned to watch bustling maids, butlers, cooks, and tailors scurry across the entryway. "Yes, sir. It's been like this for weeks. But the new Lord Hallson assures me it will die down after tomorrow."

"Is Marcellus—uh, Lord Hallson—around?" Em inquired as she scratched behind Bob's ears.

"I believe he and his bride-to-be are conferring with the head cleric. Some last-minute wording changes. But it could be hours before they emerge."

"In that case, we might just keep to ourselves for the evening," Liam said. "Sorry to interrupt."

"Not at all. Good to see you, sir. And you, Miss Strider." Fisher bowed quickly and headed toward the back of the house.

Em watched him leave and then shifted in her chair. "Feels different," she said. Her voice sounded strange in her head. Higher pitched.

"Being here? I suppose," Liam said.

They sat in silence for a moment. Em still felt nothing. An utter lack of emotion. Numbness. She wondered if that was normal. Wasn't a person supposed to feel something when their certain death had been pronounced, then merely delayed? Shouldn't she be crying? Terrified? Enraged?

She glanced at Liam. He was certainly feeling something. Relief, maybe. But his leg bounced as if he could barely sit still.

"Do you wish you'd stayed here? Kept your title?"

"No. Obviously not." He flashed her a smile.

"So you would be content to stay in Brookerby? Even when I—" But she couldn't complete that sentence. Even when she was executed for treason. After she failed her impossible task. She wondered why she was even asking? Was she trying to make this worse on the man who had just saved her? She shook her head and muttered the only thing she'd been able to say on their short walk from the palace: "I'm sorry."

"We can figure this out," he said, shifting on his seat. "We'll find out everything we can about this ring and then we'll track it down. Three months is a long time. I mean, great deities, you found a tree solution in a few weeks." Liam leapt from his chair and began pacing. "Her Majesty is right. You're resourceful. Maybe it isn't impossible. Your parents may even have the thing sitting in their warehouse. Even if they don't, I bet they could help you look. *The Standard Book of Anything* would help too."

Em shook her head. He was right. But . . . "It's an old fairy tale," she said. "'The Great Ring of Power.' Gram used to tell it to me. She reads it to the children in town. It's about the first emperor's magical ring that can create any reality he desires. It's nonsense."

"You don't know. Fairy tales had to come from somewhere. I need to make a list. All the places it could be. Where to research. Who to ask." He darted out of the room, no doubt in search of ink and paper.

Em stayed where she was. She wanted to join in. Start the search that might save her life. But her body didn't move. Couldn't.

Her hands were shaking, and she squeezed her eyes shut. If nothing else, at least her numbness had worn off.

CHAPTER 6

The national religion of Esnania requires prayers during the spring planting, the harvest, and the solstices. In addition, life events like births, weddings, and deaths are marked in a place of worship. Otherwise, the rituals are observed by temple caretakers and largely ignored by the populace.

"Why Is This Temple Here?
And Other Tourism Questions"
The Standard Book of Anything

Eight Weeks and Six Days until the Solstice

Marcellus and Cass were married the following day. The wedding ceremony was lavish, especially compared to the rites performed in Brookerby.

A short ceremony was what she had expected, but Em had been kneeling inside the massive temple—on the stone floor—for what seemed like hours. The city rituals lasted much longer, apparently. Her dress was made of a delicate material that provided no padding against the unyielding floor. Her right leg was starting to go numb.

The head cleric had a great deal of sacred text to read—not all of it regarding marriage. He floated around the dais in his bronze-and-red robes, clearly in no hurry. She studied the rafters of the triangular building, its peak extending into the sky as if the deities lived among the clouds and would notice the protruding wood and iron and remember they had supplicants below. She squirmed, and Liam gave her an apologetic look.

Brookerby had no place of worship. A trusted friend or neighbor would speak the expected ritual at a funeral, or a wedding, or the birth of a child. The words were short, and usually involved thanking the deities for their goodness and asking for their blessing. This felt entirely foreign to her. She shifted again.

"I forgot to warn you about the kneeling," he whispered.

"No kidding," she grumbled.

An elderly woman shushed them, and Liam penitently turned forward again.

Marcellus and Cass were holding their palms together as the cleric bound their wrists and forearms with a velvet rope. He intoned, "May you be forever bound, thus."

"I hope not forever," Em giggled.

Liam shushed her before the older woman had the chance.

Her cheeks flushed, and Em smothered her heckling and focused instead on the pain in her knees. Perhaps that was part of it. Transcend pain and become more in tune with the deities. There was probably a metaphor there about enduring the pain life gave you to find the beauty beyond.

But Em had not transcended. She thought only of the moment when this would be over.

Marcellus and Cass were now walking together around the perimeter of the temple, slowly, as they were still connected by the rope.

"This is the ritual of traveling through life together as one," Liam whispered.

Em nodded and watched them float around the edge, never taking their eyes from the other. They both held serious expressions but glowed from within, as if their happiness could not be contained in this austere temple. Cass looked more lovely than Em had ever seen her. It was like one of Gram's fairy tales come true, watching those two be in love.

Finally, they finished their journey around the temple, and the cleric was speaking once more as he untied their bonds. It sounded like he was wrapping up. He called out a final blessing, and the wedding guests repeated the last line: "Go with grace."

The room exploded in chatter as Marcellus and Cass disappeared through a side exit and the cleric left the dais.

Em struggled to her feet, shaking her right leg to regain the feeling. Then Liam was at her side, helping her up.

"Beautiful, yeah?"

Em nodded, not wanting to criticize. She was surprised he was moved by the stuffy ceremony.

Liam beamed. "The temple really lends a solemnity to the proceedings. Makes it feel more official, don't you think?"

Em shrugged. "I've always liked our simple country ceremonies. Feels truer to life."

Liam didn't respond. He gestured to the side door. Wanna get out of here? Head to the Lanesby estate?

She nodded. But then stopped. "Actually, we should try and talk to the cleric about the ring. Might as well, since we're here."

They had spent the prior evening brainstorming where to start with the search for the ring. The temple was at the top of the list. Legend said the deities gifted the ring to the first emperor on this very spot. It might be fiction, but it was a starting point.

They made their way up to the dais and spotted a different cleric than the one who performed the ceremony dousing candles. His bronze robes were less adorned, indicating he was lower ranked. Em wasn't sure how to address the man, but she tried. "Excuse me, Your Holiness."

The cleric looked up, surprised. "Sister, I apologize for correcting you, but only the head cleric is addressed in that manner."

Em flushed. "Apologies, sir."

"Brother Silas is fine, my sister."

"Thank you, Brother Silas." Em paused a minute, wondering how to phrase her query. "We wanted to consult with one of the clerics about a matter of curiosity. Do you have a moment, or should we return another time?"

"I always have time for one who seeks," the cleric said. He gestured to the steps of the dais, and they sat side by side.

Em began. "We are curious about a relic, which in the tales is connected with the deities and this very temple. Do you or any of your brother clerics have any information on the Ring of Clavonion?"

Brother Silas started, then smiled indulgently. "I confess, I expected a spiritual question. But your inquiry is reasonable. We have received it a few times over the years from historians, and others interested in the myth."

"So, the story is true?" Liam interjected. "It was gifted by the deities to the young peasant man who would become the first emperor?"

"It is true that the first emperor of the House of Clavonion built this temple. I can show you the capstone. The legend says the ring's stone came from this very spot, inspiring the founding of this temple. But unfortunately, we have no proof that this is true. We've searched the archives for early writings, but nothing has been uncovered to verify the origin."

"So, it's just a story?" Em asked.

"Just a story?" Brother Silas laughed and stood. "Indeed. But stories sometimes contain great truth, sister. After all, we learn from that tale that great power is granted by the deities alone. And when that power has been gifted, we should, in turn, honor those gods with our time and treasure."

Em nodded, distracted, and stood also. "You said archives. Would it be possible for us to explore those texts? With supervision, of course."

"That would be a request for the head cleric, sister, but we typically do not allow visitors in the archives. Some of the texts are quite delicate and need to be handled with great care."

"I understand. Thank you, Brother Silas," Liam said.

The cleric strode back to his work. Dismissed, Liam gripped Em's hand and pulled her away.

"He was no help," Em growled.

"We can try again later. Today is about Cass and Marcellus. Let's try to be happy tonight and research tomorrow," Liam said with finality. He was right, of course, but Em still felt time ticking. Each moment brought her closer to the solstice. Closer to failure and death. Numbly, she allowed him to guide her to the side door of the nearly empty temple.

THE RECEPTION WAS HOSTED by Cass's family at the Lanesby estate. Em and Liam arrived by carriage and found the avenue in front of the grand house crowded as they approached. The windows were trimmed in bunches of roses, and the entryway was swathed in tulle. It made for a charming picture in the late afternoon sun.

The manor was a large one, with a grand staircase at the entrance leading into an open room with high ceilings. The grand ballroom from Em's previous visit had been totally transformed into a banquet hall. Tables were draped with blush-colored tablecloths and greenery and adorned with hundreds of candlesticks.

They paused in the entryway to join the receiving line. Mr. and Mrs. Lanesby, Cass's parents, greeted Liam warmly and offered a kind nod to Em. She supposed it was a generous greeting and very polite of Mrs. Lanesby to not remark on the last time she attended an event at their house. On that occasion, Em had been arrested by imperial soldiers.

Then Cass and Marcellus stood before them, beaming. Liam shook his brother's hand and pulled him in for a quick hug.

"Congrats, Marce."

Em shook Marcellus's hand next. "I'm glad you're here, Miss Strider." He grinned. "And I'm glad my brother seems so happy. Must be your doing?"

Em smiled, but she didn't quite meet his gaze. Her insides roiled. Unbidden, the empress's words to Liam came back. *Wasting your affection on the unworthy.* She wasn't wrong. How long before Liam believed it also?

Liam grasped Cass's hands and gave her a quick peck on the cheek. "I always knew you'd wear him down," he teased.

Cass laughed, her eyes dancing. Then she pulled Em into a warm hug. "If you hadn't said anything . . . or resolved that tree business, we wouldn't be here," she said quietly. "Thank you."

Em felt her cheeks redden as Cass stepped away. If anyone in the world deserved happiness, it was Cass. And Marcellus wasn't so bad either. She had nudged the man toward Cass in Brookerby, but giving Em any kind of credit for the union was ridiculous. She smiled quickly at them both, and then she and Liam were ushered along so the next guests could greet the bride and groom.

Em clutched Liam's elbow, and they descended into the grand banquet hall below. Guests were milling about the room, remarking on the decor and gazing hopefully at waiters carrying trays of appetizers through the room.

Em had been in many crowds. In Brookerby—at the mercantile— the press of bodies and shouts of greeting were comforting. Joyful, even. In Brookerby, Em knew she mattered. That she belonged to the people pushing in around her.

But she didn't belong here. In this crowd, she had a feeling she could pass among ten different conversations without speaking a single meaningful syllable. Without anyone caring whether she participated. In that realization, she felt more isolated than if she were sitting in a room by herself.

Liam was immediately accosted by some distant relative. Em tried to be sociable. To join in. To be happy, as Liam requested, but after ten minutes without any acknowledgment of her presence, Em ducked away, swiping a glass of champagne from a passing tray. She was being foolish, she knew, and mentally flogged herself for not sticking it out, but it would be strange to go back now.

She found herself wandering the small groups without a destination. What was she doing here?

Liam was passing from group to group. Greeting old friends. He was more animated than she'd seen him in months. It was clear he belonged here. And she did not. She tugged at her flimsy yellow dress, trying to straighten the gauzy material clinging to the underskirt. Giving up, she sat at one of the perimeter tables and drank her champagne in two gulps.

Why hadn't she begged off? As she sat there, she was barreling toward almost certain execution, with a limited amount of time to find an impossible item. She should be researching. Searching. Asking questions. But of who? Would anyone here know anything? She scanned the room, wondering if the Lanesbys had invited any clerics or historians.

Her throat felt dry. Her champagne was gone, so she reached for another. Was that number two or three? It hardly mattered. Maybe it would help her tolerate the evening. She stood and strolled to the high windows to gaze over the garden. She felt a little dizzy as she turned to watch Cass and Marcellus at the top of the stairs. The receiving line had ended at last, and they were laughing at some private joke, her hand on his shoulder. They sparkled together. And they had their whole lives ahead of them. They would live in Hallson Manor. Maybe have a few children. Bicker and make up. Snuggle by the fireplace in the parlor. Grow old together . . .

She drank her champagne in a single gulp. Suddenly Liam was at her side.

"Whoa there. You okay?"

Em traded her empty for a full glass and took another sip. Liam's hand was warm on her shoulder. Dear, sparkling Liam. She was unworthy of him.

"I'm just celebrating. While I still can."

"Not funny," he scolded.

She sipped at her third—or fourth?—glass, and while she felt the heady buzz of the alcohol, she felt no relief.

"Em!" He stooped to meet her eye. "What is going on with you?"

"I'm fine. Go back to your friends." Her voice was flatter than she intended.

"Come meet them. They'll love you, I promise," he coaxed.

"They won't. And it doesn't matter. Because I'll be dead."

Liam's jaw hardened. He tried to take her hand, but she moved away, spilling a few drops of her champagne onto the polished marble floor. She quickly set the glass down.

"Do you want to go?" he asked.

Em felt her eyes well with tears, embarrassed that she couldn't keep it together for one night. "You have to stay. You're giving a speech."

"I don't have to do anything. If you're not feeling—"

"I've already ruined it. You gave up your life for nonstop work in my backward little town, and I'm not worth it. I'm not worth giving up all this." She gestured to the fine room around them.

Nearby, a few guests had stopped talking and were openly staring at them. Liam looked frustrated, but he took a breath. "You've had a difficult day . . ."

Em let out a huff of angry laughter. "A difficult everything. I blame the empress—she ruined everything for me." Perhaps that was a little too loud. There was a gasp. Had someone started whispering? "I knew who I was before, and I was okay with it. And then our warding tree fell—her fault it was there in the first place—and she put that oath on me, and now this impossible task. And I feel like I'm dragging you down with me." Liam had backed up a step, eyebrows knitted. He was going to try and fix this, but she just needed to get out before she ruined any more of this beautiful evening.

"I'm leaving," she growled. "Don't follow."

Em turned and swished toward a downward staircase. Away from the prying eyes of the crowd. She vaguely remembered there was a pantry down here that she could hide in. Now—for sure—Mrs. Lanesby would never invite her back.

CHAPTER 7

The waitstaff were ferrying dinner trays up the stairs when Em emerged from the pantry a good while later. Her body felt wrung out, but she had finally calmed down enough to consider rejoining the party. The champagne had worn off, and she was feeling the twinge of a headache.

She stood against the wall watching the trays go by. The food smelled wonderful, but she wasn't particularly hungry. And she had no desire to return to the party to be gawked at. She also didn't think she could make polite conversation for the whole evening. But she would have to walk through the banquet hall, filled with now-seated guests, to get to the exit. Humiliating. Maybe there was another way out.

She turned right into the kitchen. None of the culinary staff glanced her way as she cut a quick path through the chaos, aiming for a door at the far end. Perhaps it went to another part of the house? She could surely find another door, or a window to crawl out of.

She found herself in a narrow hallway behind the kitchen. After peering in a few of the doors and finding small, plain bedrooms, she reasoned it was some kind of staff quarters. She passed a washroom at the end of the hall, and then another staircase leading upstairs yet again. At the top was another hallway—and an external door. Breathing a sigh of relief, she yanked open this door and found herself at the back of the house in a tidy vegetable garden, hidden behind the shrubberies of the Lanesby's impressive flower gardens.

The sun was kissing the horizon, and a chilly breeze reminded Em she couldn't remain in the garden all night. She followed a cobblestone walkway through the topiaries, toward the front of the house. Several times she had to duck to avoid being spotted through the large windows of the banquet hall. She felt mortified hiding like this, but all the guests were seated, listening to speeches. If anyone looked, they would certainly notice a woman in a lemon-yellow dress wandering outside, and the gossip would start. She was protecting Liam as much as herself by staying hidden.

Liam was planning to give a lengthy and heartfelt toast for his brother. She hoped it went well, and felt a twinge of sorrow that she would miss it. If only she hadn't let her emotions—her panic—run away with her, she would be there now, supporting him.

Maybe she could just go back. Maybe no one would care. But her feelings revolted at the thought. After the scene she made earlier, she didn't want to explain herself to hundreds of strangers. It was good she was leaving.

But poor Liam. How could he forgive her after this? *Unworthy* repeated in her brain like a drumbeat.

She arrived at the front of the house and found their rented carriage. With a few quick instructions, she was inside, and the vehicle pulled away from the Lanesby estate.

THE CARRIAGE DRIVER, under protest, left Em near the temple. She sent him back to the party to wait for Liam, with a note explaining where she had gone. She didn't want to deprive Liam of a way to get home, and she didn't want him to worry.

She had to get into the archives. If they had something about the

Clavonion ring, she needed to find it. She didn't have time for bureaucratic petitioning or pleading with the unyielding clerics.

After scanning the mostly empty plaza, Em crept to the A-frame temple and crouched by the side door. She gulped. Practicing lock-picking at the Gray Horse was one thing, but performing an actual break-in introduced a whole new set of variables. The wind was biting now that the sun was down, and she still wore her yellow dress—hardly appropriate for breaking into an imperial building. She felt exposed. There were no evening services at the temple, so any person milling about would instantly look suspicious. She needed to get inside quickly.

She only hesitated a moment before concentrating on the locked door. She sharpened her focus, directing that spark feeling toward the dead bolt. Probing the mechanism. It felt like a standard door lock. Fairly new, but the design was familiar. She turned the knob as she concentrated.

A click came from the door, and, shivering, she pushed into the building.

The inside was pitch-black once the door was closed, except for one oil lamp burning on the altar table. Behind it was the simple wooden door where Em had seen the cleric disappear earlier that day. The back rooms—including the archives—must be through that door. Em bumbled her way to the dais at the front of the room, nearly knocking over a candlestand in her path. The oil lamp was her only guide. A religious metaphor, no doubt.

"Nearly there," she whispered, rounding the altar. She grasped the door handle and turned it slowly. It was also locked. She nearly cursed aloud but bit her lip instead. Most of the clerics would be gone, but there was a chance one or two observed evening prayers. Em needed to be stealthy. After listening for a moment or two, she began working her mind against the door.

Em focused, breathing deeply to calm her nerves. Again, she conjured a small spark that she directed toward the shiny steel pins and tumbler. After a moment, the lock gave a small click. She pushed the door open and stepped in.

· · ·

THE LIGHT FLICKERING from the oil lamp on the altar couldn't penetrate the dark beyond the door. She nearly stumbled down an iron staircase immediately before her. She kept a hand on the door-knob and steadied herself. Assuming she could stay on her feet, she would have to step quietly and listen for clerics. She closed the door behind her and directed that spark feeling toward her own feet—just like Farrigan had taught her—to muffle her footsteps on the metal stairs. She started descending, clutching the thin railing.

Her heart was fluttering. The fear of discovery was palpable. Every creak and distant rattle had her stopping to listen for the telltale sound of footsteps. This was maybe the dumbest thing she had ever done. Breaking in like this was highly illegal, but she couldn't deny the rush of adrenaline that coursed through her.

Em often wondered what it would be like to adventure, to pilfer magical items like her parents. They had carved out a life for them-selves and—arguably—had kept magical items out of the wrong hands. But Em couldn't square the thieving with what she believed to be right. Which was . . . not thieving?

What Em believed to be right had also put her head on a chopping block. So maybe all it took to throw out her morality was the threat of execution.

She reached the bottom of the second flight of stairs, and a faint light glowed around her. She stood at the point of a triangular room with several doors on each side, and a single archway directly oppo-site her. Another dim oil lamp hung from the apex of the archway.

But which door led to the archives? Em squinted at the doors in turn. Finally, discovering no difference between them, she arbitrarily chose the second on the left.

Turning the handle, she found it unlocked, and she ducked inside.

A series of shelves greeted her, lit from the hall light. On those shelves were jars. And something was floating in the jars. Lumps of—

Em gasped and quickly backed out of the room, pulling the door shut. Were those animal organs? Or human? She thought she saw a brain in one jar. She shuddered, feeling her stomach turn. Why would the temple have those? Was it some obscure ritual? She didn't want to know.

She drew back from that door and chose the second door directly opposite; it was as far from the jar room as she could get.

Inside were scrolls and books and shelving. Maybe this was it? She spotted a squat candle on the table, and a stone dish with matches. She lit the candle's wick and closed the door. The light cast a glow just strong enough to read the titles on the shelf without straining.

Em began searching a barrel stuffed with scrolls. They all seemed to be maps and religious iconography, so she quickly moved on to the books. She scanned the spines of the books on the shelf, searching for any hint of the ring, or the early Clavonion king, Tranton I. Any clue that could point her in a direction.

After what felt like hours, she made it to the lowest shelf, which seemed to contain large binders—temple ledgers with labeled dates. She pulled out the first volume. The dates coincided with her schoolroom knowledge of Tranton I's early reign, and from the temple's construction in 462 RQ. She placed the binder on the worktable by the lamp.

The early entries detailed the construction process and cost. Em found herself engrossed in the architectural drawings and descriptions of construction challenges and solutions. After seven pages of this, she stopped herself from reading further and flipped beyond construction. The tome thoroughly described visits by the first emperor, but his ring was not mentioned.

Finally, the scribe noted his death in battle in excruciating detail. He was nicked with a knife while fighting the Northern tribes. After he declared victory and returned home, the wound had festered. Again, the specifics were nauseating. Em was ready to move on to the next ledger, when she saw a few sentences that made her gasp.

After the High Emperor died, the temple clerics detailed the items that were to be buried with him. Among them was listed a silver-and-amber signet ring, a gift from the deities—for a thing of such power should be belong with the one man who could wield it.

"So it's in Tranton's tomb?" Em hissed in despair. The marble tomb stood a stone's throw from the palace, buried deep in the earth, with a mausoleum above, and was guarded by no less than twenty imperial soldiers. Getting inside would truly be impossible.

But she read down farther, and there was a second list of items that were actually buried with him. It seemed redundant, until Em realized the ring wasn't included. There was a footnote, written in tiny script.

Before the final entombment ceremony, the signet ring was taken by the secundarius, the supporting cleric and a scheming man. It was gifted to mercenaries, with the aim of providing power to the Northern tribes so that they might not be absorbed into the empire after their recent crushing loss. The cleric was caught and executed, but the ring was never recovered. It is believed to be lost somewhere in the Antillei Mountains.

Voices sounded outside the door. Em quickly doused her candle, grabbed the ledger, and ducked down behind the worktable. She was next to the bookshelf where the ledger belonged, so she quickly shoved it back on the shelf. Seconds later, the door opened, and the hallway lamp light spilled into the archives as someone stood on the threshold.

Em held her breath. If the cleric on the threshold lit the candle again, she would be discovered. She didn't know the penalty for breaking into the temple, but considering the religious expenses were covered by the empire, she assumed it would be another trip to the throne room. If the empress even bothered with her this time.

The cleric in the doorway was finishing his conversation with another cleric and turned to step farther into the room.

This was it. She was caught. Em wondered if Liam was still at the Lanesby estate. Perhaps he wouldn't even hear of her execution until after it happened. Then she remembered Farrigan had taught her some simple misdirection magic.

Em had used this magic once before when she'd summoned a fire as a distraction to save Mendel's life. Farrigan had been impressed at this tale, but he'd admonished her to only do the minimum amount necessary. She didn't need something fancy now. Just a noise to distract the cleric while she escaped. A broom handle falling. Or a dinner plate slipping off the table.

Or a jar of human organs crashing to the ground.

It was easier if you could see the thing you were influencing, but not essential. Em focused all of her spark on nudging a jar in the other room to slide off the shelf. She felt it move in her mind's eye and doubled down as her focus started to waver. The cleric was starting to light a match when a spectacular crash came from the jar room. Startled, the cleric and his companion—who had been standing in the hallway—rushed for the other room.

This was the best chance Em would have. While their backs were turned, she silenced her feet with another focused spark and darted out of the archives and toward the shadows around the stairwell. Her body felt strangely exhausted, perhaps from the mental effort of the magic, but she managed to move without stumbling.

The two men were entering the jar room, calling out for the invader to reveal themselves as Em silently dashed up the stairs.

She reached the top in what seemed like two heartbeats, exited into the temple hall, and flew out the side door.

Em gasped, finding that she hadn't breathed deeply since the archive room was breached. But she still wasn't in the clear, so she quickly jogged away from the temple and into the city proper. She had succeeded. She had found the archives, and a clue about the great legendary ring. Somewhere in the Antillei Mountains.

It wasn't much to go on, but it was a start. She flagged a passing cab and—rather than returning to Hallson Manor—gave the driver an address down by the wharf.

CHAPTER 8

Although Gillamor is a tourist-friendly city, we advise visitors to avoid certain parts of town where criminal activity is markedly higher. It is unknown whether degenerates flock to these areas, or whether the area itself creates lawbreakers. Imperial scholars are studying the effect.

"A Guide to the Capital City"
The Standard Book of Anything

The waterfront was seedier than she remembered. It was fully dark now, and a crescent moon did little to light the nefarious activity in the shadows. Shouts spilled out from the few open taverns. Not happy shouts. Em quickened her pace, feeling eyes on her at every dark alleyway she passed. A small group sailors loitered at the pier, watching her with uncomfortable interest. She supposed her floaty lemon-colored dress wasn't helping her blend in.

Finally, she found a familiar warehouse. She knocked on the nondescript metal door in a syncopated pattern and waited. And waited. Maybe this wasn't a great idea. What if they were out? How would she get home? She didn't have her bag, any of her tools, or the map. She had spent the last of the coin in her pocketbook on the cab here. If they didn't answer, she might as well go surrender to that gang on the corner. As she contemplated turning around to face her fate, the knob finally twisted.

"Em?"

"It's me," she said, relief spilling out through her words. "Can I come in?"

Her mother, Anne Strider, opened the door and quickly pulled her in. "What are you doing here? It's not safe at night."

"Yeah, I realized that."

Anne closed the door, engaged the locks, and turned to study her daughter. "Are we hosting a party we didn't know about?"

"No. Just had a rough evening. Ur, ah, rough couple of days, I guess. Long story."

"Em?" Farrigan's voice echoed from somewhere in the cavernous warehouse. "Were we expecting her?"

"Not tonight, Far!" Anne shouted in reply. Then said, to Em, "You know you're always welcome."

Anne guided her toward the living space at the back of the warehouse. "You do look uncharacteristically dressy. Wasn't the wedding this evening?"

Farrigan interrupted with a hearty greeting as he came into view. He had books and old documents spread on the coffee table before him, and a comically tiny loupe covering his right eye. Anne led Em to one of the lumpy brown chairs and offered her a cup of hot tea and a knitted shawl. A game board with a half-played round of sticks and stones sat on the corner table. It wasn't like Grady's game. This one seemed to have etched metal rods as the sticks, and colorful glass as the stones. An expensive set. The electric lights draped above set the cozy living area apart from the cold and dark of the rest of the warehouse, which contained rows and rows of metal shelving.

Em felt the tension slink out of her. She had needed to see her parents. Another flash of embarrassment went through her as she realized anew why she wasn't at the wedding reception.

Gripping her chipped and faded teacup, Em began to fill them in. The summons from the empress. Death for treason. Then the softening of the penalty—an impossible task—the Ring of Clavonion in exchange for her life. Brother Silas's information. Em's meltdown. Breaking and entering at the temple.

Farrigan whistled, long and low.

"I know. It's a lot," Em said, staring into her now-lukewarm tea.

"Well, yes. I knew you were an overachiever, Em, but the temple archives?" Farrigan laughed. "I guess if you're going to take up a life of crime, you might as well go big."

"We've never attempted it," Anne offered. "Once or twice we considered . . ."

"What did you see?" Farrigan asked.

"They have human organs in jars," Em said. "At least, I think they were human."

Anne and Farrigan exchanged a meaningful look. Then Anne held out a hand. "You lose." As he grumbled and reached in his pocket for some coins, Anne explained, "I heard a rumor they did. He didn't believe it."

Em laughed. "What are they for, do you think?"

Anne shrugged. "I heard a few of the clerics were dabbling in divination and darker magical arts. I suspect the empress would be livid if she knew. We've been . . . keeping an eye on it."

Em shivered anew, trying not to think about the many ways her temple break-in could've ended badly. She wondered what "keeping an eye on it" meant, but changed the subject.

"Liam thought you two might have heard of the ring in your travels. Maybe you even have it in your warehouse."

Anne was already shaking her head. "We have a few rings, which we can go look at now. But I've never caught wind of anything like that Clavonion ring. Believe me, I would've dropped everything to go find it if I had."

"Do you think it's true, then? That the ring can create any reality you desire?"

Farrigan harrumphed. "It's just a legend. If such a thing did exist, there would be traces. Footprints everywhere. Unless the owner doesn't know what they possessed, there would be a trail of magic and wealth and power leading right to their doorstep."

"I did find some information in the archives," Em offered.

Her parents looked at her expectantly, so Em shared what she had discovered about the secundarius taking the ring after Tranton's death and sending it north.

"That's not much to go on. It's a huge area to search." Farrigan frowned. "We might have a map of the mountains you can have."

Anne hopped up. "No sense in doing nothing. Let's go look at our collection." She snatched a black book from the table, her inventory, and guided them through the rows of shelving. Em had to jog to keep up.

Ring number one was a small golden band that held a delicate opal. Swirls were worked into the gold, and a tiny clasp swung the opal setting open to reveal a lock of dark hair. Anne handed the ring to Em for inspection. "We haven't been able to totally decipher its use, but we believe the ring can transfer strength from the wearer to the person whose hair is contained within."

"This is, of course, conjecture," Farrigan cut in, "but we did test it once. I felt very tired, and Anne had a remarkably healthful day."

"Plus, we've been able to trace it to a similarly described device owned by a noblewoman whose son was a war hero," Anne said.

Em tapped her lips with her finger. It was an interesting object, but it wasn't *the* ring. It didn't look like something the first emperor would wear. She expected the Ring of Clavonion to be heftier, with the Clavonion crest etched somewhere. Also, it was supposed to be silver, according to the temple archives. "What else do you have?"

Ring number two was a single piece of jade. Anne laughed as she picked it up. "This renders the wearer into the most stunningly beautiful version of themselves. No makeup or hairdresser required."

Em tilted her head. "Have you worn it?"

"Once or twice." Anne grinned. "Once when I had to charm my way into an Aglenian royal ball. Once for a night on the town with your father."

Farrigan waggled his eyebrows, grinning.

"No details, please," Em interjected.

Ring number three was a rough-cut topaz stone on a thick bronze band. It looked like the right type of ring, but it was the wrong material. Anne explained that it only provided additional light, like a mini lantern, when you swiped your finger across it.

Ring four was familiar: the feathered ring that Em had previously worn. When falling from a great height, the ring allowed the wearer to flutter down safely instead of smashing into the ground. It had saved Em's life when Sam Monterey had blasted her out a second-story window. She brushed the etched golden feathers fondly before turning away.

"That's all we have in storage right now," Anne concluded, closing her inventory.

They walked back to the living area, where Farrigan produced a map of the Antillei Mountains. He started writing on the map as he spoke.

"I think there is a small group of mages who live in caves on the eastern side, one of the largest peaks near the ruins of the Silver Nightingale fortress. We've encountered rumors in our travels of their colony."

"You think they'd be willing to help?" Em asked.

"Oh, dear. Don't get your hopes up. Rumors. Far and I couldn't even find them. And if they do exist, I can't imagine they're friendly."

Em's mind was already whirring. "Are there other potential places in the mountain range? Old deer trails or trading roads? What road would the mercenaries have traveled by?"

Farrigan circled multiple locations and wrote notes in the margins of the map. He stopped to consult a daily journal once or twice, but his mind was sharp, and he seemed to remember minute details of their adventures—even some that happened more than ten years ago. When he finished, there were over three dozen potential settlements in the mountains. That didn't even count the towns skirting the base of the mountain range.

Anne patted Em's shoulder. "You might have to spend a great deal of time searching."

"I know. But it's the only lead I have," Em said.

Farrigan lifted a cane that was leaning on the wall. "You could use this? The fast-map will get you to the mountains, but it will not be precise once you're within them. This is our jumper cane. Tap it three times in the same spot and it will transport you to a new location within eyesight. It might take some practice but could be very useful when hiking."

Em took the cane, focused on a spot across the warehouse and tapped the stick three times. Her eyes had drifted a bit on the last tap, and she ended up several feet from where she intended. And she felt a bit dizzy. Still, it was a useful tool. "Thanks."

Farrigan nodded. "Will save a lot of time."

"Oh, we're also giving you our bag of holding. Just for the trip, you understand. We do hope to get all of this back eventually," Anne said as she ducked inside their other living space to retrieve the bag.

Em was surprised at this last. The bag of holding was a gift indeed. It could hold an infinite number of items without getting any heavier or bulkier. Usually, Anne kept it close so they didn't have to limit their item selection. Em looked at them both, a bit stunned. "Thank you both. For the research. For the items . . ."

Anne stepped forward to give her a quick squeeze and hand her the bag. "We would go with you. It's just that, well . . ."

"Prior engagements. We'd only get in your way. You know. All the flimsy excuses we can muster," Farrigan finished with a quirk of his mouth.

"No. It's fine. You've done so much already. I can handle this."

"We know you can," Anne said. "We really would go. A find of this magnitude is—"

"Monumental," Farrigan said. "But we have a lead on something at the moment that can't be delayed."

"We can find out why the empress wants the ring. Subtly, of course. After all, why now?" Anne offered.

Em nodded. "I didn't think of that. I suppose it would be good to know…"

"What are parents for?" Farrigan laughed. "If not to infiltrate imperial intelligence?"

~

Farrigan and Anne dropped Em off at Hallson Manor later that evening. They again offered to help, but Em noticed the hesitation in their offer and quickly assured them she would fine. Clutching the map, the bag, and the jumping cane, she said goodnight and thanked them again.

Then Farrigan pulled out his pocket watch and wound the gear on the back. Anne took his offered arm, and they vanished with a small popping noise.

Em turned toward the townhouse, tapping the map against her leg. She had thought her parents might jump at the chance to join her. Weren't they all about adventure and magical items? But they were working on something else. Something that could not be delayed. She felt a wave of exhaustion, and any confusion was replaced by the desire to sleep.

Em wasn't eager for a heart-to-heart with Liam about her behavior. Luckily, nobody was back from the reception yet. The house was quiet when she slunk in the side door through the garden. She went straight to her room, belatedly realizing she was still wearing the knitted shawl Anne had given her. At first, she thought it might be magic, too, but there was no telltale rushing underneath the surface. Just a normal shawl; it was endearing that her mother owned some normal things too. Em's yellow dress was dirty and ripped along the hem. She slid out of it, kicked off her shoes, and pulled on a nightgown.

Then she dropped into bed like a stone, both ashamed of her behavior at the reception, and grateful for her parents' assistance. She had behaved like a madwoman. She realized that now, but in the moment, declaring her mortality and ranting against the empress felt like the only sensible thing to do. She could only hope no one felt the urge to report it to Her Majesty.

But her parents were so calm and capable. They had heard the story and immediately jumped to help, with all the skills and items at their disposal. Without them—and without some thieving—she wouldn't have the glimmer of hope she now felt. And who cares if they didn't want to come? They had given her a map, a jumping cane, and a bottomless bag. And if she really needed help, she could probably still ask them. Or Liam.

She would talk to Liam tomorrow and apologize. He would understand the stress of certain death does strange things to a person's emotions. He would forgive her. He would understand her need to act—to scour the mountains as soon as possible. After all, that might be the only way to keep her life.

CHAPTER 9

Finding lost items can be stressful, but these simple steps will help you locate the item you misplaced:
1. Retrace your steps. When was the last time you saw it, and what have you done since?
2. Think about likely scenarios that would've caused your item to go missing.
3. Look in unexpected places.
4. Search thoroughly. This may require you to notice small differences, or move objects that may be covering your missing item.

"How to Locate Your Lost Item"
The Standard Book of Anything

Eight Weeks and Five Days until the Solstice

*S*he and Liam returned to Brookerby early the next day via the traveling map. Em had immediately apologized for her behavior. Liam assured her he was not angry, but he was unusually quiet. Bob didn't seem to notice his master's mood as they spun back home. They arrived at the sycamore clearing, and Bob raced around the perimeter, as if he finally felt free to run after being cooped up in the big city.

Em and Liam started back to his apartment above the bakery, and she filled him in on the night before. He said not a word as she explained the temple break-in. She shared the information she found in the archives, and detailed her plan to explore the Antillei Mountains using the map Farrigan had noted. That was when he finally spoke up.

"That sounds really dangerous."

Em didn't disagree. But it was the only lead she had, and it was less dangerous than the gallows.

"Are the Striders going with you?" he asked.

"They couldn't."

"Seriously?" He sounded incredulous. "Isn't this kind of their thing? Tracking down items?"

"I guess. They offered, but I could tell they didn't actually . . ." Em fell silent. When Liam was outraged, it made her more confused. She had understood her parents' decision the night before, but now it did seem flimsy. Maybe she hadn't explained the deadline? Or the death sentence? Or maybe, they just weren't very attached to her. They had only met her a few months ago. She was barely an acquaintance at this point.

I only met Liam a few months ago. The intrusive thought dangled like a knife between them, cutting the scant threads that held them together. Why was she dragging him into this mess alongside her? *Unworthy* drummed in her brain, the rhythm growing familiar.

"You should stay here. Run the shop."

"You don't want me to come?"

She did. Exploring the mountains was undoubtedly safer with two. But to pull Liam away from his work, to upend his life further, and to expect all this after their short time together . . . it was too much to ask. No. She would do this alone. She would fix this.

"I can handle it. I'll bring the map. If anything truly life-threatening happens, I can just transport out of danger."

Liam pressed his lips together, as if stopping himself from saying something. Em wasn't sure whether this was better or worse than a scolding. She wondered if she had broken their bonds beyond repair.

"I'm sorry," she said again.

"You need to stop apologizing," he snapped.

She shut her mouth. When they arrived at the bakery door, he unlocked the side stairway and turned to meet her gaze. He was not inviting her up. She knew what that look was. This was a grim "what now?" expression. Em needed to let him cool off.

"I think I'm going to talk with Gram. Can I come by later?"

Liam's eyes widened at this declaration. Then he nodded wearily.

She turned and headed back toward the clearing. She heard the door close quietly behind her, and she shouldered her bag, tears welling in her eyes.

She hoped he would hang on. Then she would make it up to him.

GRAM WAS PREPARING for story hour when Em arrived at the cottage.

"Ah, the wayward daughter has returned," Gram declared, her brassy voice filled with cheer, but Em caught the undertone. They were still at odds.

"How was the wedding?"

"Fine," Em said. She dropped her bags by the door and plopped down on the overstuffed chair by the hearth. "I need to tell you something. I'm sorry. And you were right."

Gram had been placing cushions for the story-time children, but now she paused, a pillow in hand. "Ilna may have mentioned the summons. Don't blame her. She was worried. How bad?"

"If I don't complete an impossible task by the solstice, I'm dead." Em leaned her head back and closed her eyes.

"How impossible?" Gram asked, sounding remarkably cavalier.

"I have to track down the Ring of Clavonion."

Gram coughed, then coughed again and lunged for her tea to quell the fit. Finally, she cleared her throat and said, "Is that all?"

Em shook her head. "I should've just asked for a swift death."

Gram crossed the room in two steps and wrapped her arms around Em's shoulders. Em clutched Gram's arms and tried to keep it together. They hadn't spoken more than a few terse words in so long. Em had missed her—and now this.

She spilled out the entire encounter. "The empress said I was innovative. Creative, she said." Tears welled in Em's eyes as Gram kept her arms around her. "Maybe she thinks I can really find it."

"If anyone could . . ." Gram murmured, giving Em a squeeze before letting go. "It is odd that the empress would ask this of you. She knows your parentage, yes?"

"Yes. Do you think this is extra punishment for something Anne and Farrigan did?"

Gram tapped her chin, eyes seeing something Em could not. Finally, "Nothing else to be done. You'll have to complete the task. We can check my book."

"*The Standard Book of Anything*? Couldn't hurt. I also have a lead from the temple archives." Em wiped her tears with her fingertips as Gram waited, eyebrows raised. Em quickly explained what she had discovered. Then she produced the mountain map from Anne and Farrigan.

"See. You're already making progress." She turned from Em and scanned the bookshelf for an old, tattered book. Em let out a slow breath. She had expected another fight after revealing her dangerous plans to search the mountains. But Gram was taking this all with remarkable equanimity.

Finally, Gram plucked a seemingly fragile tome from the lower left corner and handed it over.

Em wasn't fooled this time by the delicate binding. She had taken this book halfway across Esnania with her, and it held up better than she had.

Em started to flip it open, but Gram clucked. "Maybe wait until after story time? I might need to prime it with the original tale. Also, the kids will get distracted if you're reading something else."

"Prime it?"

Gram nodded. "It works better if it can overhear more about the topic you're wanting. Fewer cross-references and a clearer answer."

Em nodded and placed the book down on the small table beside her.

Gram plucked her book of fairy tales from the shelf just as the first child arrived. She bantered with the children, teased the parents dropping them off, and when she had critical mass, she began reading.

~

THE GREAT RING OF CLAVONION

There once was a poor miller, his wife, and their three children. The family had enough to eat each night, but they lived in an old cottage that barely sheltered them from the elements. The children grew until they were old enough to help and soon, they cast about town for a way to be useful.

The eldest was as tall as a spruce. She had long, willowy arms and an enjoyment of the outdoors, so she applied to work on an apple farm. The farmer admired her reach and happy countenance, and in short order she was given supervision over all the other apple pickers. So the eldest found her way in the world.

The second child, a young man, was of diminutive stature and built like an ox. He soon found work as a stone mason's apprentice. He could lift a whole stack of stone blocks with ease and was a quick study with building plans. Soon he was traveling over the whole countryside with the stone mason, building wherever they went. So the secondborn found his way in the world.

The youngest was neither tall nor short. Weak nor strong. But he was clever. However, he soon discovered no one truly wants a clever laborer. He was argumentative and forever dreaming up better ways to do the work that didn't involve his own muscle and sweat. He was fired over and over, never lasting in a job for more than a week or two. Finally, after a year of trying to fit in, the youngest announced he would leave to seek his fortune in the wider world, and off he went without a backward glance.

He traveled far, but soon learned the world was very similar to his own village. No one wanted to hire a clever young man with more wits than muscle. And in time, his food and savings began to dwindle, and he lost hope, and began to spend his last coin in taverns of ill repute. It was in an inebriated state that he met a mage who would change his destiny. The ancient man wore no outward sign of skill, and yet our clever young man could tell something was different about this person. So he followed him from town to town, watching as the mage created flowers where there was only mud. Watching him craft magical items from ordinary tools.

Finally, the old mage confronted the young man. "What do you seek?" he demanded. The young man explained that he was trying to find his way in the world, and that he didn't seem to be suited for the ordinary pursuits that his brother and sister had found. The mage considered him for a time, and then reached down to collect three small stones, which he handed to the young man.

"Use the dark stone when you are hungry. Use the light stone when you have found your life's desire. Use the amber stone when you need the deities' help." The young man took the stones, puzzled. Then the mage vanished before his very eyes, and the young man was alone again. He pocketed the stones and continued on to the next town.

By then, he had run out of food, and his stomach turned with hunger. Standing on the outskirts of the village, watching the evening candles twinkle, he pulled out the dark stone. "I am hungry," he said to the stone, feeling foolish. Suddenly before him was a banquet table, filled with roasted meats, savory and sweet breads, and exotic fruits. Never before had he seen so much, so richly displayed. He sat down to feast. By this time, the poorest of the village had crept to the table. The fatherless children. The out-of-work laborer. The underpaid and underappreciated. All were invited to partake.

The stone continued to work as the young man traveled, providing daily feasts. And with him, an ever-larger crowd amassed. They followed him, for he had consistent food that he was willing to share. They formed a large traveling party, their own society of the unwanted, who found solace and society in one another. The young man began to settle disputes among the traveling folk. They sought him out for sage advice and gave of what they had. And he found that he was good at this kind of work. That evening, while camped on the shores of a great ocean, he pulled out the light stone and spoke to it. "I desire to be a leader of people."

In a rush, the air swirled around the young man and his large traveling group, and they observed a gleaming city of stone constructed along the hill-side, ending at the ocean's shore, where nothing had been before. The people joyfully moved into the houses, of which there were just enough, and the young man found a domed golden palace at the center. He was declared the leader of this city, and each night a feast was held to celebrate their new home. A marketplace was constructed.

But ruling a city was different than ruling a nomadic band. There were disputes about resources, warring trade guilds, even personal disputes about property and unfair dealings of many kinds. Over time, the people forgot their origins. Instead of sharing the nightly feast together, people would grab everything they could from the banquet table and slink away back to their homes to eat alone. The young man, now approaching his middle years, felt the weight of his responsibility. His life's desire contained many problems too difficult for even a clever man. He walked to a grassy field near his palace, knelt down, and took out the final amber stone. He confessed to the stone, "I don't know what to do. I need the deities' help."

The air once again swirled around him, and the elderly mage appeared before him.

"You have given up?" the man asked.

"Never," the younger man declared. "I want to be the best leader I can, and your gifts have provided for their physical needs. But it still is not enough. I don't know how to help them anymore."

The old mage pulled a heavy silver ring from his own finger, placed the amber pebble in the center, and slid the ring onto the younger man's finger. "You now have everything you need to try and make a better world. The knowledge and potential of your people rests within the stone. I pass this responsibility on to you. Thank the deities for this gift and be content."

The younger man held up his hand, feeling the weight of the ring and staring into its depths. He felt a rushing of power along the ring's amber stone center, and he glanced up to question the mage further. But the old man was gone.

The leader stood, and he recognized that his people needed society, *structure, mutual trust. With his ring, he spoke into existence the fall and spring festivals. The summer and winter solstice celebrations. Basic laws of their society. Flowers, where there was only mud before. He ordered a temple to the deities built on the very spot where the ring was gifted. This ruler would become Tranton I—or Tranton the First—of the Clavonions, the first emperor of the Pewter Age, and the founder of Esnania. He reigned for many years in peace and prosperity, with the Great Ring secure on his finger.*

GRAM CLOSED THE BOOK, and the children began to squirm. One child, Violet, raised her hand. Gram nodded to her.

"Why didn't the old man give him the ring in the beginning?"

Gram laughed. "That would've been easier, huh? But I think sometimes, you have to go without something to learn the value of it."

A chorus of "huh?" echoed from the kids.

"Like when you go a few days without seeing a friend. Doesn't it make it better when you see them again?" A few kids nodded. This made sense.

"Or when I don't get cookies!" one kid shouted. Gram laughed.

A little boy, Xander, shouted, "That old man was really a deity?"

"Maybe." Gram shrugged. "We don't know."

Another kid said, "I don't think the people were very nice in the story."

Gram tilted her head. "Why do you say that?"

"They just kept getting free stuff. And fighting. And the emperor was trying his best, but they were still mad."

Another chorus of "yeah" from the children.

"That's interesting," Gram said. "Why do you think they were not nice?"

The kids looked puzzled. Finally, one small girl spoke up. "They were scared."

"Interesting, Lavonia. Why do you think that?"

"They were used to not having food, and they were scared it would happen again, so they didn't want to share."

"That makes sense. Sometime people behave badly when they're scared. Anyone else?"

"I like the part where the city gets built," one boy called out.

"I like the tall sister picking apples," another kid said.

Gram nodded. "All good things. Okay, that's enough story for today. You can read on your own until your parents come to get you." The children leapt up from their pillows and crowded around the bookcase.

Gram returned the book of fairy tales to its shelf and made her way to the chair by Em. She raised an eyebrow as she sat down. "So?"

Em shook her head. "It's a fairy tale. Maybe even some propaganda in there. Probably none of that happened the way the book says it did."

"Probably not. But it's a start. Why do you think Her Majesty would want this mystical ring?"

Em bit her lip. "Emperor Clavonion needed it to better govern. To have the knowledge and potential of his people. Whatever that means. Wouldn't Regina want to do the same?"

Gram's forehead wrinkled. "The ring appeared at a time where the emperor felt out of control. Helpless. The question is, why now? Why would the empress seek out this item now instead of early in her reign?"

"Anne and Farrigan are looking into it. But does it matter? It might've just been the most impossible thing she could come up with in the moment. She didn't expect Liam to save me like that."

Gram picked up *The Standard Book of Anything* from the side table and drummed her fingers on it. "It might. When you do find the ring—"

"If."

"*When* you find the ring," Gram continued, "You have to figure out what it actually does, and whether it's wise to give it to Her Majesty."

Em's eyebrows shot up. "I don't really have a choice, Gram. It's the ring or my life."

Gram didn't respond. Instead, she flipped open *The Standard Book of Anything* and turned to a specific chapter. Em got up from her chair and came around to hover behind Gram as she read.

Myth and History: One Scholar's Perspective

    by Ronaldo F. Ganderhope

    Many of the early histories of Esnania have been passed along orally through fairy tales and mythologies. It is believed these stories were shared this way so they would be easier to remember, and entertaining enough to share, even by children at an early age.

    But how does a historian parse fact from fiction? For example, in the myth of the three wolves, it is difficult to conceive that the young heroine of legend actually spoke with the deities, but it is more plausible that some catalyst led to the discovery of crops that now populate the High Plains of Esnania. In the Great Ring of Clavonion, the very rules of the three stones gifted to the young emperor defy the known rules of magic—the creation of something from nothing—but perhaps there was some magical method by which the young man gathered followers and kept them fed and housed. Further, it is possible the stones and ring exist, but do not contain all the qualities that the story imbued.

    We wish to believe in the magical power of our folklore, but it is likely the mystical elements of these stories, in reality, had much more scientific explanations. (See "Mundane Explanations of Supernatural Events.")

Em stopped reading and backed away. "Well, that was no help."

Gram swiveled. "I disagree. It told us a lot. There is truth in the story, so we can infer the ring is real. Which is good news. Pair this with your lead from the temple archives, and you have a chance of finding it. And the mundane commentary means it likely isn't the all-powerful ring of legend, so you don't have to worry about handing some kind of weapon to the empress. She shouldn't have anything too powerful."

Em glanced around at the preoccupied kids, suddenly paranoid that some of them might have heard. "You can't say things like that out loud. What if word gets back?"

Gram stood, placing the book back on the side table. "I'm allowed my little treasons. No one is going to be swayed by the rantings of an old woman. Not even you." She shot Em a knowing look, and Em had the good grace to be embarrassed.

"I'm sorry again, Gram. I still think I was doing the right thing."

"Perhaps you were," Gram allowed kindly. "But it wasn't the smart thing."

Em bristled. Gram had won. Why keep needling? At that moment, the first parents showed up to collect their children, so she swallowed her retorts and ducked out of the cottage.

CHAPTER 10

*Clothing covers us and protects us from the elements, of course. But from its
earliest use, clothing has also been a form of self-expression. The material,
form, line, color, and shape with which you adorn your body tells the world
who you are, and who you wish to be.*

"Cultural Garb and the Fashion We Choose"
The Standard Book of Anything

Em had been meaning to visit Mendel since she saw his store in Drecovia, so she trekked down Main Street to the tailor's shop. She wanted to see him before she left town, and she hoped to borrow his magic waterskin. The little container could conjure nearly any liquid you could imagine and never ran empty. It was quite useful for a long journey.

The bell tinkled when she entered, and Mendel looked up from pinning a pattern on a dress form. His face lit up. Despite her catching him in the midst of a sewing project, the man was impeccably dressed, and his dark brown skin nearly glowed, as if he had just returned from spa treatments at the Gray Horse. Tilly, his new apprentice, must be easing his workload.

"Your timing is impeccable. I just completed a gift for you." Mendel stood and glided toward the back of the store.

Em inwardly groaned. Mendel was always trying to nudge her toward more stylish attire, but she didn't need another flouncy dress that she couldn't wear anywhere. "That's very kind, but—"

She was currently wearing a heavy wool skirt and a simple blouse, but at least they were clean. Wasn't that enough?

He bustled into the room again, carrying a pile of fabrics. "It's so untidy back there, and I couldn't see a thing in that dim light, but I know it's in here somewhere."

Em nearly snorted. Mendel's storerooms were always immaculate. Fabric and notions were sorted by color and type along the gleaming shelves. He considered it untidy if a single button was out of place. But seeing an opportunity, she leaned in to his delusions. "If you have a dim light, I could take a look? Maybe you need a repair? Or a better light fixture?"

"Oh no, my dear. My lighting is perfectly adequate. I just need a younger pair of eyes." His dark eyes met hers over the tops of his spectacles with a knowing look.

Em smiled. "By the way, I saw your flagship store in Drecovia. Very fancy."

Mendel continued to carefully fold back fabric from the pile, searching for his mysterious gift. "Ah, yes. It is a bit grand, to be sure. Although Drecovia is quite a bit larger than Brookerby."

"It was an impressive building. I didn't realize you were such a big deal. A lovely blue dress in the window too."

The tailor smiled at this unexpected compliment. "I can have one made to your specifications?"

Em laughed. "No, thank you. I don't need it."

"Pity," he sighed. Then he let out an "Ah!" and pulled something from the pile. It was a dusky blue-gray, nearly the color of Em's eyes. When he handed it to her, she felt a soft yet sturdy, thick cloth. She unfolded the garment and held it up. A cape with a hood. It had a dark woolen lining and piping along the edges. "A cloak?"

"You've been traveling so much, and the weather's getting cooler. I thought it would be . . . useful."

A departure from his usual bows and ruffles. Mendel had made her a garment that was beautiful, but also practical. Not fussy. It was exactly what she would've picked out if every cloak in the world were before her. She needed a new one anyway, especially as she searched the mountains. She looked at him, her heart full. "It's wonderful."

Mendel patted her shoulder affectionately. "Your old one was looking a bit tattered. I can't allow you to traverse the countryside in rags."

Still beaming, she rolled her eyes at him. There was the Mendel she knew and loved.

EM VISITED Liam's apartment that evening. The bakery was closed. Liam hadn't had time to bake that morning, so he was taking inventory of his supplies when Em arrived. Bob was following his every step—thinking he was helping, but really just being a trip hazard. Liam nodded her upstairs and she feared she was in for a dose of silent disappointment.

A white tablecloth draped his tiny table, and silver candlesticks stood on it like sentinels, waiting for the candles they held to be lit. His living space was small—only two rooms—and always tidy. But tonight, it felt immaculate. Had he cleaned for her?

She set her bag of holding down and picked up the book lying on the side table. She never knew what kind of books he liked. He was usually too busy to read, but today was a rare day of rest for him. To her surprise, it was a swashbuckler. This particular novel was borrowed from Gram's bookshelf and involved pirates and a damsel in distress. She forgot that Liam craved adventure as much as she did. She wondered if he preferred her to be this kind of damsel, instead of what she was . . . also in distress, but not willing to just sit there and wait for rescue. Then she spotted his knapsack, partially packed and propped by his bedroom door.

She heard his footsteps on the stairs, and quickly set the book down.

"You came."

Em smiled. He had a dusting of flour on his dark pants. "I wasn't sure you wanted me to."

He shut the apartment door, then crossed to her, putting his arms around her. Instant warmth flooded her. Em leaned in to his embrace, wrapping her arms around his middle and placing her head on his chest. Tension leaked from her body as he held her.

She stepped back finally, feeling a bit calmer.

Liam cleared his throat, as if wanting to say something, but he turned into the small kitchen instead. "I wanted to order something from the mercantile. But I wasn't sure when you'd be here."

"We don't need anything fancy. Leftovers from the bakery, maybe? Some cheese?"

"I can do that." He stepped quickly around the kitchen, lighting the candles and placing the bits of food on the table. After producing a bottle of wine, he motioned for Em to take a seat and poured two glasses. "A toast," he said, raising his own glass. "To you, squirrel. The only rodent for me." Em giggled. That was certainly true. He'd seen a mouse trying to enter the bakery last month and had gone full military on the thing. He placed traps at every entrance and window and sealed every external crack and crevice. Em had teased him about his distaste for rodents, and he amended that squirrels were perfectly fine.

"And to you, the inventor of the double-stuffed pastry twist with extra pears," Em responded, clinking her glass with his.

While they nibbled on bread and cheese, Em asked about the bakery. She found comfort in the mundane details. Running out of oats. Improvising on pastry fillings. Bob attempting to slyly lick a vat of dough. They laughed and drank through the bottle of wine as the candles burned shorter and shorter.

Liam asked about her day. She filled him in on Gram's "I told you so," and the gift from Mendel. The mood grew somber, and Em figured she should lay out her plans.

"I want to start looking as soon as possible."

He nodded. "I thought you would."

A silence fell between them, the easy comfort of the meal sapped by the enormity of Em's task.

Em broke through the tension. "How did your father gain a favor from the empress?"

Liam grinned. "Hallson charm, of course."

"No, really."

Liam tilted his head. "He told us he had a boon when he was dying. She might have been in love with him."

"But he was in love with someone 'unworthy'?" Em asked.

"My mother. She was his everything. I didn't realize the empress had hoped—" He fell silent, considering the implications.

"You'll have to tell Marce you used it on me."

Liam studied her. Reading the bitterness in her tone.

"I understand, you know."

"You understand what?"

"When we first met, remember? I tried to take charge, and you almost left me on the roadside. That whole 'master of your own quest' thing. I get it. But I don't agree with it."

Em glanced down at her hands resting on the tablecloth. She had to consider the possibility that her insistence on searching alone was driven by ego. She didn't know what she was trying to prove. But maybe that wasn't it at all. There was something dangerous and wild about being alone in the mountains. Did she secretly crave that? Or maybe she needed to go alone, so if she failed, it wouldn't be his fault. But, knowing him, he would blame himself no matter what. So why not bring him along?

His hand reached across the table and covered hers. She looked up.

"I'm coming—not because you need me, but because I can't stand the waiting. Plus, it'll be fun. When do we leave?"

No hesitation. He was the person who would always rush to back her up. No concern for how this quest could break them in so many ways.

Em grasped his hand and looked up, eyes welling with tears. "I know I'm not supposed to apologize—but I can't help it. I'm so sorry. If it weren't for me—"

Liam was out of his chair and cupping her face with his hands, kissing her forehead and temples as she tried to explain herself.

"—I just wanted to fix—"

He knelt by her chair, fingers caressing her hair. Her words became fragments of ideas.

"—you deserve—"

And finally, his lips met hers. Soft, comforting. Em melted, responding. Threading her fingers through his hair, kissing him back with every bit of herself. Warming from her core to the tips of her toes.

Then he pulled back and met her eyes. Asking a question.

She dodged. "I love you," she said. "And I promise I will find this stupid ring."

He smiled and gave her another kiss. "*We* will find this stupid ring. Let's leave at sunrise."

CHAPTER 11

Eight Weeks and Four Days until the Solstice

*E*m left early the next morning before the first light crept in. Technically, she could use her map to fast-travel from her bedroom, but somehow that didn't feel right. Her journey would not begin until she had physically left the cottage behind. She planned to slip out quietly, but Gram was waiting for her in the kitchen.

"I had a feeling you'd leave today," Gram said, sliding a bowl of porridge in front of her.

Em hesitated for a moment. She didn't want another spat with

Gram, and she needed to get going. She glanced at the window, but the light of dawn hadn't appeared yet. She realized she had some time before sunrise, so she sat and started to eat.

After a few minutes of silence, Gram shifted in her chair. "Will you take *The Standard Book of Anything?*"

Em raised an eyebrow. "Should I? It wasn't much help the last time."

"All the same, I would feel better if you took it."

Em nodded, and Gram slid the book across the table.

"Don't forget to prime it. And remember it's telling you something, even if you think it isn't."

Em placed the book in her bag and took another bite of porridge.

Gram cleared her throat and spoke haltingly. "I also want to ask you to be careful. Please."

"Of course," Em responded reflexively. Why wouldn't she? But her actions of the past months were not careful, and Gram now had to provide rudimentary advice. Em swallowed another spoonful and leaned away from the table. "Of course I'll be careful," she said again.

"If you get stuck, or something feels off, leave. Come back home, and we can figure this out together."

Em nodded tightly. Gram was worried. Gram thought she would make bad decisions, and the woman was prepared to help her out of whatever mess she got into. Em stood, shouldering her bag and hiding her clenched fists. "I need to get going. Bye, Gram." She crossed the room in three steps, pushing out of the house and closing the silent door behind her. *Come home and we can figure this out together?* Gram didn't think she could do it. Was practically waiting for her to mess this up. Em growled in frustration. She had found the archives lead by herself, hadn't she? Everyone else was just telling her she couldn't.

She tromped through the fallen leaves, kicking them as she went. After a short walk, she had calmed down enough to notice the nip in the air from inside the warmth of her new cloak. The leaves were brilliant golds and reds, even in the low light, as she ducked toward the wooded area surrounding the creek. The bag of holding carried provisions for at least a week, including rolls Liam sent with her last night, her tools, a rope, a lantern, the jumping cane, a bedroll, a few changes of warm clothes, mittens that Gendry had knitted for her, Mendel's magic waterskin, matches, her wood chip from the warding tree, the fast-travel map, and the detailed map of the Antillei Mountains with Farrigan's notes. And now, *The Standard Book of Anything*.

She hoped this would work. Despite centuries, as the ring had gone from a reality, to history, to myth, Em had to believe it was out there. That it was as real as any of the other items in her parents' warehouse. And if it was out there, she had to believe that she was clever enough to find it.

She arrived in the clearing by way of the footbridge. She could see a few of the shops on Main Street, dark and unoccupied. Everything had a fresh coat of paint. The ruts in the street were repaired. The bakery had a light on; Liam was getting ready. He was supposed to meet her here at dawn.

But she couldn't take him. She knew that now. Last night, she had fooled herself into thinking it would be fine. That he wouldn't mind following. That it would be like a vacation.

But after what Gram said . . .

She needed to do this, alone. He would be angry at her, she knew, for leaving him behind. He wouldn't understand. She said a silent goodbye to him, face crumpling. It wasn't enough. She rummaged through her bag and produced a scrap of paper and a pencil. She hastily scribbled a note and left it folded on the bench for him, hoping he would find it. Hoping that he would accept her garbled explanations. If all went well, she could come back and make it right. But not before.

Then Em pulled the fast-travel map of Esnania from her bag. A lone bird warbled as she double-tapped the southern end of the Antillei range.

The world swirled around her, in the colors of leaves and the dawn-gray light, and finally her feet touched ground once more.

Em had never experienced the mountains up close before. She

glanced up, hardly believing how this massive land towered over her in the pre-dawn sky. To the west was a thick forest of coniferous trees. Nearby, she spied the green shrubs in the foothills. Then she looked back to the rocks above her. They loomed, deadly and cold, and she knew if she took the time to ruminate—about the task before her—she would rush back to Brookerby to wait for Liam. So instead, she put away the traveling map and unrolled the mountain map to study it in the dim light.

Her strategy was to systematically hit each marked settlement or location. One by one. And then mark them off her map after she had thoroughly investigated. The nearest site was an old mining town in a valley between the first and second peak. She memorized the landmarks near the town and then swapped the map for the jumper cane. She would have to leap from landmark to landmark to approach the valley, but if she could see a place to stand, she could reach it.

She decided to skirt the first mountain on the western side. Fewer trees and better visibility. She spotted her first destination in the distance, a clearing of grass between several spiny-looking bushes. She focused her attention, straining not to look away, and tapped the cane three times.

Then her stomach was in her windpipe. It felt like the floor had dropped out from under her. But just as quickly, the dry ground rushed up to meet her feet. She stumbled as the ground crashed into her, and she almost fell sideways into an evil-looking thorny shrub. Regaining her balance, she dropped her pack and the cane to breathe calm into her roiling stomach.

Finally, when her gut settled, she looked around, trying to reorient herself. It seemed she landed where she intended. Difficult shrubbery surrounded her, and the only way out was the way she had arrived, by leaping through space. "Here we go again," she muttered, recollecting her bag and jumper cane. She eyed a smooth patch of ground maybe half a league ahead, still near the base of the mountain slope, and triple-tapped her stick.

Again, the ground dropped out and rushed up just as quickly. Em's stomach rebelled, and she heaved Gram's porridge onto the ground. Then last night's dinner. Groaning, she slumped to the dirt. Five minutes into her search, and she was ready to quit for the day.

After a few moments, she stood, still feeling queasy. "Maybe I'll just walk for a bit."

Em began picking her way among the foothills. She continued to skirt the mountain, and there was a small walking path that she joined with great relief. But the light was still dim, and it was slow going. The scenery to the east of her—the massive shadow of the first mountain—blocked the rising sun.

Liam would be reading her note now. Or maybe he had gone back to the bakery. But it wasn't too late. She could go back. She felt the squeeze of wrongness in her gut, yet she knew the damage was already done.

After an hour of walking, the small path turned and plunged into a forest, and Em decided to follow it, keeping the mountain shadow nearby.

By lunchtime, cedars and pines gave way to shrubs and larger rocks again. Her path had disappeared, and Em was now climbing over large fallen rocks, avoiding thorny weeds. After clambering over a particularly large boulder, Em sat, took a sip of water from her always-full waterskin, and surveyed the magnificent vista before her. The valley spread out below, and she had arrived at the first place indicated on the mountain map, the abandoned mining town. After she had taken in the view, she stood and approached a sharp cliff edge, glancing down its sheer side to the buildings below. From this height and distance, she saw no movement, and no actual way to approach the town. Maybe she had chosen the wrong side of the mountain to skirt. There was no way to get down there . . . except the jumper cane.

Groaning, Em pulled the stick from her pack. It wasn't worth going two days out of her way to get to the other side.

Gulping air, Em focused on the grassy flat near the first buildings. They were bug-sized from where she stood. She tapped the stick three times, and then came that dreaded sensation of weightlessness, followed by the ground crashing into her. She kept her feet this time, luckily. The nausea hit her, but she had nothing in her stomach and the feeling passed after a few dry heaves and steadying breaths.

The mining town had seen better days. There was a single street of crumbling wooden shacks—barely enough to be called a town. Still, no movement or sound. Not even a ruffling breeze in this sheltered vale, which was lucky. Any wind might blow the ramshackle buildings to the ground. She checked the map again. Her parents had indicated this town likely was part of the route the ring took from Gillamor to the North. She had to search. She approached the first decaying building and knocked on the entrance. No answer. After some time, she turned the latch and pushed her way inside.

HOURS LATER, Em was ready to admit defeat. She had entered nearly a dozen storefronts and homes, all abandoned, all breaking apart at the slightest touch, and none containing anything of value. Her stomach rumbled, reminding her that she had lost breakfast and forgone lunch. She found a bit of shade and a weathered bench under an awning and pulled out one of Liam's rolls, some blackberries from the garden, and a bit of hard cheese. She wondered about the abandoned place and if the town had dried up when the trade route changed. That was likely. It had been sitting idle for at least a hundred years. Em scanned the street and resolved to check the last few buildings, just to be thorough, but it was unlikely the ring would be here. The place was picked clean.

She pulled out *The Standard Book of Anything*, wondering if it could point her in the right direction. The table of contents listed "Theatre from the Age of Magic," "Famous Quotations from the Mountaintop," "Silver Mining in the Antillei Mountains," and "A Discussion of Trade Routes and their Discontents." Em flipped quickly to the mining article.

The Antillei Mountains have a rich vein of silver that runs the span of the mountain range. In the early 700s RQ, this vein was heavily mined by the sovereign through use of mining shares sold to scores of opportunistic entrepreneurs. The silver was exported to Zanit at great profit, but it was also used in the science of photography and other budding sciences. (See "Uses of Silver in Everyday Objects.") Several Clavonion emperors boosted the sciences as a foil to magic users, who were quite powerful during this period.

Nonsense. She supposed the ring was made of silver, but the time period was wrong. As she was putting away the book, Em heard a scratching noise. It sounded like Bob when he dug holes in Gram's garden. An animal, perhaps? Or maybe she was imagining the noise, her mind filling in the silence with something random.

She shouldered her bag, peered around the corner, and gasped.

It was an animal, but nothing so benign as a dog or squirrel. It looked like a hyena—at least how Gram described them—a bit like a dog, but disfigured somehow. The creature had an arched neck and protruding ribs, and it was bigger than Em expected—at least as tall as her waist. It was farther down the dirt alley, scratching at the side of a building as if trying to get at some small prey inside. At Em's gasp, it froze and looked up. The beast's eyes were black and ravenous. It let out a low growl and took a step toward her.

Em backed away, reaching for her cane while she ran for the entrance of the building. The hyena-beast rounded the corner, snapping at her heels. Em dove inside, slamming the rotting door behind. The wild animal smashed into the wood and began scratching at it. The sound of the rotten wood splintering had Em wondering how long the door would hold.

Quickly, she peered out a broken-paned window, trying to find a safe place to transport. The main road was in sight, but treacherous to land on. Time and weather had made it uneven and pocked with deep holes.

The wood splintered, and Em swiveled to see a dark claw pulling at a hole, making it larger. Em had to jump. There was a small yard by the last house in the row. Em tapped her cane, but at the last moment, she heard a growl, and her head swiveled toward the noise.

She dropped through the air and landed. Still in the house, next to the disintegrating door that was seconds away from being ripped to shreds by the beast. Em cursed. She had shifted her focus. And now she was in danger of hurling up her lunch.

Running back to the window, she tried again. A huge crack and a much louder growl sounded behind her, but Em focused her eyes outward and tapped. Pain tore through her hip at the moment she dropped, and she found herself on the lawn she had aimed for.

She stumbled, glancing down at the burning sensation. Three razor slices—claw marks—had shredded the side of her pants and the skin underneath. Blood oozed from them. Em hissed, both from the pain and the visual. That did not look good.

She heard the creature growl from the house down the street and saw it leap out into the main thoroughfare. It was following her. She had to get far away, and fast.

Em leapt to the road leading east out of town, to the farthest point she could see. Ignoring the sharp, stabbing pain in her hip and the roiling in her gut, she twisted to look behind her. The beast was still running in her direction. It was a bit farther away, but not enough.

She leapt again, to the crest of the hill.

Again, to the fold between the mountains, the road entrance into the valley.

Again, along the base of the mountain.

And again, partially up the second mountain slope to a small ledge. She could no longer see the beast, and she doubted he would be able to climb up here anyway. She collapsed, her whole side burning and her stomach heaving her recently eaten lunch down the mountain face.

She wiped the side of her mouth with her sleeve and then collapsed again, utterly exhausted. That had not gone well.

THE CREATURE GAVE up and went in search of easier prey. Em could make out its hairy form trotting back to the abandoned colony. As the afternoon waned, a chilly breeze rushed through the mountains, and Em shivered as she set up a small fire and settled deeper into her cloak.

Once she had warmed a bit, she turned her attention to her wound. She inched her pants down below her hips, trembling as the cold hit her legs, and winced when the shredded material brushed the wound. She reached for her pack, wishing she had brought ointment or medical supplies, and then she remembered Mendel's magic water-skin. She used water to wash the wound, which stung and bubbled, then directed the waterskin to make salve. It produced an oily substance with a woody smell, which she poured on her hip. The wound reacted badly, burning painfully and constantly, so she ended up washing most of it away with more water. Then she made a bandage out of one of her extra shirts, a ruffled puce that she wasn't sorry to part with.

She flipped open *The Standard Book of Anything* but found nothing new in the articles. After attempting to read a play written in an archaic version of the common tongue—something about love and betrayal that she couldn't quite understand—she shoved the book back in her bag with a sigh. She reached for the small wood chip and turned it over in her fingers. A ritual, to remind herself that everything would be okay.

Her small campfire was no match for the mountains, and Em shivered through a cold night on the ledge. She considered traveling home. To a warm bed. To safety. She missed seeing Liam today. Telling him the silly musings of her brain and hearing his. Getting his advice. Even if she didn't intend to follow it, she wanted it all the same.

But she had left him behind.

She heard Gram's voice on repeat in her head. *Come back home and we can figure it out together.* Yes, she was angry. After everything, she was still being underestimated.

It was reckless of her, she knew. In traveling home, she would have to face them all. Face the fallout of Liam's anger. Face Gram's criticism. Sit idle in a town that didn't need her, knowing she had failed at the one task she'd been given. And that was much scarier than the pile of rocks she now sat upon.

And she could do this. She had to do this. And if she didn't succeed, then she better learn how to survive on her own anyway, because she was not going to march quietly to her death. And because she wasn't going to drag anyone down with her.

CHAPTER 12

The three main categories of rocks are igneous, sedimentary, and metamorphic. Two of these are formed under ridiculous circumstances (See "Emotional and Physical Rock Formations"), and the igneous rock tries not to be seen in public with either of them.

"Mineralogy for the Casual Scientist"
The Standard Book of Anything

Eight Weeks and Three Days until the Solstice

She didn't sleep. Only lay there. Fighting cold and the pain from her wound and her own mind. And when the sky lightened, she found she was tired of her racing thoughts and all the anxieties that had flooded every part of her. She sat up, collected her bedroll, and prepared for another day.

The next closest point of interest was a smuggler's cave, tagged with a question mark on Farrigan's mountain map. It was halfway up a small slope, just to the north of her current location. His notes indicated the crevice was unlikely to contain what she was looking for. But it didn't hurt to be thorough.

Em folded the map and stowed it away. She would forgo breakfast, despite her rumbling hunger—she didn't want to give any fuel to the nausea caused by jumping. Standing, she scanned down the northern slope and identified a landing point.

SEVERAL JUMPS LATER, Em was sucking in breath, trying to calm her innards. She didn't think she would ever get used to the terrible motion of the jumping cane and the mess it made of her stomach. Gaining control, she finally straightened and glanced around. She was near the cave entrance, according to the map, but she didn't see an opening.

It must be well hidden, which made sense for thieves and criminals. They wouldn't want their hideout discovered. They had used the cave just over a hundred years ago—completely the wrong time period—while traveling the mountain road to transport illegal goods north. But perhaps the structure was older than the indicated use. It seemed likely enough for Em to check.

She hiked around the slope, looking for any kind of opening. She was just above the tree line, and a mountain meadow spread before her, dotted with wild grasses and boulders. She briefly thought of Liam's wilderness cabin, which sat in a very similar meadow. He would've liked to see this.

Em approached a large pile of rocks and spied a small crevasse. Perhaps . . . She cleared a flat stone that had been balanced on end, and an opening appeared. It was wide enough to crawl in, but no larger. Em lit her lantern and dropped to her belly, shoving the light in front of her as she crawled into the opening. Ahead, the lantern showed a long tunnel. She pushed inside and inched her way down the tunnel.

After crawling for at least ten minutes, her wounded hip scraped on an uneven, rocky wall, and she had to stop until the pain subsided. Em wondered if she had made a mistake. The hole continued on indefinitely, and she saw no larger cavern up ahead. This very well may have been an underwater stream, or a hole made by an animal.

The space was tight. There was no clearance to turn around, and Em wondered how long it would take her to back out. Fear rose in her. What if she were trapped here? Or an animal crawled in behind? Her thoughts flashed to the hyena-like creature from yesterday, and a clawing panic seized her.

Out of desperation, she fumbled in her bag until her hand closed around the traveling map. It was imprecise, but it would get her out quickly. Dousing the lantern, she double-tapped the map near her current location in the Antillei Mountains. The cave spun.

Em landed belly-down on a pile of rocks and felt the sunshine warm her back. Her bag clattered beside her, items spilling out.

EM LAY in the pile of warm rocks and considered not getting up. Her hip hurt. The claw marks from yesterday didn't seem to be clotting, and Em briefly worried if infection was starting to set in. The front of her body was, no doubt, covered in bruises from the crawl and the rough landing. And something deep within her—nothing physical she could pinpoint—was bruised also. She was almost certain that was not the smuggler's cave, so she couldn't even check a location off her list. She felt so tired. It would be easier to just lay here for a while.

After her moment of self-pity, she rolled to her unmarred side to stand, suppressing a grunt. Better to get on with it. She spun to take in her location. The traveling map had landed her in an endless field of rock. Pebbles. Boulders. No plants in sight. And it wasn't marked on her map. Where was she?

She put away her lantern, then swapped her traveling map for the mountain map and studied the horizon, trying to match the three nearest peaks with those on her paper. She was hopelessly turned around. There were at least four areas that matched the looming rock around her. She needed to leap to see more. To get her bearings. But she dreaded the sensation. So, she walked.

The stone crunched underfoot. The sun that burned down upon her was high in the sky, giving no directional clues. She occasionally had to clamber over a large boulder or alter her path around a formation too large to climb. As she walked, she thought.

If, indeed, the Great Ring existed, it would've been known by all in that era. Even though the secundarius cleric had acted in secret, he had transported a famous item. It was extremely unlikely that it had fallen by the wayside without the influence of outside forces. If it had been dropped down a ravine, the messengers would have moved literal mountains to recover it. A simple "losing" was unlikely.

Smugglers and thieves were a good guess. But wouldn't the caravan have defended the ring with their lives? If so, smugglers would have recognized its great value. If they could not wield it, they would have sold it for a fortune. If they could use the ring, they would've used it extensively. Both choices would have left a footprint. The latter would've shown up in history as an outpouring of magic so extensive as to rival the Age of Magic itself, leaving clues that could be used to trace the item and result in its recovery.

But it was not recovered.

So what, then? Someone acquired it who did not use it? Did they not realize what they had? In that case, it could've been sold anywhere in the wider world. But eventually, it would have fallen into hands of someone who *could* use it. And then, a footprint would have emerged. But it hadn't. Not to Em's knowledge, anyway.

Did someone find it and destroy it? Or bury it? If so, would it really be here in the mountains, just waiting to be discovered?

The more she thought about it, the more unlikely the ring was just going to be sitting on a mountain ledge. Somebody had taken it. Em should be searching for traces of magic in the history books, not scouring rocks and stones.

She arrived at the end of the rocky field where a lone weather-worn tree stood, offering a scant amount of shade. Em sat and pulled out her mountain map again. She needed to travel somewhere where people still lived. Perhaps they had knowledge of the ring, or could point her in a direction that didn't involve dead-end caves and hungry beasts.

There were several settlements still marked as occupied. The first, a quarantined village. Em knew nothing about the diseases contained therein, but she assumed if the good people living there needed to be quarantined, they were contagious.

The second was a nomad encampment on the western side of the mountain range. The map showed a wide area where the nomads might be. Em knew next to nothing about this group, but if they had been established in these mountains for a long time, they would probably have knowledge of the other occupants. And where to look for a valuable item.

The third option was a small settlement of mages—the one her parents had mentioned—buried deep in the mountains at the foot of the Silver Nightingale fortress. That was the impenetrable citadel where Bronwyn Featherweight made her last stand against the empire, before she was captured and executed. Em recalled her history: soldiers laid siege to the place for a long time before Bronwyn finally surrendered. Perhaps some of her followers stayed, had families, and started a life in the mountains. But mages in Esnania would likely not welcome visitors to their home. Not when the empress's edicts had driven most magic users into hiding.

The nomad encampment seemed the best bet. If she could find it. She rolled up Farrigan's map and then fast-traveled to the southernmost area assigned to the mountain wanderers.

WHEN SHE SPUN into the new location, she scanned the landscape for signs of people. Seeing none, she used her jumping cane to travel north along the swath of land at the base of the mountains. After several jumps, and suffering through her roiling stomach, she saw fires in the distance. She jumped once more, to a spot within a short walk of the settlement.

The nomads camped on an open plain, just beyond the shadow of one of the larger mountains. They had colorful cloth tents and wooden wagons arranged in a circle around several cookfires. Children ran through the camp chasing a ball made of rags, while several women gossiped at a stewpot. Em didn't see any men, and assumed they were hunting or scouting. They looked like the people Em had seen from Aglen, a southern neighbor of Esnania. Deeply tanned skin with nearly white hair. These nomads seemed to keep their locks long and in bundles of tiny braids.

Not wanting to frighten them, Em called out a greeting as she reached the edge of their camp.

Immediately, the women straightened, reaching for their cook knives.

Em held up her hands. "I just wanted to talk. Can anyone speak the common tongue?"

After conferring among themselves, a diminutive woman with a snowy braid stepped forward. "I speak. What purpose do you have?"

"I am looking for an artifact. Something very old. Or history about the Northern peoples. Where should I go?"

"In Northern areas?" The woman wrinkled her brow as she considered. "You hurt Northerns?"

"No! I will not hurt anyone."

The woman considered further. "You alone?"

Em didn't like this line of questioning. She darted her eyes over the woman's shoulder, to the other nomads watching their conversation. There was no warmth in their gazes, and Em felt a shiver run up her back. "No. My friends are just over there." She gestured vaguely. Then she pulled out her map of the mountains. "Where can I find information?"

The woman stared at the map, then pointed at the Silver Nightingale fortress. "Treasure and books here. Difficult to get in."

"Anywhere else?"

The woman tapped the fortress again. "Best place. They know things."

Em thanked the woman and pulled out four of Liam's rolls from her pack to offer her. The woman stared, grabbed at them, and bobbed her head in thanks. Em backed away, not turning her back until the woman had gone back to her cookfire.

The uncertainty of whether a person would help or hurt was

frightening. Liam would've handled that whole encounter better. But the woman was very insistent that the Silver Nightingale had what she needed. Em tried to recall what she knew about the place. Bronwyn's last stand had occurred only fifty years before—long after the ring's transport—but Em knew from her own history lessons that the Silver Nightingale predated the mage by centuries. Perhaps it had been standing when the ring passed by in the fourth century.

Farrigan's note was no help. It said:

Tried to find entrance, no luck. Warded.

Em rolled up the map. It was the best lead she had. The fortress was several peaks north of where she was now, but she could use the fast-travel map to get close, then leap the rest of the way.

If she found nothing at the fortress, she would have to find someone else to ask. But that was a problem for tomorrow. Today, at least, she had a plan that was better than endless rocks and bruises.

CHAPTER 13

Mazes are rarely used as a defense when a thick, solid wall will do. But if your city or castle lord or lady is a real go-getter, they might enjoy the daily maintenance, feedings, and regular clearing of the bodies.

"Mazes or Moats. A Manual"
The Standard Book of Anything

*E*m had no difficulty finding the mountain on which the Silver Nightingale stood; the fortress was visible from leagues away, nestled into the mountain like it had emerged as part of some natural process. Several turrets rose high above the mountain's peak, and a pristine flag fluttered from the battlements. She was too far away to see the details, but Em made out a silver bird on a dark background.

Someone must be there. Or someone was recently in residence. Otherwise the flag wouldn't be so tidy.

Getting to the castle was another matter, however. From where Em stood, it appeared the fortress was surrounded on all sides by sheer cliffs. Not even a handhold for a climber with a death wish. There wasn't even a pathway approaching the castle.

Em reached for her jumper cane, thinking to jump to a flat-roofed area. But when she tapped the stick, nothing happened. She tried again. Nothing. She tried to move five feet to the right and the stick obliged. She couldn't account for the malfunction, except to guess that the building was probably unevenly warded against magic. Farrigan's note indicated the wards, so at least she was in the right place.

There had to be a way in. Em scoured her mind for the history of Bronwyn's standoff with imperial soldiers. How had they eventually gotten inside? She couldn't recall. She knew only a few scouts had breached the fortress, so perhaps the entrance was hidden. Or not large enough for a whole army. Perhaps the entrance had collapsed, and the settlement was near—not actually in—the fortress. But the woods around the mountain showed no signs of civilization. She was convinced that if she found the entrance, she would also find the people. She needed to start a more detailed search.

Em scoured the foothills around the crag, leaping to a place using her jumper cane to explore the nearby areas, then leaping again after a thorough search.

In this manner, she found a perfectly round tunnel, tall enough to stand in, hewn into the rock on the northern side of the mountain. Tree cover and some strategically placed rocks had hidden it well. This had to be it—the way inside.

Em entered, shrugging to adjust her bag on her shoulder. She wasn't sure what to expect, but it was likely the castle's defenses were still intact, and that they amounted to more than just camouflage.

The tunnel was very dark, and much longer than she anticipated. At one point, Em turned and could no longer see daylight behind her.

Finally, the tunnel opened into a high-ceilinged cavern lit by some unknown source. It looked like a natural cave, except instead of stalagmites, massive walls divided up the space. The perimeter was rough-hewn rock, but the inner walls were polished pale stone with no markings that Em could see. Each wall stretched up to the cave ceiling, and each was turned on an angle, as if beckoning Em to enter a hallway. Nearly a dozen of these hallways stretched along the flat of the room where the tunnel emerged. There were no other markers or directions.

Em spent several minutes trying to find a light source. The hallways seemed to be well lit from above, but no lanterns or torches were visible.

Em jogged down the length of the room, glancing into each corridor as she passed. There were uniform squares high on the hallway walls that glowed—the source of the light. She studied the hallways as she ran, not knowing what she was looking for, and she was only able to verify that each hallway looked to be made of the same material. Some had immediate turns visible, and some dead-ended after a short walk.

"A maze?" she wondered aloud. That made sense. For enemies wishing to enter the Silver Nightingale, this would absolutely slow them down. She wondered if the settlement she sought was beyond this maze. If she could solve it, she would gain entrance. It was worth a try.

THE MAZE TRIGGERED A MEMORY: a hay-bale maze from her childhood. One of the farmers had created it in the empty field next to the schoolhouse for the children to play in after their last day of the semester. Em was in her first year of primary school and just as excited as the other children as she raced toward the massive straw labyrinth alongside her schoolmates.

But she quickly lost her way. She stopped to examine a caterpillar, and the other children left her behind. The day waned as little Em wandered through the bales, finding dead end after dead end.

Convinced she would never find her way out, and seeing the setting sun in the sky above, Em sat down and howled. Her crying had alerted nearby adults that someone was trapped inside. A quick head-count verified it was Em.

Gram came into the maze to find her.

"What's the problem, missy?" Gram asked in a businesslike tone.

Em whimpered about being lost and how all the hay bales looked the same.

"That shouldn't have stopped you. You're a big girl now, you can figure this out." Gram knelt down and wiped Em's damp face with her handkerchief. "I'll tell you a little trick, and then you're going to lead us out, okay?"

Em stared at her guardian as though she had sprouted three heads. "How?"

"When you're in a maze, the best way out is to keep going."

Em frowned. "That doesn't help," she whined.

"Okay. How about this? Keep your hand on the left wall. Then, no matter how many dead ends, you'll eventually get out."

Em thought about this for a moment, and then raised her chubby little arm to the nearest wall. "Okay," she said.

It took them a quarter of an hour, and the sky was nearly dark, but Em finally found the exit. Gram was so patient, only reminding her to keep her hand up when they hit a dead end.

EM REMEMBERED that day as she stared at the massive stones before her. She had since learned that Gram's left-wall trick was the very slowest way to solve a maze, but it never failed. It certainly beat trodding the same path again and again.

"It's a little different than hay, but I suppose the same principle applies," she muttered.

The memory hit her differently now. When she was small, Gram had believed in her. Had allowed her to fail, taught her how to think and move through the world. But now . . . what was so different about removing oaths? Gram didn't trust her where the empress was concerned? Didn't believe she could figure this out?

Yes, Em was still angry at Gram. She chose a hallway at random, and raised her left hand to brush the wall.

The hallway went on and on, until it ended abruptly in a T-shape.

Keeping her hand raised, Em followed the left wall and turned to the left. At least there were no agonizing decisions to be made. Just keep following the left wall. After winding through multiple turns, false paths, and dead ends, Em realized she had been walking for nearly a quarter of an hour. She began to wonder how long this method would take. How large was this maze?

She rounded a corner and spied another dead end. Sighing, she turned and reached for the opposite wall with her left hand. At that moment, she heard a metal screech and a clunking noise. Turning toward the dead end, she saw nothing. Then a whooshing noise above her made her jerk her head upward. Deadly spikes were flying down from the ceiling, directly at her. She had half a second to respond, and she leapt as far out of the corridor as she could manage. She fell to her stomach, panting.

The spikes landed with a clang, barely brushing the ground. Em dared to lift her head and turned to see the pointy metallic spikes were a mere hand's width apart from each other, spikes she had narrowly avoided by diving out of the way. Almost. Her foot lay perfectly between two of the spikes—a near miss. Too close for comfort. She slid her foot out carefully as the spikes began to retract into the ceiling.

What had happened? She had clearly triggered some kind of booby trap in the dead end. But there had been other dead ends in the maze without deadly consequences. She was very lucky to have escaped this one.

She wondered if it was pressure on the floor, or maybe movement that triggered the trap.

She couldn't rely on luck. It was bound to run out, and she really didn't want a spike through her foot. Or her skull.

Standing, she reconnected with the left wall and continued, back-tracking a path she had already trod. But then she arrived at a new corner. Potential for another dead end. Another trap.

She reached into her bag and felt around, rejecting items until she landed on a handful of nails she had tossed in while packing, just in case. If it was movement, or even light pressure, that triggered the trap, these might work. And she didn't mind losing them if they were smashed. She gathered them up and carefully tossed one around the corner. Then she waited.

No metal door. No grinding. She glanced up, wondering if she could spot the outline of traps on the ceiling, but the high walls blocked her view. After a few minutes of no sound, Em cautiously peaked around the wall and scooped up the nail she had thrown. It was as good a method as any, until it proved ineffective. If that happened, Em would have to come up with a new safeguard. Unless she already had a spike through her body.

She wound through the maze, stopping at each blind turn to toss a nail. She was starting to wonder if the trap had been a singular event when, at her current corner, she tossed the nail and a clanking sound responded. Not from the ceiling this time, but from the ground.

Spikes from the floor? Em took a hasty step back, but then curiously peered around the bend to see a dead end with a gaping hole in the floor. No spikes emerged. However, Em did detect a hissing sound. It didn't sound like snakes. More metallic. Like the sound of a cicada or a cricket, amplified.

Em backed up. She did not want to see what deadly insect was in the pit. Instead, she turned, put her left hand on the wall, and hurried quickly away.

There were no more traps for another half hour. But since Em's nails had worked with the insect-pit trap, she continued dutifully tossing them one by one around every turn.

She had lost track of her time in the maze when she rounded another turn and found herself back at the beginning. The row of hallways.

Maybe it just looks like the beginning, but it's a whole new room, Em thought with a desperate hope. She ran for the tunnel. It would either lead her farther into the mountain, or—as she feared—back outside. When she saw sunlight streaming at the far opening, she knew that her maze navigation had led her in a big circle.

Em cursed. She had a sinking feeling as she made her way back to the row of hallways. She didn't remember which one she had entered or come out of. Had it been the same hallway, or two different ones?

She quickly counted, and there were nine entrances. Either nine potential options with eight that circled back on themselves—or four loops and one that continued through. Or some combination. She felt dizzy. Gram's maze logic had not prepared her for this. Em dug into her bag and retrieved a piece of chalk wrapped up with her tools. She would mark the hallways she entered (and exited). Barring someone wiping her marks away, she should be able to narrow down the correct path.

Knowing she had already blown it on the last path she tried, and forgetting which path that was—one of the middle ones?—she selected the hallway farthest to the left. She placed an *X* on the stone and entered the maze again with her hand on the left wall.

The maze offered an immediate left turn. Em used her nails to identify traps, but nothing happened. It was monotonous. She twisted and turned through the maze and found herself growing weary. Maybe there weren't traps in this part. Maybe this was the correct path. But no sooner had she thought that than she rounded a corner and triggered another one.

Her nail had produced no effect, but as soon as she spied the dead end, she heard a clicking noise. Like a lock releasing. A door in the dead end swung open.

Em surged forward—this could be the way out—but stopped just as suddenly. A beast was emerging through the door, and behind him appeared only to be the animal's cage. The beast looked very similar to the hyena-like creature that had chased her out of the mining town. Only this one was larger. And hungrier. She could count every single rib protruding from its thick hide. It growled and eyed Em, licking its chops.

Em whirled and ran. She almost forgot to keep hold of the left wall, which might've made her hopelessly lost. But at this moment, she was more concerned about avoiding those teeth and claws. The beast lurched after her, and Em remembered how much faster the mining town hyena had been. In desperation, she pulled out her jumper cane for a quick jump, hoping the palace's wards didn't apply in here.

They didn't. Em raced around corners, heedless of traps, and used the cane to traverse long corridors. This kept her barely out of reach of the ravenous beast. She finally found herself in a dead end. She realized that no trap had been triggered—her luck again—but she didn't know how to get away from the animal now rounding the corner and charging down the hallway.

At the last moment, she tapped her stick and transported to the end of the hall. The beast smashed into the wall with a thud and a whimper. Em didn't stop. She kept running. She rounded several more corners and found herself in another dead end. The beast was still following, more cautiously this time. There wasn't a way to shake it. She would either have to disable or kill the beast to be free of it. Or complete the maze at this dangerous pace. She recalled the hissing pit with a shudder. Surely her luck was running out.

The beast entered her vision. Searching and hungry. Sniffing. It spotted her and growled, a low echoing sound. She prepared to tap her cane again, but the beast's leap was faster—it grabbed hold of the stick with its razor-sharp teeth just as Em was tapping, preventing her from jumping away.

Fighting her own rising panic, Em held the stick at both ends, trying to push the beast away as it snarled and snapped at the wood. But it was heavier than it looked, and its jaws were iron.

The cane snapped in two. Em felt an icy stab of fear in her gut. In two seconds, she would be dead. But the beast was still struggling to detach its teeth from the wood-pulp fibers that pulled long as the two ends of the stick peeled apart. Enough time for Em to find something to help in her bag. Fingers flailing, she reached for a tool. A blunt object. Anything.

Her hand closed around her hammer.

She readied herself by holding the tool in both hands, cocked back above her shoulder. When the beast lunged, she swung with all her might. A crack sounded as the hammer head struck the animal's jaw. The beast whimpered, then let out an angry growl and lunged again.

Em swung once more, striking the hyena on the head. It dropped to the ground with a final weak snarl.

Em didn't wait to see if the beast was moving as she scooped up the pieces of the jumper cane and ran past it. At the far end of the hallway, she glanced back to see the prone body of the beast. Had she killed it? Her heart was thrumming at an alarming pace, and she paused at the turn to lean against the wall. She had never killed anything. Ever. Not even the spiders that scuttled into their cabin. Gram wanted those to live in the garden and eat other bugs, so Em would always carefully scoop them up and carry them outside.

And now she had murdered a living, breathing thing. She was a monster.

It was trying to kill you, her logic argued back. *You were just defending yourself.*

But was she? If she had been smarter and quicker, maybe she would've come up with a better way to shake the beast off her trail. She glanced back at the hairy, lifeless form. "I'm so sorry," she whispered. "I'm not sure who put you in here. But this wasn't your fault. You were hungry and angry."

She looked at the hammer in her hand, splattered in blood, and shoved it back into her pack alongside the broken pieces of the jumping cane. She needed to keep moving. She took a few deep breaths and put her left hand on the wall again.

She would have to ask Liam for fighting pointers when she got home. He at least had military training. Em had her wits, not much muscle, and very average reflexes. Maybe if she could've outmaneuvered the animal, she wouldn't have needed to kill it. Maybe there was a way to stun animals without hurting them? Not that she ever planned on being in this situation again.

She continued her left-wall path, tossing a nail around each corner to trigger any traps.

The beast was a trap. But the nail didn't trigger it. Should she be worried?

Em found remains of humans—mostly bones and disintegrating

clothing—as she methodically traversed the maze. She wondered how long they had been here. How they had died.

She rounded another blind turn after tossing a nail, only to pause at a rustling noise. The beast again? Or had her hardware triggered a trap after all? She slowly tilted her head to peer one eyeball around the corner. She saw nothing. Just a climbing plant in the corner, twining its way up the wall, with magnificent orange blooms. Em kept her distance but stooped to collect her nail. A small vine shot from the plant and entangled her foot.

"Stars, you're quick," she said to the offshoot, trying to untangle it from her boot. But it only wound tighter and faster, yanking Em closer to the main plant. Then Em spotted something tucked into a coil of vine and leaves. It looked like a human body. A decayed hand with blackened fingernails, wrapped in tendrils, brushed the ground. Em's luck had apparently run out.

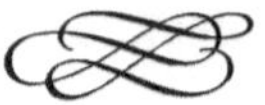

CHAPTER 14

*E*m struggled more frantically with the vine, attempting to break it. But her efforts only seemed to make it grip tighter and pull her more insistently toward the main plant. Her gaze darted again to the corpse. It was decomposed, but she saw hair and clothes still draped on the unfortunate person. The bleached skull had a mess of vines wrapped around it, a single orange flower blooming out of one eye socket. Em's sense of horror did nothing to help her grappling.

The vine was wound so tightly it was cutting into her foot now, but she barely registered the pain. Why had she not brought a knife, she wondered as she dug through her pack, looking for a solution. She was now within a few steps of the larger plant, and she was running out of time.

She realized she was still gripping the nail she had thrown around the corner. Removing her hands from her bag, she held the nail in her fist, point down. Then she crouched, trying to drive her makeshift shiv into the base of the vine entangling her. But the stem was too thin, and the metal kept sliding to the side. She held the vine and tried again, but the nail wouldn't penetrate the tough skin of the plant.

Another tendril shot out and wrapped around her knee, yanking her to the ground. She grappled again in her bag as she slid nearer. The jumper cane! She grabbed it but then remembered it was broken. Em continued to search, the all too familiar terror clutching at her again. Perhaps this was her end. She dug for the fast-travel map, only finding blankets. Food. Matches.

Matches! Em snatched one, lit it, and leaned forward to hold the tiny flame under the smallest vine. It sizzled and smoked as it burned through the vine, leaving the bit attached to Em's boot lifeless and loosened.

The match snuffed out, just as another vine twined toward her arm. She jerked her arm back and reached for another match. Two more vines were winding around her legs. She lit a second match, aiming for the vine squeezing around her knee. But she couldn't keep up. Throwing caution to the wind, she snatched her blanket roll and set it ablaze with her dying match.

It burned, the flame grew, and she moved it toward the vines, which seemed to shy away from the heat and light. She shoved what was now the burning log of her blanket between her and the larger plant, which was no more than an arm's length away. The vines holding her began to burn, and their holds broke. The blaze grew and caught the main plant. Em heard—or imagined—screeching from the plant as a dark smoke filled the air.

Em, still on her backside, slid backward, collecting her discarded nail and broken jumper cane as she went. She pulled up her trouser leg to reveal red welts and cuts where the vine had tightened. The blaze grew, and Em coughed as the smell of burning filled her nostrils. She pushed to her feet, wobbling as she realized how damaged her foot and legs were. Then, like a newborn colt, she struggled away from the dead end, keeping her hand up to the left wall.

THE REST of this maze path was uneventful, thank the deities, but it led right back to the beginning: the row of hallways once again. This time, there was a whisper of smoke coating the air. Em was careful to mark the hallway she emerged from with the chalk—different from the hallway she had entered at the far left, the X clearly visible. So, the path began and ended in different places. Four loops, then, with one spare pathway that led somewhere else.

Em studied her remaining options, feeling exhaustion set in. Her lacerated legs were starting to bleed through her pants, and every step was agony on her clawed hip, which was looking quite angry. But she couldn't quit. She felt it. She had nearly figured out this maze. The nails were working to trigger the traps. But given her experiences with the beast and the plant, she knew she might still have to fight off whatever the traps released.

She chose another hallway, marking another chalk X before entering. This one second from the right, since she was fairly certain she had entered and exited her first unmarked route somewhere in the middle.

She wound through the turning hallways, losing track of how long she had been in the cave. Everything smelled of smoke, and Em was starting to feel sleepy. So maybe that's why she didn't detect the whoosh of air and the strong floral scent—like Gram's hydrangeas—after she tossed a nail around another corner. She rounded the bend to retrieve it, and standing in the dead end was Liam.

She was so tired—she must be seeing things. She shook her head. She was delirious from smoke. From pain.

But there he was. Looking really good. Rested. Strong. Looking like he had expected her to round the corner.

"Li—"

Her voice came out as a croak, but the sound seemed to free his voice as well. "Emaline. My love."

"You're here?" She stumbled toward him. Deities, she had missed him.

"I knew you would need my help."

"You knew—" She stopped. Something wasn't right. Something about his smile. It didn't reach his eyes. "Are you okay? Are you still angry that I left?"

"Of course not, darling. How could I ever be angry at you?"

Now she knew something was wrong. Was he drugged? He had been angry at her plenty. And he had never called her "my love" or "darling" or even "Emaline." It was always "Em," or "squirrel" if he was feeling sentimental. She took a step back. Was this—

"Come on, Emaline. I can take you home."

She didn't know how, but she knew the thing standing before her was not Liam. She then noticed the sickly sweet scent. The floating mist, slightly lighter than the smoke she had caused. This was a trap.

At her realization, the thing before her shifted and morphed, until it looked like Gram.

She turned and ran, as well as she could on her torn legs. She kept her hand on the left wall. The sound of Gram's voice followed her, pleading. Cajoling. "If you get stuck, or something feels off, leave. Come back home, and we can figure this out together."

Then Gram's voice began saying the most awful things. Em tried to block it out. That thing was not Gram. But a few of its words hit closer to her heart than she was comfortable with:

"This is more than you can handle, Em.

"Come back where it's safe; stop behaving like a foolish child."

"You're not clever enough for any of this."

Still Em ran, stopping only to toss a nail at blind corners. But with every shouted dagger, her breath hitched, and she found herself crumbling on the inside.

EM TRIGGERED another trap half an hour later. Some kind of sleeping gas. She had very nearly laid down and succumbed, but she spotted an unmoving human form farther into the corner of the dead end and shook herself just enough to push away, toward clear air.

After what seemed like hours, every part of her burning with pain and exhaustion, she spotted the exit. Expecting the starting corridor of hallways, she found herself instead before a stone archway, the room beyond it lit cheerfully.

Em stopped. Was this part of the maze? Another trap? Another mind trick? She looked around for mist, for a scent, for a murderous plant. Was this really it? She had begun to doubt the maze had a solution, and had resigned herself to wandering the deadly labyrinth for days until she collapsed from exhaustion.

But the cheerful exit did not waiver. It was a wide staircase leading up into the rocky cave. She had done it. There might be a settlement up there. Food. Sleep. She only had to enter.

But it felt too easy to be real. Em started to tremble. She tossed a nail on each step, climbing higher and higher, expecting a trap. Spikes or something. But nothing happened except the clatter of metal echoing on stone.

Em inched forward, ready for something horrible to leap out at her. Wary of the bright lights. Of anything at this point. Nothing was safe.

At the top of the stairs, she emerged through an archway into a bright round room. Torches hung at regular intervals around the walls. The ceiling was domed and enchanted to look like the night sky. Twilight, really. If it reflected the actual sky, then Em had spent the whole afternoon in the maze. Or maybe longer. She had lost her sense of time. She had an impulse to keep her hand on the left wall. But it was absurd that she would lose her way in here. The room had only two exits—the arch she had come through, and a door on the opposite side.

Four shortened pillars stood in the middle of the room. A ewer sat atop each of the three. On the fourth was an empty stemmed goblet.

Another trap? Em wondered. She made for the opposite door, only to find it locked. She attempted to pick the lock with the magic she had learned, but the lock was unyielding. Shielded. More games. Deities, she was tired. Her hip was throbbing, and she glanced down at the claw wound to find it weeping some kind of liquid. Blood from the cuts on her leg had dripped down to soak her pant hem and sock. That couldn't be good.

Shaking her head, she refocused on the room. Clearly there was some kind of puzzle or choice here. Em had read many fairy tales when she was a child. Three items. Three siblings. Three tasks. On and on, the stories went. Always three. And usually, the special person central to the fairy tale would choose correctly. Or be lucky enough to be born third. Like in the "Great Ring" story. But Em had no siblings. She wasn't some special chosen one destined to shake up the world.

But she had a feeling she would have to choose something—choose correctly—or the door would not open for her. She would be trapped here, or would have to leave via the maze. The thought propelled her to the center of the room to study the ewers.

One was a delicate blue-and-yellow glass, with elegant twists and swirls on the handle. The craftsmanship could only be Brildonian. The second was a simple farmhouse pitcher, taller than it was wide, made of sturdy ceramic and painted with leaves and flowers. It reminded her of the one Gram kept in their cottage. The third was made of clay, round with a small lip at the top and etched with symbols and geometric shapes. Pottery from the Northern tribes. The liquid inside each had no apparent color or odor, and Em hoped it was water.

Em studied them without insight. She was to select one, and what? Drink whatever was inside?

None stood out as particularly different. They were all different. One from the North. One from the high plains. One from the South. They were all made of different materials. Different designs. Colors. The shapes of each were unique.

There was an inscription on the pillar where the goblet stood. Em read the engraved words.

Only the worthy will drink from the font.

At that moment, Em decided she could stand no longer and slumped to the ground, dropping her pack beside her. She hadn't eaten all day, so she rummaged in her pack for a loaf of bread, one of Liam's sesame rolls he had gifted her the night before she left. She took a bite of the roll, only to taste a mouth of sawdust. "Ugh," she spat, studying the roll. Was Liam so upset by the empress's sentencing that his baking had suffered? Her mind flashed back to fake Liam from the maze. His insults. Had she ruined him? Them?

She reached for her waterskin and took a swig to wash out the sawdust taste, only to discover that the waterskin was empty. Was it broken? Or was the magic blocked? Frantically, she reached for an apple, only to discover it also turned to sawdust in her mouth.

"Are you kidding me?" she shouted at the room. She suddenly felt quite parched. Could she return to the maze to drink? But as soon as the thought occurred, she glanced behind her and realized the entrance archway was no longer visible. When had that happened? While she studied the ewers, or the inscription, perhaps? It didn't matter when. She was trapped. Unable to retreat. And she couldn't drink or eat.

She assumed she could drink the mysterious liquid in the pitchers, but how was she to prove she was worthy? The answer had to do with the pitcher she chose. And there would probably be consequences if she chose incorrectly. At least there weren't any corpses in here. *Not yet,* she thought morbidly.

She felt dizzy. From lack of food. Water. From smoke inhalation. Yet she needed her mind now more than ever. *What would Gram do?* she wondered as she struggled to her feet to study the ewers once more. The question made her think of the Gram-like creature below, and she shoved the invading thoughts away. Real Gram would tell her to keep going. To not give up.

How could she even begin to make a choice?

Em circled the pedestals, looking at each of the ewers in turn. Searching for . . . she knew not what. Something different?

The liquid inside each appeared and smelled the same. Each vessel was unique in so many ways, it was difficult to compare them. And yet, she needed to make a choice in order to leave this chamber. This tomb.

The pedestals holding each pitcher were identical. She sent a spark toward them, hoping to reveal hidden magic. But there was nothing. She pondered the inscription again, trying to parse out its intention. What did it mean to be worthy?

Perhaps the worthy were brave. The correct ewer was random, and only the brave would dare drink without certainty. That seemed reasonable, but then Em's mind flipped. Surely great thirst and fear of death would force a choice out of everyone eventually. If the result were random, why bother to test bravery? You were merely testing luck.

Perhaps all the drinks were dangerous. Poisoned, maybe. And the worthy were those strong enough to withstand its effects. But then she reasoned it would be unnecessary to offer a choice. In that case, a single goblet would do.

No. The worthiness was in the choice. Something about choosing the right vessel made her worthy. A shared heritage with the creator, perhaps? Or an indication of character, based on the ewer chosen.

Em gravitated toward the farmhouse pitcher. The one that reminded her of home. Like it belonged on Gram's table. Purchased from the mercantile at a discount. She reached out to brush the handle. It felt ordinary. She paused. It was familiar to her, but that meant nothing here.

Following a hunch, she brushed her fingers along the Brildonian glass. It was very beautiful, but also ordinary. Then she crossed to the Northern tribe pottery. As she ran her fingers along the geometric pattern at its swell, she felt something different. A tingle. A telltale sign of magic within the object. It was a difference. Maybe *the* difference that only the worthy, the mages, were able to discover.

It was something. Finding no other clues, Em lifted the pot and poured its contents into the goblet on the fourth pedestal.

Quickly, before she could lose courage, she drank from the goblet. The liquid tasted like water from a mountain spring. It was cold, clear, and refreshing. She drank it down, and then she set the empty cup back on its pedestal and waited.

She felt nothing.

After a moment, the inscription vanished, and the locks clicked loudly. Glancing back, Em realized the archway to the maze had not reappeared. She could not go back. She must continue forward into the next room.

～

THE NEXT ROOM, up another staircase, was similar. Another domed room with a door. She tossed in a nail before entering. Then, once she was inside, the archway closed behind her. The new exit was also locked and warded. In the center of the room sat three pedestals in a semicircle. On each rested an elaborate pastry.

By now, Em's mouth was watering with hunger, and the pastries before her were even more beautiful than the ones Liam concocted. She recognized the one on the right as an éclair: a long, airy shell filled with delicious fruit and crème. Liam made them once a week in his shop, and Em was always first in line.

The treat on the middle pedestal appeared to be a tiny, layered cake, but on closer inspection, the layers were thin pastry with cream laid neatly between. The top frosting was yellow and blue with a white spiky flower decoration piped onto it.

The pastry on the left also looked familiar. One of Liam's experiments, perhaps? She couldn't remember if he had fully worked that one out. Flaky dough was folded intricately around a center of strawberries and glaze.

Em's stomach rumbled. She longed to devour the masterpieces before her. But she held back, only in recognition of a pattern. Pedestals and locked doors meant she had to make a choice. She wasn't entirely sure what would happen this time if she chose incorrectly, but she could assume. If these tests were devised by the same devious mind that built the maze, she knew the consequences of an incorrect selection could be deadly.

She approached the pedestals, searching for a clue, or an inscription. She found the latter on the base of the middle plinth.

Those who hunger for greatness may enter.

"Ha, I see what they did there," Em rasped, her voice raw from the smoke in the maze. She felt delirious with hunger. Facing down the baked goods before her, she had no idea how she could narrow her odds. What about a pastry would indicate greater aspirations? Maybe the answer was obvious. She placed a finger on each treat in turn, hoping she would feel that same spark indicating magic. But none of the pastries held the flowing tingling feeling. They were what they appeared to be. Dough, sugar, and deliciousness.

Em thought of Liam. How would he appear if he were serving up these sweet treats? She could picture his face, grinning with barely contained glee as he offered her a flaky croissant, warm from the oven. She ached at the thought of him. Not the fake in the maze. The real Liam. The one she had left behind.

Skirting that gnawing hole, either hunger or regret, Em tried to recall if he had shared information about any of the treats sitting in this room. But she couldn't remember. Couldn't think of anything that had happened before the horror of the maze. This place where she was forced to make a choice. The impossibility of it. And the necessity of staying alive.

She wondered if—after all this—she would find out anything about the ring. Maybe she had entered the fortress and its maze foolishly and would have nothing to show for it. But where else could a legendary ring stay hidden for so long?

In her exhausted mind, the only thing standing between her and the Ring of Clavonion was this. If she chose correctly, the door would swing open, and the ring would appear, unguarded and free for the taking. She had proven herself worthy. She would take it to the empress, who would heap praise upon her and give Em her life back. She could go home. She could live in the town she loved with the man she adored, safe in the knowledge that she would never have to make this kind of decision again.

Something clanged inside her heart. Was that the dream, then? It felt rather . . . limiting. Was she really just hoping to return to a quiet life of fixing leaky roofs? Although it was rebellion against that simple life that had gotten her into this mess, her sense of adventure had been awakened, and deep down, she knew she had to chase it.

Yet, weren't her parents doing the same? Chasing adventure at the expense of all else? Em remembered how hurt she was when they didn't want to come along on this quest. How sad she'd felt even a few months ago when they chose their own adventures over coming back to Brookerby. Wasn't she doing that too? But to Liam?

This was an uncomfortable thought. And not the right time to ponder it.

She turned from the pedestals and paced the perimeter of the room again. Surely there was some clue to the choice before her. Pastries were not a common-knowledge topic. Either the designer of the test only wanted bakers to enter, or there was something about the pastries that would draw a certain kind of person.

The walls were the same as the prior room's. Stucco, with a vaulted ceiling and torches lighting the space at regular intervals. There were no frescoes providing clues.

She circled the room faster. The air was a bit stale. Em wondered if she should concern herself with air quality. This room was certainly less hazy than the smoke-filled maze.

She thought of all the fairy tales Gram had told over the years, and never did she recall a story about three pastries and a choice. *The Standard Book of Anything* would know. This was exactly the kind of puzzle the book could help with. It had so much useless information about baked goods and pottery that surely it could point her to the correct pastry. She gleefully rummaged in her bag and pulled out the book. Flipping open its pages, she hoped for a clue. Instead, she found blank paper.

Page after page was blank. She kept flipping, finding nothing. She closed and then opened the book. But there was nothing printed inside it. Had she broken it? Giving up on the book, she returned it to her bag and resumed pacing.

After a few moments, Em looped back to the center of the room, studying the pedestals anew. She had been thinking the pastries were poison, but if they weren't magic, how did the door unlock if she chose correctly? There had to be some kind of mechanism. Or maybe a trap if the wrong sweet was chosen. She ducked until she was eye level with the pastries and observed a tiny crack on the platform, almost covered by the éclair, but not quite. She moved to the other two and observed the same hairline crack. Was it a pressure plate that could sense which pastry was being selected? Some kind of button that sensed a shift in weight?

If that were true, as soon as she picked up one of the treats, a trap (or unlocking) would occur. Before she took a bite. And then Em had a flash of insight. If she took all three, the door would most certainly unlock. Could she just grab them all and run for the door?

It was possibly the dumbest idea she'd ever had. Gram would suggest the human slingshot idea she'd attempted at age ten was a close second. Both had the potential to get Em killed. She would need a way to quickly retrieve all three pastries and get out of the way. And she shouldn't stand right in the center of the semicircle, like the devious creator-mind clearly wanted her to. Grabbing her bag, she pulled out the rope, accidentally grazing her wounded hip with the rough fibers. She stopped, feeling suddenly dizzy and off-center. That was getting worse. Had she lost too much blood? She held her feet until she had mastered the spinning room and then began methodically knotting the rope.

This would work. She draped the finished loop across all three pedestals, careful to not bump the treats but ensuring they were loosely circled. Then she uncoiled the long tail of the rope and walked it over to the locked door.

Em breathed in. She breathed out. Then she yanked.

The rope loop dragged all three pastries off their stands, pulling them to the floor in front of Em. Then came a mechanical clicking noise, and three things happened at once. The floor dropped out around the éclair. Had she been standing there, she would've fallen to whatever horror lay below. Arrows flew diagonally across the chamber, piercing the air where she had stood in front of the pedestals. And the door immediately behind her clicked open.

She recoiled her rope and fled the room, leaving all three treats on the floor.

EM CLIMBED another staircase and entered a third room. Another locked door. Three pedestals. If she were in a fairy tale, this would be the last and most important room. On each pedestal sat a flat, round cushion, and on each cushion sat a small hoop of material—gold, silver, and wood—with no adornment.

The middle column had the description:

To the victor, the crown.

They were circlets, then? Small crowns, meant to be worn by rulers. What did they mean? Em passed her hand gently over each, and none contained a magical spark. The cushions seemed normal. Em couldn't see the platforms, or any potential mechanisms, because of the pillows.

Was it the same system? Could she do the same as before, and just pull all three circlets to the floor? That was probably not the way this particular puzzle was supposed to be solved, but Em was tired, and hungry, and her hip was starting to throb.

She unfurled the rope, draped it around the circlets, and once she stood by the door, she pulled. The metal and wood clattered to the floor, echoing around the chamber.

Without waiting to see what traps were set off, she turned and exited as soon as the door behind her clicked open.

CHAPTER 15

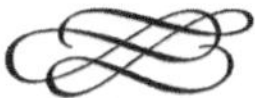

*E*m stumbled into a long hallway, similar to the one at the beginning of the maze. But this hall contained furniture. Multiple doors. Had she made it through? The corridor was silent. Echoing. Where was the colony of people? Her body ached. Her eyelids were leaden. And her hip was burning.

Em slumped against a wall, coiling her rope with the last of her strength. Everything was dark, but the soaring stone and metal archways above her supported glass ceilings that bathed the hallway in starlight. It was quite nice. Perhaps this was the Silver Nightingale Palace proper. She had made it.

Her body sagged sideways. She could go no farther. Everything felt fuzzy, and her eyes closed of their own volition. Maybe just a few minutes of rest.

EM AWOKE GRADUALLY. Light hit the backs of her eyelids, and the air smelled of vinegar and baking bread. Had she dreamed it all and actually fallen asleep at Liam's apartment? The bread smelled different than what he normally baked. Rye, maybe? She fluttered her eyes open and encountered a whitewashed ceiling with sunlight rectangles spreading across it. She started, alarmed. Where was she? A tiny bed that was not her own. Tossing back the covers, she saw a simple white shift on her body. Where were her clothes? And even more concerning, how did she get into this shift?

She rubbed her eyes, taking in her surroundings. Sunny high windows. A three-legged wooden side table holding a basin and an undecorated wooden chair were the only other items in the small bedchamber. There was no art on the stone walls, and no rug on the floor. Nothing to tell her anything about where she was. She didn't see her own clothes or bag anywhere. She pushed out of the bed, but when her feet hit the cold stone floor she stumbled, her muscles inexplicably quaking. Where . . . ?

"Good. You're awake," a youthful and cheery voice intoned. Em's head jerked up from the ground and she saw a young man entering the room, carrying a tray. She scrabbled to a corner and cast about for something to use as a weapon.

"Where am I?" Her voice cracked, betraying the indignant tone she had aimed for.

The man responded with a surprised laugh while setting the tray on the chair. Heat steamed off the dish, and it smelled delicious. Em kept her focus on the intruder.

"Where? Weren't you trying to get in here? The Silver Nightingale."

Em blinked. Yes. The maze. The three choices. It came back to her in a rush. She eyed him, assessing his threat level. The man sported a shock of dark hair, a patchy attempt at a beard and mustache, and slightly darker skin than her own. Maybe about her age? He looked like he came from the Northern territories, but he seemed friendly. "Where are my clothes? My bag?"

"Phoebe took 'em off to clean your wound, I guess. You were burning with a fever when we found you in the hallway. That was two mornings ago."

Two days! Em couldn't process this. She hadn't been sick when she sat down in the hallway. But her hip was not feeling great. And she had lost some blood. And the smoke from the fire . . .

"Those were nasty claw marks. They'd festered, huh? You get those in the maze?" Apparently, this man knew her business. Em didn't respond, and he didn't seem to mind. He gestured to the cabinet in the side table. "Spare clothes in there. Your bag too. Eat lunch, then they're all waiting for you in the Gathering Room. Just down the hall. See you soon!"

As the young man exited, Em tentatively tapped her hip. There was pain, but also a large, padded bandage where the hyena had clawed her. Her leg wounds were also bandaged. This Phoebe must be their healer?

Her thoughts drifted to the steaming tray. She felt ravenous. She inched away from the corner to get a closer look. A whole plate full of food, including a slice of the bread she'd been smelling and some kind of seasoned meat. She had a fleeting fear that maybe the food was poisoned, but she figured if they had wanted to kill her, they would've had ample time during the days she was unconscious. She dove in with enthusiasm.

Once the plate was clean, she turned to the mug. The hot drink within tasted of honey and lemon. It was soothing on her dry throat.

Two days? How had she been so careless? Now, for good or ill, she was indebted to the strangers who lived here. Em faced that prospect with less unease now that her belly was full. She padded over to the cabinet and pulled open the door. Her bag was tucked inside, next to a mismatched linen tunic and trousers. She pulled out *The Standard Book of Anything*, only to remember that it wouldn't work inside the warded fortress and all the pages were blank.

She hastily dressed in the clean clothes, and after a moment of searching for footwear, she found her old boots under the bed. Pulling them on, she left the room, bringing her bag just in case. She would have to find the Gathering Room to meet her hosts.

As she inched down the hallway, the food sitting warm in her belly, she began to wonder what her story should be. If they knew of the ring, would they freely give her the information? Should she lie? Or just leave the ring and the death sentence out of it? Should she simply pretend to be a lost traveler? That wouldn't work. They'd never believe that she had braved the maze under that pretense.

She should attempt to secure herself some free time to explore without arousing suspicion, to discover where their knowledge was kept. She could pose as a historian seeking out knowledge of the Clavonion era. It seemed weak. Em didn't know enough history to sustain the ruse, so it would fall apart at any detailed questioning. But she wasn't sure she could devise a better story. Also she wondered if she should hide her identity. According to their notes, Anne and Farrigan had never made it inside the Silver Nightingale, but they were infamous all over Esnania. She didn't want another situation where someone prejudged her because her name was Strider and her face—so like her mother's—triggered Anne's reputation.

The hallway was as she remembered. Dark and sparsely furnished. The skylight let in the noonday sun, but even sunshine couldn't disperse the gloom over the place. There wasn't a single knickknack or painting. It was as if the place had been looted long ago, then reoccupied by minimalists. Or clerics.

Voices echoed from a door at the far end of the vast hallway. The Gathering Room?

Em delayed, trying every door she passed. Hoping for some kind of information about her hosts. But the doors were all locked and warded. When she sent a spark through the keyhole, it rebounded, as if ricocheting off an impenetrable surface. She could attempt to pick the locks the old-fashioned way, but she hadn't brought the right tools. She wondered if the locked doors indicated her hosts had something to hide.

The voices were closer, but Em couldn't make out words from where she stood. Perhaps she could listen in before meeting them. But as she crept closer, a voice rang through the hall, beckoning her forward.

"Come in, young lady. We don't bite."

Caught, she moved into the room, hands strangling her bag's

shoulder strap. She didn't need to be worried. After all, they'd helped her. Healed her. She had nothing to fear, did she?

~

THE GATHERING ROOM was a misleading name. The label elicited visions of cozy furniture around a fireplace. Perhaps a poetry reading, or a lively discussion would occur. What Em found was an austere audience chamber. Hard surfaces and dark colors dominated the echoing space. It looked like a throne room. Perhaps this palace had once been occupied by royalty, before it was the bastion of renowned mage Bronwyn Featherweight. But who occupied it now?

A woman with long black hair, streaked with silver, wearing rich purple robes sat on a stone chair in the center of the room. Em tried and failed to pinpoint her age. Somewhere between Ilna's and Gram's ages? A woman in her prime, yet her gaze was ancient. A silent group —maybe half a dozen people, mostly young, most with Northern features—stood around the woman. All eyes watched Em as she walked through the group. She offered a small bow to the woman in the chair.

"Welcome to our new arrival. We are delighted to see your health improved." The woman's voice slid over Em like silk, but there was a spikiness to her gaze. Em was instantly on guard, but hid it with another quick bow. She noticed a few of the others wore the same linen clothes in mismatched colors that Em now sported.

She realized the lady was waiting for a response, so she spoke, her voice cracking. "I am grateful for your hospitality, my lady."

A beat of silence, as if they wished her to say more. But Em could not think of anything polite, only probing questions, so she held her tongue.

Finally, the lady spoke again, more acerbically. "You are eating our food and sleeping in a bed we provided. Explain how you traversed the labyrinth. Were you instructed by a former initiate?"

Em kept her countenance. Barely. Initiate? Was this some kind of cult? A school? "No, ma'am," she murmured. "I discovered the entrance on my journey. There were rumors of a settlement at the foot of the Silver Nightingale, and I wanted to speak with its inhabitants."

A low din arose from the others, who had been silent until this moment. The lady in purple leaned forward, and they quieted. The pearls on the woman's sleeves clanked on the stone armrests of her chair. "You mean to say, you passed the maze—nearly unharmed—through luck alone? That is"—she let out a small laugh—"impossible."

Em felt a shiver at the base of her neck. Danger glittered in the woman's eyes, oozed out of her very being. Em feared to speak, for her next words might unhinge the lady entirely. So she said nothing.

"The most talented mages suffer severe injuries when attempting entry. Most do not succeed at all, even if they have received instruction. Even if you get lucky in the maze, there is instant death in the winnowing chambers, unless you had the proper instruction. Speak, girl. Who sent you?" The observers had grown deathly quiet as the woman's tone sharpened to a point.

"Begging your pardon, lady. I did not escape injury. I was informed I have been sleeping for two days as a result of my injuries."

"From an injury sustained before you entered the maze, or so my healer says. Apart from a few cuts from the constricting plant and smoke inhalation—of your own doing—you were unharmed. Do not toy with me; it is quite rude, Miss—"

"Stonehill." Em felt the threat in this place. Her name—her parents' name—would do her no favors. "Emily Stonehill."

The woman's eyes narrowed. "You seem familiar, but the name does not. Do you have any magical gifts, Miss Stonehill?"

"I can do a few small things," Em offered. "But I have never been properly trained."

The woman leaned back with a small quirk of her mouth. Em's lack of training seemed to put the lady at ease. "You have a place here, Miss Stonehill, by virtue of passing the maze. I offer magical training and combat training. But as you probably can surmise, we are not open to the public. If you leave this place, you will not reveal our location or its secrets to anyone, or I will hunt you down. I should also warn you, any magical items you carry will not work under this roof. The wards only allow magic that is created here, by me or for the purpose of training. Do we understand each other?"

"Yes, my lady. Thank you. I only seek knowledge." The woman raised an eyebrow and waited for Em to continue. "There was a caravan traveling through these mountains, many centuries ago. They carried something of historical interest that I wish to trace."

"A treasure hunter, then. Come to plunder us . . ."

"Oh, no," Em protested. But whispers from the observers had grown thunderous.

The woman waved her hand, and the group quieted again. "Miss Stonehill, if you wish to join our training exercises, you are welcome. If you wish to enjoy the hospitality of the Silver Nightingale before continuing on your way, you are also welcome. We expect you to contribute to the cooking and upkeep while you are here—you will not be waited on. But if you take something that does not belong to you, you will die. Bronwyn Featherweight is not merciful to thieves."

Em's eyebrows shot up. Bronwyn Featherweight? Renowned mage, planter of warding trees, and notorious traitor? She was hanged nearly fifty years ago. Em's face must've shown her confusion, for the woman rose from her throne with imperiousness that matched the empress herself. "You may address me as 'The Lady Mage' or just 'Lady Bronwyn.' Dismissed, Miss Stonehill."

CHAPTER 16

The nightingale is a bird known for powerful song, even during the darkness of night. The bird sings to defend their territory from invading species.

"Birdwatching in the Northern Territories"
From the library of the Silver Nightingale

Eight Weeks until the Solstice

*A*fter that awkward interview with a presumed-dead mage, Em watched the others file out. Her mind was dashing through all the details, and she tried not to dwell on the fact that Bronwyn had offered to teach her magic. Bronwyn Featherweight. She cursed softly. That might be too good an offer to pass up, despite her looming deadline.

Was the woman even the real Bronwyn? She was supposedly hanged, and Em assumed the empress knew what her nemesis looked like. It's not as if she had hung someone else by mistake. So, then, who was this? An imposter? An imitator?

One burly man remained in the now-empty chamber. His light hair was cropped close, and he wore an expression of readiness. Em exited the chamber, hoping to explore the rest of the palace, only to hear the man's quiet footsteps behind her. She veered to the right, as if to let him pass, but he stopped. Waiting.

"Are you my jailer, then?"

"Not a jail, Stonehill. Go where you want." His voice was clipped and quiet.

"But you'll follow me," she said.

He bobbed his head.

"Don't trust me?" she teased.

"No."

Sighing, she turned toward the nearest door, only to stop again. "Can you at least tell me your name? Maybe give me a tour? That would be better than you guarding me."

The man seemed to consider. Finally, "Cal."

Good enough for now.

She tried to get more than a few syllables out of the man as they wandered the corridors that afternoon. She asked about his upbringing. Where was he from? Was he a magic user? How did he find his way here? Did he go through the maze? All were met with silence, or a single word. "North." "Yes." "Brought." "Yes."

She probed about Bronwyn, and he said nothing, before finally suggesting she ask the others.

All the while, she entered any room that wasn't locked. None contained any decor except for the most austere of beds, tables, and chairs—nearly identical to the chamber in which she awoke. She discovered an outside field surrounded by gardens, with a high rock wall on one side and a frightening drop-off on the other. This was where they practiced incantations, Cal confirmed with minimal syllables. Inside, a large hall once used for dancing was now used for sparring. Cal's eyes glittered, but he said very little as he presented the room. Em scanned every new place for knickknacks or trinkets or books. Nothing. Books would be the most useful since *The Standard Book of Anything* wasn't functional within the wards.

"Is there a library somewhere?"

Cal nodded.

"Can you show me the way?"

He hesitated, but then—after deciding it didn't violate some unwritten rule—he nodded again. "This way."

At last, somewhere interesting.

THE LIBRARY WAS ALSO UNDECORATED. The simplest of shelves. No comfy chairs or footstools, to Em's chagrin. Only hard stone floors. But there was no dust, and the books seemed to be well maintained.

The books on the shelf were unique to the fortress. Em found a whole shelf on the history of the Northern tribes. She guessed the empress and her book bans hadn't found their way here. Another section contained magical instruction, both theoretical and practical, also banned within the empire. She flipped open one promising tome to a random page:

Magic necessarily requires an energy source, a target, and intention. If one of these is lacking, the cantrip will not work as intended. The infusing entity selects a target—either an item or a living being—and saturates the item with flows from the energy source. Then intention is clearly stated, with all contingencies considered, and—if needed—long-term energy specified. These are the fundamental rules of magecraft. If a target is lacking, the mage is attempting to create something out of nothing, a clear violation of the axioms—

Em reshelved the book with a sigh. It was as if she had stumbled into a deep pool and she hadn't yet learned to swim. Bronwyn mentioned training, so she would just have to wait until those lessons occurred.

She continued to scan the titles. Another shelf contained books on political philosophy, then religious texts, followed by folk tales. It was a finer collection than even Cornelius's store could boast. Her fingers itched to read every volume. She spent ten minutes skimming every shelf, mentally calculating the likelihood that traces of the ring could be found in one of these volumes. Finally, as she reached for a ledger of accounts, Cal cleared his throat.

Em jumped back. "What?"

"Dinner. The dining hall."

"Now?" Em said. "Can I bring a book with me?"

"No."

Em nodded and followed him out of the room. But not before casting a final longing glance at the shelves.

DINNER WAS NOT ready when they arrived in the large fortress kitchens. The long wooden table in the middle of the room sat empty. But the stoves were lit, the fireplace was ablaze, and the same group from earlier—sans Bronwyn—was bustling around stone counters, chopping and stirring.

She turned to Cal with a quizzical look.

"Everyone helps," he said. Then, without a backward glance, he rolled up the sleeves of his linen tunic and stepped forward into the fray.

Em hesitated. She didn't see Bronwyn, but everyone else from the Gathering Room was here. She spotted the young man with the patchy facial hair who had brought her lunch. He was chopping carrots, so she sidled up next to him. "Can I help?" she offered.

He grinned. "Can you peel potatoes?"

Em said that she could. She found a sack of potatoes, and a knife was placed in front of her. She carved thin slivers of skin off the root, being careful to cut out any bad spots. When she finished peeling one, the young man took it, quartered it, and tossed the pieces in a large cookpot with the other vegetables.

"How long have you been at the Silver Nightingale?" she ventured.

"'Bout a year now. My brother, Elias, has been here for three."

"Elias. Which one is he?"

The young man pointed out his brother across the room. He was a sinewy man, roasting a cut of meat on a spit over the fire. He had the same shock of dark hair as his brother, but he was also missing two fingers and had a hard look about him that his younger brother lacked.

"Ah. Elias. And you are . . . ?"

"Silas."

Em nodded, trying to commit the names to memory. "You're from the North?"

"Yeah. Northern tribal lands. Elias insisted I come. But I didn't for a while. Didn't want to leave Meme and Pop behind."

"Was it dangerous?" Em tried to recall all she knew about the tribal land conflict, and realized she didn't know much more than generalities. Surely it didn't affect the normal people who lived there.

"Yeah. Lots of my friends joined up with the resistance when they were old enough to hoist a weapon." He chuckled. "I'm not a fighter, but I probably should be. Just out of necessity, ya know?"

"Sure," Em said, agreeing without quite understanding. She wished she knew more about the conflict, but she didn't want to show her ignorance by interrogating Silas. Not when there were books in the library she could study later.

They finished chopping the vegetables and set them to boil. Em followed Silas to the large table at the other end of the kitchen. They set out glasses and a jug of water for the table. Em noticed the jug looked like the Northern pottery in the maze room with the three pitchers.

When the Silver Nightingale was a regular castle, this was probably where the servants ate. But Em realized this cozy setup was a standard dinner for the—what did Bronwyn call them?—initiates. A short but solid middle-aged woman set the table, while a gentleman with perfect posture and a slight sneer followed behind adjusting the silverware precisely.

"That's Phoebe. She's really good with the natural magic. She healed you, by the way." Silas indicated the middle-aged woman. "And he's Otto. Stuck-up git." The last part was whispered with a grin. Em smiled. She tilted her head toward Cal, raising an eyebrow.

"Great guy. Can't get him to say more than two words an hour." Silas snickered. Em nodded in agreement.

Em glanced around. All of them had dark hair and tanned skin. All Northerners. She knew everyone's name, except for one younger woman with kohl-lined eyes and pursed lips. "And her?"

Silas's voice suppressed a chuckle. "Cora."

He was about to say something more about the woman, and but he was cut off by Elias marching through the throng carrying the cooked meat on a platter. Everyone "oohed" and "aahed" as he placed the platter in the table's center. Phoebe set a basket of rolls next to it, and Silas returned to the vegetable vat to spoon them out into a bowl.

Em backed up a step, waiting to sit until the others had found their usual spots. By count of place settings, either they had set a place for her, or they were awaiting someone else.

"Is the Lady Bronwyn joining us?" she asked.

All eyes swiveled toward Em, and she suddenly felt like an ant on the wrong end of a magnifying glass.

"The mistress should not dine with her students." Otto sniffed.

"She knows she's welcome anytime," Phoebe said. "But she chooses to dine alone."

Em wondered at this. Did Bronwyn intentionally keep herself apart? Was she to be treated like a monarch? She said nobody here was waited upon. Was Bronwyn the exception?

Silas carried the vegetables back to the table and climbed over the bench seat to his spot—next to his brother and across from Cora. Em slid into the last open place, on the end next to Cal.

The food was simple. Well-prepared, but the bread didn't hold a candle to Liam's baking. The vegetables were salted, and the meat was seasoned well enough. But after her ravenous hunger in the maze, it felt like the finest meal she had ever eaten. She noticed Otto picking at his food critically, but the others ate heartily.

Phoebe was the first to ask Em a question. "I think we've all been wondering how you got through that maze. Want to share your secrets?"

Em raised an eyebrow. "Did you all have to go through it?"

They all nodded. Silas said, "I had some instructions on how to get through, so I didn't have much trouble. Almost picked the wrong pastry, though."

"A guide brought me. I was led through quite easily," Otto huffed.

"A guide brought me too," Phoebe retorted. "But he nearly died when we took a wrong turn."

"I went through alone," Cal said softly. The others grew quiet.

Em could only wonder at what Cal had seen. She smiled grimly. "I followed the left wall. And I threw nails around every corner to trigger any traps before I stepped into them."

"Seriously?" Cora spoke, her musical voice dripping with sarcasm. "Did you trigger the hyena-beast? Because even with your tricks, you're not outrunning that animal." She pointed to a scar on her forearm shaped like claws and teeth.

Em nodded but said nothing. She didn't want to relive that moment with the hammer. Ever. So she pushed on. "In the first choice room, I chose the pitcher that was magical. The other two were not."

The others around the table bobbed their heads. Since they had magical gifts, they would've discovered that as well.

"In the second room . . ." Em wondered if she should lie, but she still had no idea which pastry was the right one. "I noticed the mechanism below each pastry and worked out that removing the right one would trigger the door. So I removed all three at the same time. I still have no idea which was the correct one. Same with the crowns."

Silas laughed. Elias was studying her appraisingly.

Cora scoffed. "She didn't pass the trial, then. If she didn't pick."

"Maybe she revealed a flaw in the tests," Elias said. "Better her than an imperialist."

Em watched this exchange, feeling as if she were being sized up by each of them. "So . . . which pastry was correct?" she asked.

No one said. An awkward silence fell.

Okay. They didn't have to tell her. "Could you at least tell me how Bronwyn survived a hanging fifty years ago? We were taught she was dead. There was an army at the Silver Nightingale. A few scouts made their way in and brought out Bronwyn. She was transported to Gillamor and hung."

This seemed to reanimate the group once more. They spoke over each other, eager to share the tale.

"You do not know? It's a delightful story."

"She never was taken!"

"Most of the scouts who found their way into the maze were killed. But one—"

"Bronwyn allowed one to live—"

"She enchanted him to look like her. She's a prestiger. One of the best!"

"To be silent—"

"The fool imperialists!"

"The empress couldn't tell the difference!"

"Whoever that scout was, they hung him!"

Em tried to take this all in. Bronwyn had sent someone else to die wearing her image. That seemed cruel. But also . . .

"So brilliant. The woman is a genius," Elias declared, lifting his glass of water. "And we get to learn from her." The others raised their glasses and clinked them before drinking.

Em felt a spark, not of magic but of ambition, flashing within her. She could learn from this woman. She could learn to do extraordinary things. To be called brilliant by rooms full of people. To fool the empress. If she could learn that trick, maybe she could evade her own execution. It was something to consider.

LATER THAT NIGHT, Em thought about dinner. She was definitely the outsider; the residents didn't trust her yet. But she could feel the warmth and the trust between them. She hoped she could find what she needed without causing problems for this cozy group.

As she stared at the ceiling in her tiny room—toying with the small wood chip from the warding tree—she thought of her own family dinner, and smiled at the first time Liam had come.

It was a week after Em had returned to Brookerby with him beside her. The warding tree was destroyed, her oath lifted, and the town healed. Still, she was nervous. Up to that point, she had protected Liam from nosy questions and demands about his intentions.

But Gram had insisted on dinner. Loudly, now that she had her voice back. So Liam came.

Em had tried to explain the tradition to him. Family dinner was a weekly occurrence. No, none of them were actually related. Yes, they dressed up a bit. (Sometimes under protest.) But they had held these dinners since Em was orphaned and placed under Gram's care. They all wanted her to have a family to lean on.

But now she and Liam stood immobilized on the stoop, as Em imagined the myriad of ways that her found family could embarrass her in front of this titled gentleman. "I'm sorry in advance," she said, squeezing his hand.

Liam laughed. "Stop apologizing. Believe it or not, I'm excited to meet your family. And I do know how to interact with other people."

"It's not you I'm worried about," Em muttered.

"Come in, Lord Hallson," Gram hollered through the open window. She faked an uppity accent as she said his name, and then cackled. Em turned beet red and quickly opened the cottage door.

Mendel met them as they entered. "Oh, Lord Hallson, how fine you look! Are those trousers from Groussens? I adore their patterned jackets. Have you seen the latest season's designs?" Unfortunately, Mendel's snobbery was not fake.

Liam was politely replying, but it was all gibberish to Em, so she ducked past them, trying to pull Liam with her.

"Emaline! Were you planning to change, my dear? Surely your young man would like to see you in something nicer? Maybe that silk dress I gave you yesterday? Hmm?"

Em scowled. But Liam grinned devilishly. "I would, actually," he said.

Em shot daggers at him, but he only winked as she tromped to her room to change out of her dusty work clothes. Then he turned to Mendel and began to speak of men's fashion and whatever the hell

Groussens was. Em groaned. She was supposed to shield him from all this, but he seemed just fine without her.

She emerged a short while later in the delicate blush dress and slunk to the table. Mendel could've at least made the neckline a bit higher. Her face only reddened further when Liam leaned over and whispered, "You look amazing."

Gram had made a roast, and Em immediately dribbled some on her dress. She attempted to hide the mess as Ilna explained the latest foreign policy initiative using carrots for the Brildonians and potatoes for Esnanians. Liam listened with great attention.

Gram told a somewhat bawdy story about one of their old neighbors, who had since moved away. She waved her gravy-covered spoon as she told the tale—much of it entirely made up, Em found out later. Mendel leaned back to avoid the gravy splatters on his new gray checked shirt. Ilna giggled, and Liam's eyes glowed with happiness while Em slid down in her seat, wondering if she could hide under the table until it was over.

When dinner was finished, Gram raised her glass of cider. "To family." They all toasted, then Ilna commented to Liam, "Now we all share something that has been on our mind."

Gram expressed her gratitude at having her voice back, and expounded on all the things she was excited to do now that she could speak again.

Mendel expressed relief at finding an able apprentice like Tilly and talked about his plans for further expansion of his fashion empire.

Em spoke briefly about the town repairs, and how she was learning to delegate to get more accomplished. It was at this moment that Mendel noticed the gravy stain on her new dress, and shrieked in disappointment, blaming Gram's spoon-waving for the splatters.

Liam stood for his turn. "I haven't had a true family in quite a while. I have my brother, but we were estranged for several years. And now, my relationship with him is improving. And I find myself here, with Em and with all of you. I want to thank you. For welcoming me. For allowing me to be a part of your lives. I've wanted a family again for so long, and tonight feels like the beginning of something really special."

Em's fears about Liam judging her family and her family finding him wanting melted away. She met his eyes, seeing only warmth and love shining back at her. He could belong here, if he wanted to.

The memory replayed brightly in her mind. She was an outsider to these Northerners, but she had her own family waiting. She hadn't left things with Gram on good terms, or Liam either. But she knew deep in her heart that they loved her, and when she came back, things would be as they always were.

CHAPTER 17

Crafting magical items is a delicate and thoughtful pursuit. One must have a thorough mind that considers every contingency. One incorrect phrase or improper metaphor and the item will more likely maim you than work properly.

"The Art of the Craft"
From the library of the Silver Nightingale

Seven Weeks and Six Days until the Solstice

The next morning, Em attended the daily magic training in the outdoor clearing. She had brought her cloak, expecting it to be chilly in the outdoor garden, but she discarded the garment quickly. Something about the wards let in the sunlight and kept out the cold.

Bronwyn was not present. Instead, Phoebe—the middle-aged mage who was skilled at natural magic (whatever that meant)—stood before them. A small pile of stones sat nearby.

"Today, I've been instructed by the illustrious Lady Bronwyn to review the basics of crafting magical items."

Em felt a shiver of anticipation. But the others seemed less enthused.

"The basics?" Cora whined. "We're all beyond that. Except for her." Em felt their eyes, and she tried to look apologetic. She wished they didn't have to review on her account, but she appreciated that today's lesson wouldn't be beyond her.

"It will be a good review for many of you. Difficulties in the fundamentals create larger problems down the line." Phoebe said this gently, but Cora made no further objection.

"Miss Stonehill, since we don't know how long you will be with us, I expect the lady mage wishes you to build a solid foundation while you are here."

Em nodded her thanks and tried to temper her enthusiasm. This was exactly what she wished to learn. The basics. The foundation of it all.

"Now, who can tell Miss Stonehill about magical energy and magical intent?"

Silas was quick to jump in. "Any magic cast, or magical item created, needs both an energy source and instructions for how it should behave. Intent, that is. Energy can either come from the mage, or the thing being enchanted. But intent must come from the mage."

Phoebe nodded. "Well said, Silas. You followed that, Miss Stonehill?"

"I'm not sure," Em said. "Can you give me more specifics on the energy? Is that the spark feeling?"

Phoebe gestured to Cora, and the girl started rapidly reciting details, sounding bored. "An item can receive energy from the creating mage. These are short-term objects, as the mage doesn't have an unlimited source to give. Objects that create their own kinetic energy through mechanical means can feed off created energy and can be used by anyone. An item can be created to draw on energy from the user of the item, whoever that may be—so long as it's a mage. If an object lives—plants for example—the magic implanted can power itself."

Em tried to keep up. If she created an item and used her own energy, it wouldn't last very long. Good to know. And the kinetic energy thing was interesting. Maybe that applied to Ilna's printing press? Items that could only be used by mages drew upon the user's energy. *The Standard Book of Anything* could only be used by mages, so maybe the book exhausted her, not just frustrated her.

She thought to the broken jumping cane in her bag and raised her hand. Phoebe nodded to her. "When a magical item breaks, what causes the magic to leave?"

Phoebe's smile grew a bit brighter. "That would happen in either of the first two instances. One, the item stops working because the magic was limited from creation. Or two, the kinetic process providing energy no longer works, and it interrupts the cantrip."

Em pondered this. Was there a kinetic process from the jumping cane? She supposed being slammed on the ground at each jump created a certain amount of energy. As was the triple-tapping. But she still was a bit fuzzy on how it all worked. She tried another question. "What about living things? Enchanted trees, for example?"

Phoebe's eyes sharpened and the honey-sweetness left her voice. "Encountered one of the warding trees of protection, did we?" Her directness knocked Em off-balance, but she didn't attempt to deny it. She wondered if this conversation would make its way back to Bronwyn. The warding trees were the mage's most visible legacy in Esnania, and it was not a positive legacy. At least, in Em's view.

Phoebe tone was clipped. "That's more advanced. A lesson for another day."

Em's brain returned to other magical items for categorization. She thought back to her parents' warehouse full of items. Some required a mage, and those must siphon energy. Probably small amounts, but she recalled feeling exhausted after using a large number of the items from the shelves.

She thought again about Ilna's printing press, back in Brookerby. It must gain energy from its own movements. She had fixed it once when the parts needed to be oiled . . . before it had fully broken down.

And the warding tree. It was living, so maybe it drew from itself? Or it drew from the town? *Another day,* Phoebe had said.

But Phoebe was moving on to a practical portion of the lesson, so Em put her rumination on hold.

"Today we will do something quite simple, in theory. Each of you will select a stone from this pile, provide it with energy, and then imbue it with a list of instructions. The stone should detect a person approaching and give you a signal to warn you. After you have created your stones, we will test them."

Everyone moved to collect a stone. Em was stunned. That's it? How would she possibly do that without any further instruction?

"One more thing," Phoebe said. "Please use your own energy to imbue the stone. Just enough for today, or a few days if you like. I don't want these existing in the world forever."

Em reach down to pick up the remaining stone from the ground, smooth and the size of a walnut. Phoebe waited as she straightened. "This is the part where you might require some additional instruction, yes?"

Em nodded. "Please."

"All right, then. First, you must craft the instruction in your mind. What is the very clear picture of what you want it to do? Focus on that. Who do you want it to detect? All people, or just those who have not been noticed yet? From what distance? How will the stone inform you of this approaching person?"

She gave Em a moment to craft this in her mind. Em wanted the stone to detect any person who was not visible to her within the same room or approaching from an adjacent room. Maybe she should have the stone get warm. Not enough to burn her, but warm enough so that it wasn't just warm from her pocket or her hand. She pictured the feeling of a mug of hot tea. But if multiple people approached, how would she determine where they were? She decided to add a directional element. If they approached from behind only, it would get warm. It would have to heat faster or slower depending on the speed of the approaching person—

Phoebe cleared her throat, and Em realized she had been thinking on the problem for several minutes. She reddened. "Sorry, I got hung up on details."

"That's probably a good thing, Miss Stonehill. It's precise details that make a good magical object. Vague instructions can be disastrous. But for now, what you have worked out is probably good enough."

Em nodded, holding out the stone once more.

"You will now fix the rules firmly into your mind and imbue the stone with both energy and the cantrip you've designed."

"How does one imbue?"

"You know that lightning feeling within?"

Em nodded. The spark.

"You allow that to flow into the object. Direct it. This might take some practice. Imagine a small waterspout, not a rushing stream. Depending on how long and how large the flow is, you give more energy to the item. Give too much and you'll be exhausted. You'll sleep for days. Weeks, even. I once knew a mage who slept for a year and half after an imbuing was botched."

Em swallowed hard. She could direct the spark; she'd been practicing with Farrigan. But controlling the flow was new. "How do I include my rules?"

"Recite them in your head as you imbue."

Phoebe watched Em make an unsuccessful attempt, patted her shoulder, then wandered away to check on Otto, who was cursing at his stone in elevated verse.

Em gazed at her stone. Just think it and direct energy? That didn't seem so hard. She ran through the rules in her brain and summoned the spark, which she funneled at the stone. She tried to picture a tiny spigot. A valve opening and closing. Tightening the valve to a small trickle that flowed over the stone. It was like patting her head and rubbing her stomach at the same time, trying to do this while reciting her intentions. No wonder mages wrote their spells down.

Em finished, and then wondered whether she had done it properly. She felt the telltale rushing of magic on the rock, but there was no way to tell if it worked until someone snuck up on her.

Phoebe had helped Otto sort through his issue and was now calling everyone back together. She sent one person out of the room—Cora, in this case—to enter when signaled, and asked Cal to test his stone first.

Cal stood with his back to the door as Cora entered. His stone made a bell tone that got louder as Cora approached.

"Very good, Cal! Is that what you intended?" Phoebe asked.

"Maybe quieter," Cal mumbled.

"That's a good point. If you don't want the person to know your alarm is going off, you probably don't want an audible cue. Who's next?"

Silas went. His rock got very heavy when Cal approached behind him, and it nearly pulled his trousers down. The group was in stitches, and Em had to stifle a giggle. Silas flashed a smile as he tugged up his pants.

Cora's rock produced a very specific, sharp odor that Em couldn't place.

Otto's rock twitched in his pocket. He also sported a small bruise on his cheek from his practice with it; the rock had jumped far higher than he intended.

Em stepped up, ready to test hers. Phoebe's mouth twisted. "You successfully imbued?"

"I think so," Em said, sounding more confident than she felt. She waited. And then her rock felt warm as Otto approached. Success! But then she startled—there was warm liquid trickling down her leg. Had she—

Em turned and Otto smirked. Flushing with confusion, Em reached into her pocket and pulled out a teacup. Had the rock turned—

"You wanted it to turn to liquid?" Phoebe asked, trying and failing to hide a smile.

"N-no. I wanted it to turn warm," Em stammered. "About the

temperature of tea . . ."

"Ha! Newbie mistake," Cora crowed.

Phoebe offered a sympathetic pat. "I should've told you. Stay away from comparisons and metaphors. The magic will take them literally."

Em tried to wring out her pant leg, feeling utterly green.

PHOEBE SHOWED Em how to siphon her failed magic away to try again. Then they spent the rest of the morning refining their rocks. Em's pants slowly dried in the winter sunshine. On the sixth try, Em was finally able to achieve what she hoped—a noticeably warm stone when someone came up behind her. Hers also seemed to have a wider range than the others'. While testing it, she would sense an intruder even before they came through the door behind her.

She couldn't help but note that the others had designed their spells with a warning that would be apparent to the other person. Smell, movement, noise. Hers could provide an alert without notice. She was rather proud of herself, and at the end of the session, she kept the rock in her pocket. Most of the others had siphoned and discarded theirs back onto the pile.

Lunch was cold sandwiches, assembled hastily by the group in the kitchen. Em was drained from using magic all morning and would've preferred sneaking away to her room for a nap. No one spoke to her, but Em sat down beside Phoebe, trying to take part. She asked the woman when Bronwyn taught the magic lessons. She had learned so much in a single day from Phoebe, and she was excited for how much more she could learn from Bronwyn herself. She hoped she would at least get a few lessons with the mage before her time here ran short. But Phoebe's jaw clenched at the question.

"The lady is very preoccupied and has less time to train the initiates," the woman said.

Em glanced down at her sandwich, picking up on Phoebe's annoyance. She hadn't meant to offend.

"Where's she today?" Silas interjected into the awkward silence.

"Here, but meeting with several town councils," Elias offered between bites. "Lady Bronwyn has many important people coming to see her. Seeking her protection and wise council."

~

AFTER LUNCH, they regrouped in the hall where physical training took place each day. Silas used the word, "sparring." Em had not been eager for this—the idea of fighting scared her—

and was tempted to beg off and go to the library instead. After all, the clock was ticking on finding that ring, and she was confident there was a clue somewhere in this fortress.

Em had never learned to fight, but she hated feeling helpless, physically or any other way. It wasn't a problem in Brookerby, but she had several encounters this past year where defense skills would've helped tremendously. Maybe Sam Monterey wouldn't have kidnapped and drugged her if she'd had the ability to fight back. Maybe she could've held off the hyena who chased her from the mining town. She decided to stay.

Elias, Silas's brother, led the group. Already, Em had the impression that the man was dedicated to Bronwyn, but his fervor for the North was also on full display. He pounded his chest, displayed his hand with the missing fingers, and shouted about defending the homeland and taking back what was rightfully theirs. This frightened Em, but she saw the others nodding in agreement, and she tried to keep her face neutral.

Then Elias paired off the group for their first bouts, and Em felt a rush of panic. Wouldn't she receive instruction? She looked around and realized for the first time how fit this group was. She couldn't best any of them. Maybe she would only be watching today. That was all right. She could study their techniques and—

Elias pointed to Em, then to Cora. "You two. After Otto and Silas."

Em sidled up to the man, pasting on what she hoped was a respectful expression. Elias didn't return her greeting.

"I need to let you know, I've never fought before," she said. "So maybe I could just start with some strength training . . . or stances, or something?"

"We won't know where you're weakest until we see you in action," he grunted.

"Ah. Well, just assume I'm weak in everything." Em grinned. "I really wouldn't provide much of challenge."

His glare silenced her. "We spar to improve. Not much motivation to improve without the threat of pain, is there, Miss Stonehill?"

Em didn't like the way he phrased that. She had a strong premonition that Cora would knock her teeth out, which would lead to great pain. That did indeed feel motivating.

The feeling only grew as she watched the other pairs fight.

Elias and Cal fought first. They circled each other warily, darting and feinting. They almost floated, like two leaves twisting in an autumn wind. Their movements were graceful, and seemingly unplanned. Finally, they caught each other, grappling with an intensity that made Em flinch. Cal had extra muscle on Elias, but the other man made up for the deficit with cleverness. He finally pulled Cal to the padded floor with a tricky leg move. Cal fought back, reversing their positions and pressing his forearm to Elias's throat. Elias was turning red, and the others were calling for him to yield. With a quick kick, Elias was back in control, holding Cal's arm behind his back until the larger man finally tapped out. Em felt ill.

Next, Silas and Otto approached the mat. They had chosen to spar with practice weapons—each clutched a wooden dagger. The two men were not as graceful as Cal and Elias, but Em could still see the years of training in their movements. Phoebe appeared at Em's side as she watched.

"How are they so good?" Em muttered.

Phoebe responded tersely, "They grew up in the North. When you are raised in constant danger, you learn quickly."

The North was either more dangerous than Em had realized, or this was exaggeration for the sake of putting a wall between Em and the others. Em tried to picture it. A life so markedly different from her own. In their world, safety was a luxury, not an assumption. She couldn't even fathom it. Surely not every moment was dangerous.

She watched Silas, by far the friendliest of the bunch, display a fierceness she would not have guessed before now. His knife arm arced toward Otto's chest. Otto blocked with his forearm, sustaining an (imaginary) cut, but then he disarmed Silas and quickly held his own wooden blade to Silas's throat. Silas yielded.

It was Em and Cora's turn. Em's palms were sweaty. Cora brought none of the wooden sparring weapons from the rack, for which Em was grateful. Still, when Em approached the mat, Cora faced her with a stony rage that made Em freeze.

She had no business fighting. She should've gone to the library. What was she doing here?

Elias signaled the start, and Cora immediately charged.

Em tried to dance to the side, arms flailing, but Cora found her all the same. She held her wrist, twisting. Em yanked it away, only to find the other woman's grip ironclad. In three seconds, her arm was twisted painfully behind her back, and the grip forced Em to her knees. The pressure on her wrist was worrying. Was Cora trying to break her arm? With a painful tug, Em imagined something tearing, and realizing she was beat, she yielded.

She had lost to Cora in less than ten seconds.

Phoebe was frowning. Otto gazed down at her in derision. Silas looked away. Elias seemed not at all surprised. "Keep your arms close to your body," he said to Em. Some instruction, at last. But Em wished he had told her before Cora almost ripped her shoulder apart. She couldn't shrug off this failure like with the tea. She felt fury. Why would they expect her to be good at this?

She looked at each of them, something turning within her. Anger and embarrassment, yes. But also the realization that—for them— these fights weren't for sport. For them, her weakness wasn't just humiliating. It was a liability.

Maybe they weren't exaggerating the danger. In the North, maybe these skills were the difference between saving or losing a family member. The only thing protecting their homes, their land, their very existence. If that were true, then Em knew nothing about what was happening in the North. And she felt more ashamed of that than a lost fight.

But her shame was short-lived when Elias pointed at her again. "Stonehill. Cora. Go again."

CHAPTER 18

The Silver Nightingale fortress has a long and bloody history. Previously named Antillei Keep, it was built as a stronghold against Southern Esnanian invaders. As Northern territory was lost, the structure became the last holdout of a bygone era of Northern power.

"A History of The Silver Nightingale"
From the library of the Silver Nightingale

Hours later, Em limped back toward her room, nursing multiple bruises and sprains. Elias had taken no pity on her. She had fought everyone in the room multiple times, even Cal, who flattened her as the match had barely begun. At the end of each bout, Em would glance up from the floor and Elias would provide one sentence of instruction. Something she had done wrong. Sometimes, the instructions would repeat. "Keep your arms in." "Bend your knees." "Don't let them get behind you."

It all made sense. But Em was having a hard time translating that intuition to her body. So instead, she took the pummelings while internally resolving to never attend fight training again. She also needed to do some reading on what was happening in the North. Why were they so afraid for their lives? And why wasn't Ilna reporting on it?

She was sweaty, and maybe bleeding somewhere, as she approached her door. Then she noticed she was entirely alone.

Now would be an ideal time to visit the library without Cal shadowing her. She could supplement her magic lesson with the magical instruction books. She could read about the Northern conflict. And maybe, just maybe, she could find traces of the Ring of Clavonion. The sooner she found the ring (or clues about the ring), the sooner she could get out of here. It was pretty clear none of these people wanted her around anyway.

She turned, scanning the hallway. Everyone else was probably changing, washing, and then going to dinner. She had a small window where the corridors would be deserted. Darting back in the direction of the library, Em's pains and bruises were pushed to the periphery of her thoughts.

She made it to the room without encountering anyone. Ducking in, she closed the door softly behind her. Her magic stone would tell her if anyone was coming. She might have all evening to search the tomes. She picked up a friendly-looking *Magic for Novices* book.

Mages specialize in one of several areas, based on their interests and natural talents. Artificers, for example, focus on the creation of magical items. A master artificer can create complex items that can function for centuries. This is the most common specialization as basic magecraft is taught using the principles of making magical items. Once learned, these principles can be adapted to other specialties.

Elementer magic uses the principles of energy and intention, but applies them to the elements of earth, air, fire and water. This practice requires great control and massive amounts of energy.

Prestiger magic is the application of energy and intention toward oneself for the purposes of altering the perception of others. Not a common specialization, but quite useful for politics and espionage.

Most mages are proficient in a single specialty. But those with strong magical bloodlines are able to perform cross-discipline cantrips.

Em thought back to her training. They were learning how to make things. Artificers, the book called it. At least the training followed how this book said it should go. But elemental magic? Did that mean, if she specialized there, she'd be able to control wind? Cause earthquakes? Set fires?

A twinge of remembrance: She had set a fire once. She had also learned the trick to keep her feet quiet. Was that prestiger magic? They said Bronwyn was a prestiger. What did that mean? That the mage could sneak around the Silver Nightingale? Or look like someone else? Bronwyn had done that, Em reminded herself. The woman had enchanted someone else to go to the gallows in her stead.

Shaking her head, Em scolded herself. This wasn't going to help her find the ring.

She would start with castle records or history. The building had been here for centuries, long before Bronwyn took up residence. She traced the spines searching for the correct dates corresponding to Trenton Clavonion's reign. She also sought maps of the Silver Nightingale. Maybe there were additional rooms that contained arti-facts. And if she found nothing, at least she had thoroughly checked the fortress before shaking the dust off her feet and leaving the place behind.

She wished she could stay for the magical instruction. For the books. But the rest of it? She didn't belong here, and she knew it. She needed to find the ring and get back to Brookerby. She needed to return to normal life, where her face wasn't being shoved into a sweaty sparring mat. Where she didn't feel completely out of her depth.

~

Seven Weeks and Three Days until the Solstice

EM SEARCHED every castle log within three hundred years of the time the ring went missing. It took her several days, and it was exceedingly dull, her sources detailing visitors, finances, food preparation, and everyday decisions made by the ruling lords and ladies who lived here. On a whim, Em went forward in the records. When had Bronwyn taken the castle? Had it been gifted to her? Was it sitting empty, and she simply commandeered it? But the records stopped a hundred years ago, and Em was left to wonder.

Em continued to attend magic and sparring lessons, but found time to sneak away to the library after her daily dose of humiliation. She re-crafted her rock several times as the energy ran out, but she liked having the stone in her pocket. Sometimes she caught resentful looks from the Northerners, usually Cora, that made her glad she would have warning if any of them tried to ambush her. Not that she could defend herself properly if they did.

Em shifted her focus to the Northern histories. She justified the swerve, telling herself a Northern magical footprint would point toward the ring. These books were enlightening. She learned the difference between the disputed territories (traditional lands of the Prutian Tribes), the Northern colonies (traditional Northern lands officially annexed by Esnania), and Fridera (a separate country where many of the Prutians had migrated.) Em had always gotten these territories confused during geography class, and for good reason. The border kept changing. Esnania regularly invaded the territories and annexed more disputed lands each year.

As for the history, it was everything Em had heard. Centuries of oppression along the border, with occasional outbreaks of rebellion from the locals. They had wanted the right of self-rule, but that had run afoul of Esnanian ambition. This was all familiar to Em, but the actual details of the recent conflict were horrifying in ways she could not have anticipated.

She read about this decade's flare-up. The North had previously experienced ten years of calm. The empire had troops stationed in the colonies for that duration of that peace and would regularly raid homes of respected Northmen who were too prominent. Too successful. So everyone was kept from climbing too high. The stationed Esnanian soldiers would make an example of any young man or woman calling for independence in the public squares. These unfortunate youths would lose a finger for minor infractions, a hand for major, and their tongue if they ran out of digits. Em thought to Elias's missing fingers with horror. Was that how he had lost them?

When open rebellion began again, more soldiers were sent to subdue the population and to claim more territory land as part of the Northern colonies. Their methods were brutal.

One leather-bound tome recorded every skirmish from the past ten years. As Em flipped through the pages, she traced the conflict on a map of the North she had found. It touched every town. Every settlement. In one town, about the size of Brookerby, the soldiers gathered the young children and questioned them harshly about their parents' activities. If a treason was revealed, the child was asked to point to their parents, who were immediately shot.

In another village, all the inhabitants were rounded up, restrained, forced to disrobe, and then forced to watch their village burn to the ground, along with their livestock, their tools, and even their clothes. This was on a particularly cold wintery day, and many of the villagers died from exposure.

Em had to put the record down, feeling truly ill. The empress had sanctioned this? Had Marcellus ever been assigned to the North? What about Liam? Would they have followed these heinous orders?

Most of the inhabitants of Silver Nightingale were from the North. What had Phoebe said? When you are raised in constant danger, you learn quickly. Had they experienced this? She pictured Silas fighting for his life, his family, and suddenly his skill with a knife didn't seem so out of character.

And then another thought hit. If they were here, learning magic and how to fight, were they planning on returning to the North to fight against imperial soldiers? If true, Em had wandered into a hotbed of treason.

She tried to imagine soldiers marching into Brookerby and terrorizing the people. She supposed they had when the warding tree fell. But the town was afforded certain privileges and kind treatment because they were solidly part of Esnania. She couldn't imagine oppressive laws or cruel acts of destruction playing out in Brookerby like they had in the North. She would be so angry. They all would be.

At that moment, the rock in her pocket grew warm. Someone was approaching. Em glanced around at the scattering of books surrounding her on the floor. She only had time to close one Clavonion history book and shove it back on the shelf before the door handle turned. Em leapt out of way of the entrance and hid behind a bookshelf, peering around the corner to the door. Would the Northerners confine their hostilities to the sparring ring, or did they feel bold enough to attack her in here?

Bronwyn Featherweight entered, and Em held her breath. She hadn't seen the mage since earlier in the week, when the woman advised her not to steal anything. Would she be suspicious of Em's intentions after finding her in here alone?

Bronwyn stopped at the pile of books left on the floor and bent down to read the titles. A small smile turned her lips. "Emily Stonehill. Reveal yourself."

Feeling sheepish, Em emerged from behind the next bookcase. "How did you know?"

"Northern histories? The rest of my initiates would not choose to relive it."

Em didn't have a response. She was surprised to find herself a bit tongue-tied in front of the mage. She had heard so many stories—from Gram, and in so many books—that to find the woman standing before her still felt like an impossibility.

Bronwyn seemed aware of her effect and kept her tone easy. "The question is, Emily, are you loyal to us?"

Em shivered. "I am friendly," she replied. "I have no interest in being your enemy, my lady." And it was true. The woman before her could probably destroy her with a snap of her fingers, something Em wanted to avoid.

"But loyalty. That is something you have not agreed to. Troublesome. On top of it all, you look familiar. I cannot place it, but I haven't met you in the North, I am certain."

Em felt startled by this. "We have never met, I can assure you."

But Bronwyn studied her face furiously. "Are you a spy for that spineless empress?"

"What—No, ma'am," Em said with a shaky laugh. but Bronwyn wasn't laughing with her. So she sobered quickly. "The empress has never done me any favors. I would not work for her." All that was true, of course, but Bronwyn's question hit close to the mark. Technically, if Em found the ring, it was going to be taken to Her Majesty, which could be viewed as "working for her." However, Em didn't intend to reveal the continued existence of the lady mage, which was probably what this inquiry was about.

Bronwyn looked slightly mollified. "And your people? Where are they from?" The woman hadn't deciphered Em's motive, and she clearly did not like to be in the dark.

Em wished she had developed an elaborate backstory for Emily Stonehill. She was a terrible liar, and coming up with a fabricated history on the spot would be a surefire way to raise Bronwyn's red flags. So she opted for something close to the truth.

"I'm from Drecovia. I am an orphan, so I don't know much about my birth family, but an older lady in my town raised me. I became interested in the history of the North and Northern trade routes earlier this year, so I'm trying to learn all I can. It led me here."

The benign story seemed to relieve Bronwyn. "Ah. Interesting." She clearly didn't think so. "You are just different."

Em hardly knew what to say. She wondered why Bronwyn was considering her at all.

"I know you outsmarted my defenses. Few are able to traverse the labyrinth without instruction. And only Northerners can—" She stopped herself. Then began again, "I know you didn't choose a pastry. Or a crown. We saw all three on the floor. That mechanical loophole is being closed, thanks to you. Yet, in the rest of the maze, you were very lucky."

Em said nothing. She had been lucky in the maze, but to draw the disbelief of the most renowned mage in recent history—

Bronwyn tilted her head, again studying Em. "And you attended training. You failed. You're a terrible fighter."

"I—" Em's mortification found a new bottom. This woman had watched her. Probably watched water dribble down her leg when her rock turned into a teacup. And watched her get beaten over and over again. But Bronwyn seemed to be self-soothing. Convincing herself of something.

Em forged ahead. "My lady, may I continue my research? While I'm here, I mean?"

The mage assented. "For now. I don't know what to make of you yet. But I am watching, Emily."

Em felt a shiver at this, but she wasn't sure why. Bronwyn was being a kind hostess and had even granted permission for Em to continue reading. But as the woman left the library, Em had a sense of foreboding. Something about the mage felt hard and unyielding, and Em had drawn her gaze. It might be best to lay low until she could find what she needed and get out.

CHAPTER 19

Mages have always presented a challenge to the power structure of Esnania. Factions of society believe that the most powerful mage should rule, as they are most likely able to create solutions and avert disasters. This was the ancient way of deciding rulers until the Clavonions seized power and established a hereditary monarchy. Even in the origin story of the ruling family, the young man—Tranton Clavonion—was granted his power (and therefore his right to rule) from an elderly mage and his marvelous stones. Even the Clavonions sought legitimacy from magic. The debate still rages behind closed doors. (See "Powerful Mages from the Age of Magic")

"Magic and Political Power"
From the library of the Silver Nightingale

Six Weeks and One Day until the Solstice

Nine days gone, and Em continued to attend training. Magic. Sparring. Library. She often waived her meals with the Northerners, but they didn't seem to mind. They rarely spoke to her anyway, except for Silas. When she skipped dinner, he would appear in the library with a plate of food for her, setting it on an empty shelf and trying to draw her out of her page turning. Once, he tried to entice her with a game of sticks and stones. But the Northern version had different rules, and Em found herself shaking her head in frustration. "I'm sorry. I need to get back to research."

She caught sight of Bronwyn once or twice. The woman was always meeting leaders from the North or traveling away from the fortress. But when she was around, the air changed, as if lightning was preparing to course through the hallways. Once, Em was returning to her room when her rock grew warm. Ducking behind a pillar, Em saw a wrinkled and coughing grandmother hobble into the hall, glance back, and then transform into the stunning Bronwyn. So the prestiger skills were not a myth. Em wondered if she had ever impersonated one of the other initiates, but Bronwyn likely considered them all beneath her concern.

Phoebe continued to teach the magic lessons, but eyed Em suspiciously whenever she asked any question that was too specific. Still, Em learned. She learned how to create a magical item only a mage could use, and to create items that used their own kinetic energy. It had to do with how energy was infused, and specific wording. She struggled a bit, mixing up words and losing focus. One time she turned a small wooden ball she was training to bounce into a gooey mess. Then later, when alone in her room, she accidentally turned her blanket into actual fire when she was just trying to make the covers warmer. Still, every night she practiced in her room, imbuing and siphoning, until she was so exhausted she fell into bed.

The other initiates weren't much better, despite their additional months of experience. This relieved Em for selfish reasons. Making items without any backlash or unintended consequences was nearly impossible. The simplest inert items—when infused—seemed to grow a mind of their own.

Unmaking—siphoning—was also difficult. It took intense concentration, and overstuffed Em. It was an odd feeling, like she had eaten too many pancakes, yet it filled her with vigor. She believed she could scale the sheer cliff face nearby without difficulty after siphoning an item. The more she practiced, the easier it became.

Phoebe requested each student unmake what they had made during the session, citing unintended consequences and a desire to hide the Silver Nightingale Palace from discovery. Em understood this well enough. If magical items continued to flood the region, eventually someone would ask where they were coming from.

This didn't stop Em from remaking and unmaking her projects at night. Again and again. The warning rock was her favorite. It was useful, and she would remake it every few days with a small amount of her energy. She wasn't sure she got the cantrip quite right, but it seemed to be working, and she kept it hidden in her pocket most of the time.

Sparring didn't get any easier either. With each humiliation, she would receive one piece of advice from Elias, which she pondered and tried to implement. But over time, Em's buildup of bruises made each hit and grapple hurt that much more. She wondered whether she was actually improving, or whether the shock of absorbing a hit was dulling into a grim determination within her to take whatever came.

With this change in thinking, Em lasted longer in the matches. *Just ten more seconds,* she would repeat to herself like a vow, blocking out the ache of a punishing hold.

She lost consciousness once. She refused to yield while Cora's forearm was pressed to her neck. Passing out was an automatic loss, but to the Northerners, it was a more honorable way to lose.

She received a subtle nod from Elias when she came to, flat on the mat. "Work on your breath," was his advice. It was vague, but this was something she could do. She lost the rest of her matches that day. But she felt the shift in herself. Like she actually was making progress. Like maybe one day, she had a chance to win.

Em began to spend her mornings before breakfast breathing deeply. In and out. In and out. After her late nights of imbuing, it was almost a relief to think of nothing. To allow her bruised body to relax into itself. Then she would hold her breath for as long as she could. She didn't time it, so she didn't know if she was improving, but she liked the feeling of peace that accompanied a breath hold. The sense of connection to her limbs that wasn't there before.

After sparring, she usually limped to the library to scour the books for any clue of the ring's existence. She kept returning to the histories of the North. The Northern territories. The Prutian Tribes. Their politics of town elders instead of a monarch. Their cultural celebrations of honoring their ancestors, and call-and-response singing on cold winter nights. It was entirely foreign, yet somehow reminded her of Brookerby's town get-togethers.

And she thought about the ring. It was supposedly sent to them after the death of the first Clavonion emperor. Was the secundarius—the cleric who had stolen the ring—a Northern sympathizer? She suspected so. Why else would he have sent it north? Maybe it hadn't been lost in the mountains after all, and that story was spread to keep Esnanian forces from trying to retrieve the relic. She wondered if all her mountain searching had also been a wild goose chase. A ruse by the recipients to keep the ring safe.

But it left Em without any leads, except that the ring had reached its intended target. In which case, there should be traces of magic in the Northern histories. If only Em could find them.

~

Five Weeks until the Solstice

A WEEK OR SO LATER, Em was sitting on the library floor, books spread out around her, when she found what she was looking for.

During the Clavonion civil war, there were some coincidences—or perhaps magical interference—that led to unlikely Northern victories and dominion over the rest of Esnanian states.

Traces of magic in history were not unusual. The Age of Magic always had evidence of magecraft in political and historical moments of significance. From the crowning of a new emperor to the establishment of diplomatic ties, a mage was always pulling the strings.

In this case, Henrich was emperor of the Northern colonies, and a few years into his rule he sought to overthrow his brother Jerrifree and unify the empire under Northern rule. This was a ludicrous idea, considering the Northern colonies were subjugated in the prior century by their grandfather, Tranton I.

But large bits of magic indicated that either some very powerful mages had emerged from the North, or an all-powerful item was being utilized. There was no other explanation for the total shift in power that allowed the North (for a brief moment) to subjugate their oppressors. Maybe the ring had arrived in the North sometime during the split reign of Henrich and Jerrifree? But where was the ring between Tranton's death and this uprising?

The puzzle pieces weren't there. But the enormous footprint of magic was. Em thought this was a good indication that something powerful had been found or saved for that moment. And after her own lessons in crafting items, she knew how unlikely it was that another equally powerful item existed.

After the North gained control of Esnanian territory through the Sun Corridor, an internal power struggle occurred. Betrayals and assassinations. Within a few years, Esnania was retaken by Jerrifree's son, and Henrich was run through by one of his own spearmen.

If the ring existed, it didn't help Henrich hold on to power. But still . . .

If it existed, the ring was probably tucked away safely in some stronghold where Henrich had seated his government. Maybe it no longer worked? Had run out of magic? Or was it an item only a mage could wield, so it had fallen into obscurity?

Em shuffled her books, feeling a sense of progress. She had found some good information here at the Silver Nightingale, and she just needed an inventory of Northern fortresses. Surely the ring was hiding with other Northern treasure, gathering dust.

She would search for a list of Northern strongholds. And then she needed to leave. She had used up four weeks of her nine. She couldn't afford to stay longer.

Em felt a small tug of reluctance. She was learning so much here. But—she reasoned with herself—she could always come back after retrieving the ring. Right now, the pressing matter was to save her own life before the deadline.

One more week, she placated herself. That would give her time to compile a list. She may even be able to get location details out of Silas, or maybe Phoebe. And she needed to learn how living things were imbued with magic—like the warding tree. And she needed to win at least one sparring match before she left.

CHAPTER 20

Henrich Clavonion almost successfully staged an uprising against the South during his brutal rein of the Northern territories. But his paranoia prevented him from gaining loyal followers. Some Northerners reported that the man had eyes everywhere. If you plotted treason in your heart, you would find one of Henrich's assassins at your door.

"Northern Rulers of the Last Age"
From the library of the Silver Nightingale

Three Weeks and One Day until the Solstice

It had been too long. Em felt her time running out. She breathed in. Held a breath. Breathed out. Held a breath. Her pounding heart calmed. She would still have three weeks to search the strongholds of the North if she left today. Maybe another book could tell her from which stronghold the Northern emperor Henrich ruled. That would be smarter, to stay on at the Silver Nightingale until she had more information. Meanwhile, she would be safe here, despite the angry looks and sparring bruises.

But that illusion was shattered the next morning when all the initiates were summoned to the Gathering Room. Em lined up with the others as two new arrivals entered the chamber. The first was a grizzled man who exuded warmth even in the cold room. "Brought you a new recruit, Lady Bronwyn. Fairly skilled already. I taught him what I know, but I think he'll make a good mage. He's for the cause."

The other man—Em's breath snagged. He'd grown a beard and looked like he hadn't had a proper meal in months, but there was no mistaking those aquamarine eyes.

The new recruit was Sam Monterey.

Em stood statue still, averting her gaze. Maybe he hadn't observed her. She looked different too. Her physique had changed; after several weeks of sparring and training, she had started to gain some muscle. Maybe he wouldn't recognize—

She looked over at him again, and his bright eyes found her, widening in recognition.

A million feces. This was bad.

He looked away and responded to a question from Bronwyn. Then he looked back and met her gaze again, eyes narrowing.

She needed to leave. Immediately. Why had she even stayed this long? If she had left when she promised herself she would . . . Maybe she could escape after this meeting. Leave the mountain. Use her map, before he could follow.

"Emily Stonehill, explain yourself. Do you know this man?" Bronwyn's voice cut through her frantic thoughts. If he wasn't sure before, he most certainly observed her now.

"Ehrm—" Em squeaked. "Yes. I know him."

Bronwyn gestured Em forward. "How? Is he one of your allies?"

Em was shaking her head before the question was finished. "I don't think so, my lady. He is probably quite angry to see me."

Bronwyn—quite unexpectedly—smiled. "That's fascinating. So many stories you have yet to tell us."

This response—the glee in the lady mage's eyes—worried Em. Bronwyn apparently wasn't concerned with the friction. And she seemed to understand that Em was keeping secrets.

Sam spoke. "My lady? If I may—"

Bronwyn gestured for him to continue.

"Although *Miss Stonehill* and I are not friends, I owe her a great debt. Without her, I wouldn't have found my way north." He shot a meaningful look toward Em. "For that, I am grateful, and ready to join the cause of Prutian independence."

What game was he playing? The loyal soldier, until he found opportunity to slit her throat? But he hadn't known she was here. Why had he come? Was he really on board with the Northern cause, and her being here was just a coincidence?

Bronwyn spoke again. "Very well. You may stay, Mr. Monterey. Perhaps you and Miss Stonehill can resolve your differences on the sparring mat. But try not to spill blood in the castle. It's rented." The initiates chuckled politely and she smiled, pleased at her joke.

Monterey nodded. "Yes, ma'am."

Bronwyn provided instruction to the other man regarding lodging and a Northern briefing, then dismissed the group. Em was lunging for the door ahead of everyone else.

Sprinting down the deserted hall, she found her room and began to toss all her possessions into her pack. She was a step or two ahead. Maybe that would be enough time to flee before—but it was too late. Her warning rock had gone hot.

"Going somewhere, *Emily?*"

Monterey leaned against the doorframe, aquamarine eyes trained on her. He spat her false name with such viciousness that she had to take a steadying breath.

She slid the pack on her shoulder, trying to look unruffled. "As a matter of fact, I've been meaning to move on for some time. Now seems like the right moment."

He laughed. Amused, but unfriendly.

Em took a step as if to leave, as if his hovering in the doorway didn't intimidate her.

He closed the distance, grabbing her arm roughly. "You sent me to hell to freeze, you bitch. What do you expect me to do, let you pass? Make love to you?"

And just like that, Em could feel the air shift. She was about to be murdered. Inside the most secure fortress in Esnania. They would find her body and chalk it up to an accident. Gram and Liam would never know what happened to her. The empress would assume she had run.

Em's arm hurt where he gripped her. He was strong. But she had been training. She let out a breath as she twisted out of his grip and threw a side kick at his kneecap. He grunted in pain, and Em darted out of reach. She had a clear shot at the hallway and she took it.

"That's new," he wheezed, turning in the doorway to face her and placing his hand on the frame. One of his fingers was missing. The smallest one. Just above the knuckle. Em stared at it, and then back at his face. He noticed the shift.

"Ah. You know what that means, then."

"Stars, Sam. I—" She could hardly say more. She had sent him north, and some soldier had chopped off his finger because he said the wrong thing? She felt a weight of guilt piled on her chest. That is, until he jumped at her, trying to grab her again. But her reflexes were quick, and she moved farther down the hallway.

"Well done. How's your town, by the way? Have you fixed the tree yet?"

Em paused. He was testing her. To see if her unbreakable oath was still intact. Last time she saw him, he tortured her with the constraints of it. She needed him to know that would never work again.

"My town is fine. The Gray Horse is also thriving. Without you."

He tilted his head, no doubt disappointed that she wasn't writhing in pain. Then he tried again. "I learned some techniques for planting magical trees. Would you like to hear them?"

"No, thanks."

He smirked. "Huh. You got rid of the oath, then? Fascinating. Did Bronwyn remove it? Is that why you're here?"

"Excuse me," Em said, then started down the hallway at a jog. His next words slowed her.

"Are you not interested in why I'm here?"

Em *was* wondering. She pivoted to find him closing the distance between them. "I didn't bother to ask. Anything you tell me will be a lie up to the point where I find your knife in my back."

"Most definitely," he agreed. "But I didn't know you were here. I didn't come for revenge."

"So, Northern independence?" she asked, nodding at his missing finger.

He let out a "hah" and started tapping on the wall paneling. This was strange, even from Sam Monterey, and Em found herself riveted.

"What are you looking for?" she asked.

"Aha. She is interested," he said, almost to himself. Then he glanced up and down the hallway. They were the only ones in sight. "The Prutians have been oppressed for many years. Murdered. Looted."

"So you are here to fight for them?"

"Sure. That too." He continued his tapping along the wall. Em kept well back in case he decided to lunge for her again. "I spoke to an aged gentleman in an alehouse. He drunkenly shared that many of their most precious treasures were sent away for safekeeping a century ago. Nearly everyone alive has forgotten. Precious gemstones. Artifacts of great power. When they are found—after independence is won—the North will be a wealthy country."

"Sent away for safekeeping?" Em's mind whirred. She was planning to go north to look for the ring. If Sam wasn't lying to her, the ring wouldn't be there. It would be in hiding.

"Exactly. This fortress is storing all the wealth of the Northern nations. And I intend to find it. Only a few artifacts, and I can live like an emperor."

It was Em's turn to laugh. "I've been here a while, Monterey. There's no finery here. The rooms are unadorned. I've looked in all of them. Quite a good library, but no riches that I've seen."

"You've looked?" he asked. At that moment, he stopped tapping. "Maybe you haven't looked well enough." He placed his hand on the raised frame around the wainscoting and tugged. A click sounded, and one of the panels swung outward.

Em felt her jaw go slack. He watched her with one eyebrow raised. "I found that in two minutes. What have you been doing? How long have you been here, exactly?"

Em had no response. She hadn't thought about secret passages or secret rooms or anything other than what was right in front of her. How did this man always make her feel like a fool?

But Sam wasn't done taunting. "You are a simple village girl. You were just here to—what, learn?"

Em growled. But she had no comeback.

"And the fake name? Afraid the Strider reputation will burn you again? I wonder what would happen if I exposed you for the lying hag you are."

Em recognized the blackmail, but didn't take the bait. He hadn't exposed her in the Gathering Room, and she was leaving anyway.

He started to step into the hidden passage, and, with a grin, gestured for her to follow.

"If you think I'm going anywhere with you, then you must really believe I'm simple," she said.

"More for me, then." He smirked. "Watch your back, Em."

Then he climbed through and pulled the panel closed behind him.

EM STARED at the wall where he had vanished. She couldn't see the seams even after she had watched the door open and close. The drunken alehouse man must've told Sam what to look for.

Em returned to her room in a daze. Sam Monterey was here. Escorted by some trusting guide from the North. He was dangerous, and his warning to watch her back wasn't an idle threat. He would likely kill her at the first opportunity, if he thought he could get away with it. And if he actually found this hidden Northern treasure, there was nothing stopping him from offing her on his way out the door.

Her self-preservation instincts were screaming at her to shoulder her pack and leave.

But a treasure trove? In the Silver Nightingale? She remembered Bronwyn's words on the first day here—*if you take something that doesn't belong to you*—and her suddenly sharpening when she thought Em was a treasure hunter. Maybe the Clavonion ring was housed in these very walls? All she had to do was slip through a secret passage and find the very thing she needed?

She couldn't just leave. Not now.

But how could she treasure hunt without accidentally bumping into Monterey in some hidden passage? She lucked out this time, evading him when he didn't expect her to fight back. But there were many ways he could orchestrate her death and make it look like an accident. A well-placed blow in the sparring ring. A tumble from one of the turrets. Even a bout of food poisoning would do the job.

She supposed she could do the same to him. Get him, before he got her. But as satisfying as it was to imagine, Em knew in her gut that she could never follow through with it. The slaughtered beast in the maze flashed in her vision, and she shook off the memory. She wasn't a killer.

She needed to be sneaky. She needed to find the hidden rooms, before he did. She needed to locate the treasure without Sam knowing. And then, she needed to get out of here.

CHAPTER 21

"Breathing deeply is a technique that provides multiple benefits. First, it reduces the stress response by lowering heart rate and blood pressure. Second, it delivers more oxygen to the body. Finally, it can help the breather manage pain.

"Breathing for Better Health"
From the library of the Silver Nightingale

That evening at dinner, Em sat as far away from Sam as she could manage, and kept a close eye on any food he prepared. Just in case. Meanwhile, the others welcomed him and his older companion with great enthusiasm. (Em still hadn't caught the grizzled gentleman's name)

"How'd you end up in the North?" Silas asked.

Sam's eyes flickered toward Em. "I hit an unlucky stretch and lost my business to some interlopers. Had to get away. Found myself half-frozen in Fridera without proper clothing."

Cora smirked. The grizzled man guffawed, amused. But Sam was a born storyteller, and his audience was leaning in for more. Em included. She had always wondered what became of him after she double-tapped him away from the Gray Horse and into the frozen North.

Sam continued. "I stumbled, half icicle, into the nearest building I could find. It was a little tavern called the Dusty Whale. They put me in front of a fire and fed me until I thawed out."

"Fridera's dreadful," Otto commented. "Nothing but snow and savages."

"My second cousin lives near the Dusty Whale," Phoebe said with a pointed look at Otto. Then back to Monterey, "Did you happen to meet a woman named Jessamine? Round lady? One eye?"

Sam's eyes sparked with recognition. "Jessamine! She makes the best stew I've ever tasted! Told me how she lost her eye too. Nasty business."

Phoebe nodded in approval. Sam had won her over by virtue of knowing her relative. Em mentally put Phoebe in the Team Sam column.

"Then what happened?" Silas prodded. "How did you meet Merrick?"

"Well, it was several weeks before I was ready to travel. Almost died up there." Again, his eyes briefly flicked to Em's. She felt a slight pang of guilt. Very slight. After all, he had tried to kill her first.

"After I was ready, I bartered my own labor for shelter and food. Spent most of my time dodging soldiers and walking from town to town. When I crossed into the territories, I stayed in Hemnisville. Met this guy at the market." Sam gestured to the older man. "Merrick took me on. Taught me a few things about magecraft. Brought me into the cause, you know?"

Elias was nodding at this. The cause. It was the reason they all were there. All except Em, of course.

Cora spoke up. "Merrick found me too." The girl reached over and squeezed Merrick's hand warmly. It was the least sarcastic thing Em had ever seen her do.

Sam met Cora's eyes with understanding. Without saying anything further, they had bonded. Em thought she spotted a glassiness to Cora's eyes. Was she crying? She didn't think it possible. Cora was on Team Sam. Crumb.

Em needed to do something to stop this cascade of support. She turned to Merrick. "And what was it about this gentleman that made you take him on?"

"Oh, nothing at first. He looked pretty torn up. His finger hadn't quite healed. But I could also tell he was from the South, and from money, if I'm not mistaken."

Otto perked up at this last comment. Em gazed around, but the others didn't seem so put out by this information.

Merrick continued. "I watched him for a few minutes, trying to figure out if he was a threat. If we should keep an eye on him. Then imperial soldiers entered the marketplace, harassing people. You know. Like they do. And this feller here stepped in. Distracted them with silly questions so the merchants could close their stores and get away before their goods were confiscated and anyone made an example of. It was an act of kindness, it was."

Silas's eyes were shining. It was clear he thought Sam was a champion of the people. They all did. Double crumb.

Otto coughed, and Em glanced over to find him discomposed. Red-faced. Like he'd been holding back emotion.

"Otto?" Cora asked.

"My father is a merchant in the Northern colonies. He was in a territory marketplace when—" His voice wavered, and he fell silent without finishing. But he was looking at Sam like he had secondhand saved his father. Like Sam was some kind of hero.

Merrick was the first to respond. He reached across the table and patted the slender gentleman's forearm. "It's all right, lad. We know."

While Otto regained his composure, Elias was patting Monterey on the back. "Glad you're here, Sam. We can use a good man like you."

Em had lost her appetite. If he had won them over so quickly, it wouldn't take much for him to turn all of them against her. And she knew they could each best her in a myriad of ways.

She looked at each of them. They were smiling at Sam and

Merrick with a warmth and camaraderie that had never been directed at her. Cal was sitting silently. Observing. But that wasn't anything new. She assumed if the others were on the Sam boat, he would be too.

She looked at the other end of the table to Sam, who was watching her with those icy aquamarine eyes. She felt a shiver run down her spine.

And then he winked.

Triple crumb on a floorboard. She was as good as dead.

AFTER DINNER, Em retreated to her room and locked the door. For good measure, she put the chair against the knob to slow down any potential murder plot.

Sam was good. Self-effacing. Handsome. Charming. Everyone in that room thought him a true believer. A convert to the Northerners' plight and a valuable ally. Only Em knew the truth. Sam cared for Sam alone.

She paced her small bedroom, trying to plan. How could she search for the same treasure as Sam without running into him in a dark corner? She couldn't search in broad daylight. Although she did have sneaking-around magic Farrigan had taught her. And her warning stone. She wondered—

Her thoughts broke off with a panic. What if there was a secret passage into this room? She'd be murdered in her bed. That terrifying prospect had Em on her knees inspecting every knothole and base-board. She knocked on the walls listening for—not quite sure what . . . a hollow sound?—something different. But finally, she sagged. There was nothing wrong with the walls. Just something wrong with her brain.

Sam Monterey had returned. The very last person she expected to see here. To be honest, she always thought he would turn up at the Gray Horse, or somewhere in Brookerby. Maybe that's why she had felt so on edge the past few months. She expected him to find her eventually. Ragged, angry, but unable to do anything, and his ravings would gain him no sympathizers.

Em had pictured him ranting, and then some cooler mind would prevail. Get him to calm down. "She didn't kill you, m'boy. She even fixed up your resort while you were gone. Why not let all that stay in the past?" Then Sam would nod his head and allow himself to be led away. Maybe back to the Gray Horse. Maybe not. But the whole messy business would be well and over.

But here? Sam was learning magecraft. He was controlled and lucid. But from the venom in his eyes when he looked at her, there was no chance for the imagined calm-down scenario. It would be war. And Sam was gaining power that would only make their inevitable clash uglier—more deadly.

So she had two choices: Run. Run right now, and never stop running until he found her. Or stay and fight back.

It was unlikely she could take him in the sparring ring. She had the element of surprise on her side this afternoon. That advantage was now neutralized. And his magical training likely would equal or surpass her own because of Merrick's lessons.

That left tricks. Misdirection and distraction. She either had to get him to unveil his treasure-hunting plan within earshot of the others, or she had to slow him down and keep him out of the way while she searched. And she had to prod him to reveal enough of his horrible personality that the others would cease their hero worship.

She began compiling a list in her head of ways to keep Monterey off-balance. She added to the list as she absently scanned her illegally taken library books for the rest of the evening, and added to the list as she blew out her candle and climbed into bed. And for the first time since Sam's arrival, she didn't feel like cornered prey. She felt like the hunter.

CHAPTER 22

Magical disciplines can only be used by those who are born with the magical gift. (See "Magical Genomes and Probabilities of Mage Offspring"). It was discovered before the present era of rationalis quingentae (RQ), and knowledge has been passed down orally from mage to apprentice for centuries.

"Fundamentals of Magical Studies"
From the library of the Silver Nightingale

Three Weeks until the Solstice

In mage training the next day, Sam shared a story of his Northern training with Otto and Cora, who listened intently. Meanwhile, they were instructed to take an ordinary kitchen spoon—provided by Phoebe—and make it stir a pot of water on its own, which Em was attempting in a small alcove of the garden, away from the others. Otto let out a snigger that interrupted her concentration, and Em noticed Otto, Silas, and Sam laughing quietly together.

Were they laughing at her? About something she had done? Em

supposed it didn't matter, except Sam was growing closer to these people, and that meant danger for her. It wouldn't be long until they were keeping watch while he lured her to a dark, deadly corner. She had to do something to halt the warm relationship they were building. Something drastic. Something offensive.

Em turned her attention on Sam's spoon across the lawn. She infused it with an additional skill that would occur at the same time as Sam's stirring cantrip. It was more difficult, infusing from a distance and adding to an existing magic, and she wasn't entirely sure it had worked.

When the time came for each of their spoons to be tested, Sam presented his. He set it stirring in the pot of water that Phoebe had prepared, and it started to sing a rude children's song about the Tribal Prutians. No one was sniggering now.

"That's quite enough, Mr. Monterey," Phoebe snipped, snatching the spoon out of the pot. Several of the others were red in the face, either from anger or embarrassment.

Sam shrugged. "I didn't intend for that to happen."

Phoebe quickly motioned for Silas to test his spoon, tossing Sam's back at him. "I hope you understand why that song is so offensive."

"I would never—" Sam began to protest, but he had lost them. They were subtly turned away from him, their body language saying what they were unable to. He was an outsider. His eyes darted to Em, who kept a neutral expression.

The class concluded in total silence.

There. It would take him days to rebuild the goodwill he had lost in that single moment. Em had bought herself some time.

Two Weeks and Six Days until the Solstice

AT SPARRING PRACTICE the next day, Elias paired Sam and Cal. The Northerners were still giving Sam a wide berth after the spoon incident, and Cal was apparently harboring some silent anger at the man.

Sam ended up flat on his back with a bloody nose. The others clapped for Cal, and Em joined in. Suddenly, Sam was on his feet and talking to Elias.

"Stonehill. You've been challenged."

In sparring, anyone could challenge anyone else in the group. It was rarely used, as Elias did a fair job of pairing similar skillsets and allowing people to test their skill against those who were slightly better. But it was an acceptable way to put some hurt on someone who was irritating you. Em had seen Otto challenge Cora with wooden staffs after she'd said something snarky about his family crest.

Now, Em felt a sense of dread as she squared off against Sam. He was much larger. He probably wasn't as deadly as Cal or Elias, but he could badly hurt her and make it look like an accident. She accessed every piece of advice she had received from Elias. Bend your knees. Don't let him get behind you. Breathe. She breathed in. Held the breath. Breathed out. Then Sam charged.

He was coming at her full force, and rather clumsily, she recognized. She sidestepped him and stuck out her leg to trip him. He stumbled, but quickly pivoted and grabbed her outstretched leg. Em was wrenched off-balance, and they both went tumbling to the mat. Immediately, he was on her, yanking her leg behind her and twisting her wrist to meet it.

As he held her pinned to the floor, Em realized the others were shouting encouragement to both of them. Elias demanded over the din, "Do you yield?"

"No!" she shouted. She would be damned before she yielded to Sam Monterey.

Sam pinned her leg and arms to her back with his chest, and she kicked back with her other leg, catching him in the groin. He groaned, and his hold loosened a bit. Em was able to shove him off and roll away. He grabbed for her again, but she was able to capture and twist his arm behind him. She put her knee on his back, pushing his chest into the mat.

"Do you yield?" she gritted.

"Never."

She leaned her mouth close to his ear. "I can defend myself this time, asshole."

He growled back, just loud enough for her, "I don't care. I will never stop coming for you until I've done to you what you've done to me."

At this, he kicked out of her grip, and then muscled her to the mat below him. He sat astride her hips with one arm across her shoulder and throat and the other holding her free arm down. She tried to kick his back but couldn't reach. The spectators continued to shout encouragement and advice. But Em was trying to breathe slowly and not pass out from his arm blocking her windpipe.

He was breathing heavily, but a wicked twinkle came into his eyes. "Finally—you beneath me where you belong," he cooed.

"Bastard!" The edges of Em's vision were turning dark, but she couldn't regulate her breathing anymore. Since he was winning, she did the only thing she could do. She spat at him, and his eyes narrowed. Then the pressure on her windpipe lasted beyond her stored breath, and she blacked out.

She came to on the mat moments later. Monterey had stood and was spinning in a circle with his arms raised, accepting applause for his victory. She was tempted to kick him between the legs again, but then a hand entered her field of vision. Elias was trying not to smile as he pulled her to her feet.

"You fight worse when you get angry," he commented.

"Thanks," Em snarked. "I'll remember that."

AT DINNER THAT NIGHT, Em infused Monterey's dinner roll with magical instructions to roil his stomach. She watched out of the corner of her eye as he picked up the bread and took a bite. She waited for him to eat more, but he paused, held his other hand to the roll, then quickly put it down and spat out the bite in his mouth. He glanced her way, an eyebrow raised, but she feigned interest in the lively conversation that was bouncing between Silas and Elias. They were arguing about the true rules of sticks and stones, but it sounded like yet another Northern variation that she wasn't familiar with. Internally, she wasn't listening at all. She was filled with a sense of vengeance and self-satisfaction. How dare he threaten her? Try to drive her away from this place?

She lifted her own roll and broke off a piece. Then the bread in her hands began to tingle. She dropped it so quickly that the conversation around her paused.

"Still hot," she said to the curious glances.

They resumed their discussion.

Sam's mouth was tilted in amusement. As if to say, "whatever you do, I can do it right back."

She narrowed her eyes at him, trying to fill the look with every bit of hate she held for him.

Silas and Elias were standing to go look for a game board, and the others were clearing their own plates, chattering happily. No one noticed the silent war still being waged at the table.

As she darted out of the kitchen, Cal was immediately next to her.

"I'm just going to the library." She spotted Sam surreptitiously checking a corridor for latches and levers and decided he needed a chaperone. "Oh, Mr. Monterey, you seem to be looking for something. Can we help?"

Sam's head swiveled. His eyes narrowed when he saw Em. "Just admiring the construction of these corridors. You don't see design like this anymore."

"Don't you?" Em asked, trying to saturate her question with innocence and sweetness. Then, as if she had a sudden thought, "If you are interested in architecture, perhaps you would like a tour?" Then to Cal, "He didn't get one this week, and the fortress is really quite large."

Cal glanced at Sam, as if assessing the truth of this statement. Then, nodding, he gestured down the hallway. "Follow me."

Em watched as Sam trailed helplessly behind Cal. He looked so annoyed. But Em's methods guaranteed that he would have no free time until tomorrow, at least. And she would be safe to search, knowing he wouldn't be waiting with a knife in some dark corner. Stars, Cal was predictable.

~

EM SPENT her evening scouring the corridors for secret passageways. She briefly explored the passage Sam had revealed earlier that week, but it only spanned the length of the hallway, then popped out in the antechamber of the Gathering Room. Good for listening in. Bad for storing treasure.

She found three more. Each in a long passageway and built into the paneling. No luck on any hidden Northern treasure. She used her warning rock to evade the approach of Otto headed to the sparring room, then Sam—finally free of Cal—searching for hidden areas late into the evening. Anytime she felt the rock warm, she ducked behind furniture or columns. On one occasion, the rock warmed as Em was examining a passageway. She escaped into a window alcove, then peered back through the curtain just as Bronwyn appeared. The woman had snow in her hair and wore a furious look as she strode away from the dead end of the blocked-off wing of the Silver Nightingale. She paused when she spotted the hallway passage ajar. Em hadn't fully closed it in her haste to hide. But Bronwyn didn't seem surprised. She pulled it open, glanced inside, and then shut it before storming away. The lady mage knew about the passages, then.

After several more evenings of searching, Em began to wonder whether this secret treasure room was a ruse. It did sound ridiculous, except she could actually picture Bronwyn keeping Northern valuables in this place. But why would she put them where any initiate could stumble on them? She didn't seem worried when she saw that open panel. Was Sam simply trying to get her hunting for nonexistent treasure, then when she least expected it, hit her from behind and leave her body to decompose in the walls?

It was a gruesome thought. One Em didn't indulge for long. Still, she kept an ear out, and her warning rock in her pocket. Meanwhile, in her head, she counted the weeks. Her deadline was approaching with no leads other than Sam's wild tale of treasure. She decided if she hadn't found any additional clues by week's end, she needed to leave and seek the ring elsewhere.

CHAPTER 23

Prestiger magic is the least respected of the three branches. Far from creating something useful, like the artificer, the prestiger may only trick, spy, and muddle minds. As much as a prestiger demands respect, they are never granted positions of high authority. After all, who would trust a mage who specializes in manipulation and disguise?

"Magecraft: Benefits and Discontents by Branch"
From the library of the Silver Nightingale

Two Weeks and Three Days until the Solstice

Em had been skulking around the Silver Nightingale late into the night, and she couldn't stifle a yawn as she entered mage training one morning. It was then that she noticed the rest of the group was silent. Waiting.

"Am I late?" she asked.

Elias hushed her, just as Bronwyn swept into the training grounds, her dark blue robes billowing behind her, hair loose and wild, and a shimmering pendant necklace brushing her sternum. Every eye followed the woman as she took Phoebe's normal spot at the front of the group. The senior mage studied each of them with an exacting stare before she spoke.

"You will learn from me today, a rare privilege, about infusions on living beings."

Em heard Phoebe's quick intake of air. This was a surprise, then?

"What I am about to teach you is difficult, rarely taught, and—if used carelessly—deadly. I rarely teach this to initiates, but many in this group may become mages in Northern cities, and all of you have demonstrated adequate skill. I share this information in exchange for your loyalty and obedience. You shall never use this magic unless I have commanded it."

Em's mind snagged on the word "loyalty." Bronwyn had mentioned it before in the library. A running concern for the famed mage. Loyalty in exchange for rare magic instruction. Each of them nodded solemnly, and Em joined in. Not only would she learn magic directly from Bronwyn but she would also finally understand magical impacts that she hadn't before. The warding trees. The unbreakable oaths. She fervently agreed this magic should be used sparingly. However, she caught a predatory gleam in Sam's eye. She wondered how long it would be before he tried to harm her with it.

"This is a long-lasting form of magic. It will stay with a living being, so long as they continue to breathe. There is no way to remove such a thing. Only I can teach you how to wield it properly, so if you think you've learned before, you were mistaken."

Em wondered at this. She was able to break the unbreakable oath. Was that a contradiction already?

Bronwyn began strolling up and down in front of the group, like a general addressing her troops.

"The three elements of magecraft. First, energy, coming from you. However, with living things, you can siphon energy, or even attach the magical instructions to the person's own energy for future powering of the cantrip. Two, a target. The other living thing. Three, intentions. Must be carefully thought out. If you have a lesser mind that cannot hold complexities, you may choose to write these down."

Em thought of the warding trees of protection and nodded. There were certainly ill effects from the trees. She also recalled the paper documents that were used at planting—including the one that Mendel had passed on to her. Had the trees backfired because Bronwyn didn't write anything down? Did the woman not plan well enough? A darker thought occurred, that perhaps Bronwyn had wanted the ill effects.

"Living things have a will that you must overpower. Alternatively, the subject can submit willingly."

Bronwyn went on to explain the process of overcoming the will of another living thing. Em reinterpreted the mage's jumble of flowery and self-praising statements: the mage pushes past a protective barrier using infusion as the drill. That seemed straightforward to Em. She wondered if Bronwyn could also explain the basics of defending your own mind against the attack of another. Em thought this seemed rather important, and was prepared to ask some questions, but the theory part of the lesson was already over.

Bronwyn stepped to the side and gestured to the geraniums that grew along the edge of the training field. "You will start by overpowering the will of those flowers. Do not attempt to alter them with rules, simply break through the barrier of the geranium's will."

Several of them laughed uncomfortably. It didn't seem to be a fair fight. But they lined up and targeted their focus.

Very quickly, Em realized this would not be as easy as it sounded. The flowers were impenetrable. Apparently, their bright red petals concealed an impressive inner strength. Em focused her infusion to a single point on the flower, probing at the mental membrane, and after a quarter of an hour with no signs of breaking, the flower finally relaxed and yielded.

Gasping, she felt relief from her own strain as she stepped back. That was exhausting. It took a great deal of energy to focus the spark thus. A few others—Phoebe, Cora, Elias—had also succeeded, and were looking similarly winded. Sam let out a whoosh of breath and looked up, also apparently successful.

"So difficult," Bronwyn purred. "I forget how weak you all are."

Em tried not to take offense. Compared to the lady mage, they probably were. But it didn't seem like a very good teaching method to point it out.

"For those of you who were successful, take a moment to catch your breath, then pair up and attack. It is unlikely you will succeed, but try. Phoebe, with me. Cora and Elias. Then Sam and—"

Before Bronwyn could finish speaking, Em felt something sharp and angry slam into her consciousness.

She staggered, took a second stumbling step, then regained her balance in the squatted stance she'd learned in sparring and mentally slammed a shield of iron around herself. Bronwyn hadn't taught this, but, thankfully, the idea of a shield around her mind seemed to manifest as some kind of actual magical shielding.

Monterey would destroy her if he could get in. She knew this as surely as she knew how to patch a thatched roof. Stars, he was strong. His attack pulsed like a headache. He would crush her mind, leave her drooling and nonsensical, and chalk it all up to a training accident. Em grunted in pain, feeling his angry energy trying to drill into her. She fought him off, second by second.

Her eyes briefly flicked to Bronwyn. Had she noticed? But the mage was locked in her own battle with Phoebe, who was whimpering on her knees. Neither had noticed Sam's aggressive attack. Em was on her own. And the brief shift in focus was costing her.

She felt tiny spiderwebs start to form in her defenses. She wasn't sure how, but she knew he was moments from breaking through. Trying not to panic, Em took a deep breath. Held it. Let it out. The cracks stopped spreading. Again, she breathed, in and out. The cracks were shrinking, sealing themselves together with her very breath as the paste.

Em glanced at Sam—the man who wished her nothing but ill—and felt a strange calm. He would not get in. She took another breath in. Hold. Release. The cracks—the few that remained—were hairline. In. Hold. Release.

Sam met her gaze, and instead of the smirk or scowl she anticipated, she detected a flicker of something else. Fear? Uncertainty, at the very least.

In. Hold. Release. She was a limestone wall. A metal lockbox. A blacksmith's anvil. He would not get into her mind. Not today. Not ever.

How long had it been? Longer than the geraniums. Nearly an hour. Around them, the others had broken. Cora let out a gasp as Elias stopped attacking. They nervously chuckled together, breaking their standoff with camaraderie. Phoebe bemoaned her weakness as Bronwyn ceased her attack. Sam didn't let up at all. Even after Bronwyn issued an order. He was starting to strain. Sweat was beading on his temples, but he showed no signs of stopping.

Suddenly, his attack ended and the intense pressure on Em ceased. Bronwyn was standing between them, holding the oval pendant necklace she had been wearing. It cast a shimmery shield around each of them. It looked like they were both encased in a soap bubble.

"Fools," she growled, looking first at Sam, then Em. "Everyone else, get out."

The others filed off the training field, watching the trio with curiosity. Bronwyn did not remove the shield; instead, she compressed the bubble, the hard shell forcing them both onto their hands and knees. Em was trembling, wondering if the lady mage intended to crush them.

"When you come to the Silver Nightingale, you are mine to command. There is bad blood between the two of you. You made that quite clear from the moment of his arrival. I don't care. My plans are bigger than your petty vendettas, and I don't want to lose mages to a grudge match. I will turn you both into drooling, half-conscious turnips if you continue to challenge each other under my roof. Do I make myself clear?"

"Yes, my lady," Em said.

Sam bobbed his head.

Bronwyn pushed the shield down farther, knocking them both on their stomachs and holding them firmly against the grass. It felt as if Bronwyn had placed a solid board on top of them and was pressing down. To their credit, neither of them cried out. "I could squash you both like the insects you are. Instead, as punishment, you will assume all cleaning duties for the next week. You will work together to complete the list, and if I hear of any altercations, you won't get another warning. Now get out of my sight."

The pressure lifted, and Em rolled to her feet, staggering for the door.

~

EM STUMBLED TO THE LIBRARY, still feeling lightheaded and weak after her mental battle with Sam, and the near crushing from Bronwyn. In her panicked moments after leaving the outdoor clearing, Em's only thought was to keep searching. The sooner she found Sam's hidden treasure heap, the sooner she could be safely away.

It was awful and terrifying. She ceased to think of Bronwyn as a benevolent benefactor of the Silver Nightingale, but instead, its avenging wraith. What might the woman do if Em discovered the ring and stole it? Em hoped to be long gone before she found out; Bronwyn would clearly show no mercy. Returning for additional magical instruction was no longer an option. Not after that experience.

The library was empty, which wasn't a surprise. Em took a slow breath, embracing the quiet of the room, the calm after her terror. Not wanting to leave, and knowing if she sat her exhaustion would overtake her, she busied herself checking for passages.

Em searched the perimeter, hoping for a latch or an out-of-place knothole. There were some cracks in the stone floor over in the left back corner. She had noted them before, but assumed that all castles built into mountains crack and change with age. But perhaps those cracks were something more.

She moved to the corner and examined them. They were far too regular a shape to have occurred by chance. But if it were a door, she had no idea how to unlock it. Maybe hidden behind the books? She started pulling books off a nearby shelf, looking for a lever. On the third shelf she emptied, one book was surprisingly rigid. When she began to pull it, it lurched forward, triggering a lever that must've unhooked the door in the ground.

The cracks in the floor widened with a gear-grinding noise. Em took a step back as part of the floor swung down into the hole, revealing a twisting staircase descending to the level below.

Quickly shelving all the other books, Em checked the title of the trigger, a thick periwinkle volume: *Flora of the North: A Memoir*.

"Sounds riveting," Em snarked. But maybe the lever was built into that book because the odds of someone wanting to read it were low.

She wondered if she should re-hide the passage and come back when she was less likely to be discovered. But no one came in here this time of day. And the passage was behind the back shelves where nobody ventured. She flexed her sore, crushed muscles and hoped that was true.

No time like the present.

She started down the stairs, which dropped into darkness. Pausing, she reached in her pocket for her warning rock and quickly infused it with the ability to glow. It didn't light up the stairwell as much as she hoped, but it would keep her from stumbling.

The walls were stone, and bare. The staircase turned at right angles with no landings, climbing ever lower into the mountain. The air grew cooler, and Em shivered. How long had it been? A minute? Five? Twenty?

Finally, she found the bottom. A stone floor spread out before her, and the rock encasing the staircase appeared to have been a small column in a large cavern. She couldn't see how far the room went on —she saw nothing other than stone and darkness. If there was indeed a great Northern treasure, it was not visible yet.

Em stepped carefully, finding the floor slightly uneven. The sound of dripping echoed from somewhere farther back in the hollow. She felt—rather than knew—that she was deep within the mountain. What purpose would the builders of the fortress have for creating this passage?

She shivered again. The temperature was quite cool in this cave.

But she kept walking, determined to explore the entire space. After all, the ring could be hidden down here, quite easily. A small box shoved into a cranny, or under a rock? It would remain hidden for centuries.

But as she drew deeper into the cave, she began to think that this was not a storage room at all. There were no signs that anyone had been here, or that humans had ever used this hole for anything.

Until she spotted the vegetables. Carrots. Onion. Canned tomatoes and peaches. Cabbage. Apples. Barrels and barrels of flour, beans, rice and sugar, and other kitchen staples. She stared at the feast surrounding her with bafflement. What the—

Then she spotted the second stairway—a narrow opening in the rock led to a stairway very similar to the one from the library. When she inched up it, she saw faint light from above and heard the sounds of the initiates preparing lunch. The kitchen.

This was a root cellar. Or whatever you called a cold room in a cave. Anyone who retrieved food would know about this cave.

Feeling foolish for thinking she had discovered a new place, she started to creep down the stairs and back to the library when she heard her name in the kitchen above.

"Em didn't tell you?"

It was a masculine voice. Was that Sam? She paused on the steps. Tell who what?

"She keeps to herself, mostly. We weren't even sure we could trust her." Definitely Phoebe's rich, round tones. Phoebe's opinion of her wasn't a surprise.

"She gave you the wrong name, you should know. Also, she and I, well, we were involved."

Em ground her teeth in fury. He was blowing her cover, but she expected that. The other thing? How dare he imply—

"But she jilted me. For some lord with money and a mansion in Gillamor."

"Seriously?" Cora's voice. She sounded more annoyed than usual. "Is she still with this lord guy?"

"Well, she's here, so maybe not. Anyway, that's why there's been tension. That's why I went north, to try and forget her. She's done me great wrong, but I still have feelings for her."

"That's awful of her to leave you just for some rich guy."

"It hurt me, I confess."

"I saw the tension on the sparring mat the other day. Also this morning."

Em had heard enough. She marched away from the stairwell, angrier than she'd ever been. How dare he? Sharing blatant falsehoods. About him and her, no less! What game was he playing?

She marched back across the cave and up the library stairs in a huff. Should she just tell Phoebe and Cora that he was lying? Would they even believe her? She had been standoffish, and she had lied about her identity. That didn't mean Sam Monterey could march in and define her to everyone else. Could spread lies that make her look like a heartless money chaser. It was too much.

If it was a ploy to gain their sympathy, it sounded like it was working.

Em's fury didn't abate as she reset the library shelves and retracted the staircase. Her brain was so full of rage that she nearly bumped into Silas as she was leaving the library.

"We missed you at lunch. Get caught reading?"

Em nodded, trying to conceal her anger.

A silence hung between them, but then Silas tried again.

"Can I ask, what are you reading about? Must be really interesting. And you said you were looking for information."

He reminded Em of Bob, chasing his tail and bounding along without a care in the world. It was maybe an unfair comparison; he was the only one who had been kind to her. Em decided that it wouldn't hurt to have an ally, since Sam was poisoning everyone against her.

"I'm reading about Northern history," she confessed. "It's banned where I'm from."

Silas nodded. "I'm not surprised. The empire would want to conceal their actions over the years."

"A lot of what was going on doesn't make its way down South. And it seems important. But the constant fighting . . ." She stumbled a bit trying to explain. It was more to her now than just discovering traces of the ring. The history felt like a lost artifact too.

Silas stopped and faced her. "Do you understand why?"

"Not really. I could trace it back to Emperor Jerrifree and his brother Henrich. The civil war. But I don't understand why the conflict has continued. The empress can be overbearing, but my own village has never felt the need to fully rebel. We leave them alone, and they leave us alone."

"Must be nice for you." Silas's voice had gone cold, and Em realized she must've said something wrong.

"I am trying to understand," she said. "I want to listen if you'd be willing to share your—"

She fumbled, but Silas nodded and stopped in the middle of the hallway. He looked uncharacteristically angry, and Em was desperate to make it right.

"The right to rule . . . no." He stopped himself, coughed, and ran a hand through his messy hair. "We have our own lands, despite the invasion and regular skirmishes at the border. Everything north of the mountains was part of the Prutian ancestral tribal lands."

Em said nothing, only nodding for him to continue. She was surprised they claimed so much territory but didn't want to voice that. Didn't want to upset him further.

"They have taken so much of our land for no other reason except they want it. Imperial soldiers march in and issue orders. They shut down our ancestor remembrance rituals. They interrupt our weddings and new child ceremonies and funerals and tell us that we must give up our savage traditions and adopt yours. They want us to burn our heirlooms and swear unbreakable oaths to the empress. They have killed so many. Not just rebels. But old men. Young children. Mothers. It's clear they want our land, but not us."

His voice rose, and Em was rooted the spot. Of course she knew some of this from books, but to hear it spoken aloud was somehow horrifying in a new way.

He continued. "How could we not fight back? And we have. But the soldiers double in number. And their actions become more inhumane. And more of our land is taken. And we can feel the empress's fist tightening around us until we can't breathe. We aren't even living anymore. We are surviving. Trying to find brief moments of joy before, one by one, each of us is snuffed out."

Em couldn't even imagine. All at once she was ashamed of herself. Chasing her own anger against Sam. Even living her own happy life when somewhere else, people were brutalized by her country.

"I didn't know," she said.

He was unable to meet her gaze. "We have a hard time with you. Here to read our books and eat our food and learn from us, and then you'll return to whatever pampered life you came from. And we return to *that*."

"I'm sorry, Silas."

He looked up, finally. Master of himself, but his open expression mingled with the pain of what he revealed. "That's why we're here. Training. Fighting back."

She nodded in understanding. "I would do anything to keep those I love safe."

He studied her, then finally his mouth turned up a fraction. "Yes, exactly."

They stood in silence for a moment. Then he tilted his head toward the kitchen. "I think there's a sandwich or two left, if you're still hungry."

Em nodded and drifted past him to the kitchen, properly shamed. She was resolved to do better. To help. But she wasn't sure what that even looked like.

CHAPTER 24

Everyone has a point of view. Or a belly button.
But not always both.

"Wisdom from the Mountaintops:
One Man's Journey to Enlightenment"
From the library of the Silver Nightingale

After uneventful sparring, Em made her way back to the kitchen and found Sam waiting by the cleaning supplies. She seethed, his lies about their involvement fresh in her mind. What do you do with two people determined to hurt each other? Put them in a room together and make them do chores. It made a twisted sort of sense, so long as you didn't care whether one or both of the people ended up dead.

He seemed chastened by Bronwyn's rebuke. And she was resolved to put a lid on their conflict after her chat with Silas. Yet, nothing was resolved. Despite the truce, she was determined to never turn her back to the man.

"What's first?" she asked coldly.

He read from the cleaning list. "Sweep and mop kitchen. Wipe down all surfaces."

"Okay." She nodded. "I can sweep and mop."

He ducked his head in agreement, and they silently began.

She looked over at him. He was scrubbing the counters and very determinedly looking anywhere but at her.

She was so angry the words came tumbling out before she could stop them. "Why did you say those things to Cora and Phoebe?"

"What things?"

"That we were involved."

He continued scrubbing. "You heard that, huh?"

Not even a hint of remorse. Em contained her ire. "You know as well as I do that it's never been like that between us. You are making me out to be a villain. Why? What do you gain?" Em's voice rose an octave, and she swept much more vigorously than she needed to.

"Maybe you *are* a villain, Strider. Why did you lie to them about your name?"

This counterpoint surprised Em. Why did Sam care? But it was a fair question. "You know better than anyone, my parents don't always make a good impression."

"You're not here to take advantage of them? To swindle them?" He had stopped scrubbing now.

Em flushed. He thought she would do that? She remembered what Silas had said about the Northerners having trouble with her. "No. I didn't understand the Northern conflict like I should've, but I wasn't trying to make anything worse for them."

He met her gaze, his fury bouncing against her indignation. Then he broke eye contact and turned back to the counter.

Em tried her question again. "Why would you tell them we were involved?"

"I don't know."

"Take a guess."

Sam started scrubbing again. "I'm sure you've told them things about me."

"I haven't."

He turned again, eyebrows raised. "Really?"

"I haven't told them much of anything about me at all. So you've had the first crack at telling them what scum I am. I guess it doesn't matter."

He was silent as he brushed a pile of crumbs from the counter into his hand and flicked them into the rubbish bin.

Em swept her little pile of dirt into a dustpan, then glanced up again. He was watching her with curiosity. She preempted whatever he intended to say. "I meant what I promised, you know. I'm done with"—she gestured between them—"whatever this is."

He moved on to the cupboards, and Em shifted to sweep where he had been standing.

"So why are you here, then? I know it isn't just to learn. Otherwise, you would've befriended all of them by now. And you keep sneaking off to look for hidden passages when you think no one is looking."

Insightful. He had been keeping an eye on her. "I'm surprised I don't have a knife in my back."

He laughed. Not sinister. Just amused. "I considered it. I'm not as angry as I originally was."

"Why not?"

He held up his hand and waggled his missing finger. "Perspective," he said.

And despite everything, Em believed him. She certainly didn't feel visceral fear around him. She didn't know if that was pure stupidity, or if the act of fighting back—of knowing she could—made her feel less helpless. Or maybe Bronwyn's violence gave her an illusion of safety around Sam. Or maybe something fundamental had changed within him, and she had begun to sense the shift.

"So you truly came here to help the North?"

He didn't hesitate. "Yes."

She believed him to be sincere, and she flushed. Embarrassed by her own self-interests. "You are a better man than I gave you credit for."

Sam spoke into the silence. "I'm sorry. For the umbrella. For messing with your oath. For all of it. I took it too far."

Em snorted. It was the understatement of the year, but she didn't want to scoff at what seemed a genuine apology. An apology she never expected. She felt she should return the goodwill, but she really didn't want to apologize for any of her behavior last fall, when most of her actions were simple retaliations against his bad behavior.

"I'm sorry I sent you to Fridera without a coat," she finally said. He nodded in appreciation. Then she remembered something else that went too far. "And the roll thing. That was a bit childish."

The edge of his mouth turned up. "You dropped that roll so quick!"

In retrospect, it was funny. But Em didn't give him the satisfaction of a laugh.

Sam had finished wiping down the cabinets and moved on to the table. Em had finished sweeping and was filling the mop bucket with sudsy water.

"So, what's the deal with you and Lord Hallson?"

"We're still together," Em said briskly, not wanting to discuss this topic.

"Really? Good for you two. I have to say, I'm surprised. Very surprised."

Em could tell he was baiting her, so she bit her tongue and started to scrub the sticky bits on the floor without commenting.

But that didn't dissuade him. "Interesting that he didn't go for a high-society type girl. Surely he won't want to stay in Sticksville forever. He'll want a cozy mansion in town and a quiet life. And you? You've changed. You're more devious than you were."

"I'm not discussing this with you," Em clipped.

"Fair enough. I'm just giving my observations. Although"—he grinned wickedly—"you didn't tell me I'm wrong. And you're here, so . . ."

Em lifted the mop and flung water in his direction, which made him laugh but shut him up.

"I screwed things up," she finally admitted. "He's been great.

Patient. And I did something stupid that led to whole pile of consequences. I'm here trying to fix that."

"How?" he asked.

Em shook her head and kept mopping. Sam had finished wiping and now sat on the counter as she worked around him. "Doesn't matter. Now that I'm here, I'm starting to understand what they're fighting against. And I can't help but think that maybe I should be on their side."

Sam raised his eyebrows. "Treason, Strider? You *have* changed."

She shot him a dirty look.

He shrugged. "Since we're being honest with each other, I've considered it. Joining the resistance, I mean."

"Looks like you already did." Em nodded to his missing finger.

"I did. A little bit. And in really stupid ways that had more to do with me and my own issues than actually helping anyone. But the distraction in that marketplace—which Merrick saw—that was a new tactic. But not enough. They need an army. The empire needs to fear them enough to back away."

"I thought you were just here for treasure?"

His eyebrows waggled. "That is also very appealing. Can't I help them *and* take some compensation for my efforts?"

Em tried to hide a smile and squeezed out the mop. Considering she was also looking to take the ring if she could find it, Sam and she were more alike that she cared to admit. But there was no way in all of the deities' creation that she was going to tell him that.

One Week and Six Days until the Solstice

BRONWYN CALLED them all to the Gathering Room several days later. Sam gave Em a quick nod when he entered. Perhaps their truce would hold, which was a relief to her. They had spent each day cleaning silently in the same room without bloodshed, so that was progress.

Silas sidled up next to Em. "What's this about, then? You and Monterey destroy a wing of the castle or something?"

Em laughed, happy that Silas was still speaking to her. "Not lately. No idea why we're here. Maybe someone new showed up?"

But there was no one else there. Phoebe and Elias had filed in, and they didn't seem any less confused.

Finally, Bronwyn swept into the room, and sat on the stone chair in the middle of it. They all watched her expectantly.

"I can no longer wait for you to absorb the trainings I have generously offered. I must tolerate using your weak skills. Scouts have reported additional troops on the border. We expect them to cross into the territories very soon, and there are whispers of a full-scale assault on Fugea within the week. The resistance is spread too thin to reconvene in time."

Cora was whispering something frantically to Elias at this announcement. The others had let out some loud expletives. Em turned to Silas. "What is it?"

"Fugea is one of the largest towns in the territories. A lot of us have friends and family there. An attack on a town that size and that far from the border is unprecedented."

"It could be deadly?"

Silas nodded. "It's like I said. The empress has long thought it would be easier to take the territories if there weren't so many people fighting back. They kill who they can, then they set themselves up in the new land they've acquired."

Em bit the inside of her cheek. How could the empress possibly justify that? She felt a tiny flicker of rage inside her. This wasn't okay. It couldn't be explained away, and she couldn't ignore it.

"How can we help?" The voice was Otto's. His ever-present sneer was gone, and he seemed just as worried as the rest of them.

"At least you're willing." Bronwyn scowled. "We can slow down their arrival with some defensive magic, allowing Northerners a chance to hide or flee. We can also provide some objects to fight back. I will leave three days hence with anyone who wishes to come. But"— she looked first at Sam, then at Em—"do not come unless you truly wish to join the cause. Unless you are loyal. If you are spotted by imperial soldiers, then you are forever linked with us traitors. It would make it difficult for you to return to Esnania. And if you are not loyal and you come, I will have to kill you myself."

Em felt other eyes on her. And she felt the weight of the choice. What were the odds she would be recognized? She didn't know. But to never see Liam, and Gram, and all the others? But if Bronwyn decided she wasn't on their side . . . Em wasn't ready to make that decision. She tried not to shift. Three days? She had less than two weeks until her deadline. She shouldn't go. There wasn't enough time.

THAT AFTERNOON, Em and Sam were assigned to wipe down the sparring room. As they worked in silence, Em tried to keep the weapons rack in her periphery. Just in case Sam was playing some kind of long game that involved killing her with wooden swords when she least expected it.

She was sweeping the corners when he finally spoke. "Are you going?"

She didn't need to ask what he was talking about. The trip to Fugea had been bouncing around her brain all day. She was thinking herself in circles. She should help. She wanted to help. But was she ready to risk injury, death, or worse, being recognized? Putting all her loved ones in danger? Putting yet another death mark on her head? Missing her deadline? Was she willing to risk Bronwyn's wrath if she didn't go? She shrugged. "Are you?"

Sam was wiping down the sparring mat and paused to meet her eye. He was reading her. Trying to figure out something. He gave up, shrugged, and went back to cleaning.

After a few minutes of silence, he spoke again. "Can you tell me about the Gray Horse? What's going on with it, I mean?"

He asked haltingly, as if afraid of the answer.

Em was equally cautious in her response. "I repaired the damage.

Right after—I mean. I also fixed a few things that we didn't break. You're welcome."

He didn't thank her, but her mention of their previous fight didn't seem to trigger him. So she continued. "We spoke to the employees. Most of them wanted to continue running the place, so we helped them set up a rotating management schedule with a profit-sharing option. They seemed to be pretty happy about it. I also returned the stone—the lucky one—to your desk drawer."

Sam scoffed at the profit-sharing mention. Em ignored this and continued. "I've visited a few times a month since. The spa is thriving, and the hotel always seems busy."

Sam nodded and said nothing. Em couldn't tell if he was grateful, disappointed, or annoyed. Maybe a mix of all three. After all, she had just reported that his large, complicated resort could operate better without him.

She scooped up a pile of dust and dirt into the dustbin and moved to another corner. "Have you found any more secret passages?"

He chuckled. "So you're interested?"

Em scowled. She shouldn't have asked so directly. "Not particularly. Just making conversation."

His lips turned up in a mocking smile. "Sure. I've found a few." Then he started polishing the sparring weapons. Irritated, Em moved away, looking for something to clean on the opposite side of the room. There were little ledges at the tops of columns that probably needed dusting, and she moved that way, grabbing a stool so she could reach.

She still had to stretch to reach the ledges and nearly fell off at his next conversation starter.

"Want to know how I lost my finger?"

Em turned, stunned. He was still polishing the weapons but watched her with an amused expression. He was testing her. "If you want to tell me," she said carefully.

His voice took on a musical quality, as if he were spinning a yarn around a campfire. "I traveled to the Northern territories after some time recuperating in Fridera. There's a town called Hemnisville right along the border. A larger village than what I had been in, and I stayed with a relative of the people who'd saved me. I did odd jobs for them, and they gave me room and board, just like I had in Fridera at the Dusty Whale. On the side, I worked jobs around town trying to earn enough to travel by public coach back to Arrenmore."

Em stretched to dust with her back turned to him. She was afraid to comment. Afraid if she spoke, he would stop.

"Since it was a border town, there were a lot more imperial soldiers than I'd seen before. In Fridera, they were a nuisance, but these were meaner and more plentiful. One carpenter I sorted hardware for lost a whole pile of lumber when they all—ah, relieved themselves on it."

Em shuddered in disgust, then swiped her dust rag over the ledge.

"One older lady would pay me in soup if I would go to the market to do her grocery shopping. I think she was afraid to go herself. The soldiers were regularly harassing vendors and shoppers. Ruining merchandise. Kicking people around. I kept my head down and kept out of their way, but they still targeted me. Trampled all the vegetables I had bought once or twice. I had to use my savings to buy new produce for the lady, because I didn't want to go back empty-handed.

"One day, they were harassing a boy. Maybe ten or eleven years old. He was carrying a dozen eggs, and they took them. Made him stand there while they pelted him with them. They laughed when he started to cry. They called him things. Awful things. Things I heard as a kid, mostly from my father."

Em started. His father called him names? She snuck a glance at Sam, who had paused, reliving some uncomfortable memory.

"Hearing that . . . something in me snapped. I hit one of them. Kicked another. And then they beat me. I have a scar"—he pointed to a spot under his beard—"where they split my chin open."

Em had abandoned all pretense of cleaning. She stood on the chair, holding her dust rag and watching Sam's face as he continued to speak.

"I started fighting more after that. It was so stupid. It would always end in me getting my ass kicked, bleeding. But somehow, I felt like I was doing something right. One day, I tried to get the other merchants to join in. To fight with me. To defend themselves. That's when those soldiers held me down and took my finger. For inciting others."

Em closed her eyes, imagining this man fighting for others. Recognizing injustice that didn't directly affect him. And in that moment, she knew the Sam in front of her was not the Sam she had met many months ago. "It hurt?" she asked the obvious.

He winced. "The worst pain I've ever felt in my cushy, sheltered life."

CHAPTER 25

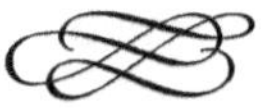

Emperor Henrich retained multiple strongholds during his short reign, but he spent most of his time at the Antillei Keep. The fortress was impenetrable, and he liked to keep the Northern treasures safe within its walls.

"The Life and Times of Henrich Clavonion"
From the library of the Silver Nightingale

Em didn't sleep that night. She flipped her warding tree wood chip over her fingers again and again. Her candle burned low as she paced her tiny bedchamber running through all the scenarios of a visit to Fugea.

What if she went? She had enough magical knowledge to help, and maybe she could actually save some people. After all, if Sam had helped the cause, shouldn't she? But then, what if the soldiers spotted her? Reported back to the empress? Her whole world would implode. Goodbye to her life with Liam. To Brookerby. The town and people she had worked so hard to preserve. Would the empress punish

Brookerby until Em turned herself in? Would Liam come with her into exile? Would Gram?

She shouldn't go. Then what? Stay in the Silver Nightingale while everyone else leaves and continue searching for the ring? That seemed logical, but what if the ring wasn't here? She would already be a fugitive, and Bronwyn would surely expel her from the fortress for not being on their side. She remembered Silas's face as he explained the brutal world his people endured. *I didn't know.* No doubt they had suffered massive injustice. But did it necessarily follow that she must give up her chance at a future to help them?

Perhaps she could work out a trade. The ring for her services? Too coldhearted. And that bargain would tip her hand to Bronwyn. Who would just kill her.

Em sat on the edge of her bed, exhausted from pacing. This whole dilemma was a repeat of the unbreakable oaths. She tried to do the right thing. The humane thing. And because it defied the empress, she faced the consequences. Alone. None of the people she saved had spoken for her. And really, what good had she done? She helped very few, despite her months of work. All she had to show were several broken relationships and a death mark on her head.

What was she doing here? What was the point of any of it? This endless exertion, promising to help, giving your life breath for those who don't know you and don't care.

Wouldn't it be better to hide away, as Bronwyn had done? Pursue enlightenment at a safe distance while the world burned? It did sound nice. She could learn so much. But she had a feeling Bronwyn wouldn't allow that. These Northerners wouldn't allow indifference. She had to choose a side.

But then her thoughts drifted to Sam Monterey. His story. What he had seen. The scarred stub of a finger that proved he had tried to do the right thing and suffered for it. He was a better person now than if he had turned away and cared for himself alone.

Retrieve the ring and the empress would pardon her. Retrieve it, and she could retreat to a quiet existence of repair jobs and building a life with Liam.

Help the North, and the empress would condemn her. Help them and die alone.

Em paced her room, thinking in circles. She even flipped open *The Standard Book of Anything* for advice, only to find blank pages in the non-working book. Perhaps she should stay. Or she should find the ring and leave. Or she should go home right now, ringless. She could plan her next move in safety. But it all just delayed the inevitable. Either way, without the ring, she was dead in two weeks.

One Week and Four Days until the Solstice

"WHAT HAVE YOU DECIDED?" Sam asked. They were weeding and trimming the outdoor garden that bordered the training field when he threw the question out in the midst of their working silence. Em had been trimming a hydrangea with hedge clippers, and she paused. The blooms had already shriveled, and she wondered if Gram's garden was wilting too. It was late in the year, so probably.

The wind had kicked up, even in the shelter of the wards, and Em wished she had worn her cloak.

She realized Sam was still waiting for a reply. "I don't know."

The same arguments had cycled in her mind the past two days, and her brain was starting to feel fuzzy from lack of rest. But she couldn't go. Her deadline was looming.

Sam knelt to pull weeds. He didn't comment on her indecision or the dark circles under her eyes. For this, she was grateful. Em found it strange that she was comfortable working alongside this man who had once tried to kill her. But since the apology and his story, they had been—not friends,—but something akin to it. Or at least Em felt that. It could've simply been another ruse from Sam to lull her into trust before he struck. She would discover the ruse only after he betrayed her again. If he did. Until then, she would enjoy the camaraderie.

Sam was pulling at something over in the corner, behind a massive evergreen tree. Em paused her work to watch. He yanked but nothing came up. It clanked against his tools.

"What is that?"

He didn't answer, using his small shovel to clear the packed dirt and rock. She walked over to watch. "What is it?" she repeated.

He pulled on the metal again. It looked like a rusted circular door pull. His tugs dislodged pine needles and crusted dirt went flying. He grinned up at her. "Trapdoor. Doesn't look like it's been opened in years. Should we see where it goes?"

Em glanced around. No one was watching. All the times they had cleaned together, no one had come to check on them. But to disappear into a hole in the ground with Sam? Em hesitated only a second before she smiled. "Lead the way, Monterey."

His eyes crinkled at the rhyme. Then he reached for the rusted iron ring and pulled, lifting the door with great difficulty.

The opening revealed a stone stairway that descended into darkness. Cobwebs hung everywhere.

"Why are there always stairs," Em muttered.

Sam looked up, surprised by the comment. "Always?"

She rolled her eyes. A slip of the tongue. She was too tired to lie; she might as well tell him. "There's a cave passage between the library and the kitchen's root cellar. Nothing down there, of course, but lots of stairs."

A grin spread across his angular face. "What else did you find?"

She gestured for him to start descending, and she followed after him. He produced a candle and lit it while she pulled the trapdoor closed behind them. And then she began to detail her non-finds. The corridors that ran parallel to the hallways. Sam commented on the ones he had found, and they discovered that—between them—they had searched every possible hallway.

"Well, looks like we're even," he said. "A whole lot of nothing for both of us. I also found a passage in the sparring hall after you left yesterday. Secret door near the weapons rack. It came out in the Gathering Room. The base of a pillar twists to open the stairs. Empty, though."

Between the two of them, they had searched most of the rooms in the Silver Nightingale—at least of the open wing. The other wing had been bricked off to all residents but Bronwyn, and the lower belly of the castle was being used for the labyrinth.

"Do you think there's treasure in the maze somewhere?" Sam asked.

Em shuddered. "Not likely. They wouldn't risk an intruder finding it."

"So this is it, then," he said. "Gotta be something here, in this passage."

"What about private quarters?" Em asked.

"I checked mine."

"Yeah, mine didn't have anything either."

They continued climbing stairs in silence for a bit. Maybe this really was the last passage. Then Em came up with another possibility. "What about Bronwyn's quarters? The other wing?"

Sam laughed. "That mind of yours! Just when I think you are naive and wholesome you come up with something so devious. Are you suggesting we break into legendary mage Bronwyn's private rooms and just poke around?"

Em didn't think it was that crazy. "Why not?" she challenged.

"For one thing, I never want to make an enemy of that woman. She would've crushed us into the dirt of the training field without a second thought."

Em agreed. The woman was frightening in a way she hadn't encountered in anyone before. Not even the empress. But Bronwyn's quarters seemed a likely hiding place, and Em kept toying with the idea as they descended deeper into the mountain. Sam's candle cast a wavering glow on the rock walls that enclosed the stairs. If the ring was there—in Bronwyn's room, or even at the bottom of these stairs— it would fix everything. She could return to the empress, receive her pardon, and go home to the people who loved her. Escape this whole messy business.

"What have you decided?" she asked. She realized that she hadn't reciprocated his question from earlier, and discovered she was curious about the answer.

"Yes," he said. "I'm going."

Em felt a wave of shame. Helping felt like the right thing to do, and if Sam Monterey was compelled to pitch in, Em would be the most selfish being on the continent if she did not.

But Sam was still talking. "Originally, my goal was to get back to the Gray Horse. Get revenge."

She nodded in the dark. She suspected as much.

"But I worked through some—" He cut himself off, as if he was about to share too much. "The things I saw up north. They just felt wrong. And I acted. And then for the first time in my life . . ."

Em finished for him. "You felt like a good guy."

He stopped and turned, the candle lighting his angular jaw. "Maybe. I wouldn't put it like that. Was I ever a bad guy?"

"Ah, yeah. Absolutely you were."

He studied her for a moment, then shrugged. "I guess it's a matter of perspective."

Em badly wanted to delve deeper on that one. Perhaps they would never see eye to eye on what happened at the Gray Horse. But she bit her tongue and only let out a small "Hah."

His voice was quiet. "It's funny. I never loved that place. I felt this pressure to keep it going. My father's voice in my head. I didn't want to be the weak link in my family. But I felt trapped most of the time. And now . . . seems they're fine without me."

This admission was news. But remembering the run-down state of the Gray Horse when he was in charge, and his own prickly demeanor at that time . . . it felt true. And based on what he had said about his father, that voice in his head was probably not a kind one. But why was he telling her this? By way of explanation for his bad behavior? To let her know it was okay he was no longer there? "So I did you a favor?" she joked.

"In a roundabout way, yes. I do wish you'd let me grab a pocketbook and my coat."

"Next time," she promised. He shot her a glare, and she felt the hollowness of her own joke. "Kidding." Mostly. If there were a next time, it would be infinitely more complicated, given that they seemed to be—almost—friends.

The ground leveled out up ahead, and Em prepared herself for another empty cave.

But it wasn't empty. In the candlelight, the room sparkled. Sam let out a whoop, handing off his candle to Em and drifting closer to the glittering piles.

The Northern treasures were wall-to-wall, floor-to-ceiling. In piles. In trunks. Spread throughout the room in a dizzying array. Kept secret in the Silver Nightingale until this very moment.

THEY HAD BEEN DOWN THERE AT LEAST an hour, and Em was sorting through a pile of precious knickknacks, separating the magical from the mundane. She could still feel that telltale rushing of magic beneath the surface of each item but didn't risk testing them all. After all, magic was rarely safe. There were a few with instant effects, which told Em that the room was outside the wards of the fortress. A magical mirror showed her what she would look like twenty years hence. She wasn't shocked to see she looked like her mother. A magical accordion played a dancing tune the moment she picked it up. Momentarily enchanted, she started bouncing along until Sam told her to put it down for deities' sake.

It all looked ancient. There were no new designs or technologies. Everything was at least a century old, based on the dates on the coins, the embellishments on the items. The tarnish on the silver. Either the stash had not been taken care of, or this chamber hadn't been breached in recent memory. This idea made Em more eager that her legendary ring might actually be here. Lost in a hole in the ground.

She only partially focused on her sorting; she was more concerned about inching closer to the jewelry box on the nearby wall. She had purposely started several piles away, because she knew Sam would be hyper-focused on the first things she inspected. If the ring was resting with the other jewelry, perhaps she could slip it in her pocket once his attention wandered.

That seemed a good possibility. Sam had a silvery top hat on his head, tilted at a jaunty angle. He picked up each of several gem-encrusted goblets clustered on a richly carved table and made a toast.

"Here's to the raven-haired upholsterer's assistant in Arrenmore. Never has a woman done more with velvet."

Em rolled her eyes.

"To the busty seamstress on Hickory Street in Gillamor. Never have I owned a finer suit, or had such fun paying for it."

A bit too suggestive for her tastes. Em set the final knickknack, a small standing clock, in the mundane pile and moved on to a heap of rich fabrics. One pile away.

"To the ladies wearing the latest fashions, and to all the things the ruffles don't hide."

"Mr. Monterey!" Em scolded. She could ignore entendre, but not blatant scallywaggery.

"Oh, come now, Strider. I'm having a bit of fun. Those ruffles were meant to attract eyes. Don't pretend you haven't selected a dress to hook a man."

Em's eyebrows shot to the ceiling. "Hook a man? Could you be any cruder?"

"I could." He grinned.

Sam hadn't been drinking but his filter seemed to have disappeared from the moment he put the hat on. Probably something magical that was loosening his lips. Em decided to have a bit of fun instead of telling him to take it off. "Have you ever tried to 'hook a man'?"

Sam shook his head loosely. The chapeau slid sideways as he did, looking even more ridiculous. "I haven't that inclination. Although . . ." he trailed off.

Em grinned. There was a story in that "although." "Hook a lady, then?"

"What have I just been talking about, woman? Should I tell you more about the velvet?"

Em shuddered. No. A thousand nos. "I meant, for real. Like a woman you didn't want to lose?"

He shifted and set down the goblet he'd been holding.

"Once. A few years back. She . . ." His face took on a melancholy twist.

Em recognized her mistake. Old flames were not a good topic. He had gone from manic to depressed in two heartbeats, no doubt aided by his current headwear. She had to stop him before he started crying. She couldn't handle that level of friendship just yet.

She shot him a stern look. "Find anything else over there? Apart from the mood-altering hat?"

Sam started, then slipped the thing from his head with a sheepish smile. "You're a sly thing, Em. You knew it was doing something to me."

"Ah, but you were having such a good time," Em laughed as she sorted through a pile of woven fabric.

"Nothing else over here but gold cups and silver forks. Pretty dull actually." He set down the hat and began to move toward her.

"You can look through the knickknacks over there. I sorted them into magical and nonmagical. Are you planning on choosing something?" Em asked it casually, wondering if he had any specific item in mind.

"Actually, I've been eyeing that jewelry box."

Crumb. A string of curses fluttered across Em's mind. Now she could either show her own interest or let him open it alone. "I'm curious also," she admitted, coming alongside him as he placed his candle, now in a glass candelabra, on top of the chest and reached for a drawer. The cabinet was large enough that it reached Em's shoulders and was of crafted mahogany with some kind of metal inlay and numerous drawers of different sizes.

Sam pulled open a first drawer to find a string of black pearls.

"Magic?" Em asked.

"Nope." He shoved them back into the drawer and opened another. Gold hoop earrings and a nose ring. The nose ring was magical.

"You want to wear it?" He held it out to Em.

"Not really my style."

"Shame." He set the nose ring aside and continued riffling through drawers, pulling things out and placing them along the front of the table, occasionally offering a bauble or pin to Em. There were no silver rings with amber. Then Em spotted it. Next to a pendant with a substantial ruby sat a silver box, the size of a ring.

Sam picked it up, and Em tried not to wince. Maybe he wouldn't . . .

"Want this?" he offered. "Feels magical."

Em held out her hand. "Maybe." He dropped it in her palm and continued sorting through the jewelry. She studied the box, decorated with the geometric shapes and etched symbols of the North. Was this it? Was the ring inside? There didn't seem to be a hinge or a way to open it.

"What does it do?"

Crumb. She might as well stand under a signpost lit with electricity for all her subtlety. "No idea," she said. "It just reminds me of a ring box my mother used to have."

Sam set down the rose-shaped brooch he'd been studying. "Em."

"Hmm?" She didn't meet his gaze; instead, she continued looking over the box.

His hand closed over the top of hers, and she instinctively jumped back, but his hand grabbed her so firmly that she couldn't pull away.

"Strider, despite your recent turn toward villainy, you're a terrible liar."

"What?"

"First off, you didn't meet your mother until this year. You have no idea what ring boxes she had. Second, that's the first thing you've shown interest in, out of this whole room." His other hand now gripped her elbow. "Is this what you were looking for?"

"Who says I was looking for—ow!" He was now holding her arm so tightly she thought she might have a bruise.

"I may be many things, but I'm not an idiot." His aqua eyes glittered with amusement, but there was hint of danger in them. The old Sam Monterey lurking in their depths. Em didn't want that guy to come back out. She didn't know if she could tell him a convincing lie, but she could slip out enough of the truth for him to trust her.

"It's a long story. But I'm not even sure this is it. If there's a magic ring inside, and it matches a description, it's going to save my life."

"More fortune tellers, Em?"

Em recalled the fortune teller at the Rashorbuj festival who had predicted her death. She wondered how Sam knew—oh yes. He'd had her followed. She shuddered. Old Sam. Let's keep that one locked up. And the only way to do that was to share some of the truth. "No. Not more fortune tellers. Soon after our last encounter at the Gray Horse, I figured out how to remove my unbreakable oath."

Sam looked impressed but puzzled. "You figured out—seriously? I thought infusions on humans couldn't be removed. That's Bronwyn-level magic. Does the ring—"

Em held up a finger to forestall his questions. "I started helping other people, all over Esnania, remove their oaths. The empress found out."

Sam let out a curse. "How are you not dead?"

"She said she would let me live if I tracked down a magic ring for her. Within a certain amount of time."

Sam released her arm but kept his other hand on hers. It was surprisingly warm despite the chill of the vault. "And here I thought you were a treasure hunter like me."

Em wasn't sure how to respond to that. He sounded almost disappointed. Like he'd hoped they had similar aims. "I'm not my parents."

He seemed as if he wanted to debate this last statement, but instead asked, "How do you get it open?"

"No idea. I could take the box with me."

"You should open it here." He said it pleasantly, but the underlying threat was clear. He wasn't going to let her leave without showing the contents and spilling her secrets.

Em tilted the small silver box this way and that. Something clattered faintly inside. It sounded like a ring. Maybe this was a puzzle box, like the kind the blacksmith in Brookerby used to make. Move a piece in an unexpected direction and it allows another piece to shift out of the tangle. She prodded at the various symbols until she brushed concentric circles on the bottom that began to glow. Suddenly, the box was prodding her mind. Not forcefully, like Sam had done in the clearing—nearly a week ago now—but politely. Asking for her to open the gates willingly.

"No." Em set down the box and backed away.

Sam watched with amusement. "Too difficult?"

"It wanted in. What if it scrambles my mind?"

He shrugged. "Do you want the ring or don't you?"

That was a good point. But the item inside may not even be what she was looking for. Was it worth risking her mind? She leaned against the wall, feeling shaky.

"Do you know what it does? And how long did you have to find it?"

"I have one week and four days left. The solstice. And no, I don't know what it does."

Mercifully, he said nothing. Em took a few deep breaths. In. Out.

"I can pull it out of your hands. If it looks like it's hurting you," he offered.

This actually was a decent offer. Did she trust him? Not fully. But with this? Before she could second-guess, Em nodded and walked back to the table. She lifted the silver box and pressed the concentric circles. Again, the gentle prodding.

Against her instincts, she imagined opening a gate, allowing the prodding force in.

Her vision became hazy, and then sharpened. She was somewhere else. In a void. A dark room. Before her was a long table, lit from some unknown source above, with many items displayed. She approached carefully. A waterskin. A glittering dress. A deck of fortune cards. A chocolate croissant. A fishing pole. A map of the mountains. On and on. The items appeared at random, and the table stretched into the void as Em walked along it. As she looked at them, she realized they weren't quite random. They were items from her life. Things she had used.

What were all these here for?

Choose.

A whisper in her mind. The box was asking her to pick an item. A test. Maybe it wanted to understand her. It had pulled her memories, and was asking her to pick the most important thing from them.

At that moment, the outline of a door glowed beyond the table.

Choose, and enter.

There was something beyond the door. An unknown test to come. She found herself drifting toward her tools. Lifting her hammer. With this, she would be fine, no matter what was on the other side.

Through the door, there was a pile of wood. A pile of nails. As if in a dream, Em hefted her hammer and began to build. A bench. Something beautiful to fill the empty clearing. Then somehow, a new room for Grady's treehouse. Then a shelf for Mendel. Hammering, designing, planning. The wood was always the right size, and it leapt to her hands with eagerness. Yes. This was wonderful.

Then suddenly, she was standing back in the glittering room with Sam Monterey's hand on her shoulder and the silver box open before her.

Inside lay an amber ring. It was held in place by vining silver mounted on a thick band. The amber itself was of uneven quality; in some places opaque and orange, and in others clear and cinnamon. She picked up the ring, and on the opposite side of the band, the Clavonion crest was etched in tiny, perfect detail. By description, this was the lost ring.

"What happened?" Sam asked.

Em held the ring gently. Magic rushed below the surface, more wild than any item she had felt before. Stronger than the warding trees. Em studied every detail with a mixture of relief and awe. This thing meant she could live. It felt powerful. Important. She felt the swirling of magic, and swore she could see the amber itself swirling within its setting.

"Em?"

She closed her hand around the jewelry. "The box wanted to test me. To see what kind of person I am. I think it was a security measure. I chose a hammer, and then I built a lot of things."

At this, he patted her shoulder and stepped away. Em slid the ring and box separately into her pockets. "Are you going to take anything?" she asked.

"I don't know. Maybe." He scanned the room, looking.

"Not much of a treasure hunter if you don't," she said, moving toward the stairs. When she reached the first step, she felt the box vanish from her pocket. Spinning around, she saw it reappear on the jewelry table. The ring was still in her pocket. She tried again with the same results. "Uhh. Don't think I can take the box. Another security measure, I guess."

But Sam wasn't listening. He kept picking things up and putting them down. Finally, he grabbed his candle and started toward the stairs, empty-handed. That in itself seemed strange. Em had expected at least a grab for the ring, if not a shoveling of gold pieces into his pockets. But it appeared he was going to let her walk out with this thing without a fight. It felt . . . odd.

"Sam."

"I can't. Doesn't feel right." He turned to face her.

"You aren't going to tell anyone, are you?"

He looked at her for a moment, his eyes searching hers. Then a smile curled his lips. "Not sure. That depends on you."

Em wasn't certain, but she thought the room grew a little darker at his words. "How do you mean?"

He sat on the steps, a casual posture, but Em knew he was intentionally blocking her only means of escape. She had trusted him, and what? He was going to blackmail her now? That definitely was an Old Sam trick. Why did she keep making this same mistake over and over? Was she that susceptible to his charm and good looks?

"You have a week and a few days before you need to leave for Gillamor. I know you can travel fast. You have that map."

Em didn't attempt to deny it.

"Come north with the rest of us. For one week. Come north and use all of your skills to help Fugea. If you do, I won't tell anyone you're taking that." He nodded at the lump in her pocket.

That was it? He was blackmailing her to . . . help people? There had to be a catch. "Who are you, and what have you done with Sam Monterey?"

He smiled but it didn't reach his eyes. "They need your help up there. The North needs help. And I owe them. I need to go. And since I'm going, I want someone who's good in a crisis. That's you."

Em worked her jaw, trying to conjure a response. But Sam had more to say. "Also, you said you aren't your parents. I need you to prove it. Anne and Farrigan would run—with everything they could carry from this room. Prove to me you aren't a thief—help the cause—and we part ways as friends."

Em wanted to defend her parents, but Sam was right. They would've stolen every magical item that wasn't nailed down. And she was doing the same, she realized. Accept food, shelter, mage training, and then take what wasn't hers and flee. She didn't want to be that. She remembered how happy she was—in her mind—building things for others. That was who she was. Who she wanted to be.

She needed to help. She could stay out of sight. Create magical weapons and help the Northerners flee without letting the imperial soldiers see her face. She could make this work. Then home to Liam with her ransom paid, a clear conscience, and a few new magical skills to boot. Everything would work out. She met Sam's eyes and nodded. "You have a deal."

CHAPTER 26

Fugea is one of the most established Northern cities. Although small, compared to Gillamor, or even Abingdon, it maintains a consistent population and a thriving trade, thanks to its indoor marketplace and the high-quality roads that intersect in the center of town.

"The Northern Route: What to See & Do"
From the library of the Silver Nightingale

One Week and Three Days until the Solstice

They met the following morning in the Gathering Room. All of the initiates were coming, and everyone was wearing heavy cloaks and carried their packs. Em wore her cloak from Mendel and her own clothes, which made her a bit homesick. She would get back to Brookerby soon. She could feel the outline of *The Standard Book of Anything* in her bag, and she hopped from foot to foot. Soon, she would be able to see more than blank pages—once they traveled outside the wards.

She felt for the shape of the ring beneath her mittens; the strong magical rushing of the ring was tangible, even through the thick material. She had originally packed it in her bag, but it felt wrong to let her lifeline out of her sight. So after testing for any immediate effects, she resolved to keep it on her and hidden.

Silas gave her a friendly wave, which she returned. Cora had a look of shock when she spotted Em and started whispering something to Elias. They'd all expected her to run the other direction. She supposed that was a fair assessment. That had been her plan, until Sam's deal.

She sidled up to Sam. He gave her a nod and looked about to say more when Bronwyn raised her hand for silence.

"We will arrive on the outskirts of Fugea after traveling by gate-port. One of the villagers has offered their home for you to stay in during our mission. If you have family, you may also stay with them. Report to me each morning for your assignments. There will be a large group of mages and a few resistance fighters joining us in our efforts. If the empire attacks, we will defend, but our tasks are creating weapons and fortifications for the town to cover their own retreat.

"Mind your energy levels. When you can, make items that draw off the energy of the thing itself, as you have been taught. That is the most efficient use of your breath. I will demand larger tasks during our stay and expect there to be energy reserves to draw on. No grandstanding. Follow my every order. Disobey me and face severe consequences. Are we clear?"

They all murmured their assent.

"Very well. Follow me."

Bronwyn pushed past the group and led them out of the Gathering Room and down the corridor. They were a quiet bunch as they walked, but the longer they moved, the more they began to whisper.

Sam leaned close to Em. "Still in?"

Em nodded. "Yeah. Where is she leading us?"

"Gate-port in the other wing. It's how Merrick brought me here." He flashed her a quick smile and said nothing more. That was news to Em. Sam hadn't gone through the maze?

They had reached the blocked-off wing of the castle and halted before a large stone wall that ran across an arched hallway. Bronwyn tapped a few of the rocks in a complex sequence and the stones rearranged into a door-sized archway. She gestured them on with barely a backward glance.

The hidden wing was similar to the one they had been occupying. Stark walls, cold and impersonal. But Em caught a glimpse of a few of the rooms that were open and saw lush furnishings and knickknacks. Perhaps this was where Bronwyn lived. It made sense that the mage would not deny herself luxury, even if her initiates lived simply.

Finally, they made a hard left into an audience chamber similar to the Gathering Room. Raised platforms were scattered throughout the room, with large, empty picture frames hanging above each one. The frames were all different materials and sizes. Some nearly brushed the ceiling, and some were no larger than a cabinet door. The platforms had names of cities etched at their base. Em recognized a few; they all seemed to be cities in the Northern territories, or in Fridera. Bronwyn stood in front of the platform labeled "Fugea."

Without any additional speeches or fanfare, Bronwyn motioned and the picture frame behind her flashed and swirled, like a liquid-bronze pool hanging vertically within the frame. She stepped through first and disappeared. The group queued to follow her, one at a time.

Em had never seen a gate-port before, much less a whole room of them. She had heard about them but had believed only one or two existed in the whole of Esnania. Items that rare and valuable generally ended up in the hands of the richest citizens. But here—Bronwyn had at least a dozen and was using them to visit towns in the North. Maybe Bronwyn had been traveling through these the whole time?

The energy to transport someone a week's journey away would be massive. The costs to make such a thing seemed enormous. Was that energy already paid by the maker? Or would the frames siphon energy from anyone who used them? Bouncing with anticipation, she watched their small group disappear, one by one, into the swirling bronze.

She supposed her traveling map carried the same questions about energy. She wondered if some of the spinning feeling she got when using it fed the energy needs of the map, but she also felt a bit tired each time too. Perhaps this frame would pass on a similar fatigue.

Em's turn had come. She stepped up and placed a hand to the swirling surface before her.

"No trick," Phoebe said. "Just walk through." She was the only other person waiting. She watched Em's uncertainty with uncharitable amusement.

The bronze rippled as Em put her hand on it. It felt like diving into farmer Earl McBean's pond, only sideways. And she wasn't getting wet. She took the plunge.

On the other side, she first caught sight of weathered wood and ice, and then felt a shocking blast of cold air.

Em had never truly experienced cold before now. It snowed on occasion in Brookerby, and the thermometer took a dive from time to time, especially around the winter solstice. But this cold was blinding. The kind of cold where you always feel exposed, even in the warmest cloak, and a chill so deep you wonder if you can ever find warmth again. That was Em's impression as she stepped out of the old lean-to that housed the Fugea portal and into the narrow streets of the Northern town. All the buildings seemed tired and huddled together for warmth.

Sam waited for her, watching her reaction to the temperature.

Bronwyn was ahead, leading the small group forward, but she turned around and flicked her hand to deactivate the portal after Phoebe stepped through. It became an ordinary wooden frame in a shed, huddled in an alley between two squat cabins.

Em trotted along behind the group, feeling a bit dazed. Was it always this cold here? Had the portal taken some of her energy and that's why she was so chilly? She tucked her mittened fingers into the pockets of her new cloak and sent a silent thank-you to Mendel. But she was still fearing she wouldn't make it inside before she lost some toes.

Sam was beside her as she moved, hopefully toward shelter. "You get used to the chill," he said.

She met his eyes and realized what they were both thinking. She had sent him here. Without a second thought. Without a coat. She felt the weight of that for the first time. And he watched her realize it.

It was a strange moment. She winced. He raised an eyebrow. He wanted her to come here—maybe to help—but more importantly, to understand what this felt like. The isolation and the cold. He may have been a black-hearted villain, but when she fought back, she had matched him blow for blow. He had caused pain? Tried to kill her? She had done it right back.

Words weren't forming, but she offered him a nod. She understood. He patted her on the back, a friendly gesture, as if to say, *Now you know.*

Bronwyn led them to a small house on the southeast edge of town —their lodgings. Em studied the town as they moved and compared it to her mental map, based on the one she looked up in the library. The town had two major roads, one running north to south, and one running east to west. They intersected in the middle of town, and each quadrant was a huddle of houses, sheds, and business with narrow alleyways between. There were four gates, stationed on the perimeter of town on the major roads. Most people entered through the gates, but any intruder could enter at any alleyway along the perimeter. Em wondered that better fortification hadn't been built, and then realized that might be their purpose in coming. She felt a twinge of excitement. She could definitely build a wall, so maybe this was her chance to get on Bronwyn's good side.

The mage then left them on some unknown business. Silas, Elias, Cora, and Phoebe had darted away to find their friends and family who resided in the town. That left Em, Sam, Otto, and Cal to duck inside and claim their sleeping spots.

Otto commandeered the single bed in the cabin, his aristocratic sensibilities offended by the idea of sleeping anywhere else. Cal claimed the sofa, and Em and Sam each found cots near the fireplace. Em didn't have a bedroll (not after setting hers on fire in the maze), so they found some extra quilts in a trunk for her.

The others bustled about investigating the cabinets for food and the closets for extra scarves and hats. Em fed the fire with the stack of logs nearby, then padded back to her cot and wrapped herself in a quilt. She was just starting to thaw when Cal moved to the door.

"You're going out?"

"We are. Meeting all the other mages near the south gate."

Em let out a slow hiss of air. Out there? Again?

"Come on, Em!" Sam cheered, pulling her blanket away and yanking her to her feet. He was clearly enjoying her discomfort. "No better cure for what ails you than fresh air."

"You've got to be kidding," Em muttered. Sam laughed as she followed them back out into the cold. She only had to survive for a week.

Bronwyn watched their small group, the initiates from the Silver Nightingale, Merrick, the older man who had brought Sam to the fortress, and a large gathering of others Em didn't know. At least fifty people, of all ages. She presumed most were the other magic users, and from the way they were hanging on Bronwyn's every word, perhaps former students?

A few of the Northern crowd carried weapons and sported numerous scars. Many of them had a white armband tied around their upper arm. Em supposed these were resistance fighters. Or at least the ones who were able to make it to Fugea.

The town sat just north of them. The south gate turned out to be a weathered wooden fence that stood wide open to any travelers coming to town on the main road. In all directions, there was blinding white snow, flat and untouched. Em scanned the horizon and saw the mountain peaks far to the southwest. Otherwise, nothing broke the white void except a handful of trees and boulders scattering the tundra.

Bronwyn was explaining their task for the day. The invading soldiers would mostly likely come by the road, and so they would create devices to slow them down. The townspeople could leave by the opposite road or exit through the gate-ports and wait the soldiers out in the Silver Nightingale.

Em was disappointed. Not a fence? But she pivoted, her mind was already building hypothetical devices. There were no trees nearby, but there was plenty of snow. What if she dug a pit, covered the top with an illusion of snow, and then when the soldiers were on top of it, the snow would disappear and they would tumble in? Or was there any wildlife around here? She could enchant creatures to protect the town. But some of them might be killed, which didn't sit right with Em. What about a barricade of discarded wood and large furniture? She could infuse the items so that they held together, making a large, immovable mass. That surely would take time to climb over or skirt around. Or even a line of fire barricading this side of the town? That wasn't magical, but Em supposed not everything needed to be. A wall of ice? She could build a frame, fill it with snow or melted water, and that wouldn't require fuel.

She was about to voice her ideas when Bronwyn declared, "We will be making small explosives out of found objects and burying them in the snow on and around the road. Not enough to kill, but enough to maim the soldiers and halt their advance. Infuse the item with enough energy to be triggered by someone stepping on it. Fill it with gunpowder."

Em felt immediate disappointment. She liked her ice wall much better, and it didn't injure anyone. But maybe they could do both. She approached the mage.

"Lady Bronwyn, I have another idea, if you'd be open—"

"I have spoken. Obey, Stonehill." A clear dismissal from the woman.

Em frowned. "But I think my idea could—"

"Silence!" The command was so loud it echoed across the tundra, the nearest buildings shook, and the group halted, fearful. Em closed her mouth quickly.

Bronwyn spoke, low and harsh. "You will follow my orders, or I will consider you a spy for the empress and will punish you accordingly. Do I make myself clear?"

"Yes, my lady." Em ducked away, feeling confused and a little afraid. Why wasn't Bronwyn open to suggestions? Would she really retaliate because Em shared another way to keep Fugea safe? What had Em signed up for?

The others scurried about, selecting their first items and finding a place out of the wind to infuse each piece. Em chose a cracked teapot and a tarnished candlestick holder. Why couldn't they infuse inside, and then have a runner carry the items out to the road? Wouldn't that preserve their energy better than sitting out in the cold?

Em plopped down at the base of a snow dune, which kept the wind off her a bit, and started concentrating on the item. But she couldn't focus. An enemy spy? Was Bronwyn serious?

"Don't question her."

Em looked up to see Cora standing close. "What?"

Cora gestured to the ground next to Em. It took Em a second, but once she realized the girl wanted to join her, she nodded and patted the ground.

Cora did so, hauling a small planter (surely for an indoor plant) and a lampshade alongside her. "She's in charge and doesn't like to be questioned."

"I didn't intend to make her angry. I had an idea—"

"It doesn't matter what you intended. Lady Bronwyn doesn't like to be questioned. She's triggered by it, if you know what I mean."

"I guess I saw that firsthand. Scary."

"You have no idea."

Em set down her teapot. "Does that happen regularly?"

Cora looked around and, seeing no one, lowered her voice. "It goes without saying, we're all grateful for Bronwyn's training. She's saved a lot of lives up here. But she also believes she is the future queen of the Northern territories, and she expects everyone to bend the knee. Even the resistance fighters who have nothing to do with her. My cousin had a friend who spoke up, argued with her actually. A week later, he turned up dead. A hunting accident, they said. But it felt like too much of a coincidence." Cora glanced around again. Then continued in a whisper. "Another woman, talented herbalist and very beloved, two towns over, disagreed with Bronwyn in a public forum and wouldn't concede. She had a magical 'accident' the next morning. Never the same since."

"Why are you telling me this? You don't even like me."

"I didn't know if you were with us before. The fake name and all. And you're not a Northerner. But now . . . I'm warning you. If you have ideas, keep them to yourself if you want to stay alive."

Em feigned confusion. "Fake . . . ?"

"Oh, stop. Sam told us. Except for—he didn't tell Bronwyn, of course. Said your parents are thieves, or something? It made sense, but still. Hard to trust someone when you don't know their real name."

Em didn't respond. She had overheard Sam outing her, but she'd hoped they didn't care. Apparently, they did. She focused again on her teapot, and Cora picked up her planter. They sat in silence, infusing their objects.

Finally, Em spoke. "Emaline Strider," she offered. "You can call me Em."

She saw Cora's mouth twitch up. Almost a smile. "Nice to meet you, Em."

Em shifted her eyes to where Bronwyn stood talking with Merrick. Now everything she saw had the filter of Cora's words. *Future queen of the North.* She detected not camaraderie but deference and a bit of fear in the older man. He was doing very little of the talking, only nodding and bowing as Bronwyn spoke.

The weather wasn't the only danger here. But Em reminded herself that this was temporary. She just needed to keep her head down and do as she was told until she could take the ring back to the empress.

CHAPTER 27

You have been a disappointment from your conception, and I blame your weak-minded mother for your softness and lack of drive.

"Letter from Romulus Monterey to his son Samuel"
The Standard Book of Anything

At dusk, Em was near frozen as they reentered their lodgings. She flexed her fingers to warm them as Cal built up the fire in the hearth and Sam started rummaging in the cabinets for food. They were all tired from infusing explosive items all day.

They buried mines on and around the main road, as far as the eye could see, but Em wasn't feeling very proud of this job. She was still smarting from Bronwyn's rebuke, but that wasn't all of it. Burying explosives just felt like the wrong thing to do. They were dangerous for the locals and guaranteed that the road would be unusable for years, lest a careless villager or wandering child accidentally step on one. There would also be carnage as the imperial soldiers approached. That would attract the empress's ire and only bring more soldiers to the area. Unless Bronwyn was trying to start all-out war . . .

Was Bronwyn trying to start a war?

Em glanced up and noticed Otto watching her from a chair near the fireplace. She tilted her head in question.

"Not what you expected?" he sniffed. Em couldn't decide if his voice held more derision than it usually did. It raised her hackles.

"Not exactly," she said. But she supposed it didn't matter what she expected.

Sam swiveled his head from the kitchen. "I thought Bronwyn was going to take a chunk out of you. Did no one warn you not to question the lady mage?"

"No, you didn't. She wasn't like that at Silver Nightingale."

"She was. Remember when she tried to crush us? That was insane. Why do you think I was so afraid to make an enemy of her?" Sam said as he carried a tray of sausage, hard rolls, and dried fruit over toward the fire. He set the tray down on a small table and flopped to the ground in front of it. "Dig in."

Cal prodded the fire once more, then turned around to grab a roll. Em sat in the chair opposite Otto, still baffled.

Otto leaned in. "She's fearsome, to be sure. And I don't like the idea of exploding imperial soldiers. My father wants to continue trading here, but he won't be able to if there's a real war."

"So no one wants to question her?"

"We want to," Cal murmured, "but we won't."

"I personally would like to keep all my organs inside my body," Sam said before taking a bite of sausage.

Em was quiet. She had observed Bronwyn for the rest of the day, and now she considered what she had seen. The woman had lost her temper twice more for petty reasons. Most of the Northerners averted their eyes and were overly subservient around the woman. In the afternoon, she had taken a few mages for a different project. They were led away to a house on the southwest side of the village, out of view, and returned an hour later looking like dried-out husks. Those mages were excused to rest but were expected to return the next day.

No one was brave enough to challenge her. And Em was starting to think Cora's tales of "accidents" might be true. But it didn't make sense. If the North wanted the best chance of surviving, shouldn't they consider all ideas and pick the best ones to implement? What made Bronwyn think her ideas were better than anyone else's?

Em's toes and legs were starting to tingle as her body finally warmed. She reached for a dried pear slice. "Otto, what does your father sell?"

"Spices, mostly. Rich cloth. Things he imports from Brildonia and Zanit."

"Did you work with him?"

"Deities, no. He's quite ashamed of me actually. Calls me a layabout."

Em wasn't quite sure how to respond to this. Self-deprecation from Otto was new. "How'd you end up at the Silver Nightingale?"

"Father was selling goods in Tucarit last year when a gang of imperial soldiers approached. They must've been off-duty because they decided to have a bit of fun with my father's goods. They shot holes in his fine silks and did foul things to several barrels of spices. Because they could. Roughed him up a bit too. They might've been drunk. But my father didn't look the other way. He was incensed. He wrote to the empress demanding retribution, and she did nothing.

"He isn't a vengeful man, but from that moment, he lost faith in Her Majesty's ability to rule justly. He has been contributing to the Northern cause ever since. I'm part of his contribution, I suppose. Send me to the fortress where my mother learned magecraft and make me into something useful."

The last he said with a wry twist to his lips. He never wanted any of this. And yet, he was here.

"Why didn't you just leave?"

"Father threatened disinheritance. Otherwise, I'd never choose this arduous lifestyle over the wealth back home. I'm just waiting for him to relent. Or I somehow find a way to earn his respect."

Em shifted in her chair, pulling her legs underneath her. She had never considered the other initiates had their own reasons for training. Sam and Cal were silent. Not unusual for Cal, but Em had a feeling that Otto was sharing information that no one had heard before.

"I had nowhere else to go," Cal said into the silence.

This admission surprised them all. Sam recovered first. "What? Strapping lad like you? Impossible."

Cal shook his head. "Merrick sent me in, after I became a target. For the soldiers. I . . . lost control of my magic a few times." He ducked, red-faced. It was the longest sentence that Em had ever heard him speak.

"What does that mean . . . 'lost control'?" Otto asked.

"I infused things I didn't mean to. When I was scared. When I was angry. Like soldier's weapons would heat up to the point of melting in their hands. Fires. Things like that."

Em thought of the time she had set a fire without knowing what she was doing. She had done it under extreme stress, and she supposed Cal—if he grew up here—would have plenty of occasions of stress. Was he a—what did the book call it—an elementer?

Cal continued. "Soldiers knew it was me. They wanted to arrest me. For violating Southern laws that regulate mages. Probably would have executed me. If they could've caught me."

"So, you're already a fugitive?" Em asked gently.

"Dunno. I've been at the Silver Nightingale a long time. Several years. Maybe they've forgotten about me."

Sam snorted. "Unlikely."

"Anyway, I'm grateful to Bronwyn. For taking me in. For training me. I didn't have anyone before." It was as if a valve had broken within Cal, and all the things he wanted to say came flooding out of him.

"Bronwyn used my energy for one of her projects last year. Me and a woman named Alia. We didn't even know what she was making, but she filtered our energy into something small. It was painful. Alia begged her to stop, but she kept going. We both almost lost consciousness before she finally stopped. It took weeks to recover."

Deities. That sounded awful. And definitely not a point in Bronwyn's favor. "How does she take energy?" Em asked.

"You know what we learned with the fourth type of magic? About cracking into someone's mind, or submitting to another? We were asked to willingly submit, and then she could access it."

"Has anyone refused?" Sam asked.

"Dunno. I suppose Bronwyn would just break through their shields if they did. There have been a few mages who were permanently damaged. Maybe they were the ones who tried to fight it."

Em felt the wrongness of it. Maybe Bronwyn was doing some larger good with the siphoned energy—the gate-ports, perhaps—but it didn't seem worth exhausting and using up other mages. And to do it even when your subject refused? That seemed almost villainous.

"I'm worried," Em blurted. She'd learned some things today that did not reflect well on the woman. Were they here laboring on behalf of a tyrant?

"It would be foolish if you weren't worried," Otto remarked.

Sam cut in again, chewing a piece of sausage, "We're here to help Fugea. Help those people get safe. Protect the town. If you can do it while avoiding the notice of the soldiers and—apparently —Bronwyn..."

"That's all any of us want," Cal said.

Em reached for a roll and wondered if she could stay subservient around the lady mage. It was not her primary mode of functioning. She had ideas. Better ways to do things. What's more, she hated to see the strong preying on the weak. Hated it so much she might do or say something imprudent.

But she couldn't withstand a battle with Bronwyn. The woman had incredible power and knowledge. Em had to remind herself of that next time she was feeling noble and mouthy. Remembering Cora's warning also triggered another thought.

"By the way, my name is Em Strider. Not Emily Stonehill. Sorry for lying."

Cal and Otto both rolled their eyes. "We know," they said.

Em shot Sam a dirty look. He'd told all of them. He was gnawing on a piece of sausage, but stopped long enough to catch her look, grin, and wink. Infuriating lout.

~

LATER THAT EVENING, Em flipped open *The Standard Book of Anything* and found an awful letter from Sam's father to Sam, his only offspring. It was cruel, and it verified the few words Sam had said about the man. Em supposed the book had been primed by Otto's father talk, but she had really been hoping for a clue about how to activate the ring. After skimming through several other useless articles, she finally gave in to her weariness and dropped off to sleep.

~

One Week and Two Days until the Solstice

THE NEXT DAY, Em awoke early and—after no help from the book—decided to test out the ring. She started layering her clothing for the wind and weather outside.

"Backing out of our deal already?" Sam was awake, but he watched her with a sleepy look. His hair was tousled, and Em tried not to think about how cozy he looked at this moment.

She shot a glance toward the couch. Cal was still fast asleep. She wiggled the ring at Sam. "I wanted to test this before we started today."

Immediately, Sam was emerging from his blankets and pulling on his boots. "I want to see what it does. Must be something spectacular if the empress wants it so badly."

"Shhh," Em hushed him. "Don't go saying that. Try keeping a secret for once."

He offered a not quite sincere look of shame and pulled on his own cloak. "Okay, let's go."

Em put another log on the hearth, stirring up the embers, and then tiptoed out the door with Monterey behind her. She circled to the far side of the house where there was a snowy field. Shivering sticks of some long-dead crop rustled in the morning wind.

"How do we test it?"

"Not sure. I've been wearing it for the past day, but I don't feel any changes." Em thought back to the Ring of Clavonion fairy tale. "Maybe I can make something happen? Like . . ." She focused on a spot in the earth and imagined a table with all kinds of breakfast foods. She stared at the stop until she was nearly cross-eyed, but nothing happened.

"Are you doing something? I can't tell," Sam commented, leaning against the cabin's exterior wall.

"I'm trying to make something appear."

Sam shook his head. "Nope. Can't make something out of nothing. Rules of magic, Strider."

Em sighed. "Okay. What if it makes me super strong? Or nimble? Or smart? How would I test those?"

"Want me to administer a math test?" Sam grinned.

Em wanted to kick him. She settled for calling him a crude name and started to pace. The stone in the ring was the third item the king received in the story. She tried to remember what the old mage told the king . . . something about "the knowledge of his people." Maybe it shared information? Like *The Standard Book of Anything*. But how? It had no pages or words. She held the ring up and studied the stone.

"What if it shields you?" Sam offered.

That didn't feel right. It didn't fit with the story. But Sam didn't know the story. She supposed he was just thinking of random powerful things it could do. Then Em felt a sharp prodding at the perimeter of her mind. Sam was doing his own experiments. It certainly didn't feel like she had any extra protection; it was just as uncomfortable as when he had done it back at the Silver Nightingale. "Stop it," she growled.

"Nope. No extra shielding," Sam said with a cheeky grin as he ceased his mental attack.

She held the ring up again. "What do the people know?" she asked it. It was silent in her fingers.

Sam guffawed.

Em glared at him. "If you aren't going to be helpful . . ."

He was still laughing. "Deities, Em. That's the last question the empress would ask."

"What do you mean?"

Sam shoved his hands in his pockets and continued to lean on the cabin wall. "The empress wants this, right? Therefore, she must know what it does. It probably does something she would find useful."

Em nodded. That made sense. "Okay. What would the empress find useful? She likes controlling people. But she already has the fountain for administering oaths."

"Which you've figured out how to break," Sam offered. "Maybe she needs a new method."

"She doesn't like magic users. Maybe this controls all the magic users."

"Try it." He held out his arms again, as if inviting a blow.

"Make Sam walk in a circle," Em said to the ring. Nothing happened.

They tried a few more iterations before Em was ready to call it quits. She was cold and irritated that this legendary ring wouldn't reveal itself. She and Sam went back inside to get ready for the rest of the day.

Otto and Cal—now awake—eyed their return curiously but said nothing. Em wondered if Cora or Phoebe had gossiped about their supposed love affair, and now it looked like they were returning from a stolen tryst. She felt a flicker of rage anew. Why had Monterey started that rumor to begin with? But then her ire abated when she realized it was a good cover story to keep the ring a secret. But she wasn't about to thank him for it.

Breakfast was hurried and simple. Cold biscuits and jam before they bundled up and trudged through the snow toward Bronwyn and the larger group.

"I wish I knew what she was planning today," Em muttered, to no one in particular. When she spoke the sentiment, she felt a flutter from the ring, still around her finger. They all nodded in agreement, ignorant of the excitement rising within her. The ring had done something.

She walked a few steps farther before muttering something about an outhouse and fell back from the group. Darting around the corner, she pulled off her mitten and stared at the ring on her icy finger. "I wish I knew what Bronwyn was planning today," she repeated.

The amber started swirling, and orange-tinted ghostly images appeared in the large stone. They were wispy like smoke and emitted no sound, yet she could make out details and understand the main points of a conversation, as though they were being fed directly into her mind. First it showed Bronwyn as she explained a new item to craft—another kind of explosive—and held up a shovel. Then it displayed Bronwyn collecting Em and two others from the lunch line for a special assignment.

As the wisps of smoke in the stone drifted away, Em whistled, low and soft. The ring told the future. Maybe. That would be of great use to the empress. Or to anyone, really.

She stuffed the ring back into her mitten and hurried to catch up with the group.

CHAPTER 28

*Strategy extends beyond individual acts of violence or peace. To truly play
the game of international sticks and stones, you must understand how your
actions will be perceived by your adversary, and how they will respond. Once
you can force their reaction, you control the game board.*

"Strategic Thinking in a Time of Conflict"
The Standard Book of Anything

The ring was correct. Bronwyn wanted a perimeter dug around the town, and explosives triggered when soldiers crossed the line.

Em found it hard not to criticize. More explosives? And so near the buildings? Wouldn't this make the town uninhabitable? And it wouldn't keep the soldiers out. It would just maim the first few who entered. Also, it was too much like the assignment yesterday. Couldn't they try something more interesting? Em thought of her ice wall, or the deep pit with imaginary snow on top, and resolved to implement at least the second one. Bronwyn wasn't keeping a close enough watch

235

to realize if she deviated. And it would work better than a shallow pit with explosives.

She grabbed one of the shovels and chose a spot as far away from the mage as possible—around the southwest corner and up almost to the west gate—and began to dig. A deep trench required her to dig through the snow and into the frozen ground. She softened the earth by infusing it with magic. She also infused her shovel to cut through the dirt more easily. Once she got deep enough, she climbed inside and continued to dig from inside the trench. She hoped Bronwyn wouldn't stroll by.

Within an hour, she was exhausted but had a trench taller than her height, and several shovel lengths wide. She climbed out and motioned to Otto, who dug nearby.

"Come look at this," she said, waving him nearer.

He strolled over, and Em stuck out an arm to keep him from the edge. He stared as she infused a thin layer of snow with a bit of energy. She directed it to drift over the pit, and the finished product looked like undisturbed snow.

"That's—" he stammered.

"Clever, right? They won't see it coming, And we don't have to explode anyone," Em said.

"Lady Bronwyn hasn't seen this, right?"

Em saw his fear and reassured him. "No. I'm not going to tell her."

"Don't. But yes. It's brilliant." He flashed her a quick smile, but quickly returned to his own trench.

She followed. "I can help you dig. Do the same thing with yours."

He leaned on his spade and studied her. "Do you have a death wish or something?"

Em pressed, "You said you didn't approve of exploding soldiers. This is an alternative."

He bit the side of his lip, then finally nodded. "But if Bronwyn comes, use your snow trick to make this look like the shallow trench I'm supposed to be digging. I don't want to end up on the wrong side of her temper."

Em flashed a smile and swung her shovel into action.

BY LUNCHTIME, Em was numb and sore. She had infused a great deal of energy into her shovel, and it was still backbreaking work to remove all the loosened dirt. To her surprise, Otto kept pace, digging and magicking alongside her. Em's estimation of the young man grew. Perhaps there was more to him than spoiled and rich.

They had a trench nearly five houses long, curving across the wide west entrance to Fugea. Em put the finishing touches on the thin layer of ice, and marked the perimeter in the snow, so no one would accidentally fall in.

She and Otto walked back toward the south gate, where the locals had set up a lunch line to feed the volunteers. They were chatting idly about the blisters on their hands when Em spotted Bronwyn. The mage was first in line for food and sported a resting scowl.

The ring had warned her. Bronwyn would seek her out for a "special assignment" over the lunch break. In other words, the woman was going to drain her—leave her an energy-less husk for the next week.

"Not if I can help it," Em muttered. She did an about-face and headed back toward the west gate.

Otto let out a surprised question at her outburst, so she covered.

"Forgot something. Go ahead without me." She started jogging back along the edge of town, hoping that her luck would hold and Bronwyn wouldn't come looking for her.

She leapt over her own trap and reentered Fugea from the west. Her jog had warmed her, but the sweat was now chilly against her skin. Deities, she was cold. If only she could find a place to warm up for a few minutes and get something to eat.

Maybe a marketplace was nearby? A mercantile equivalent?

She wandered the weatherworn streets, getting her first real look at the heart of Fugea. The buildings were squat and huddled together, as if to keep out the chill. Streets signs were so faded she couldn't read them, and the main street and alleys were a slog of icy mud. Maybe when the fighting was over, Em could come back and make repairs. After all, upkeep must be difficult in this climate, but she could use magic to help. Maybe special pavers on the main roads that would melt the ice? And protection on the wood so it wouldn't warp as badly. She was so pleased with her ideas that she wished someone were around to share them with. But the streets were completely deserted. Em hadn't laid eyes on a single Fugean, except for those who were helping the mages. Maybe most people had evacuated.

At that moment, wind rushed through the narrow gaps between buildings, and Em ducked deeper into her cloak but found little relief from the bite. While she was huddling, she nearly missed a faded "Market" sign hanging over a small barn-like building. She hurried over to the structure and entered quickly to escape the wind.

She gazed around at the open rafters and the hay-strewn floor. The interior looked like a barn, too, but instead of animals, there were vendors. Ten stalls sat in this room, a few occupied with merchants. It didn't take Em long to discover that the entry structure was only the beginning of an endless winding hallway filled with vendors of all kinds. Not all of the booths were full, and there were very few shoppers, but Em still found plenty to draw her attention. There were shops selling spices, like Otto's father did. But there were also hats and scarves and mittens and homemade baskets and jewels mined from the Antillei Mountains, crafted into fine wearables, and meat pies and roasted nuts and spiced wine and hot tea and everything you could possibly imagine.

"On a busy day, this whole place would be packed," a merchant commented as Em studied a row of small stone figurines at her stall.

"Has everyone evacuated?" Em asked.

"Some. Those who have family nearby." The woman gestured toward a string of empty booths farther down. "Some merchants are still in town, but with no customers . . ." She clicked her tongue. "Me, I'm an optimist!"

Em chuckled with the merchant. "I know the feeling. Can I ask—I'm not from around here—what person these represent?" She held up one stone figure.

The woman squinted at the piece, then at Em. "That one is a matriarch. An ancestor. In the North, we like to seek wisdom from those who come before us. We light incense and pray for guidance and protection. Highly illegal, by the way, so don't go shouting it about."

"Illegal? Why?"

"Got me there. But the empress, she don't like it. It's the deities or nothing with her, never mind that we have our own traditions."

Em held the little figure in her palm. It was simple and round, but with some obvious female characteristics. She didn't know much about her own ancestors. Her parents weren't around when she was young, so she didn't hear stories. Her great-grandmother Emaline— her namesake—was a mage. Em felt a strong tug to learn more about her, and about all the women who had come before her. And the men, too, she supposed.

The merchant interrupted her thoughts. "Are you one of the mages come to protect us, then?"

Em nodded, ducking her head. "I don't know too much magic yet, but I wanted to help."

"But you aren't a Northerner." The woman's voice held a hint of puzzlement. Em wasn't sure how to explain to the woman her circumstances—her bargain with Sam and her understanding of the conflict. She didn't want the woman to perceive her as some kind of hero, because she definitely wasn't. She was coerced here. So she shrugged and held up the figure once more. "I don't have any local coin. Do you take Esnanian money?"

"I'll take whatever you've got, hun."

EM STROLLED FARTHER through the unending wooden tunnels. The stone figure and a stick of incense were safely tucked in her pocket next to her coins. Her stomach rumbled, so she searched for a food vendor among the empty stalls. She finally purchased a meat-and-rice dish that smelled wonderful. The vendor, an ancient man, winked at her and rolled up her dish in a thin bread so she could hold it and eat as she walked. It was delicious and warmed her from the inside out.

She continued to wander the rickety corridor, looking at the structure overhead and trying to guess when the market entered a new building, and in what part of Fugea she would find herself when she finally exited. It was impressive infrastructure, and far superior—considering the weather—to an outdoor market.

She found a quiet corner behind a whole row of empty stalls and leaned against an external wall. She was curious if Bronwyn's actions had changed since Em had thwarted her original intent. She asked the question again of the amber ring, and it fluttered.

But it showed her the same image. Bronwyn directing the volunteers to make explosives, and Bronwyn collecting Em and two others out of the lunch line for an energy draining. But it was no longer possible. Em wasn't in the lunch line. She was here. Hiding.

She felt a prick of shame. Someone else would take her place with Bronwyn and be drained instead. She should take her turn, same as everyone else, right?

But then defiance rose to the surface. Em was under no obligation to do anything for Bronwyn. Granted, the woman had housed her for a month or so. Taught her some magic. (Actually, Phoebe mostly taught her, not Bronwyn.) But Em wasn't one of her subjects. She hadn't sworn fealty or obedience. She had volunteered. And she should get to decide what she did or didn't do for the cause.

Feeling more steadfast—freer—Em continued through the market. She heard a familiar voice and turned to find Merrick several booths down, conversing with a pie vendor. Em hadn't spoken with him much in the brief time he was at the Silver Nightingale, but Sam and the others thought highly of the grizzled man.

Em called out a greeting.

"Ah! One of the mages. Emily, is it?" A broad smile spread across the scruffy face.

Em returned the grin. "It's Em, actually. Good to see you again, sir."

He introduced Em to the vendor. "Jordy was telling me there's no fortifications on the eastern side of town. Folks are starting to get worried. None anywhere else, either, except the explosives on the southern road."

Em jumped in. "That isn't entirely true. There are some enchanted trench pits by the west gate."

Merrick studied her. "Did Bronwyn order that?"

Em flushed. She had intended to hide her own involvement, but Merrick's shrewd gaze saw through her vague words. "Not exactly."

Jordy spoke in a creaky tenor, "Does it matter, Merr? The gal's doing what needs to be done." It sounded like her work solved a problem, so she supposed these two at least would not broadcast her mutiny. She let out a breath.

"True." Merrick scratched his beard. "You think you could do something on the eastern side? Soldiers use that just as often as the south. Don't want you to offend the Lady Bronwyn, though. That woman doesn't like to be . . ." He stopped his words, as if afraid to say what they were all thinking. It was dangerous to ignore orders from Bronwyn. Even more dangerous to work around her plans. But his words were a confirmation that he would keep Em's activities secret.

"I can try," Em said. "I was thinking about an ice wall. Might need some wood and tools to make a frame for the snow and ice. But I bet we could get it built in a few days."

Merrick told her where to find tools and scrap wood and clapped her on the back with gratitude. Jordy was ready to gift her a meat pie for helping, but Merrick bought one for her instead. "Maybe share it with your roommates, eh? Thanks, lass. We'll keep her away, if we can."

Em waved goodbye and started in the direction she had come. Then, realizing she was hopelessly turned around, she asked directions of the nearest vendor—an artist who created metal decor out of scrap—and found an exit near the southeast quarter. She ducked back out into the cold, reinforced by her warm lunch and new plans. She marched in the direction of her lodging with the meat pie, wrapped in paper, tucked beneath her arm.

~

EM HAD BEEN GONE a long time. Her foray through the market and stop at the cabin brought her back to work several hours into the afternoon. When she returned to the trenches at the west gate, Otto dropped his shovel and rushed over.

"Where in the dark demon hole were you?"

Em held up her hands, placating him. "I went exploring and lost track of time."

"Bronwyn was raging mad. Apparently, it was your turn to be used by Her Ladyship."

Em already knew this, and her face must've shown it.

Otto's expression twisted in disbelief. "You knew? Were you . . . hiding? It's going to be worse when she gets ahold of you."

"That's the least of my worries. How do you feel about some justifiable insubordination tomorrow?" Em explained her encounter with Merrick and Jordy at the market and her plan to build an ice wall along the eastern edge of the town. "Will you help?" she pressed.

Otto's face flickered with fear but then hardened. "Yes. I'm with you. I'd wager Cal and Cora will be also."

"Maybe Sam too," Em said. It was speculation, but she trusted him enough to bring him into the scheme. He had changed since his trip to the North. Or at least she hoped he had. Otherwise, he had fooled her so completely that she was setting herself up for a stunning betrayal.

She picked up her shovel, and Otto followed her lead. "Let's get the western side finished so we can focus solely on the wall tomorrow."

THEY LABORED the rest of the afternoon, stopping only to rub feeling back into their hands and stomp their frozen feet. As the sun dipped below the rooftops, they surveyed their line of trenches, spreading across the west side of town. They placed a trench in front of every minor road and alley spreading from the southwest corner up to the main road cutting across Fugea. Any soldier trying to enter from the west would surely fall in, unless they ran beyond the road before cutting in. Unlikely.

Em was exhausted, but proud of their work. She pulled Otto through the middle of town to avoid the large group of mages on the southern side, including Bronwyn.

When they reached the cabin, Em paused at the door and turned to Otto. "Should we have a plan? I don't want to spring the idea on them right away. Maybe I mention the defenses, but mix it in with other stories. Then you could say you heard one of the locals talking about the east gate. After—"

At that moment the door swung open. Sam and Cal stood grinning on the other side. They had clearly heard every word. Em reddened.

Sam yanked them both inside and closed the door. "Out with it, Strider. What wild scheme are you planning?"

"We're in," Cal said bluntly.

"Just like that? Don't you want to know—"

"No," Cal said.

Sam nodded. "Bronwyn drained two Fugean mages today and screamed at three Northerners who tried to ask about the other defenses. She was moments away from sticking needles under Silas's fingernails when she realized you were missing. It's time a few of us went rogue. But we'll have to watch our backs."

Em grinned and led them to the meat pie she had been gifted. And then she pulled out her magic waterskin to pass around. While they ate and drank, she described her encounter with Merrick and sketched out the most magnificent ice wall her mind could conjure.

CHAPTER 29

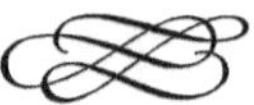

The Prutian Tribes hold sing-alongs that require call-and-response from all attendees. This gives them something to do on cold nights. Avoid these if you are able. They are long and boring.

"Northern Oddities and Their Logical Explanations"
The Standard Book of Anything

One Week and One Day until the Solstice

The next morning, Em awoke and immediately checked the ring beneath her blankets. *What will Bronwyn do today?* She had checked it twice more the evening before, but the images hadn't changed. But today, the image swirled and revealed Bronwyn assigning different explosives to the smaller crowd of mages. Then Em saw her discover the trenches by quite literally falling into one.

She let out a giggle, then stifled herself. She hadn't told Sam what the ring could do, and she knew he would be irritated that she kept it a secret. For that matter, she didn't know what the others would do if they knew she had stolen a ring from the Silver Nightingale.

She poked her head above her blanket, and her eyes met Monterey's aquamarine ones. He had heard. Was watching as he lay in his cot a few paces away. But then his eyes crinkled and he was laughing at her.

Em smiled. She didn't exactly trust him, but Sam was her friend now. Might as well tell him what the ring did. She stuck her hand partially out of the blankets and wiggled her ring finger. That should be enough for him to know she had learned something, and she didn't want to tell him in front of everyone.

His eyebrows raised, and then he gave her a subtle nod. He understood. They would chat later.

The others were stirring now. Em heard Cal shift on the sofa and Otto tossing his blankets aside from the bedroom. She sat up, pulled her mittens over the ring, and started layering up for the day.

EM WENT EARLY to gather the wood and tools Merrick had offered. Otto was able to get a note to Cora, and they all assembled on the main road near the eastern entrance.

"I thought you said to keep my ideas to myself," Em said quietly to Cora.

"Yeah, well." Cora looked down. "Somebody needs to do something."

Em smiled at the girl. She was afraid, but she had shown up anyway.

"No Silas or Phoebe?" Em asked, scanning the group.

Otto wrinkled his nose. "We couldn't tell Silas without alerting Elias. And Elias scares the piss out of me. If he didn't like what we were doing, he could destroy us all."

"Phoebe's with Bronwyn," Cora said. "She would give us away."

Em nodded. She supposed that made sense. Phoebe had been

teaching for Bronwyn for a long time. Loyalties grown over decades were not easily broken.

"Okay. Well, the plan is to build a wall to keep imperial soldiers from entering from this side." Em showed them all the hastily drawn plans from the night before. "I'll make some wooden frames, and we can start packing snow into them to make snow bricks. Then we can stack them and pour water over the top of the structure to make it sturdy and impossible to climb. I'm thinking a wall as tall as Cal might be best."

Otto spoke up, "How do we connect the wall to the city, so they don't just go around it?"

"Yeah, can we even make a wall this long and tall by the end of today?" Cora asked.

Sam jumped to the rescue. "We can attach the wall to one of the houses on the southeast edge and seal it with water. And we don't have to do the whole thing, just from the southeast corner to the eastern road. That's enough to discourage any soldiers who skirt the explosives."

Cal offered, "I can magically melt the snow bricks together without needing water."

It would save time; the others nodded their assent. They started shoveling snow with the spades Em had found in Merrick's shed, and Em began building wooden frames. This was going to work.

By MIDMORNING, they had a whole field of snow bricks. Em had built the snow frames so they could roll and create the bricks in a long row without much manual intervention. Cal, Cora, and Otto had broken off to start stacking the wall while Em and Sam began rolling the frames on each new row. The others had quickly innovated, finding a piece of wood to slide under multiple snow bricks to carry over to the wall and then infusing the wood to be slippery at the right moment, so the bricks would slide off and into place. It was exhausting work, but Em didn't even register her fatigue. She glanced around at the row of snow bricks with a swelling in her chest. This was going to keep people safe.

Sam set his frames next to hers and started them turning. He shot her a grin and asked, "What does it do?"

It took a moment for Em to register his question. The ring. She knew he would find a time to ask her, and she decided to be truthful. "It tells me what someone will do next." After glancing around to make sure the others were behind them and out of earshot, she pulled off her mitten and held her hand in front of them. Sam stood beside her, their shoulders pressed together to block the wind as she demonstrated. "Show me what Bronwyn will do next." It showed the same wispy image as this morning—Bronwyn directing the explosive-making and falling in a pit. He laughed as the mage dropped out of sight.

"It only works once a day and then resets. And I think once I see these things, I can prevent them from happening."

"How do you know?"

"I saw yesterday that Bronwyn was going to pull me aside for a 'special project.' Only I wasn't there. So it didn't happen." Sam wrinkled his brow, and Em returned her chilly hand to its mitten.

"Those were the pits you and Otto dug yesterday, right? On the west side?" Sam voice was barely louder than the wind gust that pulled at Em's cloak.

"Yes. Why?"

"I'm wondering. If Bronwyn just discovered those . . . well, she's a smart woman. Wouldn't she figure out that someone is doing extra things. And she knows who is missing . . ."

Em let out a string of curses. "She's going to come check this side and catch us all."

"Unless we can stop her from falling in the pit," Sam reasoned.

Em pulled out the ring and watched Bronwyn fall again. She couldn't tell what time of day it was. Maybe it hadn't happened yet. Maybe someone could keep her distracted so she never wandered to the west.

Sam glanced at their group, at the two dozen snow blocks, then nodded, as if deciding something, and strode south.

"What are you going to do?" Em shouted.

"Keep building," he yelled over his shoulder, then broke into a run.

EM HAD QUICKLY REINFUSED her warning rock, this time with a loud bell clang noise so they would all be alerted if anyone was within sight of the wall. They had worked through lunch and late into the afternoon, and Sam still wasn't back. Em was starting to worry, but it seemed like whatever he had done, he had kept Bronwyn away. The wall was coming along. It was a ten-minute walk from the southeast corner of town to the east gate. And that whole distance had an ice-and-snow wall as protection. Cal had sealed it all together. To test it, they all pushed against a small section, but it didn't budge. It was magnificent.

The others were marveling at the work, too tired to do much but collapse in the frozen dirt—where the snow had been before they shoveled it all up. Em kept glancing south, waiting for Sam or Bronwyn to appear.

They decided to call it a day; everyone wanted to get out of the cold.

"Should we go to the marketplace? Hot cider on me," Em suggested. The others agreed, and they trotted off to a side entrance of the market. Cora led the way, since she was familiar with the town. Otto trailed behind Cora, making careful conversation.

Cal walked in companionable silence next to Em, and she was shocked to discover that she liked these people. Maybe it was the shared goal, or simple proximity, but Em felt foolish for keeping to herself at the Silver Nightingale. Even Cal, who initially seemed like a threat, turned out to be as gentle as a puppy, and as kind as anyone back home.

Back home. Em felt a wave of longing as she thought of Liam. She wondered what he was doing right now. Was he still angry at her?

Had he continued baking, or had he gotten fed up and returned to Gillamor to live with his brother and sister-in-law? Would he be proud of what she had done here? What she had learned? Or impatient with her for dallying so long after she found the ring? Had he ever been here, in his soldiering days, maybe?

She tried to picture him doing the terrible things imperial soldiers did in the North—at least what she had heard and read—and she couldn't fathom it. She hoped he hadn't. Surely he hadn't.

She pictured his warm brown eyes spotting her behind the row of customers in his bakery. She always came at the end of the day, and when he saw her, a smile lit up his face. She noted the energy with which he moved to serve each customer until he got to the end of the line—to her. Then he would flip the sign in the window to closed, take her face in his flour-covered hands, and kiss her. Then they would sit at their normal table by the big mixing bowl, holding hands. He would ask about the mundane details of her day. She would laugh at the impressions he did of certain customers. It was a small ritual, but it was theirs. And Em missed him so much her heart ached. Yet she dreaded their reunion and what it might bring.

She couldn't leave Fugea until Sam said their agreement was fulfilled. Or until the soldiers attacked. But it was more than the agreement that kept her there now. She couldn't leave until she was sure the people would be safe and Sam knew that she wasn't her parents.

THEY ARRIVED AT THE MARKETPLACE, and Cora led them to a drink vendor who had a few small tables next to his booth. The others moved the tables together while Em ordered a round, dropping her coins on the counter.

A short while later, she had a tray full of steaming mugs, which she ferried to the group.

"I'd like to propose a toast," Em said as the mugs were handed around. "To my friends from the Silver Nightingale. By your sweat, and shivering, and brave actions today, you have made the town of Fugea a bit safer. Thank you. And cheers."

They all raised their mugs and their voices to those words. Warmth crept back into Em's body, from the drink and the indoors, but also from the feeling of rightness, and belonging. Something she hadn't felt since she had left Brookerby.

"What's this now? Out for a drink without me?" Silas leaned against the wall behind them. A chorus of cheers went up as they shifted their chairs to make room for him. Em jumped up to buy another cider for him.

"Interesting that you're here," Silas commented. "I haven't seen any of you all day." He looked at Em, "Or yesterday."

Em offered him a wry smile from the counter. "Side project," she said.

Cora hooted with laughter. "She's gone rogue! I guess we have too."

Silas's eyebrows lifted. "And you didn't invite me?"

Cora patted the seat next to her. "You're invited. We didn't think Elias would approve, so we didn't want him catching wind of it."

Silas agreed. His older brother was not a rule breaker.

Em placed the newly poured drink in front of him and began explaining their plans. Silas studied her with a glint in his eye. "This is brilliant. I'm in."

"Did you see Monterey with the main group? He didn't come back," Otto said. Cal looked at Silas, waiting.

"We had an inkling that Bronwyn might get suspicious and come looking for us. He was going to keep her from doing that," Em answered. Then she sipped her cider, trying not to look worried. Had Sam betrayed them? Or had something happened to him?

The others didn't respond, but they exchanged concerned looks.

Silas coughed. "Actually, he was stuck to her like glue today. She kept shooing him away, yelling at him, and then finally she pulled him away for a "special project." And by "special project," I mean she drained him for her energy stores."

Em let out a soft curse. The others were silent.

"Can we do anything? To speed his recovery?" Em asked the group. "Give up a little bit of our strength to help him?"

Cal bobbled his head. "I don't know if that would work."

"We've always assumed those selected would just have to rest for the next week. No one has tried to speed it along. It would make Lady Bronwyn angry, and you could massively wreck someone's brain," Otto said.

"What is the deal with you and Sam, anyway?" Cora asked Em. "He told us—"

"Yeah, I know what he told you." Em rolled her eyes. "It wasn't true. Well, the fake name was true." She turned to Silas. "I'm Em Strider. Nice to meet you."

He smiled back at her, not shocked by the news. Sam must've told him too.

"So you're not into him? Not even a little? Girl, those blue eyes . . ." Cora said.

"We were never anything romantic. The first time I met him was at his family's resort in Arrenmore. He drugged me and held me there against my will."

"Ooh, spicy," Otto said. Silas snorted.

"No! It was terrifying and infuriating," Em spat, then she softened. "We were mortal enemies when he showed up at the Silver Nightingale. But I don't know. He's changed." She thought about him jogging away to distract Bronwyn so they could keep building the eastern wall. So they could keep the town safe. "I think he's turned into a good guy." And she realized it was true. The old Sam would've never sacrificed himself for the greater good.

"To Sam and his dreamy eyes," Cal said. Cora giggled.

"To Sam," Em responded. They all clinked their glasses and drank.

THEY SAT around the little table with the wind howling outside, telling stories and making each other laugh. A few villagers stopped by to thank the group for their work on the wall, patting them on the back and buying a round of drinks. This made Em's heart swell, and she was glad they had done it. Bronwyn be damned.

Em bowed out when they started singing Northern drinking songs. She said goodnight and reminded them to be back at the east gate tomorrow to finish the job. The rest barely waved and continued with the bawdy limericks they were creating.

Laughing to herself, Em strode along the marketplace alley, looking for the southeastern exit she had used yesterday. The market was mostly closed and dark, and rather eerie in the late evening. She wondered if she should've waited for Otto and Cal to walk home with, but she had no reason to think the city unsafe. Nevertheless, she quickened her pace and found an exit that looked right. But when she got outside and found the main roads, she realized she was in the southwestern quarter. She would have to walk at least ten minutes in the cold to get to her lodgings. She ducked back into the darkened marketplace and kept walking.

"Out late, lovie?" A deep slurred voice sounded to her right. She turned and saw a large man coming toward her from the shadows. He was tipsy, and Em didn't like the way he was approaching her.

"Stop," she commanded as she held up a hand. "Go home, sir."

But he did not stop. He came close enough for Em to smell the liquor on his breath as he said, "Come stay with me, sweet—" and tried to grab her wrist.

Even six months ago, Em would've frozen. From shock. From fear. From the belief that most people were good, and surely this man didn't mean her real harm.

She didn't think that way anymore.

And she had learned a few things in the sparring ring.

She leapt away from his grasp, casting about for a weapon. Nothing. He lunged for her, and she stepped sideways while grabbing his wrist with both hands and pulling it behind him as she moved. He tried to grab her with his free hand, but the impossible angle of his right arm drove him to his knees. It helped that the man was inebriated. Em couldn't have overpowered him if he were sober; he was almost the size of Cal.

Em twisted his wrist up to the middle of his back and then put her other arm across the back of his neck, pushing his face into the dirt. She had a knee on his non-twisted arm, just in case he started flailing. She had subdued him in less than a minute. Elias would be proud.

But far from feeling satisfaction and relief, Em felt rage. How dare this man? She was breaking her body day after day to keep this town safe, and he was lurking in dark corners, like a rat. He whimpered on the ground, and Em ground her knee into his arm. He was not the victim here. He was the predator.

And so, she tried something she shouldn't have done. It was the kind of thing that made Bronwyn villainous, the thing that turned ancient mages into monsters. But she was angry. And she could do it. She broke through the defenses in his mind.

It wasn't exactly easy. If a geranium had a thick membrane, this man had a brick wall. But the alcohol had made it a wobbly wall, and Em struck the same spot over and over again, as if with a hammer. The only thought was that this man attacked her in a dark alley when she was alone. That had she been weaker, or untrained, or tipsy, he would've hurt her, in more ways than one.

And when she broke through, she felt the man's energy stores—dull and pulsing—waiting for her to take. So she did. She had never done it before, but it came easily. The opposite of infusing an object. Like siphoning magic when she was unmaking an object. Like sucking the power from a person with a straw. It took only a minute or two, but when she was done, the man was trembling and unable to stand. Em gave him a push and he rolled over into a fetal position, looking utterly shaken.

Without another word, Em turned and stalked away into the dark hallway of the market.

CHAPTER 30

Underestimate the cold at your own peril.

"The Dangers of Low Temperatures"
The Standard Book of Anything

She was nearly to the cabin when she realized two things. First, she was quivering. Had that just happened? And what had she done? She felt the weight of it and realized that it was a monstrous thing to do. No matter what he had tried to do to her. She stole his energy? What was she thinking? Second, she realized how hearty she felt. She could run around Fugea five times. She could go work another twelve hours building her ice wall. Is this what Bronwyn felt when she drained people?

With her hand on the cabin door, she realized something else. She could try to give Sam some energy again. He wouldn't have to be laid up all week waiting to heal.

She burst through the door, teeming with life, and saw him on his cot, under blankets, looking utterly wretched.

"Monterey? You look terrible." Her voice was louder than she remembered, echoing through the empty house. The fire was down to embers, so she put another log on the hearth before turning to him.

"Strider." His voice was barely a whisper. Em trotted over and knelt down next to him. "She drained me. But she doesn't know . . . she thinks you left."

"You did good, Sam." Em—without realizing what she was doing—brushed his dark hair off his forehead and felt his cheeks. His skin was alarmingly cold, and his eyes had dulled to nearly her own color of blue-gray. He looked so weak. Ignoring the feeling that she should leave it alone—that she shouldn't be smoothing his hair and touching his face—she went one step further. "I can fix you. I have some extra energy. Will you let me in your mind?"

She saw a slight hint of fear in his eyes, but when they focused on hers, his expression softened. "Okay." He closed his eyes, his hand trembling up to grasp hers. His fingers were ice, and she started rubbing them to warm them. His hands were large and surprisingly rough. She accidentally brushed his knuckle by the missing finger with her forefinger and flushed, feeling a strange protectiveness that she shouldn't have been feeling. Best to get on with it.

She prodded his mental defenses. In his state, and because he was willing, they were no more than a gauzy film, and she brushed past them without effort. Then, with a brief fumbling of what to do, she started to infuse him with the energy she had stolen. His body started to warm. Color slowly crept back into his face, and his grip on her hand tightened.

Em tried to keep her mind blank. She didn't want to accidentally infuse some lifelong instructions into him. Although . . . No. He had trusted her. She finally slowed the flow, feeling her own strength ebb to what it was after a long day out in the cold. Then she left off, backing out of his mind and replacing the gauzy curtain.

His eyes were bright aqua again. Those dreamy eyes, as Cora called them, trained on her own in amazement. Em had been kneeling beside him, and now sat back on her heels, feeling exhausted. He sat up at the edge of the cot, still holding her hand.

"How?"

Em began to tremble anew, remembering the attack and what she had done. Maybe she wasn't a good person. She got a small taste of power and used it to take revenge. And then, just now . . .

"Hey, hey, what's this? Did you give too much?" Sam was out of his cot and crouching beside her, still gripping her hand. She held it back, tightly, feeling the tilt from her shifting understanding of herself.

"I took that energy. It wasn't mine." The weight of what she had done felt like an anvil on her stomach. "A man in the market—tried to attack me, and I—"

"Hey, shhh." Sam lifted his free hand and brushed her wet cheek. Had she been crying? In front of Sam? She shuddered. "A man attacked you? And you stole his energy? Strider, you've embraced your dark side."

Em laughed, despite herself, then suppressed a sob. "I shouldn't have. I'm just as bad as Bronwyn."

"Did you kill him?"

She shook her head. "I don't think so."

He brushed her knuckles with his thumb in soothing circles. "Two minutes ago, I was a husk. I didn't even know if I would survive the night. Now, look at me. You helped me. And you kept yourself safe. And you . . . let's say you reappropriated some energy that was being poorly used. You even let him live. I don't see anything wrong with any of this."

His hand still gripped hers, softened and warmed. She leaned her shoulder against his, and he gave her hand a final, gentle squeeze before letting go.

"Thank you," she said.

As they sat together on the floor in front of the fire, something itched in the back of her mind. Sam was right. She was changing. She felt angrier. But also, she was helping people, wasn't she? But none of her actions had made her safer. If anything, she had leaned into defying the most powerful mage alive.

Her mind flashed again to the man in the alleyway. And then, unbidden, to the dead beast in the maze and her blood-splattered hammer. She had done those things. Comparatively, they hadn't felt that different, except Em experienced instant remorse over the beast.

She saw herself, as if from far away, and wondered—not for the first time—if something was broken within her. Maybe it happened when the empress pronounced her death. Or maybe it started much earlier—when Gram questioned her judgment, or the moment she chopped down the warding tree, or discovered her parents had forgotten her, or when she took the unbreakable oath. Or maybe it started when the warding tree fell.

The man in the alleyway had it coming. Sam approved. But what would Liam say about it? And Gram? Because she had a feeling—if they knew all of it—they would be horrified.

CHAPTER 31

I give this book of poetry to you, you beautiful sad man, so when you read its silky words, you can remember my skin on yours.

"Note from Marissandre to Samuel Monterey,
on the title page of Rousos Sonnets"
The Standard Book of Anything

One Week until the Solstice

The next morning, they were back at the wall, joined by Silas, who praised their efforts from the day before. A wet snow had started to fall, so they all huddled out of the wind and planned their work for the day. Sam was off Bronwyn's radar; she would assume he'd be recuperating all week. And she believed Em had left town. Thus the two of them were free to continue the ice wall without fear of discovery. The others might have to worry.

"I'm not going back," Cora pouted. "I don't want to be drained."

Their heads swiveled toward Sam, who looked healthy and ready to build. "Bronwyn might be going easy on us, since the soldiers will be here soon?" Otto suggested. Em hadn't told anyone about her after-hours encounter, and Sam said nothing about the energy transfer. But Em knew they were all suspicious. No one bounced back after a day.

"Don't kid yourselves. I still feel terrible," Sam offered. The others looked dubious. Sam appeared to be the picture of health.

Em spoke, "There are a lot of mages at the south gate. What are the odds Bronwyn notices us missing?"

Otto, Cora, Cal, and Silas eyed each other. No one spoke.

Finally, Silas said, "What if we just use the warning rock again? That way we can hide if she comes looking."

"Good morning, mages! Great snowdrifts, that's something." Merrick's voice cut the morning air. They all jumped. They hadn't even heard him coming.

"Sir—" Silas stuttered. "We can explain."

"Oh, I know all about it. Em and I had a chat a few days ago." Merrick grinned at Em and gave her a thumbs-up. "It's quite impressive. Although you've had good weather until now. Not sure what you can do with this storm coming. I just wanted to say keep up the good work. I don't think the great lady mage is suspicious, but I'll keep her out of your hair today. Strategy meetings and all."

"Thanks, Merrick," Sam said, clapping the older man on the shoulder. "Are the imperial soldiers close?"

"Ah, that's what I wanted to talk to you about. They've been spotted about a day away, to the southeast, so it's likely fighting will begin tomorrow. They'll surely wait until after the snowfall tonight. I'm evacuating the villagers through the north gate today and tomorrow. I encourage you all to keep your things with you. In case you need to make a hasty exit. But perhaps you would consider staying for a few hours after they appear? Provide some opposition and help the civilians get clear."

Cora nodded. "You can count on us."

"I knew I could. Fugea is forever grateful. I'll send someone out here today with lunch."

He shook their hands, ending with Em. He spoke in a low tone, just to her. "If you ever need help, come straight to old Merr. I'm grateful for all you've done."

She nodded and thanked him.

Then he was gone, strolling back into town on the east-west road.

Em turned back to the group, and they were beaming. Amazing how a bit of praise could lift their spirits so much. Could lift hers.

THE GROUP EFFORT, and Merrick's praise, reminded Em of cleaning up Brookerby in the aftermath of the fall of the warding tree. The villagers had turned out to help repair storefronts and clear away debris. Em assigned jobs based on skills, but she had all the care of a dizzy heifer tromping through a mud puddle. Liam had quickly stepped up beside her and spoke to each person as they passed. Not about anything in particular, just an acknowledgment that they had shown up, and something personal. Something Em hadn't bothered to do.

Later, when they were walking back to the cottage, Em brought it up. Liam shrugged.

"No, it was a big deal," she insisted. "I might've had a mutiny. You made them feel appreciated. I should've done that."

Liam looked bemused. "It wasn't intended to be criticism. You're harder on yourself than they would ever be."

He was right. She was hard on herself, but that's how she improved. How she learned. "I can remember to do that next time."

Liam stopped and brushed a stray hair from her forehead. "You are magnificent. The only reason I walked up there was Gendry had made me a sweater, and I wanted to thank her. I don't think I've ever owned anything knitted like that. Much less with a croissant stitched on it."

Em laughed. Gendry's sweaters were legendary. Liam was now officially part of the town.

Liam continued. "I just wanted to talk to them. It wasn't any kind of commentary or correction on what you were doing."

"Really?"

"Truly. But I wonder how much you take to heart that wasn't intended to be a judgment. I want you to know that I see that about you. That I think you are fine the way you are. That you don't have to keep proving your worth to us. To me."

Em had kissed him. Told him he was perfectly fine too. But his words bounced around in her brain for weeks afterward. What did that mean? She was constantly trying to improve, but did he think she was trying to prove something? Trying to earn love from the town? It didn't paint a very good picture of her, and she wondered how on earth she could correct something like that. One thing was for sure: she wouldn't forget to thank people who had showed up.

BY THE TIME JORDY—THE merchant Em had met in the market— brought hot soup for lunch, they had created enough bricks to finish the wall curving up toward the northeast edge of town.

Cora and Otto were stacking the snow bricks, but they were doing a lot more giggling than stacking. Em leaned over to Silas and said, "Are you seeing what I'm seeing?"

"Oh yeah," he replied. "Otto's been sweet on her for ages. Been too afraid to make a move. Until now, anyway." He wiggled his shoulders suggestively, and Em laughed. Silas didn't miss anything. She wondered if Otto had said something to Cora at the market the night before.

"Talking about those two?" Sam asked. "They've been cozy all morning. It's adorable."

She waved them over, sorry to disrupt their flirting.

They all sat at the base of the ice wall slurping the hot potato-and-leek soup. Sam plopped next to Em, his shoulder brushing hers.

"How are you feeling today?" she asked, half expecting the energy she had transferred to have worn off.

"Just fine. A little cold, but aren't we all?" His eyes were bright in the falling snow, and Em felt a twinge of relief, and a twinge of something else she didn't care to name as she looked at him. She glanced away and realized the group was watching their interaction with barely concealed smiles. They were getting the completely wrong idea, and there was no way she could shout that at them without raising more suspicions. She inched away from the warmth of his shoulder and diverted her attention to her soup, brow furrowed.

A silence fell over the group as they ate. Em made a list in her head: Finish the wall. Return supplies. Prepare to leave. Avoid Bronwyn.

"Before we get back to the wall, maybe you all can go home, warm up, and collect your things?" Em suggested to the group. They were too busy eating to do more than bob their heads in agreement. Except Cora whispered something to Otto and he smiled at her, then whispered something back and she giggled.

They were giddy together. How had Em not seen that before?

Sam leaned in and said, quiet enough for only her to hear, "Have you checked the ring today?"

She shook her head and whispered, "We should. After lunch."

Silas stood. "Not you two also. Maybe Cal and I will go smooch behind the market after this."

Cal smiled and wickedly raised an eyebrow. Silas burst out laughing and patted Cal on the shoulder. "Sorry, guy. I've got a town to evacuate." Cal shrugged his shoulders and went back to his soup.

Em started to protest. She and Sam were not—crumb. Silas was already gone.

She finished her soup and stood. "I'm off to the cabin. Cal? Otto? Sam?"

"I'm going to help Cora's family get packed up first," Otto said.

Cal patted the bag beside him. "Already got my things."

Sam stood. Em's brain was waving large warning flags. Of course they would think she and Sam were an item if they were always running off alone together. "Cal, you can still come get warm," she said, desperate for a group instead of a pair.

"I'm good."

Darn him. She gave up, and she and Sam trudged through the new accumulation of snow toward their lodgings. She thought she heard a wolf whistle from the group and resisted the urge to throw a snowball at them.

As soon as they were away from the other mages, Sam spoke, "I've been thinking. The ring only works once per day, right? We should check on the imperial soldiers instead of Bronwyn. Might be nice to know when they show up. If they do. And where they will try to enter the town."

Em agreed, and as they walked, she prompted the ring to reveal what the soldiers approaching Fugea would do.

The ring swirled, and the amber muddied. It showed the gold-and-blue crest of the empress on miserable soldiers caught in a whirl of snow. Em almost felt sorry for them. Then the picture changed and it showed darkness and the same group of soldiers approaching the southeast corner of the town. Explosives triggered, and the whole group shifted away from the south gate and toward the east.

"It's a good thing we built that wall," Em muttered. She saw in her mind's eye the ease with which the soldiers could've marched into town. Bronwyn had not provided good protection, despite her fine speeches and school of mages. Was the lady mage really that blind? Or was there another reason she had left the east and west unguarded?

"When will they come?"

"Tonight, it looks like. After dark, but I can't tell what time," Em said. "We should inform Merrick and the other town leaders. It's sooner than they thought, and a lot of people haven't evacuated."

Sam nodded but said nothing as he pulled open the cabin door. They ducked inside to find the embers from the hearth fire had gone cold, and the air nearly as chilly as the outside. Em could see her breath. She approached her cot and surveyed the space. Some of her extra clothes were neatly folded below the bed. But her tools, map, and *The Standard Book of Anything* were tucked away in her knapsack. The last time she opened the book, she saw a steamy note from one of Sam's former lovers, and it had made her blush so furiously that she hadn't opened the book since.

She spotted the little figurine she had bought at the market, lying by her feet. The female ancestor. She swept it up into her bag along with the borrowed blanket from her cot. Then she stood and brushed crumbs from the low dining table into her hand.

Sam grabbed his pack and was scanning the room for anything left behind. His focus found Em, and she realized he was watching her clean.

Em tilted her head at him. He had been unusually silent. Somber even. He stood with the bag loosely held. His eyes were bright, nearly glowing, and his dark hair was ruffled from the wind.

"This is it, then?" he asked.

It? Em felt a surge of confusion, then realized he was talking about their bargain. She supposed she had fulfilled her end. Come to the North and help. Prove she wasn't a thief.

"Yes. I only have a few days to take this to the empress. If I don't, I'll have a death sentence to outrun." She tossed the crumbs into the cold hearth and turned to him again.

He hadn't moved. "And what about you and me?"

Em smiled. Her feelings toward the man were so different now. "We part as friends."

He took a few steps closer, setting his pack in one of the chairs by the fire. "That's it?"

"What else is there to say? I'm grateful, you know? That we got a second chance. That we—" Her rambling was cut short when he took her hand and held it to his lips. Em felt a hot wind course through her. Was this just a friendly gesture, or was he—

"I've never met someone like you, Strider," he murmured, still holding her hand in front of him, brushing it with his thumb. "I hated you. The most thieving, conniving—" He broke off with a soft chuckle. "Especially when you're trying to poison me with dinner rolls."

Em let out a small laugh. Their whole revenge cycle at the Silver Nightingale was petty. But it seemed comical now.

Sam's smile shifted to something more determined. He was trying to say something important. "When you confided in me. You allowed me to be a hero. You gave me energy . . ." He dropped her hand, looking embarrassed. "I don't know what I'm trying to say. Just . . . to earn your trust, and your help . . . it's been a privilege. I hope this isn't goodbye."

In the chilly room, Em's skin was strangely warm where he had touched her. She wanted to close the gap between them and take his hand again. But that might be a step too far. Encouragement that led somewhere she couldn't go. She had to break this tension, before something bubbled over that she couldn't fix. So she flashed a cheeky smile. "I guess Bronwyn did something right. Forcing us to work together."

"I guess so."

"Maybe the Gray Horse will take you on as a housekeeper," she teased.

Sam laughed again. "Not you. You're terrible at mopping, incidentally. You missed all the corners."

Em flipped him a rude gesture, and the exchange returned to playful banter as they finished packing. In Em's mind, they were out of the danger zone.

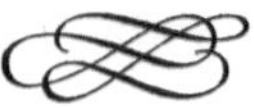

In the Northern territories, elders are elected from each family group to represent the clan's interest with the local governing body. Although not necessarily the oldest member of the clan, an elected individual is considered the wisest. It is confusing, therefore, that their decisions are regularly ignored by the populace.

"Northern Political Structure"
The Standard Book of Anything

When twilight fell, the small crew had built the wall to the northeastern edge of town. Em suspected some magical intervention; they had completed the wall much quicker than she had expected. As Sam placed the last block, Silas started clapping, and Cal melted the last section together. They had done it.

The snow wall followed the eastern boundary of the town, thick and uniform. A slight sheen glistened off the surface; the snow Cal melted had crusted into a glossy ice shell that made the barrier unclimbable and impenetrable. It was beautiful. They had done it.

"Good work," Em said. "I hear a rumor that soldiers are arriving soon. They might attack tonight, so be careful. We should start the evacuation." Sam caught her eye as he dusted the snow off his gloves. He knew she was minimizing; the soldiers absolutely were attacking tonight. But she couldn't tell the rest of them that definitively. Then she would have to reveal the ring. She'd have to tell them where she got it, and then the goodwill of the group would be lost.

The others shuffled around the corner, toward the north gate and into a biting wind. Em collected her tools and the snow block frames, waiting for the Northerners to dissipate. She felt heavy, knowing she would be leaving without officially saying goodbye.

Silas approached. "Hey, thanks for everything. Stay safe, okay?"

Em pasted on a bright smile. "You too! See you later."

He trotted off, leaving only Em and Sam.

"Lies, Strider," he commented as he watched Silas disappear around the corner. She would be gone before she saw any of them again.

Em grimaced. She was getting better at the easy deception. But she'd also helped these people. Surely they'd forgive her for not saying goodbye. But there were still some chores left before their work was done. She turned to Sam. "Will you go through the market? Clear out the vendors," she asked. "I'll find the elders to warn them."

He nodded and with a quick backward glance, strode off. Em held the wooden frames and shovels with her frostbitten fingers and watched his back as he turned the corner. She may not see him again either. She had the strange urge to call after him. They could go together. He could come with her to the empress. He could . . . what? Come live in Brookerby? Become close with her family and friends? She pictured Sam and Liam chatting comfortably in the mercantile, and that's where the fantasy became too ridiculous to imagine further.

She took a steadying breath, then rounded the corner herself. She hoped she could track down Merrick and the elders before the fight began. Give them some warning of what was to come.

THE SKY WAS GROWING dark as Em moved toward the long wooden building in the northwest quadrant that was the meeting place for the town elders. The snow had turned to sleet, and Em ducked her head into the hood of her cloak to avoid the sting of the wind. There was a tension in the air. She passed villagers carrying bundles and bags as they streamed toward the exits. A few resistance fighters ran the other direction. The temperature was dropping rapidly, and there were elderly and young among the stragglers. How far would they be able to walk? Was the next town near enough? Brownyn should've opened the gate-ports. All of them. Then the villagers could safely hop to any number of towns in the North. Why hadn't she?

Em arrived at the long house and pushed into the antechamber. There was a floor-to-ceiling curtain painted with snowy tundra scenes that blocked the entrance from the main chamber. Em peeked around the divider and saw men and women, mostly middle-aged or older, seated on opposite wooden benches that ran the length of the room. The lofted ceiling had exposed wooden beams, and the wind made the wood creak in an alarming way. The elders were still in session, their voices raised.

"It's not sustainable," a woman called out. "We cannot keep running and cowering."

"We can't blow them up either. That will bring the whole weight of them upon us," a warbling voice called back.

"We cannot rely on magic to save us anymore. Lady Bronwyn has done more than enough."

"Like hell she has. Put us in a pickle. Only defending the south end. They'll walk right in the side gates."

Em recognized Merrick's voice as the next speaker. "The east and west have protections, thanks to some of the other mages. But our defenses will only slow them down. We must evacuate."

Em moved into the room, alongside the other silent spectators. Maybe she could whisper her report to Merrick so he could update the others.

"And what of the attack in the marketplace? I found Felix barely alive this morning. We have dangerous people among us if they would drain a person so callously."

Em started at the statement. Felix. Her attacker had a name. At least he wasn't dead, thank the deities. She again felt the wrongness of her actions in the clench of her chest at his mention. How long before he revived and described her? He was drunk, but perhaps he remembered details. Her gender. Her face. The fact that she didn't look like a Northerner. That would identify her for sure.

She flicked the fear away. She would be gone before he could speak. Meanwhile, she needed to warn Merrick of the impending invasion, so she moved toward the front to wave him over. But her movement caught the eye of more than just him.

"Young lady, this is a closed assembly," came a nasally remark from the benches. The other spectators turned to stare at her, and some stepped away, leaving Em exposed.

Merrick came to her rescue. "This woman is responsible for the eastern and western defenses. She deserves our thanks."

Em tried to gesture to Merrick. She needed to tell him something, but several voices called out, "Report!" Em scanned their faces, feeling suddenly as if she had gone about this all wrong.

"Come forward, girl," an elderly woman commanded. "Speak up and say what you need to say."

Em stepped out from the spectators and felt all pairs of eyes watching her as she made her way to the center of the forum. She was directed to a spot designated for speakers, in the exact middle of the room. The ceiling creaked as a gust of wind blew over the building, and Em took a few steadying breaths.

"Hi—erhm—good evening. I wished to make a quick report that an ice-and-snow wall has been constructed along the eastern side of town. It spans the whole length of town and is taller than your average soldier. The sides are slick, so it would be difficult if not impossible to climb. The eastern side of town should be protected." Several elders nodded in approval, so Em continued, in a slightly stronger voice. "In the west, a series of hidden trenches, again about as deep as a person, flank the gate. If soldiers try to enter from that side, they will find themselves in a pit that is very difficult to climb out of."

"Thank you. That is most helpful," a silver-haired woman said kindly. "Miss—"

"Strider. Emaline Strider," Em supplied. "I also need to share some intelligence. I have good reason to believe that the soldiers will arrive very soon. Tonight. And they will not wait to attack. We must evacuate the rest of the citizens immediately."

At this, the room exploded into chaos.

"Who is this woman?" "Our information says they will wait until tomorrow." "How will we get everyone out?" "She might be a spy!"

Merrick raised a hand, and the group quieted enough for him to ask, "Em, could you share your source, please? It isn't that we don't trust your words," he said, daring the others to disagree, "but evacuating tonight in this weather would be dangerous. We need some certainty of your intelligence."

Em didn't expect this. She knew the information was correct, but if she revealed the ring, they might recognize it and take her for a thief. Which, technically, she was.

"I have a magic item . . ." She halted, took a breath, and then surged forward. "I have an item that tells me what will occur, in small glimpses. And it showed the soldiers attacking at night, in poor weather. They will approach the southeast corner."

At that moment, sounds of explosions came from outside, so loud that the noise dwarfed the creaking of the wooden roof. In the silence that followed, the room held its breath. Perhaps one explosive was triggered by mistake. Then another blast rocked the room. The elders eyed each other in disbelief, then fear that the soldiers were indeed upon them. And then the chatter was deafening, as the elders rose from their seats and made for the exits.

Em stood in the middle of the room as the crowd swirled around her. An ancient gentleman tugged on her sleeve, and Em made to step aside for him. Instead, he gestured for her to lean closer. She bent down, her face now level with his.

His voice was a whispered croak, "May I see your magic item?"

Surprised, Em backed up a step. "I'm sorry . . ."

"A ring? Silver with an amber stone?"

This man knew the ring. She shook her head, stepping back again. She was prepared to sprint into the crowd when he made a calming motion. "I do not wish to take it from you," he offered. "I do not wish to reveal what it is you carry."

Em must've looked relieved, for he continued. "That is the most dangerous thing in the world. It was forgotten for a reason. Take it back to the silver box, and for the ancestors' sake, keep it away from Bronwyn."

He hobbled away, but Em called out, "Wait! Please."

The man turned and raised a wrinkled eyebrow.

"Why was it forgotten?"

He limped back to her side. "In the hands of a benevolent man, it is mildly helpful. In the hands of a tyrant, it is death for us all. It wasn't worth the risk. My great-grandfather's grandfather gave his life to steal and hide it. To enchant its hiding place. Do not carelessly drag it back into the world, I beg of you."

CHAPTER 33

Explosions were cascading as Em left the meeting lodge. There were elders and villagers running in every direction, and Em felt dazed. The cold wind hurt as it pounded her face, and she wondered where Sam was. Where Silas was. And Cora and Otto. And Cal. Even Phoebe and Elias were running around in this, trying to get people out. Trying to save lives.

This last thought spurred Em into motion. She sprinted toward the south side of town, intending to knock on doors. Intending to get as many out as quickly as possible.

The explosions continued to rock the town as Em sprinted by a large group running north. The blasts were deafening. Em had to hand it to Bronwyn, they were an effective alarm bell for Fugea, but she wondered how many soldiers were being injured or killed. And how the empress would retaliate. She still carried the wooden snow block frames and her spade. She hastily shoved them into her pack, grateful for the infinite room that her magical bottomless bag provided.

She ran by Otto and Cora, who were helping two elderly women hobble toward the north gate, and skidded to a stop. They were loaded down with bags and packs and weren't moving quickly enough. If the soldiers got through, they would quickly overtake them. Damn Bronwyn for not opening the gate-ports. Em dug one hand in her pack as she wheeled around.

"Where are you trying to go?" she yelled above the sound of blasts.

"North," the woman on the right croaked.

"Luvitt," Cora shouted back. "We have family there." To the ladies, "This is Em. The one I told you about."

The ladies nodded politely, but they both looked worn out and frightened. They would be walking all night in the storm, and Em's chest squeezed with concern.

"I can get you there quicker, if you want," Em said, pulling out her fast-travel map. The ladies nodded, and Cora tilted her head at Em.

"Hold on to each other and to me. There is a little bit of spinning, but it will be over quick," Em instructed. A woman grasped onto each arm, and Otto and Cora held on to their other hands. Em double-tapped Luvitt, one of the northernmost cities visible on the map. The explosions dimmed as the world streaked around them in shades of white, gray, and midnight. Their feet touched down at the gates of another Northern city, and Em held the ladies steady as they regained their bearings. Her gaze swept over the town. It was a bit smaller than Fugea, but all the homes were clustered together in a similar manner. Lamp lights flickered from windows.

"Do you know where to go from here?" Em asked. The women nodded, a little dazed.

"That was . . . wow," Otto said. Cora was studying Em with a newfound respect.

"It was nothing. Just a travel map. Do you two want to stay here, or do you want to get them settled and come back with me?"

They opted to come back with Em, so they quickly led the ladies—Cora's aunts, it turned out—to relatives and left them at the door with instructions to warn Luvitt that others might be coming.

Then Em spun back with Otto and Cora. They landed in the middle of the market, which was nearly deserted by this time.

"Can we use that map again?" Otto asked. "I bet there are plenty of people who can't make the journey . . ."

Em paused, feeling anxious. She needed the map to get to Gillamor before her deadline with the empress. But to save people, especially the elderly, children, and those who couldn't move easily . . . she supposed she could lend it to them for a few hours.

"Yes. We need to get everyone out of their houses and to the north gate. Then maybe we sort them by destination? I don't know how many this map can take, but . . ."

Cora nodded in understanding. "We'll start sorting. Get as many as you can to help clear all the homes, and we'll meet you at the gate."

Em gave them both curt nods. Then, with hesitation, she handed Cora the map. "I want that back by the end of the night. My life depends on it. But go ahead and start ferrying people. Double-tap your location to go." Ignoring their quizzical looks, Em sprinted toward the south.

THE FIRST FEW homes she knocked on were empty. But a fourth contained a local mage who Bronwyn had drained several days ago. They had put on all their layers of clothes and packed their belongings but couldn't seem to walk more than a few steps without needing rest.

Em needed the map. Why had she given it to Cora? She just as easily could've sent her to find people while Em took folks back and forth.

Too late to change course. But how could she get this mage to the north gate? She needed to feed them a little bit of energy. Just enough to walk.

"Would you trust me to get in your mind? Just to give you some energy?" she asked.

The mage's dark green eyes widened, but then they nodded. Em prodded and found what felt like a wall of ivy, but with no stone behind it. She rustled past and then infused the mage with some of her own energy. Just a bit. And then a bit more. She backed out, and the mage's eyes had brightened.

"Thank you," they said. "My name is Gerwig Shadem, and I am forever in your debt."

"No need for that. Just get to the north gate. There are Silver Nightingale initiates there waiting to transport you wherever you need to go."

"A thousand blessings upon you."

"You're welcome," Em said, feeling touched by the mage's response. But then she realized this act could link her back to the attack on Felix in the market. "Please don't tell anyone I did this."

The mage looked confused but nodded their assent. Em followed them out the door and watched as they walked, slowly but steadily north.

Em sagged against the doorframe, feeling the cold more keenly. How much had she given? But she was still on her feet, and she had to keep going. As if to spur her on, the explosions continued just south of where she stood. How long before the soldiers made it through? She saw a woman about her own age, running toward the explosions. She wore the white armband of the resistance and wielded a long wooden staff. Em wondered if she had been born here instead of Brookerby, would she be running toward the fight like that woman? The thought spurred her onwards.

She knocked on more houses. Most were empty, but a few had cowering civilians who lacked clear instruction or a place to go. A stern-faced man answered the door at one home near the west gate. He refused to leave. "If soldiers come, I'll shoot them," he stated, nodding to the shotgun leaning against the wall in the corner. After trying to reason with him for a few minutes, Em let him be. She couldn't force anyone if they didn't want to go.

The explosion blasts finally stopped. Did that mean soldiers had pushed through? Or had they grown wise to the explosives, realizing they were only placed around the southern entrance?

Em was near the western gate, so she made her way toward it, being careful to stay hidden in alleys and behind lean-tos. But she didn't see anyone. No soldiers. No sign of anyone else either. Maybe . . .

"Strider?"

She recognized the voice and shuddered. But she couldn't place it.

"Em Strider!"

No one was around. She stood at the west gate scanning the horizon.

"Down!" the voice commanded. Em realized someone was calling out to her from very trenches she had dug and angled her eyes downard. Maybe one of the townspeople had fallen in? Then she spotted him.

Jeralt. An imperial soldier. A nasty one she had encountered last summer. What was he doing here?

Em called out before she thought better of it, "Jeralt?"

"Help me up, will you?"

Em's first instinct was to obey. But Jeralt was in a trench dug to keep Fugea safe. Was he part of the invading force? "What are you doing here? I thought you were on Captain Marcellus's squad?"

Jeralt was pacing at the bottom of the trench. "He resigned his position. I was sent to the Northern regiment. Pull me up. I was scouting and I fell in this hole. Northern bastards."

Em froze. She was about to do as he asked, but that last statement stopped her. "What are you doing here?"

"Here to subdue the local population with force. Dodged those explosives at the entry, and now things are going to get ugly for every snow-crusted rat in this frozen wasteland."

Em's stomach churned with horror. She backed away from the trench. If Em helped the man up, he'd run into the town and start shooting. He wasn't hurt, and would likely be rescued once the soldiers overran Fugea. But in the meantime, Em had to pick a side. "N-no," she stuttered.

"Strider." A warning. Jeralt held a pistol in his hand. Em backed up and out of his sight. Then she took off at a run and heard a shot ring out behind her.

It was only after she reached the crossroad in the center of town that she realized the implications of not helping Jeralt. An imperial soldier had identified her. And for being here, for not helping, she was a traitor. She was as good as dead.

The sound of explosives had long ceased. The invading force wasn't on the western side. Maybe they were attempting to get over the ice wall? It would only take half an hour if they decided to skirt the wall and approach the north gate. Em had to get everyone out before that happened. She broke into a run, hardly noticing her surroundings.

That's when she bumped into Bronwyn.

CHAPTER 34

Rebellion starts small. A stray comment. An errant thought. A wayward
action. Catch it early and cull the source.

"A Leader's Guide to Extreme Control"
The Standard Book of Anything

Em bounced off a cloaked figure. "Excuse me," she stuttered, but a hand gripped her cloak, and she glanced up to see the lady mage. Bronwyn's silver-streaked black hair whirled around her, and snow dusted her robe. The woman was stunning, in a terrifying way. And the way she glared at Em in the darkness felt deadly.

Em tried to twist away but was weak from sharing her energy. Bronwyn's grip tightened; the woman was surprisingly strong for her age. She looked no older than fifty, yet Em knew she was about the same age as the empress. And Gram, for that matter. She hadn't thought about it before and now wasn't the time to ruminate.

"You lying hag," Bronwyn sneered. "How dare you defy me!"

She was shaking Em as she spoke. Mendel's lovely cloak was

twisted around Em's throat in an uncomfortable way. She coughed. "We needed to stop the soldiers—"

"You NEEDED to do as I commanded. I told you no. And yet, I find trenches in the west. And an entire ICE WALL on the eastern side?"

"It wasn't about you. None of this is," Em said simply. It was time someone stood up to this woman to her face. The mage reared back her hand and struck her across the cheek. The slap echoed around them, and Em felt the shock first. Then pain followed. It radiated from her cheekbone to her right ear.

Em dared to hope that would be the last of it, but Bronwyn didn't release her grip. She was pulling Em toward something. Bronwyn gestured and a gate-port opened before them. Em found herself shoved through it.

Em experienced the sensation of being thrown into a pond as she landed on the other side and found herself on her hands and knees in a snowdrift. Dazed she tried to take in her new surroundings, but they weren't so different from the ones they had left. Endless snow. Darkness. Bitter wind blowing. The only difference was the lack of buildings. Or any sign of civilization. Her ears were ringing still from the near-constant explosions of the past hour, but now she heard nothing. Em touched her right ear; it felt like someone had shoved a sharp stick inside it. Her fingers were coated in blood when she pulled her hand away.

Bronwyn stepped through the gate-port and towered over her.

Em crawled backward and tried to stand, but she was too dizzy to do more than sit back on her heels.

"I heard a name tonight," the mage growled. "Your name. Emaline Strider. A name that would've invited death from the moment you uttered it. But you knew that, didn't you?"

Em was seeing spots in her vision. Bronwyn seemed to be saying something important, but Em was having a hard time following her words.

"I had hoped Sam Monterey would kill you," Bronwyn mused. Her voice somehow audible over the howling wind. "Do the Northerners a favor, because none of them wanted you there, and you were clearly up to no good. But he seems to have gone soft, or lovesick. I'm not sure. I found him in the marketplace. Helping people leave." She nearly spat the last sentence, as if it tasted foul in her mouth.

"You hoped . . . ?" Em was not keeping up. Stars, her ear hurt. The mage had struck her so hard.

"Yes. I hoped. And that was before I knew who you were. The great-granddaughter of Emaline Magnomium is a threat to me."

"My great . . . ?" The world was spinning. Deities, that wind was cold.

"And to see Sam Monterey, the fool I drained only a day ago, running and healthy? Somebody fixed him. Somebody is keeping secrets. Building power. Challenging my authority." Bronwyn's voice was building. She was raging. Toward what end, Em didn't know. "I will be empress over this land. The North must be grateful to me. Me! Me only. My mages must be wholly loyal to me. Or else, why did I spend all that time training you?"

"You didn't," Em said, disdain overcoming her confusion. "Phoebe and Elias did. You did nothing." Bronwyn's face contorted in even more rage, but Em didn't care. "Were you hoping people would die? That the town would fall? Did you want the soldiers to get in? Or did you just bungle it, like the warding trees of protection?"

"Silence!" Em's words earned another backhand from the mage. On the same side as before. And this time she felt every bit of the pain. She was bleeding. The snow around her was speckled with red. Her ear still? Or something on her face. Did it matter? Bronwyn would kill her now for sure.

While Em crouched in the snow, cupping her cheek, she felt a sudden drilling into her mind. Bronwyn was trying to get in. To drain her. Maybe to implant some kind of ill-conceived magic in her. Or kill her from the inside out. Em did not move. She did not try to run. She reserved all her strength to battle the woman in her mind. Breath in. Hold. Let it out. She felt so weak. Cracks were already forming in her wall, but with each breath, Em repaired them. In. Hold. Out. Every breath hurt. Her ear pain was so sharp she almost lost concentration. In. Hold. Out. In. Hold. Out. Cracks repaired.

How long had it been? A moment? A week? Em maintained her breathing. Her shields held. The wind battered them both.

Finally, Bronwyn huffed, and the attack ceased. "You hardly have anything left to take anyway. I'll let the wolves have you."

With that, Em listened to the mage's steps retreat, the whoosh of a closing gate-port, and then nothing but the howl of the wind.

CHAPTER 35

*S*he had to get up.

It would be so easy to just lie here. She would get cold of course.

Maybe there was a settlement just over that ridge.

Colder and colder. Then numb. Then she could sleep.

Or maybe she had an item in her pack. She could check. See what she'd brought.

Just fall asleep and it would all be over. No more pain.

Sitting up. Standing. Finding the nearest town. Finding shelter. She wasn't sure she could even do those things right now.

Just fall asleep.

Just fall...

~

EM JOLTED UP. No! She had drifted off. For how long? Hours? Only moments, she thought, for the sky was still dark and the blood was still wet on her cheek. Her face hurt. Her ear hurt. Her fingers. Her nose. Her legs. Her eyeballs felt numb from the cold. But she was not going to let this be the end.

She cycled through the list of people she loved. Who relied on her. Who cared about her. Liam, Gram, Mendel, Ilna, Gendry and her silly sweaters, little Grady, Marshall Dengett, Fern, Earl McBean . . . once she listed all the people she could think of in Brookerby, she started to name people she'd met last summer. Cass and Marcellus. Tilly. Anne and Farrigan. Liam again. Bob. Then she started listing people in the North. Cora, Otto, Cal, Silas, Phoebe, Elias, Merrick, the people she had evacuated . . . Sam Monterey.

She needed to get out of the wind, and she needed to think.

Clumsily rummaging in her bag, mittened fingers too cold to work properly, Em pulled out the shovel and started to dig. She flung the snow into great heaps around her, until she had a small circle set into the drifts, with a snow windbreak around her. She put the shovel away and dropped to the ground alongside her pack. She was exhausted, but she had decided she wasn't giving up. She need to figure out what to do next.

Her frozen fingers weren't working, so she dumped her pack out, searching. Her belongings scattered in the small space.

Her mind kept returning to the fast-travel map. If only she hadn't loaned it to Cora. If only she hadn't gone to the west gate. If only. If only.

But she remembered the look on Cora's aunts' faces. Fear to pure relief when they realized they were safe. Cora and Otto had likely ferried numerous others to safety tonight. Was that worth it? It was, the unselfish part of Em resoundingly agreed. It was.

She spied what she was searching for. Matches. And wood from the snow block frames she had hastily shoved in her pack. Her spare linen shirt from the Silver Nightingale would burn too.

In moments, she had a small fire. It wouldn't last all night, but it would provide some warmth and buy her some time.

She studied the other things from her pack in the firelight as her fingers thawed. She grabbed the borrowed blanket and wrapped it around her shoulders, grateful for an additional layer between her and the chill. The waterskin could produce a warm liquid, but not a hot one. She laid out her tools. Spade. Hammer. Screwdriver. Wrench. Nails. Lantern. She had used them some on this journey, but they were unlikely to help her survive the weather and wind.

The broken pieces of her jumper cane, destroyed in the maze. She gazed sadly at the splintered wood, wishing she had been more careful. It would've gotten her out of here. And now it would never work again.

The Standard Book of Anything lay in the snow. It could tell her what to do. Survival skills or how to make her own gate-port with no energy, maybe. She reached for the book and flipped to a random page.

> *The clarity of night, the shell of snow,*
> *Alone.*
> *Explosions within, frantic wonderings cease,*
> *Never home.*
> *Wrapped in another kind of bedroll, made of wind, and*
>   *betrayal, and sleet,*
> *Roaming.*
> *Until, at last you accept, the elements have won.*
> *"Anonymous Northern Poet"*

The poem smothered her in its sadness. Why would the book give her this? The one time she really, really needed the help. She slammed it shut and tossed it away from her. A gust of wind above her hollow blew loose snow into the fire. It sputtered and choked. Em grabbed her linen pants from the Silver Nightingale and fed those to the weak flame.

From the very beginning, Bronwyn had wanted her dead. Because of her name? Because of her great-grandmother for some reason? Bronwyn had said something about loyalty. She trained mages, and they would be loyal to her. But were they really? They feared her, certainly. Believed her to be all-powerful. But hadn't Em held her off? And Bronwyn's mages-in-training had joined Em willingly enough to build the ice wall. Were the older mages—the ones who had finished their training—similarly inclined? Or would they support Bronwyn's schemes and fight alongside her, even if it went against their own better judgment?

Bronwyn had wanted Sam to kill Em. She had orchestrated their partnership so that he could. Maybe had even spoken to him, encouraging him to stick a knife in Em. So why didn't he? He had every reason, and ample opportunity. Was he really so changed from his time in the North?

Em recalled their goodbye, those quick moments in the cabin. His words, so uncharacteristically fumbling. His lips on the back of her hand. He behaved as if he cared for her.

She shivered. A weight in her gut began to grow. Had she flirted? Led him on? She didn't think so. She told him she was with Liam. Quickly shot down rumors of anything between them. Hadn't she?

And yet she liked him. Not as a lover—but if she survived, she would have to sort out what she did feel. He was her friend. How could she hang on to that if, for him, it was really the other thing all along?

Her toes were thawed, so she rotated to warm her back. Her gaze darted to the other items spilled on the ground, including the ancestor statue and incense.

Em grasped the slender stick, lit it, and pressed the unlit end into the ground. Fragrant smoke wafted from its tip and intermingled with the flames and smoke from the campfire.

Em held the rounded stone of the ancestor figurine, studying its small features.

She knew very little about Great-Grandmother Emaline. Only that she was a mage, a powerful one, and Bronwyn's enemy, apparently. If Em survived, that would be something to look into. Ancestor Emaline had lived during the Age of Magic. Was she respected? Useful? Or did she cling to power in toxic ways, like Bronwyn did?

The little stone had been chilly from the snow but grew warmer as Em rolled it in her fingers.

"I sure could use some ancestor wisdom, Emaline. If you're offering," she said. After a moment, she sighed. Nothing happened. She ran her finger over the pleasant smoothness of the little statue and put it back in her pocket. The incense was starting to make her drowsy, so she snuffed it out. She fed the fire the last of the snow block wood and turned to warm her hands again. She was running out of time.

Think, Em.

The elder in Fugea had told her the ring was the most dangerous thing in the world. Was he jesting? It couldn't get her out of this mess. It didn't even save Fugea when it really mattered. It didn't warn her about Bronwyn, or Jeralt, or even this very moment where, without help, she would surely freeze to death. It wasn't powerful at all. She felt no qualms about giving it to the empress, who would surely use it to spy on her enemies. Once a day. With very limited information coming back. The woman was welcome to it.

Em grabbed her pack and was reloading all her tools when she noticed a rolled-up paper wedged in at the bottom. Her parents' nonmagical map of the mountains.

She unrolled it and spread it before her. She felt hope. She could use the landmarks. Figure out where she was. The map was mostly mountains, but it included some of the land around them, including the Northern regions. Fugea was on the eastern edge of the map. She stood, peering above the lip of her snow windbreak. The dark sky was lit by innumerable stars, and a quarter moon gleamed down on the white unbroken plain. She could see the mountains in the distance to her right, but no other landmarks. The nearest coniferous tree was at least a league away. She was in the middle of a vast frozen field.

The mountains appeared farther away now than they were in Fugea. She had that much. Sitting back down, she held the map to the dying firelight. It showed hills and forests, neither of which were visible from her current location.

She grabbed a piece of chalk from among her tools and drew a circle, centered on the northernmost peak of the mountain range and extending out to Fugea, around the whole map, using her hand, palm to fingertips, to measure the distance. She was somewhere outside that circle. And based on the weather and remoteness of the place, she was still north of the disputed border.

From there, she assumed that—on this clear night—she could see at least a league in all directions. Maybe more. She crossed out any place without a large open plain at least two leagues wide. That left three, maybe four possible locations.

And then she dropped the chalk at her feet and sat back. It didn't matter where she was. Any of the possibilities would require at least a half day's walk to get to the nearest town. Her strength would give out, or she would freeze before she arrived. Of course Bronwyn wouldn't leave her somewhere with shelter nearby.

The fire was no more than embers. She fed her mountain map to the flames. It caught. A flare-up of bright and heat was quickly replaced by ash. She reached down, grabbed the pieces of the jumper cane, and fed those to it. They caught, and the flame licked up again. It was useless to feed the fire. Delaying the inevitable.

She spotted a small bit of wood in the snow beside her. Her wood chip from Brookerby's destroyed warding tree. Her talisman that everything would work out in the end. It had been a comfort, but now she felt like crying when she saw it. She picked it up and tossed it in the sputtering flame.

She eyed *The Standard Book of Anything*. That would burn. It wasn't useful for anything else. *Until at last you accept the elements have won.*

Think, Em.

She stared at the tools lying in the snow. Maybe she could make a fast-travel device. Infuse her screwdriver with instructions for sending her a mile in the direction that she twisted it. She was low on energy, but she grabbed the tool anyway and began to concentrate. Twist and travel. She infused as much as she dared, retaining enough energy only to keep her eyes open and the tool firmly in her grip.

When she had finished, she gathered up her bag, stood, and gave the screwdriver a twirl, twisting her wrist as far as she could go.

The screwdriver torqued out of her hand and flew across the frozen tundra, leaving Em gasping. She had instructed the thing to travel, but not to carry passengers. Nor the manner of travel, which might've ended with Em flung high in the air and landing in a way that would break her body. Foolish mistakes. In the Silver Nightingale, the others would laugh, and then she would try again. Here, when it mattered, she had blown her one chance to get it right. She dropped down beside the waning fire, every fiber of herself wishing for sleep.

Her face was numb. A small mercy after the battering she had received from Bronwyn.

This wasn't like being stuck in a warehouse. Or on top of a roof when the ladder fell away. There was nothing to figure out. No solution to rig. No magical item to aid her. The distance was too great to conquer, and she was empty. She wondered if anyone would ever find her body, and bring the news back to Liam.

She glanced at the sky once more. How long? Were they in the wee hours of the morning?

If so, a new day had started. She could use the ring again. One last time.

She could see Liam one last time. Or Gram. Or Mendel. See what they planned to do today. One last glimpse. Or check on her friends in Fugea and make sure they were safe. Make sure Bronwyn had not done to them what she had done to Em.

She patted the ring, the silver like ice on her frozen finger, even blanketed in her mitten.

Most dangerous thing in the world. The search for the ring had certainly wrecked everything for her. But how were its limited visions more deadly than bombs and soldiers? Perhaps it had been more potent in the past, and over time it had diminished in power.

An idea drifted to her, as subtle as the falling snowflakes. Maybe the ring could show her own future. At least show her that the end would be peaceful. It might take away the sting, the fear, if she knew the ending.

Before she could tell herself the idea was foolish and a waste of her last ring use, she removed her mitten, held up the ring, and spoke.

"What will I do today?"

The amber swirled and Em pulled her fingers closer, hoping to see every detail. Instead of images in the swirling stone, she felt the world lurch. She was still seated in her snowy hole, but suddenly everything was tinted an orangish-brown. As if she was inside the ring itself. Surrounding her were ghostlike images of herself. Insubstantial as smoke—like the ring images—and too numerous to count.

One cloudlike Em was nearly on top of her, so she stood, stepped back, and watched herself. The specter curled up in a blanket on the ground, by the ashes of the fire, and stopped moving. After a moment, that smoky image drifted away. Em shook her head. Shook it harder. Faster. Was that it? Was that the end of the prediction, or had she . . . She couldn't even think the words.

She turned to another version of herself who had tunneled into the snowbank, searching for elusive warmth, but collapsed part of the way into digging. The image also dissipated. No, no. No. That couldn't be it. Where was the rest of it? The part where she stood up again. Saved herself. Devised a clever solution. Not like this. Unmoving in the snow. She waved away the image, trying to erase it from her mind, and turned to another. Then another.

Most of the wispy images were failing in their attempts to shelter or create warmth for themselves. These were no longer moving, and then—gone. A lump formed in her throat, and a sudden pressure behind her eyes. She was dying. All around her, the wisps could go no farther. A grisly confirmation of what she suspected; she wouldn't survive the night.

But maybe one or two made it. There were many other copies of herself that seemed to be leaving the makeshift campsite, heading in all directions. Em discovered that their actions played in a loop, and she could follow one image to its conclusion by simply focusing on it. Her consciousness drifted alongside one Em after another. Watching as she sought firewood, or shelter. Watching her failing body struggle in the direction of potential villages until she collapsed. None of them ended well. The shadows of herself would keel over from exhaustion, or lay down to sleep and never rise, or, or, or. She watched herself die. Over and over again. Weeping until her eyes ached, because there were so many things she didn't get to do. The way she had left things with Liam. Her childish anger at Gram. There were so many things that were unfair about this. Watching herself, filled with hope, being cut down again.

She had tried so many ways to survive. She was so brave. So resourceful. And it wasn't enough. She followed each of her shadow selves, holding vigil for the multitude of ways she had tried, refusing to turn away, even when her demise was horrifying—as in the one case where she encountered a large bear. She honored each version of herself and then returned to the campfire to follow the next shadow to its end.

It was an odd thing. The more Em watched, the more she realized her death was unavoidable. It should've caused her to mourn again. To rant and rail at the unfairness of it all. But instead, Em felt a sense of calm she had not experienced since before the empress's summons. She wouldn't make it, it seemed. But she had done her best. She had tried everything. And somehow, that made it endurable.

She followed another ghostly Em, one of the few she hadn't traced yet. This image strode away from the mountains, purposefully. Em followed, like a monk seeking enlightenment. Wondering if this Em would make it a few minutes longer. Would try something new.

But this Em did not die in the vision. In fact, this was the only wisp of Em, in hundreds, whose luck held out.

CHAPTER 36

*E*m followed the specter of herself as she trudged along. The ghostly image found a massive piece of dead wood in the shadow of several isolated fir trees. The snowy plain still surrounded her, but these few pines felt like a refuge. Her shadow dug a trench around the log, then reached for matches and set the wood aflame. Somehow, it caught. The projection added dried needles to the flame, and it sparked and crackled.

This felt different. Many of the images had found wood before. But it had been too wet to light. But this piece, protected under these evergreens, would burn for hours. The trees and pine needles would provide additional kindling and shelter, and the singular chance for Em to keep going.

Em's mind returned to the original campsite, and the amber glow of the world was lifted. Despite the hours it felt like she had spent following her ghosts, she discovered no time had gone by. The fire was still glowing, and the sky just as dark. She shivered again, feeling her body at its limit. She knew the exact distance she could go before she collapsed. She had witnessed it too many times to forget. But she also knew, if she walked the path of the singular spectral Em, she would make it. So she pulled on her mittens, gathered her things, and set off in the same direction—away from the mountains.

She found the large piece of wood in the firs and followed the same motions as the Em in her vision. Soon, she had a blazing fire. She dropped to the ground, lying as near to the flaming log as she dared. Her fingers and toes began to prickle as they thawed, and she lay with her eyes closed, just breathing. She would survive for another few hours while the massive log burned. She would be able to rest, gather strength, and maybe, just maybe, she would live beyond tonight.

A COLD WIND WOKE HER. Her eyes flew open. She had fallen fully asleep, a dangerous thing to do. The log was nearly ashes, the last little bit producing barely more than a candle flame. Rolling to sit, she looked around. It was brighter. Nearly dawn.

She felt better. Stronger. She still felt like a block of ice and chose not to examine her extremities too closely. She had heard of frostbite, where fingers and toes were amputated because they were too frozen to save. That hardly mattered right now. She was alive. She had survived the night when all reason—and the odds—told her she should be dead.

It was the same day, but the ghostly Em she followed would still be here. Maybe she would show her where to go next.

She removed her mitten again (thankfully, her fingers were still functional.) She lifted the ring, asked the question, and again found herself in an amber-tinted world filled with a whole new set of ghostly Ems. She wouldn't need a daily reset. Which meant she would have help. She would get out of this.

Following each amber-bathed Em, she saw all the mistakes. Several tried to craft an item that horribly backfired. Some started walking in a random direction and became lost and cold after several hours. One tried to scale one of the pine trees to get a better view of her surroundings, and fell from the tree, breaking her leg. Em shuddered.

Finally, she watched a wisp-Em strip a thick chunk of bark from a tree with the claw of her hammer and infuse the curved wood. Then she sat upon it with her pack beside her and it shot off into the snow. The fields were not so flat as they appeared last night—they had a gentle roll to them—so the sled gained energy as it rocketed down hills. That built-up energy then helped propel the sled up the next incline. She expected the bark to break apart or sink into the snow, but her shadow must have reinforced it, and the snow was thickly crusted with ice, so the small vehicle simply glided over the top.

"So smart," Em thought about her counterpart. She followed this Em until she reached a hilltop that overlooked a small village. Then she returned to her glen in the pine trees and followed the actions of her pre-tester. She had succeeded in creating the sled, so her fear of creating a magical item with backlash was minimal. She gave it as much energy as she dared. Then she thought very carefully about the instructions. She reinforced it. She described the motion and the kinetic energy of the thing. She instructed it to carry her and her pack. To stay on the ground. And on and on. When she could think no more about every contingency, she climbed on. And it was enough.

Sledding was very chilly, and Em mostly ducked her face into the hood of her cloak to hide from the wind battering her face. But the forward motion was exhilarating. She was tired again from infusing the item, but she knew one thing: there was a town ahead. She was going to make it.

CHAPTER 37

"Ceremonies of the North"
The Standard Book of Anything

Six Days until the Solstice

It was nearly midday when the sled arrived in the small town of Yarvule. It was a fraction of the size of Fugea, which naturally meant that a strange girl on a sled in the center of town was headline gossip in short order. She was brought into the town longhouse, seated by a brazier with a leaping flame, and questioned.

Once they discovered she was in Fugea, they brought forth two youths—cousins, who had been seeking apprenticeships in the city, and who had been transported by Cora and Otto the night before.

"Did they all get out?" Em asked.

They nodded and explained that Otto had arranged everyone into groups by destination, then Cora had transported the groups with the most elderly and young children first. The cousins were one of the last groups to be taken. The soldiers were getting close, but they think everyone got out.

Em inquired after the other mages, including Silas, Cal, Phoebe, and Sam. They shared stories of them running through the town, gathering up stragglers and distracting soldiers. But they were unclear on where they ended up. They suggested that maybe Bronwyn had opened the gate-port back to the Silver Nightingale.

"Thank goodness for the ice wall. That was so wise of Bronwyn to create it. And to transport us out like that," one of them gushed.

Em glanced down at her frozen fingers, feeling an odd blend of pride and anger. Her wall had worked. Her friends were heroes. But Bronwyn was taking credit. And she was prepared to let them all die if it helped her solidify her own power. Em was too tired to set them straight. They were only a few years younger than herself, but after the past day, she felt ancient beside them.

She nodded her thanks, and they ducked away.

Someone brought her a warm cup that smelled like cloves, and another trotted in with a map to tell her exactly where she was.

As she continued to thaw, she realized that it was a formidable distance to Fugea, but there was no point in going back there. It was probably crawling with soldiers, if they hadn't burned it down entirely. It was also likely Fugea would be added to the annexed North claimed by Esnania, which filled her with fire anew for the unfairness of it.

She noted that she was only a few leagues from Luvitt, the town where Cora's aunts had traveled yesterday. She reasoned that Cora might fast-travel to check on them, and then Em could get her map back. It was only a few days until Em's deadline, and it would be impossible to make it to Gillamor by nonmagical means. She had to hope Cora was as concerned about her relatives as she seemed the night before.

But if Cora didn't come, Em would not make it back.

She indicated to her hosts that she would like to use the privy—they directed her to a ramshackle outhouse, too frozen to be smelly. Once alone, Em pulled her hand out of her mitten to consult the ring. The world tinted, and again, Em watched versions of herself. Most headed toward Luvitt by various means. A few headed toward a different town nearby, and one or two met with accidents on the road while traveling. The projections of herself that went to Luvitt all seemed to find Cora's aunts, who remembered her from the night before and welcomed her into their family cottage. It was early evening, and Em's shadows all sat fidgeting in the tiny home, drinking the ceremonial hot spiced drink of the North, starting at every sound, waiting for Cora. She never came. Then, one by one, the wisps would rise and find various places to sleep. A local inn. The relatives' cottage on the floor. A neighbor's house.

Annoyed, Em realized Cora was long gone with her map. She watched the few versions of Em that went to other towns. In these places, she found welcoming strangers and no help in getting back to Brookerby or Gillamor.

Then she sat on the privy, shivering and thinking. How to get home?

Someone knocked on the door. "You all right in there?"

Starting, Em realized she'd been staring despondently at the ring. There had to be other options. "Fine," she shouted. She left the outhouse and stumbled against the wind back to the cottage.

She had been determined to go to Luvitt until she had checked the ring. She would've failed if she had made that choice, and she didn't have time to mess anything up. Maybe it would show her new options, now that she had changed her mind. When her hosts left the room, she tried again; she asked the question and watched the world go sepia once more. A new set of scenarios emerged from the amber.

The miraculous thing was that no time seemed to pass. She watched multiple iterations inside the ring, and then when she glanced up, her hosts would still be in the process of leaving the room. She glanced down at the ring as one of her hosts was asking her a question from the kitchen. She watched several minutes, realized what she was doing and pulled out of the orange-tinted world. The questioner had not noticed, and, indeed, was still asking the same question.

Realizing she could check the ring quickly, she no longer needed to excuse herself. She dipped in again. An entirely new set of Ems. A few still stubbornly traveled to Luvitt and found the exact same results as before. But others were attempting to make magical items or canvas the town to see if any fast-travel items existed. She watched each in turn, and several choices seemed to have decent luck with making or procuring a way out. She continued to watch, wondering how to pick between several seemingly successful methods. The projections of Em only went so far before they froze or looped back to the beginning.

She made a choice, randomly, and discovered that if she made a decision, she could follow a projection further—bootstrapping her way out of the rural North.

She experienced every moment from the safety of amber and hypotheticals, working out the best, most efficient way to proceed. All under the oblivious gaze of her hosts.

LATER THAT DAY, Em knocked on a weathered wooden door on the outskirts of Yarvule, feeling the confidence of the ring on her finger. She never would've approached this run-down cabin otherwise. The door cracked open, and an exhausted woman peered out.

"Who are you?"

"I'm so sorry to bother, ma'am. I was told you could help me."

The door started to close before Em could finish her sentence, but Em wasn't disappointed. She had seen this all play out, so she shoved her foot in the crack, keeping the door from slamming in her face.

"Please. I just need to get to Bonwhite. It's a matter of life and death. I have medicine for my uncle. Someone in the square told me to come find you."

The door pressure on her foot eased, and the woman's haggard face softened.

"Bonwhite? Well now." The woman invited her in and made friendly chitchat; she detailed the various ailments of her mother who lived in Bonwhite and refused to move.

Em wasn't here for the story. Only the gate-port.

The woman led her to a side room, where an empty picture frame hung. Very similar to what they had used in the Silver Nightingale to get to Fugea.

"Have you used one of these before, miss? Very dangerous, but it'll take you right to the center of town. A whole baker's dozen of mages had to pool their energy to make it for me so I can take care of my mother. Very kind. Yes."

Em hardly listened. This was going to work. But she needed to leave now if she was to make her next appointment.

"How do you turn it on?" she interrupted the woman, midsentence.

The woman was momentarily flustered by Em's briskness, but she shrugged and waved a hand before it as she continued to chatter. The frame swirled with liquid bronze, and Em stepped through without a backward glance.

She supposed that was rude, but so was the lady in most scenarios. She had seen (in the ring) that the woman only responded to the sick uncle story. She slammed the door when Em had told the truth, and many other variations of sob story. So, Em didn't really feel like showering her with gratitude. In any case, she needed to catch—aha. There he was.

She emerged from the alleyway onto the bustling main street of Bonwhite. A middle-aged man was hitching up a fully loaded wagon to two sturdy-looking oxen. The wagon had rails for ice and snow that could be swapped out with wheels on dry ground. Em appreciated the practicality. Also, this was her ticket out of Bonwhite. She adjusted her face to one of distress and rushed forward.

"Sir, please! Could you tell me, has the public coach to Esnania already passed? I was delayed, and now—"

The man held up his hand, distracted. "Sorry, miss. It left about thirty minutes ago."

This part required a bit of acting. Em allowed her eyebrows to rise and her lip to tremble. "I'm supposed to be married within the week. I won't"—she made as if to hold back tears—"won't make it."

The man shifted his weight, looking uneasy. Em brushed imaginary tears from the corner of her eyes. "I'm—I'm sorry. It's not your problem." She turned, surveying the town, as if looking for someone who could rescue her.

"I'm going south," the man offered.

She turned back, looking at him hopefully.

"Only as far as Hemnisville, but perhaps you can get transport there to where you're going. Or even catch the coach there."

"Truly? Oh, thank you!" she cried, and flung her arms around the man. He chuckled and patted her back. "Happy to help, young miss."

Five minutes later, Em was settled in the seat beside the man as the wagon glided out of town and to the south.

THE ONLY DIFFICULTY in lying to the man, a merchant, was that he wanted details. She had to keep inventing lies during the several hours they spent traversing the frozen tundra toward Hemnisville. Em found they came easily. She simply told him all about Liam, and how excited she was to marry him and start a new life and have four children and make him supper every single night.

They were lies, all the same. She realized as she was talking that what she wanted veered wildly from the fiction she was feeding this man. But, she reasoned, he wouldn't have offered a ride to a fledgling mage who was left for dead and now must retrieve her magical map and return a ring to the Esnanian empress before she was executed as a traitor. She knew, because she saw that version in the ring. In that version, she was still stranded in Bonwhite, or—in another version— dropped at the side of the road.

She enjoyed talking about Liam. That was real, at least. She missed him. He was steady. He made delicious pastries. He made her laugh. He talked her down when she was angry and picked her up when nothing was right in the world. Her heart fluttered a little bit when he called her "squirrel" and pressed his lips to hers. And she didn't feel lonely when she was with him, because he saw her.

That's what everyone wanted, right? Just like that ceremony at the temple. What had Liam said? The ritual of traveling through life together as one. It was beautiful. But what if one of you wanted to walk a different direction? Em supposed it didn't matter, because she was traveling alone. By her own choice. By her own stupid decisions.

When the merchant stopped at a melting stream to water the horses and change the sled runners to wheels, she shook off the cloud settling on her thoughts and lifted the ring, seeking the next few steps of her journey.

HEMNISVILLE, a border town sitting in the shadow of the looming mountains, was also the birthplace of Sam Monterey's conversion to selflessness. As the wagon rolled into town, Em scanned the icy cobblestones, foolishly hoping to catch traces of him.

Her driver dropped her close to where a public coach would arrive later that evening. She gave him another quick hug. "Thank you!" she tried to gush, stifling a yawn. "If you're ever in Exeton, please look me up! I'd love to introduce you to Liam."

The merchant assured her he'd love to visit, and they parted ways. Em let out a breath when he was out of earshot. The lies didn't feel great, but what was the likelihood that he'd actually show up in Exeton looking for a recently married "Hazel and Liam"? Not likely at all.

She waited until he turned the corner, headed for his evening lodgings. He was selling his wares at the Hemnisville market the next few days, so she would have to give the market a wide berth. And the Stone Hearth Inn, where the merchant was staying. She wanted to sleep for a week. She was ready to drop with exhaustion, and her short nap in the back of the wagon earlier only amplified that feeling. But she knew her next move; there was a singular opportunity to get out of this frozen hellhole. If all went well, she would find her next target, then get sleep and be out early tomorrow.

Leaving the public coach platform, she turned and strode toward an unassuming pub across town. The mountains were much closer now than they were in Fugea, or anywhere else she had been in the last day. The air was different. Sharper. She tried counting her breaths as she walked and discovered her mind sharpening despite her exhaustion.

When she reached the sign of the Spinning Narwhal, her heart was pumping, preparing her for the next unlikely step.

She pushed into the crowded pub, attracting very little notice. The regulars were used to travelers, and many of the patrons sat alone at their tables or were casually chatting with new acquaintances. She scanned the room and spotted her mark at a round table near the far wall. He looked more drawn than when she had seen him last and was sporting a new scar on his forehead. He was chatting amiably with another person (who hardly mattered). This man was going to get her home.

CHAPTER 38

Five Days until the Solstice

She wove through the tables, taking off her mittens and scarf as she approached the corner table.

"Hello, Merrick."

The grizzled leader of the North started, turning his gaze to her as she stood before the table. The other man looked at her with disinterest, but Merrick's eyebrows rose in surprise.

"Em! You made it out okay. Didn't think I'd see you again. Sit!"

Em accepted the chair he gestured to and turned to the other man. "Sorry to cut in," she offered.

"No trouble," the man mumbled, although clearly he was disgruntled at being interrupted.

Merrick ignored his companion and shifted to face Em. She got a better view of the cut on his forehead that was just starting to heal. "Rough day yesterday?" she asked with a wry smile.

He humphed. "You ain't lying, lass. But we got everyone out. Even all the mages are okay. Thanks to you and that wall of yours. The buildings? They may not be there. The whole swath of land probably belongs to Esnania now, but lives are more important."

"Did all of the mages go back to the Silver Nightingale?"

He nodded, taking a sip of his ale. Then, "You look like you've had a rough go. Would you like something to eat or drink?"

Em nodded gratefully, and he gestured to a waiter to bring some soup and another pint. Merrick's companion, clearly bored with the exchange, stood and wandered over to the bar. Merrick watched him go with a laugh. "Everyone up here has their own troubles. No time for anyone else's. Peter fears that Hemnisville will be next."

Em filed this information away. It seemed she had left one conflict only to charge straight toward another. "Is that why you're here?"

Merrick laughed. "Trouble seems to find me, lass. Not the other way around, I assure you. Speaking of trouble, what happened to you? I was one of the last out of there, and some of the other young mages were asking where you went. One of the gals. Cora."

Em bobbed her head. "Cora. I loaned her one of my magic items and I need it back. But we got, uh, separated."

Merrick leaned in conspiratorially. "Lady Bronwyn?"

Em nodded, but didn't elaborate.

"Lucky you survived. We should've told you to leave straightaway, rather than risk her fury."

"I almost didn't survive," Em said. "Never mind all that. Remember you said if I ever needed help, I should come find you?"

"Anything, lass. Name it."

"I need my item back from Cora. Can you get me to the Silver Nightingale without Bronwyn knowing I'm there?"

Merrick scratched his stubbled cheek. "I can always get to the

Silver Nightingale, but without Bronwyn knowing is going to be a challenge. She watches the gate-ports closely."

"Then get me to the maze, at least. I can make it from there."

"Too dangerous. I wouldn't send you there."

"I got in last time. I can do it again."

Merrick said nothing. Em's food appeared, a carrot-and-celery soup, hot from the stove. As the steam rose between them, she looked directly at the man and said the only thing that had worked in the hundreds of versions of this conversation. "Please? We can't let her have the North."

WAS IT MISLEADING? Yes. To imply that Em was going to take down Bronwyn Featherweight was laughable. Legendary mage against Em Strider. Handy with a wrench, terrible in a sparring ring, and excellent at making the exact wrong decisions. At least, until recently.

But Merrick had resisted pleading, appeals to his kindness, even the full revelation of Em's goal to carry a legendary ring to the empress. That particular scenario ended badly. Merrick's anger left her out in snow after he abruptly ended their conversation. No. The only thing that worked was the suggestion that Em could keep Bronwyn from claiming the North. That was more concerning to Merrick than a whole host of other threats, including the dangers of imperial annexation. And for some reason, he thought she could do something about it.

She lay in her tiny room—rented for the night—exhausted but unable to sleep. She kept watching the same scenarios in the amber ring. The ones where she made it into the maze and then died in numerous and horrific ways as she took incorrect turns. Over and over, she watched herself impaled, crushed, attacked, squeezed, poisoned, and bludgeoned. It was horrible. But necessary to find the right path. She had made it through the maze with luck last time. This time, she had the ring. She had nothing to worry about. And yet, sleep was slow to come.

WHEN DAWN ARRIVED, Em was packed and ready to go. Despite the poor night of sleep, she felt ten times better than she had the night before. She repeated the maze path she had worked out. Left, right, right, left, right, left . . . She met Merrick outside the pub door, and they walked toward the edge of town.

He had explained his idea the night before. There was a gate-port next to an unused shed that would take Em to the maze entrance, at the base of the mountain.

"I thought Bronwyn was monitoring the gate-ports?" Em had asked as she spooned up a large chunk of potato in her carrot soup.

"Only the ones directly into the Silver Nightingale," Merrick said. "She doesn't care about this one, because whoever uses it still has to traverse the maze. And she believes only the worthy will make it through. I've used it for recruits that I couldn't personally vouch for. Give them a chance and all. I'll guide them a bit, but only if they ask."

Em recalled this conversation now as they walked in silence through Hemnisville. She wondered how Merrick could be so blasé about sending magical recruits to a likely death. As they passed the market, Em ducked behind her cloak hood to avoid the merchant. Finally, they arrived at the gate-port shed. Em shifted her bag on her shoulder and glanced at the Northern man expectantly.

"You sure you want to do this?" Merrick asked. "After all, an item can't be worth all of this."

"Unless you have a way for me to fast-travel to Gillamor?" Em asked.

He tilted his head at her, puzzled. Em realized that request was probably not what he had expected. In fact, it was undoubtedly concerning for him. But she had to ask. Just in case.

"Sorry, Em. We don't want any speedy transit between the North and there. Do you—"

"Yeah, I figured," Em said, cutting off his question. "Then I have to do this. Thank you for your help."

He nodded, and then with a swipe of his hand, the gate-port was activated. Bronze swirled, and Em stepped forward.

"Come back? Once you do what you need to do. We could use your help again," Merrick said.

Em shivered. She never wanted to come back to this frozen hell. Forget about the injustices and the suffering, she couldn't wait to leave the biting cold behind. But would she be able to forget what she'd seen? Never. She met his eyes and ducked her head. "If I can, I will."

Then she turned and stepped through the gate-port.

CHAPTER 39

Inscriptions in stone were not chosen carelessly. Consider the source and
context.

"Statues and Monuments"
The Standard Book of Anything

Four Days until the Solstice

She was back at the entrance to the maze, a circular tunnel hewn into the rock of the mountain. Em took several breaths before entering. It felt like years ago she had stood at the base of this mountain, wondering if she should enter. So much had happened. The world felt smaller and darker than it had then. It would not be like before, she reminded herself. The beast. The spikes. The unknown death around nearly every turn. This time, she had the ring.

The chalk she had drawn on the hallways, on three of the nine entrances before her, was still there. She supposed Bronwyn would eventually have made her and Sam clean the maze. No doubt hoping the maze would accidentally kill them both. As it was, she could narrow down the correct path based on her chalk markings. Such a smart idea. She felt a tiny twinge of pride that she had navigated the deadly maze on her wits alone. Now, she walked confidently to the farthest-right marked hallway as she repeated the turns to herself. Left, right, right, left, right, left . . . At each bend, each choice, Em consulted the amber stone. She knew the turns, but just in case. She watched numerous images of her own death. Collapse from the noxious sleeping gas that she had narrowly avoided before. Dismemberment by the monster that camouflaged itself as Liam. Several other new traps and tricks that she hadn't encountered on her first trip through. She bypassed them all and arrived in the circular room with the three ewers. It had been less than a quarter of an hour and she didn't have a scratch on her.

In the first room, Em quickly selected the Northern vessel, the one with magic rushing under its surface, and poured a cup to drink.

Only the worthy will drink from the font.

Em smirked. Bronwyn would believe that only magic users were worthy of entering. The door swung open into the pastry room.

Em studied the pastries again. Crumb. Bronwyn mentioned fixing the mechanism. The hairline crack on each of the pedestals was no longer there. She didn't dare believe her trick of selecting all three would work again. She hovered her hand over each pastry in turn. The éclair. The tiny, layered cake. The pastry folded around strawberries and glaze. They all looked delicious. And deadly should she choose the wrong one. She laid a finger on each. No magic detected.

Seeing no obvious answer, she pulled out the ring and gazed into the amber depths. But nothing swirled. No ghosts of Em appeared.

Em waited for a few moments, until she finally had to accept the truth. She was inside the castle wards now. The ring wouldn't work.

Why hadn't she thought of this? Watched the whole thing from the safety of outside before charging headlong into these rooms?

She knew for sure it wasn't the éclair. Before, a trapdoor opened around that platform. So it had to be the strawberry pastry or the tiny cake. Her fingers trembled as she reached for one, changed her mind, reached for another, then backed away. She had to choose. It wasn't random. There was a reason that the others knew. Em cast back to that first conversation around dinner where the Northerners were shocked to learn how she had circumvented the test.

The Northerners knew which one to pick.

Those who hunger for greatness.

A call to their desire to rise up. She scoured her memory for pastries in the Fugean marketplace, but remembered nothing.

Had they been told? Or did they just . . . know?

Em studied the pastries again. Slowly. Looking for clues. Any kind of hint. And when she saw it, she shouted a "Ha!" to the circular room.

The layered cake had a spiky white flower decoration. But it wasn't a flower. It was a snowflake. Surely this was the signal to the Northern people.

Still, Em hesitated. Death felt so much closer these past few days. She had brushed against it in reality, and observed it an unhealthy amount when gazing at the myriad of choices she could make. What if she chose wrong?

She wished the ring worked. That she could go back and check. Just to be sure.

Shaking, she lifted the snowflake layered cake.

Nothing happened.

"Do I have to eat it?" she wondered. She supposed if she chose wrongly, she would be poisoned. And if she chose correctly, somehow a bite would trigger the doors opening. But how, if the cake wasn't magical?

She bit down.

It was fine. A bit stale. Definitely not as good as Liam's baking. But it had a pleasant flavor. And better still, Em wasn't dead. Not yet anyway. She chewed and swallowed, but the door stayed closed. Had she selected the wrong—

She walked over to the exit, still holding the cake, and the door clicked open.

Something in the frosting—chemicals? A magnet? Em wanted to

stay and investigate, but the door was open and the third chamber awaited. She set the half-eaten piece down by the door and walked through.

Three circles of gold, silver, and polished wood sat on the cushioned pedestals before her. This was the other room she had hacked before. Something new was in the room: a bust on a pedestal by the door. The statue looked vaguely like Bronwyn.

To the victor, the crown.

What did it mean? Obviously, Bronwyn wanted her bust to be crowned with the correct headwear. But which one? The circlets were identical, apart from their material. The pressure sensor had been removed, she assumed from the pedestals, so she couldn't smash and grab like she had before. She needed to choose.

Out of habit, she checked the ring. It still didn't work.

Gold. Silver. Wood.

She touched each, and they all rushed with magic. The fix was magical. Bronwyn had done something to each of these.

Em slowly circled the pedestals, thinking hard. Wood was the frame of the portals. That might be stretching logic a bit. Wood was ordinary, yet from something alive. Bronwyn had made the warding trees. Perhaps a connection? She felt her mind tumbling, as if from a high place. Not landing, just spinning midair.

Shifting, she focused on the first circlet. Gold. Not much was gold around here. Some of the treasures in the vault were gold. Nothing in the North, really. It was considered valuable. Highly desirable. Fine jewelry. Fancy palaces. Things in Gillamor were covered in gold. The Golden Lark Palace. That was something! The empress literally ruled in a golden building.

But the Northerners didn't respect the empress. Didn't submit to her rule.

Silver. Her ring was set in silver. The Silver Nightingale.

The Golden Lark Palace. The Silver Nightingale Palace.

Em felt a flash of insight, so bright it blinded her. Bronwyn was forcing mages to make a choice. It was a loyalty test from Bronwyn.

Declare Bronwyn the victor, grant her the crown of the North, and you may pass. Bow down and enter.

That had to be it.

Em reached for the silver circlet, feeling the weight of this choice. But could it be anything else?

She lifted the crown, and nothing happened.

Oh, right. The pressure sensors had been fixed. She needed to crown Bronwyn's bust.

Em crossed to the door and then hesitated. Even symbolically, she couldn't crown Bronwyn. The woman was unfit to rule. She would be a tyrant, taking no counsel and murdering anyone who opposed her.

She touched the bust and felt no magic. Only the crown held the cantrip. There was no need for interaction between the two items, then. She guessed she could crown anything—anyone—and it would work. *Anyone but her.* It was a risk, but . . . Em lifted the silver circlet and placed it on her own head.

The door clicked open.

What would've happened if the magic required the bust? Em didn't stick around to find out. She jogged over to the door and arrived in one of the long sparse hallways of the Silver Nightingale. The round chamber door swung closed behind her and clicked again. She wouldn't be able to leave from that way. Which was tricky. The only entrance was the maze. Were the gate-ports the only way out? Unless Bronwyn hid a secret mountain staircase somewhere. This was a problem for future Em to deal with.

The hallway echoed with her footsteps, and she itched to check the ring before anyone appeared around the corner. To discover her exit. But she knew full well the thing wouldn't work in here. She debated going to the garden—the secret passage with the unwarded treasure trove—but at this time of day, the initiates would be practicing magecraft in the court-yard clearing. She didn't want to risk bumping into Bronwyn.

Feeling exposed and starting to sweat, she ducked into one of the secret passages that ran parallel to the hallway. One of the ones she had found while competing with Sam Monterey for some unknown treasure. Now she realized Bronwyn had probably instructed him to egg her on. Get her in a secret room and knife her. She didn't know how explicitly Bronwyn had suggested it, but Sam hadn't taken those final instructions. Not in the end, anyway.

She needed to find Cora and Otto. She would find them, retrieve her map, and get out of here before the lady mage was any the wiser. With luck, she'd never see the woman again, and she would likely assume Em had perished on the frozen tundra.

Maybe she didn't even need to find Cora. She could just search the rooms for her map. Not that she knew which room Cora was in. And the doors were locked and shielded. Better to catch the girl as she was leaving mage lessons.

She inched along the narrow, hidden corridor, listening for footsteps, but she heard nothing. She belatedly realized her warning stone was useless in her pocket. It wouldn't work here because she had remade it in Fugea—beyond the wards. She would have to siphon and reinfuse it here. She did so quickly in the dark passage, instructing the stone to grow colder when someone was approaching her, and get hotter when she was approaching them. After infusing, the rock still sat at a perfect room temperature.

As she neared the courtyard, a sense of wrongness overtook her. Her rock was not heating. She heard nothing. Where was everyone?

She longed for the certain predictions of the ring. One false step in here and she was dead. After hesitating for far too long, she left the safety of the passage and slowly peered out a window. No one was outside. The winter sun shone brightly on the lawn, but there was no sign that anyone had been out there.

Quickly, she darted to the hidden stairway door—the one she and Sam had found nearly a week ago. It felt like a lifetime. Em brushed aside the pine needles and opened the rotting wood trapdoor. She just needed to use the ring. She didn't trust this—what she had walked into—and she needed to know. Sprinting down the stone steps in near darkness, she pulled out the ring and began to watch.

～

EM EMERGED a short time later and re-hid the stairs with pine needles and dirt. It was imperative that Bronwyn not find this treasure. She marched in the direction of the sparring room. There was a passage that would get her to the Gathering Room, and then the ring had laid out a whole plan for her. She had saved herself from Bronwyn, but the others had built the ice wall too. And Bronwyn knew it. In the ring, she saw her friends drained and weak, and there was a course of action that would free them all and evade Bronwyn. If she could follow it to the letter. Panic flitted in her chest as she infused her feet with quiet to keep them from clomping and made her way to the sparring room. A set of stairs near the weapons rack would lead to the Gathering Room. The ring showed, at the right moment, she could get in the room without anyone realizing she was there. There were other options where she retrieved the map and escaped undetected, but she couldn't leave any of them under Bronwyn's thumb. She needed to make sure her friends were safe.

As she approached the passage, her rock grew slightly warmer. The right direction, at least. A set of stairs led down to a small stone room. A spiral staircase disappeared into the Gathering Room above. She stepped carefully on the metal stairs, feet still silenced by her cantrip. Her rock was as warm as an oven-fresh roll in her pocket, and she heard a faint voice above that became clearer the higher she climbed. Bronwyn. And she didn't sound happy. This was playing out as the ring had showed. Em reached the top of the staircase and found herself inside a stone pillar. She still couldn't hear very well. Her stone was nearly burning a hole in her pocket.

The ring had suggested she stay in the pillar until a particular moment, then she could emerge undetected. However, Em must've bumped a switch while leaning her ear against the wall. Triggered something, because the room spun, and Em fell forward into the Gathering Room. She managed to keep from toppling over, and then as she straightened, she realized she had drawn every eye. Not the inconspicuous entrance she had hoped for. Definitely not the path the ring had laid out for her. Definitely not the right moment. It was a stupid mistake. But everything she saw in the ring was not going to happen now. She was stumbling blindly again.

Her friends—the other mages—stood, hands behind their backs, shock on their faces. Em offered them a weak smile. Then she turned to see Bronwyn, sitting on her stone throne, looking extremely stiff, almost wooden. But then her expression sharpened. Incensed.

"Surprise?" Em said.

Then she felt a sharp dagger pain in the barrier of her mind.

Em fell to her knees, crying out at the unexpected pain of it.

"You crowned yourself? You insect," Bronwyn seethed as she cut into Em's mind barrier over and over. What was she talking about? Oh. Em was still wearing the silver circlet. Bronwyn's attack felt like an axe carving a piece of firewood into smaller and smaller chunks.

The others just stood there. Why were they just standing there? Em turned her head to survey the initiates. The mages. She had raised a glass with them in Fugea. They had helped her build an ice wall and keep the people safe. Were they cowards? Why did they not move?

She met Cora's eyes, begging for aid. Bronwyn was starting to crack through Em's mind, and Em realized she had mere moments before the mage took everything from her. Cora looked back with a blank expression. It was then that Em noticed her withered skin. Her sallow cheeks. The deep circles under her eyes.

Bronwyn had drained them.

Glancing from person to person, Em realized that Bronwyn had sapped energy from every single one of them. Otto. Silas. Cal. Phoebe. Even Elias and Sam.

It was a miracle they were still standing.

"What have you done?" Em wheezed, swiveling back to Bronwyn with fury.

"Making it clear who is sovereign here, and who is not," Bronwyn responded with a toss of her hair. "Your little rebellion in Fugea will not be tolerated. Not then. Not ever. And since you were supposed to be dead anyway—"

She broke off as she sharpened her attack. Em barely heard the gasps at Bronwyn's declaration as she felt the cracks in her shield split open, and something within herself break. Bronwyn had won. After everything Em had lived through in the past day and a half, Bronwyn had won.

The second thought in Em's mind as her defenses broke was for the single misstep. She could've prevented this, just like she had prevented her demise hundreds of other ways over the past day. If only she hadn't bumped that switch in the column.

The sensation of being battered by wind, by hail, and by withering sun at once overtook her. So this is what it was like to be drained. She felt a day's worth of energy leave her in moments. Her body shook from the exhaustion. From the strain.

She knew Bronwyn would continue until Em lay lifeless on the floor. And no one could stop her. Em saw some of the others in the corner of her eye. They could barely stand. Silas had tears in his eyes as he watched. Cal shook. Otto's face twisted in fury, despite his wan skin and sunken eyes.

Em needed to fight back. Needed to fight for her life. But she couldn't. She could barely catch her breath. If only the ring had worked.

Another day gone from her body.

She sank down, knees splaying on the stone floor, palms holding her up for now. The silver circlet clattered to the floor.

Bronwyn's eyes gleamed viciously. She was ridding herself of a pest, Em thought as another day slipped away from her. Her head dropped. She couldn't fight back. Merrick was wrong about her. She couldn't offer real opposition to this woman. It wasn't a fair fight.

She wished she had done so many things differently. Wished she hadn't left Liam behind. Wished she had worked harder—and sooner —to befriend the other mages in this place. Maybe this would've turned out differently.

Then she heard a scuffle behind her. Suddenly, a larger body hurtled toward Bronwyn, knocking the woman off-balance and breaking her concentration. Em's head lifted. Sam?

The drain on her energy broke off. Bronwyn was shouting.

Flinging Sam off as if he were a wayward leaf, then spinning toward the rest of the group.

Oh, no you don't, Em thought. With a sliver of remaining strength, Em took a breath, held it, then let it out. And as she did, she tapped on Bronwyn's defenses. A stone wall, very similar to the fortress they occupied. Em took another breath, and as she let it out, she tapped on a stone block. Surprisingly, it moved. It didn't fall. Not yet. But Em found the woman's defenses remarkably permeable. Why?

Bronwyn flinched and turned away from Sam's prone body, back toward Em. But Em took another breath, held it, and let it out. And she pushed the stone block, revealing a hole in Bronwyn's defenses. Bronwyn tried to fight back, but it was too late. Em was already in.

She reached inside, exploring. Similar to the attacker in the market, Bronwyn's energy stores were apparent, a spiky ball of lightning. But Em also saw quite a few that didn't belong to Bronwyn. Other energies. A radiating glowing orb that felt foreign to Bronwyn's mind.

Em took it back. Not in slurps and tugs, like she had with the attacker. A single touch was enough to send the energy flying to her, almost as if it knew where it belonged. Days of vitality slammed back into her, and her heartbeat thundered in her ears. What was she doing on the floor? She stood as soon as she had the thought. Bronwyn had fallen back into her stone chair, still trying to fight off Em's attack with her mind, looking frightened.

Why was this so easy? Bronwyn was legendary, and Em had merely poked at her. A geranium put up more of a fight. She continued to prod, locating other energies within the lady mage. A strong, steady light bumped back to Cal. A bouncing glow flew back to Silas. Phoebe's luminous bundle. One by one, she flung them away from Bronwyn and back to where they belonged. But where was Cora's? Sam's energies were flickering—irregular—but glimmering. As she flung them over to him, she saw his prone form take a labored breath and she felt relief.

In the moment she took her eyes off Bronwyn, her concentration lapsed. The lady mage screamed in a frenzy of rage, and Em felt something burning and biting in her gut. Twisting, she looked down to see a bloody dagger sliding from her. Bronwyn reared back for another thrust when Elias caught the woman's wrist and wrenched the weapon away.

Em stumbled backward, holding her hand to the gaping hole in her side. Bronwyn had stabbed her. Bronwyn had—there was a lot of blood. So much blood. And great deities, it hurt. She started to shake again. Elias was pulling Bronwyn away, but Em could barely focus on that.

"Cora," she rasped.

"Here," the girl replied, stepping forward as Em slumped to the floor.

"My map. Take me to Brookerby. Find Gramalia. Get warfern."

Cora said nothing, and Em wondered if the normally unflappable girl was in shock. Otto took charge. "Cal, it's in my pack, hurry. Phoebe, rip that and tie it around, we need to slow the bleeding. Silas, check on Sam." He continued to issue commands, but his words faded as Em stared at the vaulted ceiling. How had they constructed those high ceilings? She felt cold. Where had her cloak gone? Mendel would be put out if she lost his cloak. The world was fading in and out. She willed herself to stay conscious. She breathed in. Held it. Breathed out. They were moving her somewhere. Oh, right. They couldn't use the map inside.

"Where is the exit?" she wheezed.

Someone shushed her. "Almost there. Hang on."

The world was spinning, all the colors and voices streaking around her. Then the world went dark.

CHAPTER 40

*E*m drifted awake, trying to remember where she was, and when.

Stars, her stomach hurt.

She glanced down. It was a gray winter day, and pale sunlight streamed through her bedroom window. Under the blue-and-green quilt Gram had made, she was wearing her least favorite pajamas. She felt thick bandages around her middle.

She was in her room. But how?

Oh. Cora. The map. Bronwyn.

She must've survived. They must've found Gram.

If Gram had used warfern—a healing herb with miraculous properties—why was her middle still sore and throbbing? The magical herb had offered instant relief before.

She had started to prod the bandages when Gram slipped into the room.

"Em."

At seeing her friend, her guardian, a surge of emotion so strong it threatened to overwhelm replaced her grogginess. Em flung her arms wide and grabbed Gram in a desperate hug. Something twinged painfully around her middle. "I missed you."

Gram stood at an awkward angle as Em hugged her from the bed. "That'll do, Em. Yes, yes. We've been a bit lonely too. But you'll pull your stitches out."

"But what happened? I—"

Gram sat down on the edge of the bed, and prodded Em's bandages. "I could ask you the same thing. Here I am, tending the herbs in the garden, when a whole gaggle of Northerners run up with a blood-drenched you draped across them. Luckily, the warfern was blooming. It works well, but you lost a lot of blood. You've been sleeping. You might be sore and a bit anemic for a few days. Pretty impressive belly scar too." Gram tilted her head. "Who did it?"

"Bronwyn Featherweight."

"Be serious."

Em laughed, regretting it instantly as her stomach wrenched in pain. "I wish I was joking."

Gram's smile was gone. "You're telling me that whole story. When you're up to it."

"Are we okay? We never really patched things up, and then I just left . . . "

"I know. But it's okay. Poor Liam, though."

Em felt a knot in her stomach, unrelated to her wound. Liam. She would have to face him.

"Can I get up? I need to get to Gillamor before the solstice. Gram, I found it. I can—"

Gram was pursing her lips.

"What?"

"Solstice is today."

"I need to go, then. That's my deadline. The empress wants—"

"You barely survived death. The empress can wait."

After all that, she'd nearly missed it. "She won't accept it late."

Gram patted her hand. "Give it a few hours. Eat. Rest. You can take it tonight."

This soothed Em a bit, but she was still ready to jump into her clothes and leave again. "Where is the ring?"

"Drawer in your bedside table. You were wearing it when you

came in. I didn't mess with it, except to take it off. Didn't know if your wounds were some kind of backlash. It could be drawing energy from you too."

Em reached for the table. "It saved my life. Multiple times. I'll have to show you."

She clutched at it, but Gram held up a hand.

"Show it to me later. Before you go to Gillamor. You have a roomful of people out there eager to see if you're all right."

"The Northerners?"

"And a few townies. Word got around. Liam too."

Em gingerly rolled out of bed, feeling the painful twinge in her middle as she did. She started to reach again for the drawer with the ring—but one stern look from Gram was enough to stop her. "Later," she agreed, leaving the drawer alone. Gram left her room, and she carefully changed into the nearest blouse and trousers that had been flung on her bedroom floor the night before she left. Months ago.

She exited her bedroom and took in the scene before anyone noticed her. Silas, Cora, Cal, and Sam lounged on the sofa and over-stuffed cushions by the hearth, whispering.

Ilna and Mendel sat at the kitchen table, eyeing the Northerners with some amusement. Liam stood beside them, watching Sam Monterey with fury.

Bob was the first to see her. He charged toward her, wagging his tail and jumping up to greet her. At this outburst, the others' heads swiveled toward her. She bent down to scratch Bob's ears, and he licked her face, tail whipping back and forth.

Wiping off the slobber, she was next greeted by a pair of arms, Liam's, encircling her. He folded her into a hug, and she felt every bit of his relief, but also something in reserve. Nothing obvious, but there was a stiffness in his shoulders that she could sense.

When she pulled back to study Liam's face, her calm slipped. He was still angry. The tension in his eyebrows gave it away. She lowered her gaze and stepped away, feeling wretched. Then, glancing around, she offered a small wave to Mendel and Ilna, who were observing her interaction with Liam intently. But she couldn't deal with this. Not with everyone watching.

She turned her focus on the others. It was a strange juxtaposition to see the Northerners in her home. They were eyeing her and Liam without subtlety and then glancing toward Sam. Sam was flipping through one of Gram's books and had looked up when Em entered. They were out of context—all of them—in this place. And yet, seeing them felt more comforting than if they had gone. Despite the blatant curiosity about her love life.

"Has everyone met?"

Sam looked at Liam with a smirk, and Em gave Sam a subtle shake of her head. He grinned and bobbed his shoulders. Just stirring the pot.

They all muttered that they had met, but the atmosphere was awkward.

Em looked at Cora. "Thank you." Then said the same to each of them in turn, landing finally on Sam. He had thrown his withered body at Brownyn. Such a stupid thing to do, but without him . . . "I would have died."

He looked back steadily, and understanding bounced between them.

Then she noticed who was not there. "Where's Otto? And Phoebe and Elias?"

Silas spoke. "Phoebe and Elias stayed at the Silver Nightingale. Elias is watching Bronwyn. Keeping her confined."

Cora spoke. "Otto went home. After we brought you here."

Em felt a surge of confusion. She knew he longed for the wealth back in his home, but hadn't his behavior in Fugea, in the Silver Nightingale, indicated he'd thrown his lot in with all of them? Wasn't it Otto who took charge? Who got her home in time to save her life? On the other hand, he could tell his father how Bronwyn stabbed another initiate, and surely the man would relent. It was a good excuse to get back to luxury and safety.

Em desperately wanted to talk to them all. Find out what happened in the moments leading up to her battle with Bronwyn, but not with everyone standing around like this. Not with Liam's disapproval floating over her like a rain cloud and darting at Sam across the room.

"How about a walk into town? I think I need some fresh air."

Liam quickly volunteered to walk with her. Mendel and Ilna also got the hint and stood to leave, saying their goodbyes to Gram. The Northern folks were staying at the cottage, so Em could return and chat with them alone.

As she passed Sam, she muttered, "Back soon," and he nodded his understanding.

"AND THE SOLDIERS JUST ATTACKED? With no provocation?" Ilna was shocked as Em quickly caught her friends up on the events of the past few months. It was chilly in Brookerby, and the bare trees blew gently in the winter morning air. But it was practically balmy after the climate of the North. Liam maintained his stony silence as they walked toward town.

"None at all, that I saw at least. They're struggling to survive, what with the attacks, and the cold." At this she turned to Mendel, holding up her cloak. "Thank you again for this. It kept me from freezing up there."

Mendel smiled. "I'm delighted to hear it. Although I might have to construct another. I cannot allow you to traverse the countryside in rags, after all." He pointed to a large bloody spot on the middle back that she hadn't noticed before. It was near where she had been wounded.

"I'm so sorry, Mendel!" Em said, truly saddened that her cloak was ruined.

"Yes, dear. Have a care not to bleed all over the next one. In fact, try not to get stabbed at all." He winked at her. Deities, she had missed him and his weird sense of humor.

They chatted about the Northerners until they crossed the footbridge near the clearing. The conversation turned stormy when Ilna broached the topic of Sam.

"We're just concerned, dear. It was only a few months ago that he—"

Liam jumped in for the first time. "He's a monster. And now you're saying he's earned your trust? Em, you can't be—"

"Stop." Em held up her hands. "Sam has changed. The North changed him for the better. We're friends. In fact, I would be dead if it weren't for him. I don't want to hear anything else about it."

Liam stopped as if stunned, and Em regretted her harsh tone. He dropped his gaze to Bob, who was happily circling Em's leg over and over. "Seems I missed a lot."

In the uncomfortable silence that followed, Mendel took Ilna's elbow. "Shall I escort you back to the print shop, my friend? We're glad you are all right, Emaline. We've missed you."

They walked toward the *Brookerby Leaflet*, and once they were out of earshot, Em met Liam's gaze. "Say whatever it is you're wanting to say."

"I'm so happy you're back. That you're safe and not dead. I missed you."

"But?"

"You left me. You lied to me, and when I came to meet you that morning I found *this*." He produced the note Em had left for him. A pitifully short, messy letter just saying she had already gone. The paper looked worn, and the creases were deep, as if he had folded and unfolded it many times.

"Liam—" Em began.

"There is nothing you can say that makes this okay," he said, voice raised. "I don't know if you just didn't want me around. If you don't trust me. If you don't think I'd be useful. What was it? Because if it's any of those, we don't have a way forward together."

Em was silent. It was none of those. She felt her eyes tear up, but didn't look away as he continued to rant. They stood in the clearing, in nearly the exact spot where the warding tree had stood. And again, everything was falling apart.

"You didn't come back. Even though, with the map, you could've at any time. You didn't even send me a letter to tell me you're safe. And then you return two months later, nearly dead, with a whole entourage of Northern mages in tow, plus *Sam Monterey* for some deity-forsaken reason. And I learn you've involved yourself in another cause—a military scuffle, no less—that defies the empress. I'm not even sure I know you well enough to understand that move."

A tear escaped, trickling down Em's right cheek. But she allowed him to get it all out. She deserved this. She had hurt him and hadn't tried to make it right, until now.

Bob sat next to Liam, leaning against his leg in an attempt to comfort his human.

Em let out a slow breath, little clouds forming in the chilly air. She was trying to formulate the words that would fix this, when something occurred to her. "Were you ever stationed in the North? When you were a soldier?"

He tilted his head. "Did you not hear what I said? Em, I'm trying to understand why—"

"I know. Just please answer."

He huffed in frustration, ran a hand through his hair, and then shook his head. "No. I was never sent up there. It was considered a punishment. For soldiers who didn't follow protocol or couldn't control their impulses. It's less disciplined up there, and I'm told the climate is difficult."

This relieved Em. It also explained why Jeralt was in Fugea—less disciplined, indeed. Liam was never one of those invading monsters who destroyed homes and cut off fingers of dissidents. *But he could've been,* she thought. And she would have to square that idea with what she knew of the man standing in front of her.

She realized Liam was still waiting for her excuse, or an explanation, or an apology. And she couldn't offer him anything. Nothing that would dispel all the charges left at her feet.

Em scrubbed the tears off her chin with the back of her hand. "I missed you. I'm sorry I . . ." She stopped. Her apology sounded ridiculous to her. She tried again. "It was wrong for me to leave without talking to you. I know that you deserve better. That you've wasted a lot of time waiting for me to try and figure out how to do all of this without screwing up. I never wanted to hurt you. You mean the world to me, and if you forgive me, I will never again leave without telling you in person."

Liam opened his mouth, then closed it again. He clearly hadn't expected this. She hadn't promised not to leave him behind. And he didn't like that at all.

Em offered him the out, stifling a sob as she did. "I understand if this is not what you want for your life. There are many lovely women out there who would make a better partner than me. I release you from any obligation to me, if you realize you've made a mistake."

"Em." Liam took a step back. She saw tears in the corner of his eyes that mirrored her own, and felt how much her actions and the words she had tossed at him just now had wounded him. Again.

"I'm sorry," she said. And she meant it. She had done this. Not him. But she didn't take back anything else she had said. She wasn't going to suddenly make all the right decisions, no matter how hard she tried. And he hadn't contradicted her when she said he could find a better partner. She supposed it was better they know this now.

They stood now in the clearing, both unsure what to say, a heaviness in the air between them.

"You still have to deliver the ring?" he asked, finally. She nodded, and he continued. "I'll be here when you get back. We'll talk then?"

He gave her hand a final squeeze, whistled for Bob, and turned toward his bakery.

Em watched him go, feeling her heart shatter, but knowing she had spoken true.

CHAPTER 41

We are pleased to announce that Em Strider has returned from her long journey, and has been seen walking around Brookerby with that special someone. Not naming any names, but perhaps his cinnamon bread will improve to previous standards now that our favorite fix-it is back.

Brookerby Leaflet, 12th lunar month, 806 RQ
The Standard Book of Anything

She arrived back at the cottage sometime later. It took a while to collect herself; she didn't want to return looking like she'd been crying. She took a breath, then burst through the door, cheerily calling out to the group sitting at the table, eating a stew. Gram ducked out, saying she had to drop by the bookstore, but Em knew her friend was giving them a chance to talk freely.

She slid into an empty chair between Cal and Sam and reached for her bowl.

"Tell me everything," she said without preamble. "What happened the rest of the night in Fugea?"

Silas shared how he and Sam cleared out the marketplace just as the soldiers reached the ice wall. They could hear them trying to climb it, then trying to break it down.

"It held!" Silas crowed. "We should build one around every Northern town. Just brilliant."

Em grinned at his enthusiasm and turned to Cal.

"I helped Cora and Otto. Lined up groups in a chain, so they could jump from one town to the next without coming back to Fugea."

In typical Cal fashion, he understated how much time that probably saved, and how many people he had helped. Em nodded her gratitude. "Cora, everything go okay for you?"

Cora nodded stiffly. "Everyone seemed grateful."

Em glanced down at the table, tracing a familiar knothole with her finger. "I'm sorry I wasn't there the whole time. I was clearing out houses when Bronwyn found me."

Silas's eyebrows shot up. "And you're still here?"

Em lifted her eyes to his, expecting a joke, but he looked deathly serious. She nodded. "I was very lucky. She dropped me in the middle of nowhere, and it took some time to find my way back to the Silver Nightingale."

"You didn't miss much," Sam offered. "After all the people had been evacuated, soldiers were streaming into Fugea from the south gate and burning buildings. Bronwyn caught up to us and opened a gateport."

"She drained us all," Silas said. "One by one over the next two days. We were resting when she ordered us back to the Gathering Room. I suppose that's when you showed up."

"You all seem okay now." Em glanced at all of them. Cora still seemed a bit out of sorts, but the others looked healthy.

"Don't you remember?" Silas offered. "You sent our energies back to us."

Em remembered the balls of energy she'd sent bouncing around the room. "That actually worked?"

Cal shrugged. "We're fine now."

"Gram let us sleep here, for a few days. It was really nice of her," Silas offered.

"Why did you come back to the Silver Nightingale?" Cora asked.

"I needed my map. I have to be in Gillamor by tonight," Em admitted.

Sam's eyes caught hers, worried. "Will you make it?"

"I have to," she answered.

AFTER LUNCH, Cal helped Em with dishes. Cora and Silas were clearing the table when Sam tugged on Em's sleeve and gestured for the door. "We need to talk," he whispered.

Em followed him out of the cottage, and they started up the hill on the small dirt trail. A northern wind whipped her hair about, and she wished she had grabbed her cloak. This had better be important. Halfway up the hill, he leaped off the path and pulled her behind a large fir tree.

"What?" Em barked, feeling her recently healed wound twinge in protest.

"Something isn't quite right. I'm not sure we can talk in front of the others." His eyes darted back toward the cottage, as if expecting someone to come looking for them.

"They saved my life. I can't trust them?"

"I don't know. Something's weird." Sam leaned his back against the tree and started speaking in a low voice. "Obviously it made sense for Phoebe and Elias to stay behind. But after Elias grabbed Bronwyn, the fight just went out of her. He shuffled her away, and she followed him as meek as a lamb."

"Odd."

"I thought so too. But I didn't think too much about it because I was barely conscious and you were bleeding out on the floor. Phoebe couldn't heal you. Something about that dagger wasn't normal. When we brought you here, Cora tried to take the ring from your finger—maybe she thought it was doing something to you? I grabbed your hand to cover the ring, to stop her. Then, as the old lady was working on you, stitching you up and applying those herbs, Cora and Otto left the cottage. A short time later, Cora came back alone. She said Otto decided to go home, and she took him there with the map."

"Yeah, why did he leave?"

"Here's the thing . . . Cora didn't seem upset. But since they'd gotten close over the past week or two, I thought . . ."

Em finished his sentence. "She would be more affected." She sat on a nearby boulder, trying to process. "Did they break up?"

Sam shook his head. "I don't know. She's been really quiet. Respectful. Only speaks when spoken to. But I caught her a few times trying to sneak into your room. At night, when she thought we were all sleeping."

"That doesn't seem like her. Was she the last one drained? Or maybe they did break up."

"Speaking of which, your boyfriend doesn't seem to like that I'm here."

Em sighed. "Can you blame him? Last time he saw you, you had blasted me out a second-story window and tortured my relatives."

"That was months ago. He should be over it now. Maybe he's jealous."

Em rolled her eyes. "Of what?"

"Our friendship. You saved me. I saved you. That kind of connection doesn't just happen anywhere."

He spoke seriously, but Em saw the twinkle in his eye. He was stirring the pot again. She wrinkled her nose at him and swatted his arm. "Stop. Liam was mad about something else. It wasn't just you. But you should probably lie low while you're here. Take a bodyguard if you leave the cottage."

He shrugged. "By the way, what happened in Fugea? What did Bronwyn do to you?"

Em closed her eyes, not eager to relive the ordeal. "She yelled. Hit me. Then stranded me. She gate-ported me to the middle of nowhere. She tried to drain me, but I kept my defenses up long enough that she got frustrated and just left. It was so cold, and I was drained anyway because . . . well I figured out where I was because I could see mountains, and I was able to make it to a town."

The last part was a bit of a fabrication. But Em really didn't want to have to explain the additional ring abilities. Of watching herself die over and over again. Of selecting the one single course of action that kept her alive. Not now, right before she had to hand it over to the empress. Because she knew if he knew, he would talk her out of it.

Sam let out a low whistle. "So you're luckily to be alive. Again. But you bested Bronwyn in a battle of minds? That's impressive."

"That's the other weird thing. It was really tough that night. I fought and fought, and finally she gave up. In the Silver Nightingale, I broke right in. It was really easy. She wasn't even trying to keep me out. It didn't feel like the same person."

He looked puzzled, and Em lowered her gaze to her hands. Chapped and cracking from weeks of cold. She was almost done with this whole ordeal. But everything felt wrong, somehow. Like she had missed something important.

"Em—" The warning note in his voice caused her to jerk her head up in alarm. She looked at him for two seconds before she realized what he had already figured out.

She cursed. "It wasn't the same person." And then they were sprinting back to the cottage, praying it wasn't too late.

CAL, and Silas huddled around the hearth, looking at a large diagram of a sailboat with great interest, when Em and Sam burst in.

"Where is she?" Em demanded.

They swiveled to the noisy arrivals with annoyance. "Who?"

"Br—Cora. Where is she?" Em was shaking.

Everything looked fine. Maybe Sam was mistaken.

"Cora? I don't know. She walked to town. Maybe shortly after you two left."

Em cursed, over and over, as she ran to her bedroom. Her bureau was ransacked, and her bedside table drawer was open and empty.

The ring was gone.

She stood in the doorway to her room, feeling her world being torn into pieces.

Em turned to Sam. "She saw the ring. She must've known what it was."

"But it wasn't that powerful. Why go through the trouble?" Sam said.

"What ring?" Silas asked from his chair.

Em slid down the doorframe. She was wheezing. She couldn't get air. Maybe she was dying.

Sam crouched beside her. "Breathe, Em. It's going to be okay."

"I can't," she coughed.

Cal was beside her. "What can you smell right now?"

What was he asking her? Em looked at him with confusion. "Stew? The vinegar Gram uses for cleaning. The fireplace."

"Good. What can you hear?"

Em listened. "Crackling fire. Wind. My heartbeat. Uhhh . . ."

"What can you feel right now?"

"The floor. My clothes. The bandages on my stomach. My stitches. Cold." What was this? She felt her pulse slowing.

"What can you see?"

She huffed. "Lots of stuff. What does this have to do with . . ." She pointed at her ransacked room.

"Breaks the cycle. You were panicking," Cal said simply. Em stilled, then looked at him with a new level of appreciation. His personality was a locked vault, but the glimmers that shone through were truly impressive.

But stopping her panic didn't fix the problem. It was the solstice. If she didn't show up at the Golden Lark Palace by the end of the day, she would be condemned to die. And Cora could be anywhere with the ring by now.

"Did she take the map?" Em asked, feeling defeated.

Sam reached in his pocket and produced it. "Otto gave it to me after we came here. I demanded it after Cora ferried him home." He handed it to Em, who quickly tucked it in her pocket. It was strange, but she felt more whole with it there.

"Something wrong with Cora?" Silas asked cautiously. They had all moved to Em's bedroom doorway.

Sam sat beside Em and looked at the rest. "You know how she's been acting strange? The thing with Otto. And now disappearing with Em's ring? What if it wasn't actually Cora?"

Silas's eyes widened. "Seriously? You think—"

"Yeah. We think," Sam said.

Cal's mouth was a thin line. "Cora is Bronwyn?"

Sam nodded. "The Bronwyn back at the Silver Nightingale was easy to defeat. And she behaved so strangely here . . . Bronwyn may have switched appearances with Cora. Put the real Cora under some kind of compulsion enchantment."

Silas slapped his forehead. "She *was* different. I thought it was just because she'd been drained. Otto knew. He tried to say something the other night, but then he went home instead."

"I hope Otto is okay," Sam said darkly.

"And now she's gone. With the ring," Em said, leaning her head back against the doorframe. "Although, why? She doesn't know what it does. I don't think."

"She might," Sam offered. "She seemed to recognize it."

Gram burst through the door at that moment. "Em? Ilna just told me—" She spotted them all sitting on the floor near Em's room. Then she saw the ransacked room, and her tone grew quiet. "Ilna said your friend—Corrie? Cora? She was asking Ilna about the empress. About the summons. Ilna spilled the beans about your solstice deadline. She felt guilty about it, but assumed you trusted her . . ."

"It wasn't Cora. We think Bronwyn was in disguise."

"Bronwyn. And she took the ring?" Gram's voice was low and dangerous.

Em nodded. "I don't think she knew how to use it."

"Doesn't matter," Gram growled. "It was a chance to get an audience with the empress. Under the guise of your deadline, Em. She would be very interested in that."

Em hadn't considered that. Bronwyn wouldn't slink back to her fortress. She wanted revenge and power. If she could show up looking like Em Strider, the empress would let her walk right into the Golden Lark Palace. She didn't need the ring to imagine what would happen next.

"We need to get to Gillamor."

CHAPTER 42

The most powerful mage in written memory was teacher Emaline
Magnomium. She mastered all three branches of magic, making her an
unstoppable force. Then she taught all she knew to her three little birds, her
nickname for her students.

"Powerful Mages from the Age of Magic"
The Standard Book of Anything

The Solstice

The five of them—Em, Sam, Cal, Silas, and Gram—spun into Gillamor a short time later, appearing in the green space near the temple. Gram had insisted on coming along, despite Em's protests. Bronwyn was dangerous, and Em didn't want Gram drained or hurt. But Gram would not be denied, and Em finally relented after extracting Gram's promise to run if they had to confront the lady mage.

As soon as they all regained their equilibrium, Em was issuing orders.

"Sam, do you remember where my parents' warehouse is? Can you go find Anne and Farrigan? Tell them what's happening and see if they can help."

Sam held up a finger. "Slight problem. They hate me."

Em took off her bag—the bag of holding—and gave it to Sam after pocketing the fast-travel map. It was nearly empty except for a few tools and *The Standard Book of Anything.* "They'll know this is from me. Hopefully they don't hold a grudge." Sam nodded and trotted away toward the waterfront.

Em continued. "Let's head toward the Golden Lark. If we can beat Bronwyn to the gates, we have a chance to warn Her Majesty."

Gram, Silas, and Cal followed her through the congested streets of town. It was winter solstice, in the late afternoon, and—despite the chill—the roads were full of vendors and buskers and merrymakers. It reminded Em of when she was here before, for the harvest festival. The town was a constant party, and her Northern companions were gaping at the colors and lights that surrounded them.

Em felt a calming within her. It would be okay. They would get ahead of Bronwyn, the empress would accept her story, Bronwyn would show up with the ring, and the empress would arrest her. For real, this time.

She felt Gram's hand squeeze her arm as they twisted through the crowd. "It's going to be fine," the older woman said.

"I know," she said. She was glad Gram had come. Despite the danger, there was something safe about having the woman by her side.

She spied one of the buskers sweet talking two young women who were giggling at his words. Em recognized the fortune teller from several months ago. He was still at it. She wondered if she should tell him how accurate his predictions turned out. Although, even when the man had predicted a poor ending, Em had survived. Liam had calmed her down after the certain death prognosis; he had danced with her, and she had started to fall in love with him at that moment.

The Golden Lark Palace was closed to visitors for the festival, but its gilded outer wall was already lit with torches ahead of the setting sun.

Em approached the main gate, which was open but guarded. "Sir, I must see Her Royal Majesty immediately. She is expecting me."

"Her Imperial Highness is not—" the man started but broke off when he saw her face. "Say, do you have a twin? I just admitted a lady—"

Em's mind raced. Someone who looked just like her. It could be Anne Strider, and somehow Sam had gotten her parents here already. Or Bronwyn had already arrived, and disguised herself as Em to gain admittance. Em's mind was furiously trying to recalibrate. Which was more likely? If they went inside now, would she worsen whatever situation Bronwyn had crafted? On the other hand, the empress might be in grave danger.

Cal and Silas hung back; they were wary of the imperial soldier, but Gram stepped forward. "The woman who looks like her"—she gestured at Em—"is dangerous. The empress needs help."

But the man scoffed, unimpressed. "There are many guards protecting Her Majesty. She is quite safe in these walls."

"Please," Em pleaded. "I really do have an appointment with Her Majesty. Em Strider. I was supposed to retrieve something for her by today. Just let her know I'm here."

The guard looked annoyed, but he went through the iron portcullis, waved over a passing advisor, and began furiously whispering. The man glanced their way, sniffed, then gave a curt response. The guard returned. "Her Majesty is not to be bothered this evening. Come back tomorrow."

The others backed away from the gate. To plan another way in? To re-strategize? But there wasn't time. Bronwyn could be attacking the empress at this very moment. Em wanted to just shove past the guard. But she had been in the Golden Lark before. She would never make it through the massive hallways and multiple doors if she tried to force her way in. So she tried something different.

She poked at his mind. First, gently, then more firmly. His eyes widened, and he started to call for help, but Em had already made it through the gelatinous wall protecting his mind.

She didn't take his energy. Instead, she infused him with the simple thought, *The empress is in danger. I must help these people save her.* She repeated this to him a few times, infusing a bit of her energy with the thought. Then she retreated, leaving her infusion to work.

"I know this isn't regulation," the man began, and Gram turned to him in surprise, "but if the empress is in peril . . ." His eyes were unfocused and confused. Then they sharped once more as he waved them through. "Follow me." He turned on his heel and led them toward the palace.

Silas looked at Em, wide-eyed and terrified. "Did you just . . . ?"

"Shh. We're in, aren't we?"

Gram muttered, "We're in. But mage training may have corrupted you."

"Let's just save the empress and get this whole mess over with," Em snapped back. She didn't need lessons on morality just now. After all, she didn't scramble the man's mind or take control of it. She only nudged a bit.

They traveled down the ornate corridors, pushing through several sets of heavy wooden doors toward the round throne room. Their footsteps echoed, and Em wondered if many of the palace workers had already left for the festival. Cal and Silas tried not to look awed, but Em knew they had never seen such a grand building before. Gram, on the other hand, walked as if she owned the palace.

At several points, a guard looked ready to challenge the group, but Em would use Farrigan's distraction magic to cause something to fall, or a door to bang, and the guard would scurry off in the direction of the noise.

They arrived at the throne room doors, where half a dozen guards stood at attention outside of the room.

"The empress, is she alone with the visitor?" the gate guard inquired of the nearest guard, a stout woman with deep scars on her hands.

"Yes, sir. She asked that we vacate for a few moments. She wished to discuss something confidential with the girl." It was then that the door guard caught sight of Em. "I thought you were inside?" she said, confused.

"An imposter," Em said. "We need to go in." She didn't wait for permission. Instead, she pushed her way into the round room.

The empress stood unattended in front of her stone throne, white hair braided into a crown and peacock-blue robes drifting around her frame. The setting sun through the skylight cast an orange glow on the sovereign as she moved to the center of the room. Shadows fell at the perimeter, behind the columns that circled the room. Em stood in the shadows trying to understand what was before her.

There, on the wooden floor mural, stood Bronwyn, disguised as Em, holding up the silver ring for the empress's inspection as the sovereign approached her. The illusion was so complete that Em was unnerved at seeing herself standing in the room.

Bronwyn's other hand, hidden behind her back, clutched a wicked-looking dagger.

CHAPTER 43

The sparrow is a symbol of the common people. What they lack in flash, they make up for in cleverness and adaptability. They are highly social birds and fiercely protect their kin.

"Esnanian Birdwatching"
The Standard Book of Anything

"Stop!" Em shouted, stepping toward the middle of the room and the light of the setting sun.

The empress froze a few steps from Bronwyn, her eyes narrowing at the sight of two Ems. "What is the meaning of this?"

The gate guard rushed forward and knelt. "Begging your pardon for the intrusion, Your Imperial Highness. But we believe you might be in great danger. As it is, I have allowed this group to come in and—"

In an instant, Bronwyn had transformed back to herself. Her purple dress billowed around her, hair wild like a lioness. In one swift movement, she brought her dagger across the man's throat, spilling thick, dark blood across the wooden lark that decorated the floor.

Em cried out in horror, and Gram pulled her back a step or two so they pressed against the wall. The guard's body fell to the floor, and Em felt the weight of his death instantly on her. If she had not forced herself into his mind . . .

The empress, normally an unflappable woman, was shaking. With anger or fear, Em could not tell, but her voice was all bluster and outrage when she spoke.

"Bronwyn Featherweight, how dare you come here? Guards!"

The empress did not sound surprised that Bronwyn was alive. Em had no time to ponder this as she swiveled her head to the throne room doors. But the doors did not open. The empress called again, and Bronwyn began to laugh.

"You were always an arrogant little lark, Regina. Did you believe I would come here without a plan? Without precautions? That after fifty years, I would rush in here without carefully watching all possible outcomes?"

Em let out a breath. Bronwyn's hand was toying with the ring, visible on her slender, polished fingers. Bronwyn turned her focus to Em.

"Oh yes," she breathed. "I watched it all. What a gift. And you—fool—left it in a drawer."

Silas was near the doors. The walls were shimmery, and when he pounded and shouted, it wasn't on the doors, but on the translucent barrier. Em had a feeling the guards couldn't push their way in, even if they could hear the empress calling for them. Bronwyn held out her necklace. The oval, shimmery one that she had used back in the Silver Nightingale that cast a large impenetrable soap bubble around all of them. They were trapped until she lifted the dome.

A trickle of the dead guard's blood was flowing across the floor, inching closer and closer to Em. The nightingale and the sparrow in the floor mural were now staring at a river of blood that had drowned the lark and was probably staining the wood. Em was immobile. If Bronwyn had truly watched every outcome in the ring, then she knew what they would do next. Escape or fight back, it didn't matter. Bronwyn had won.

Gram stepped forward. "Enough of this nonsense. You two have been at odds for too long, and now you intend—what—to rip the world apart?"

Em gasped, wanting to pull Gram back. She was outmatched against these two powerful women. But strangely, neither the empress nor the lady mage seemed surprised to see the diminutive Gram in their midst.

"What compromise can be had, Gramalia?" the empress shrieked. "She has always sought power. Even when we were young."

We? Em looked at Gram in shock. Had she known the empress? And Bronwyn? "Young?" she asked.

"Yes, honey, but that isn't important right now."

"Like hell it isn't! You three . . ." She lost her question as she glanced between them. They were all about the same age, but how would they have even met?

Bronwyn spoke with a sneer. "We trained together under Emaline Magnomium. Her three "little birds." As if we were on the same level. Gramalia was the charity student. Regina was a no-talent hack who received special treatment because of her family."

"No talent?" The empress practically growled in anger.

"The only reason you were there is because you Clavonions want to claim the magical right to rule as well as the hereditary one. We weren't fooled. You could barely infuse at all."

Gram held up a hand. "Water under the bridge, ladies. Surely there is a resolution that doesn't involve transfers of power and murder— this poor fellow notwithstanding." She gestured respectfully to the dead guard on the floor.

"Emaline Magnomium?" Em asked, her head still swimming.

"Your great-grandmother. The most powerful mage in recent history," Regina said. "Don't pretend you don't know. A trained descendant of Emaline would be so formidable as to threaten the stability of the empire. We all know this; you can drop the act."

"We've been living quiet lives. She knows nothing. She is not trained." Gram spoke this like a mantra.

"Like hell she isn't. You sent THIS"—Bronwyn gestured at Em—"to my doorstep, without any warning, under a false name. What else was that but a declaration of war?"

"I sent her," the empress said. "The ring was somewhere in the North. And so were you. I hoped her presence would smoke you out of your rat hole, finally. Or else you'd kill her once you learned who she was. Either was fine by me."

"Well, that backfired spectacularly, didn't it?" Bronwyn snarked.

Em's jaw dropped. All this time, they knew each other. Knew something about her. They had used her. Made her into a pawn. The empress had sent her on an impossible quest, just to rile Bronwyn. It was too much. She was so out of her depth here, and Gram —she glanced at the woman who had raised her—had protected her. Or tried to, anyway. But also, she had kept her in the dark about something very important. Gram met her gaze and mouthed, "Later."

"I'll admit, I was planning to conquer as a Northern queen. Rebel forces have endured harassment for years. I finally had those backward tribals convinced to invade and steal the empire. I've been training mages for years, collecting energy, building coalitions . . ." The last word was uttered with disgust. "But when the most powerful item in our lore—the object our teacher desired most—appeared before me, I realized it was more tantalizing, more immediate, to simply take my throne now."

"You can't win," Gram said. "Even if you kill us, there are guards just outside. And your mages won't follow you after this."

"Ah, but they will." Bronwyn turned her gaze to Cal and Silas. "A demonstration." She snapped her fingers. Suddenly, Cal's hand was around Em's upper arm, and not gently.

"What are—" She stopped, because he showed no sign that he heard her. Something wasn't right. Cal still looked like himself, but his gaze was fixed on the opposite wall as he squeezed ever tighter on Em's bicep.

"Unhand me, you lout!" The empress was also being manhandled by a vacant Silas.

"What have you done to them?" Em demanded.

"Special project, granddaughter of Emaline," Bronwyn replied, lazily holding her hand with the ring to the light. "I collected energy—prestiger and compulsion magic is quite costly—but I also infused some guaranteed loyalty. Quite clever of me. It took years, but most of the North is under my command, should I wish it."

Em felt a growing horror at the declaration. Bronwyn had altered them? Every person from whom she stole energy? All the Northern mages. Merrick. Her friends from the Silver Nightingale. Sam.

At this, she began to struggle anew. She had sent Sam to her parents. Had he turned puppet when the lady mage snapped? Anne and Farrigan could hold their own, of course, but what if they had turned their backs? Or what if they killed Sam?

Cal held firm, and Em was furiously thinking of how to escape without hurting him.

"Enough," Gram shouted. She squared off with Bronwyn. "Since you cannot be content with the North, we need to settle this."

"You forget," Bronwyn said with wry smile, "I've seen all of this. I've already won."

To the victor, the crown, Em thought bitterly.

"And you forget who I am." Gram's gaze was steely.

"What? A little sparrow from the countryside? The lucky woman who gets to protect an untrained child? And that child's untrained child, and so forth? You may have been the best of us nearly sixty years ago, but you've been baking pies in a hovel for the past fifty."

In response, Gram flicked her fingers, and a mighty wind swirled within the dome. It tore at their clothes, knocked Em to the ground, and pulled Cal with her. It was magnificent, and strange, and terrible. Em pried open her eyes against the swirling maelstrom and saw Gram standing like a goddess in the middle of it. Her white hair swirled about her, and her eyes blazed. With another flick of her hand, the wind tore the oval pendant from Bronwyn's neck and the ring from Bronwyn's finger. Both spun to the floor. As the wind died down,

Bronwyn was prone. The necklace had smashed, bits stuck in the river of blood that seeped across the floor. The bubble was gone, and the ring was flung somewhere in the throne room. The empress laughed a cruel, hacking laugh. "Not so powerful without your little trinket, are you?"

Bronwyn growled and flicked her own fingers, now bloody from the floor. The room warped and swirled around Em, as if they had boarded a rickety boat that was also melting in front of them. Em was disoriented and immediately woozy. The empress staggered backward, hitting her head on a stone column as she dropped. Silas also fell, and his eyes held a touch of confusion. Cal had lost his grip on her as he tumbled on his side, and Em fell to her knees. She crawled out of reach, hoping she could open the side door and call for help.

Gram had lost her footing, and one of her knees crashed to the floor. She steadied and pushed back up, never taking her eyes off Bronwyn. The throne room solidified, and Bronwyn was now stalking toward Gram with fury.

"Talent and smarts were nothing, Gramalia. Despite your gold stars and your talent, you were never destined to be on top. No ambition. And we all knew it."

Gram gave her a pitying look. "It doesn't have to be this way, Wynn."

"I deserve this. Me! By magical right. Not that thief girl. Not that spoiled princess over there." She gestured to the empress's prone, unmoving form. "Mistress Emaline never liked me. She suppressed my gifts. Tried to shame me for being formidable. But she was afraid. Threatened. I know that now. And I will be more powerful than she ever was. The second Age of Magic begins now."

With a flourish, Bronwyn pulled the bloody knife from a hidden pocket of her cloak and crossed to the unconscious empress. Em realized a second too late what she was trying to do and darted forward. "No!"

But suddenly, there was a wall of air between Bronwyn and the empress. The mage whirled on Gram, angry, but Gram's eyes were shut and her forehead furrowed. Bronwyn halted, bloody dagger in hand, staring back at Gram with fear, then determination. Em knew that look. They were battling. Attacking the other's mind. What if Bronwyn altered Gram's mind? Em reached out, mentally prodding, hoping to help. She felt a firm shove backward. Was that Gram? Gram was pushing her away!

"I can help," she rasped, desperate to be of some use.

But no reply came. Neither Gram nor Bronwyn gave any indication that they'd heard.

Suddenly, a shockwave of power radiated out from Gram, so strong that it warped the air around them. Em felt the wave hit her. Then the world went dark.

CHAPTER 44

*H*er back ached. That was the first conscious thought that entered Em's brain. She groaned. Her head was pounding too. She tried to roll over and catch a few more minutes of sleep. But the wound on her side panged in protest. That hurt. Where did that come from?

Then her eyes flew open. Bronwyn had done that. Bronwyn with an evil-looking dagger.

Her next breath she was calling for Gram. Was she okay?

Gram, with the wind of her own making swirling around her. Gram, somehow holding off Bronwyn Featherweight. Gram, with powers and secrets that she'd kept hidden in Brookerby. Why?

She wasn't here. The only thing that was here was a bucket in the corner that smelled foul. It was dim. Where was she?

Iron bars. She sat up, and realized she'd been sleeping on a wooden plank. This had to be a prison cell. Was she still in Gillamor?

What happened after she had passed out? Had the empress regained consciousness? Was Bronwyn in another cell? She jumped up and instantly regretted the quick movement, paying for it with a sharp pain between her eyebrows. Had she hit her head?

She moved to the bars. Was she the only one down here? What time was it?

"You're awake?" A grating voice from the shadows.

"Where am I?"

"Dungeon. Golden Lark Palace."

Em still couldn't see the man. But he had a malicious glee in his tone, and she heard a clanking as he spoke. Playing with the keys to her cell?

"Rumors among the guards say you made an attempt on the empress's life."

"Is everyone okay? Is anyone . . . ?" Em couldn't finish the sentence. Her mind flashed back to the moments before she blacked out. The unmoving empress. Bronwyn with a dagger.

"There was a woman on the floor. Died of a nasty head wound. But Her Majesty seemed just fine. A little out of sorts. Said you had done it." The man spat on the floor and then moved away, keys clinking.

Em backed into the corner of her cell, cradling her head. She remembered what had happened. The empress was unconscious. Bronwyn was approaching, and Gram intervened. She sent out this massive wave of power. Maybe the empress was okay, and Gram had killed Bronwyn.

"The dead woman. What did she look like?"

"You don't know who you killed, witch? Some peasant woman."

Oh, deities. Gram?

"Where was the body?"

"Where you left her. By the throne. In a heap."

Em took a breath. Let it out. That was the spot where the empress had fallen. Em had watched her fall. Hit her head. The empress was dead, then? And nobody knew it yet because Bronwyn was a prestiger.

Her thoughts battled her pounding headache for dominance. If Bronwyn was now pretending to be the ruler, she had indeed won. Em had no love for the empress, but she hadn't deserved to die like that. Meanwhile, what horrors would Bronwyn inflict on Esnania? More warding trees of protection with horrible consequences? Or some sinister form of mind control? Or worse, had she recovered the ring? Deities. Where was Gram?

The guard grunted at her silence. "Yeah. Let what you've done sink in. Executioner comes at dawn." He stood with a labored grunt, and then his footsteps receded as he disappeared down the cellblock row.

Em listened to him go. She had no intention of dying at dawn. If anyone else was alive, would they be down here? Cal or Silas? Gram?

"Hello?" she called out.

No response. She listened for any other noise. Snoring. Breathing. Nothing.

She inspected the lock on her cell door. It was warded. She reached into her pocket for the fast-travel map and found nothing. She cursed. They must've emptied her pockets while she was out. Looking around for something, anything, she saw only the filthy bucket and some crumbling masonry in the corner. She could chip her way out, but could she do it before dawn? What time was it now? Maybe she could infuse the bucket handle to dig faster? She approached the bucket and, trying not to gag from the stench and the previous occupant's leavings, started to untwist the handle from the vessel.

A popping noise echoed behind her, and she swirled toward the cell door.

Anne and Farrigan, dressed for a party, approached the bars.

"Thought we trained you better than this," Farrigan teased. "Couldn't pick the lock?"

At the sight of her parents, unharmed and standing outside her cell, she felt all the tension leave her body and she slumped to the floor, a small sob escaping her. "You're here. You're okay."

"That scoundrel, Sam Monterey, showed up earlier," Anne said. "We had him warded and tied six different ways when he finally squeaked out that you might be in trouble. Then we saw the bag of holding." Anne gestured to the bag, now dangling from her shoulder. The crossbody tote did not match her sparkling evening dress.

"Sorry it took so long," Farrigan offered. "Lots of chaos out in front of the palace."

Anne produced a watch chain from the bag that she looped around one of the cell bars and yanked. It cleaved the iron in two. "We heard the rumors. Someone tried to kill the empress." Anne paused at her cutting. "You?"

"No!" Em was offended she had to ask. Then she watched as Anne ripped through another iron bar. "I thought the door was warded?"

Anne shrugged. "Usually only the lock." She eyed Em kindly. "Sam said something about Bronwyn Featherweight."

Em let out a long sigh. "Bronwyn was training mages in the North. I found the ring at her palace. She followed me home. Attempted a coup." Then she said nothing as Anne continued cutting bars, crouching down in her sparkling evening gown. Somehow the whole experience felt imaginary. Had Gram really summoned wind and bested Bronwyn? Had Bronwyn stabbed Em and then followed her back to Brookerby? Or was it all just a Gram adventure story that bubbled in her exhausted brain?

Farrigan was riffling through the table by the guard station, pocketing papers and keys. "Still want this?" He held up the fast-travel map. Em nodded and reached for the paper through the bars. "You couldn't use it inside the cells anyway. We tried that once. The wards limit teleportation."

Once there was a hole in the door large enough for Em to crawl through, they helped her out of the cell.

"Thank you. About the ring . . ."

"Sam said you found it!" Anne cheered. "I knew you would. I'm so proud of you!"

"Um, actually, Bronwyn might have that. It was on the throne room floor. She's probably found it by now."

Anne's expression shifted to dismay. "What does it do?"

"It shows the future. As many iterations as are possible."

Anne cursed softly. "Then we need to get you out of here. You can tell us the whole story once we're safe."

Farrigan spoke up. "Not that it matters now, but the empress has wanted the ring for the entirety of her reign. We greased some palms and discovered that she's been asking for it regularly. But all of her advisors assured her it was a myth."

Em shook her head. "She sent me on a wild goose chase, hoping I would die." Saying it out loud seemed absurd, but the sovereign had admitted it. Because of her great-grandmother? Why hadn't Gram warned her?

But she had. Not directly, but in many subtle ways.

Deities, Em was exhausted.

The row of cells was empty. No other prisoners. Em moved down and back to check. No Gram. No Silas or Cal. Farrigan wound his pocket watch, and Em and her mother held his arms as they transported away from the Golden Lark prison with a pop.

THEY REAPPEARED on the darkened streets of inner Gillamor, half a block from Hallson Manor. Now that she was out of immediate danger, Em's mind was free to run in multiple directions. She was still trying to sort out what she had witnessed. The empress was dead? Or Gram was? Or both? Bronwyn was masquerading as the empress. Bronwyn had an army of mages poised to become mindless killers at her command. And now, the woman had the power of the empire at her command. The ring was missing, Em hoped. If Bronwyn had the ring, she had truly won. And she had no idea where Gram was. Where Silas and Cal were.

"Em. Want us to come in?" Anne's question was soft, but it startled Em. They were standing in front of the blue door of Hallson Manor.

"Why here?"

"Seems to be the happening place," Farrigan joked. The window above the door was dark. No one was awake, and Em glared at him, uncomprehending.

Anne rolled her eyes. "Honestly, Farr." Then to Em, "Sam said he'd be here. Since he came to find us, I assumed you'd established a meeting place? Also, we saw some Northern gentlemen carrying an unconscious Gramalia outside the Golden Lark. We brought them here too."

At this, Em's heart leapt. Gram was here. She turned and hammered on the carved wood until she saw interior light flick on. Marcellus came to the entryway, opening it a crack, until he saw her and swung the door wider.

"Miss Strider."

"Please. Are they here?"

He nodded grimly. "Come in."

"Can my parents come too?"

Marcellus glanced at Anne and Farrigan, eyebrows lifted at their evening wear, and then waved them forward.

Sam was sleeping in one of the new chairs in the parlor. Em started toward him when she heard footsteps on the stairs. She whirled and saw Cass in a simple robe with her hair down, drifting halfway down the main staircase. "Em! Thank goodness."

Em's thudding heart refused to soften. "Cass! I'm so sorry. I don't even know what time it is. But—is Gram here?"

Cass nodded somberly. "Follow me."

Em charged up the stairs in Cass's wake, trailing her to one of the guest rooms.

"We didn't know what to do. Two Northerners brought her." She cracked the door open, and Em saw Gram lying on top of the bedcovers; someone had draped a blanket over her. "She hasn't woken up."

Em gazed at her friend. The woman who had raised her. Ordinary, sassy Gram. She looked as she always did, but Em could never see her the same way. Not after the throne room. She turned anxiously to Cass. "But she's breathing? She's alive?"

"Seems to be. Marce knew her—had met her when he was in Brookerby this fall—so we assumed something had happened to you also. Your friend Sam came earlier today . . ." She trailed off when she noticed Em wasn't responding, only watching Gram with a steely determination. "What happened?"

Em turned, pulling the door shut behind her. "Not here. Let's go back to the parlor. I don't have time to explain this more than once."

They tromped back to the parlor, where Marcellus was making awkward small talk with Anne and Farrigan. Sam was stirring in his chair, and he shuddered when he saw Em's parents. Em crossed and placed a hand on his shoulder.

He blinked, saw Em, and was instantly alert. "What happened?"

"Was it Cal and Silas who dropped off Gram?" she demanded.

"Yeah. They were pretty shaken up. They said they had to get away, so they couldn't be used against us. Tried to get me to come too. What does that even mean? What happened?"

Em looked at them all, hardly knowing what to say. Sam stood and reached for her hand. She squeezed his, trying to convey all the emotions of the past day. Em saw Marcellus's eyebrow lift, and she dropped Sam's hand quickly. Then she took a breath and related as much as she remembered about the throne room encounter. No one interrupted. When she shared Gram's relationship to Bronwyn and the empress—or at least what she knew of it—Farrigan leaned in and Anne's jaw dropped. When Bronwyn snapped her fingers to control Cal and Silas, Sam muttered a curse. When she got to the end, the empress's unmoving form on the floor and Gram's wave of power, she paused.

"I think the wave knocked us all out. Gram is . . . as you see. Bronwyn must've awakened sooner and spun the tale for the guards. When I woke, I was in a cell, imprisoned for attempted murder of the empress."

"But why would the guards listen to her?" Cass asked.

"She is a prestiger. Bronwyn now sits on the throne of Esnania," Em said softly. "Wearing the face of our empress."

Marcellus let out a low whistle. "What can we do?"

Em shrugged. She was out of answers, and she had no ring to steer her away from the wrong moves. And yet, they were all looking to her.

"Anyone connected to me might be in danger, so I need to leave. Me and Gram."

"I'm coming," Sam said. "I don't want her using me."

Em didn't expect this, but nodded. Marcellus and Cass exchanged a look, then Cass asked again, "What can we do?"

"I'm not sure. Try to spread the word quietly that an imposter sits on the throne. Maybe leave Gillamor? I don't know. Bronwyn might also have a ring that shows her the future, so try to stay off her radar. If she uses it against you, she will win."

Cass nodded solemnly and gripped her husband's hand. Em had a flashback to their ceremony. Traveling through life together. Her heart ached that their beautiful journey had just become much darker.

"What can we do?" Farrigan's voice was uncharacteristically soft.

"Do you have anything in that warehouse that can dethrone a tyrant?" Sam asked.

Anne shook her head.

"Then you'd better lie low," Em advised. "Stay out of her way. If she hears the name 'Strider,' she will try to kill you."

Anne and Farrigan exchanged a glance. Em nodded to Sam, and they rose once more, tromping up to Gram's bedroom. The others trailed behind. At the bedroom door, she gestured to the sleeping form. "Sam, can you lift her?" He scooped up Gram and the blanket, cradling her in his arms. Gram's white hair trailed down, and she still slept.

She turned to the two couples. "Thank you. All of you. I owe you."

Marcellus shook his head. "You owe us nothing."

Anne held out the bag of holding. "You'll need this."

Em took it with a sad smile, giving her mother a quick hug, then moved to Gram's side and pulled out the fast-travel map. She grasped one of Gram's cold limp hands, trying not to think about the enormity of what was next. Then she double-tapped Brookerby on the map.

CHAPTER 45

Compulsion and other infusions on living beings are impossible to remove. A famed example might be the so-named unbreakable oaths. Many a mage has tried to rid the living of infusions, with nasty consequences. If a magic user were to discover a method, it would be as miraculous as repairing broken magic around Esnania. But both these things have never been done.

"Limitations of Modern Magecraft"
The Standard Book of Anything

They spun into Brookerby's clearing in the middle of the night. Gram still hadn't awakened. As they walked to the cottage, Em offered Sam another out.

"You could go back to the North, you know. Warn people. Try to figure out how to remove the compulsion . . ."

But he was shaking his head. "You are the only one who figured out how to remove something like that. The oaths. I'll take my chances with you."

"But that was by accident! I can't promise you—"

"Just try. Promise to try."

She nodded. "I'll try. But not now. We need to pack and leave. As soon as Bronwyn realizes I'm not sitting in a cell waiting to be executed, she's going to gate-port some soldiers here. I would bet on it." Bronwyn had been to Brookerby. She knew how to find Em and all of her dearest friends.

They arrived home, and Sam set Gram gently on her bed. Em opened the bag of holding and started shoving clothes, keepsakes, books, anything that meant something to her or Gram into the bottomless bag. She emptied Gram's bureau of clothes, not knowing what Gram would want to take. Any food in the cupboard, Em packed.

She needed to warn Ilna and Mendel. It was the middle of the night, but she didn't want to leave them unprepared for what was to come. And Liam. She'd promised never to leave without telling Liam to his face.

Sam hadn't spoken much, and Em knew his inner thoughts were screaming just as loud as hers. She gently pushed him toward the sofa. "Try to sleep an hour or two. I'm going to warn some people, then I'll be back."

"Don't leave without me." It was a plea, not a demand.

"I wouldn't dare." Em offered a small smile. After this assurance, he closed his eyes, and she slipped out the door.

ILNA AND MENDEL FIRST. In turn, she knocked on each of their doors and quickly explained the events of the evening. Mendel immediately agreed that they must leave. But Ilna argued. "You can just hide in the tunnels until this whole thing blows over! It will be fine, I'm sure."

Em gently explained that if Bronwyn possessed the Clavonion ring, she would find the tunnels with no trouble. "We need to get somewhere beyond her reach."

Ilna had offered to print Em's firsthand account of the empress's death and Bronwyn's coup, but Em had begged off. It would only put the town, and especially Ilna, in more danger. She couldn't risk them.

After warm hugs and promises to stay safe, Em walked in the early morning hours toward the bakery. It would be dawn soon. She paused as she walked by the clearing. Em felt a pang of sadness for the magnificent tree that had been there. The warding tree had been Bronwyn's creation. And Em had gotten around that, hadn't she? And the empress's unbreakable oaths? Surely she could remove a loyalty infusion. But to remove a dangerous woman from her throne? She was not clever enough for that.

She continued walking the short distance from the clearing to the bakery. She had promised not to leave without telling him. To his face. And she was dreading every moment of it.

The lights were on. Liam was already up, baking. A friendly bell tinkled as she entered. Bob was still sleeping soundly in his basket. Liam emerged from the back, carrying a tray of croissants. When he saw her, he quickly set down the tray and lunged for her, wrapping her in a hug.

"When I didn't hear from you, I feared the worst. Did the empress absolve you? How is your stomach wound? Do you want anything to eat? You're up early."

"Liam."

Something in her tone made his chatter stop. He was holding a croissant as he spun to her, the warm bread forgotten in his fingers. His face fell. "It's not over? Deities. It isn't over. Just tell me."

"Can we sit?"

He nodded and gestured to their table in the bakery. Then he tossed the croissant back on the tray and wiped his hand on his apron.

Em waited until he had joined her, then she related the events from her ill-fated trip to Gillamor and the Golden Lark Palace. She finished by saying, "The empress is dead. Bronwyn assumed the throne, pretending to be her. Gram won't wake up. I was supposed to be executed this morning. I need to leave."

"What?"

"Please don't make me say all that again. Gram and I are leaving

Brookerby. Bronwyn will keep trying to kill us both, and I don't want anyone to be in danger on our account."

Liam sat back, looking shell-shocked.

"Liam?" Something about her tone brought his attention back.

"I know. You're right. You can't stay."

"I promised to tell you, in person."

"Thanks," he said. "I'm glad you kept your word."

"And?" she prompted, with some dread. Em waited for him to wish her a good journey. To tell her to look him up when she returned. No hard feelings.

"And for the record, I don't want you to become anyone different. You don't need to try and 'deserve me' somehow, because you are already so much better than any woman I could've ever hoped for. I want you to be exactly you."

She hadn't expected this. He was continuing their conversation. From before.

"Everything's different. You don't need to be dragged into this."

He was already shaking his head. "And yet, here we are. My father loved my mother through so many changes. The tree falling. Leaving our home. Going to bed hungry in a squalling firetrap of an apartment in Gillamor. Even when he caught the empress's eye, and she was offering him the world, he stayed with my mother. Not out of obligation, but because he knew she was his and he was hers. No matter what. I want that for me. For us."

Em grasped his hand, unable to speak for a moment. And then she voiced her biggest fear. "What if I've changed too much?"

He shifted in his chair. "You may have. So have I. We'll keep changing. What matters is, do we still want this? I do. But you have to tell me whether you do."

She met his eyes and something deep and broken within her was fused back together. She nodded.

He looked around. "I'm going to miss this place."

Her expression must've been puzzled because he leaned forward and kissed her quickly. "I'm obviously coming with. I can't lose you." Then he rose and flipped the sign in the window to "Closed."

"But—the bakery."

"I can open a new one. Wherever we end up. I can't go months with you gone, possibly in danger, and coming back with a gaggle of good-looking, fit Northern guys. My heart can't take that."

Em let out a surprised laugh. "You're sure? We might be in Zanit or Brildonia for . . . I don't know how long."

"Em Strider, I love you. I want to marry you. And I can't have you believing that I expect you to be a certain way, or we don't work. I can bend. I can meet you halfway. More than halfway. Because you are more important to me than baking bread."

Em felt herself tear up. "That's the most beautiful thing you've ever said to me."

"I know." He grinned. "Now let's get moving, squirrel. I have packing to do."

~

Just as the sun crested the horizon, Em, Liam, and Sam—carrying a still-unconscious Gram—were in the cottage garden, getting ready to leap.

Liam had grumbled a bit at the sight of Sam Monterey, and Sam hadn't done anything to ease the tension. He insisted on carrying Gram, with a side glance at Liam. Some kind of man-challenge that Em had no patience for.

Bob barked and growled at Sam at first, but with a rebuke from Em, he slunk over to Liam's side and stared at the other man warily.

Em pulled out her fast-travel map. It didn't show a great deal of the bordering countries, but she eyed western Zanit, the rightmost place on the map. They would start there. Secure a place to stay. Maybe find temporary work. Learn to get along. Wake Gram. And then, somehow, develop an airtight plan to unseat a dangerous mage who could see the future.

Sam put a hand on her shoulder. Liam put one hand on Bob's collar and another on Em's elbow. Em breathed in. Breathed out. Then double-tapped.

ACKNOWLEDGMENTS

I could not have made this book without Laura Petermann, my earliest and best writing buddy. Despite having a full plate, she unselfishly took the time to untangle plot knots with me, and did an alpha read and full commentary on my story. The Lost Ring of Destiny would be something very different (and less awesome) without her influence. I am so grateful to her.

To my beta readers (in no particular order): Jan Street, Alex Huckaba, John Creager, Bev Huckaba, Becca Lozano—thank you for your thoughtful insights and your time. By the time the draft gets to you, I'm tired and can't see the forest for the trees. Your comments reinvigorate me for edits, and guide my fine-tuning.

To my cover artist, Michael Perry, thank you again for your amazing ideas and your artistic skill. Your cover design is magical, and it is a perfect companion to the design for book 1. Can't wait to see what you do for book 3!

Gratitude to my invaluable editor, Shawna Hampton of Magic Words Editing. Thank you for straightening out my prose, and being so kind and encouraging while you do. Your skill is what really makes my story shine. I'm so grateful that you continue to take me on, and I'm always tickled to find your lol notes in the margins.

Thanks to my family and family-in-law for their support as I continue to do this thing—writing—that I really like to do. Your interest and help has been wonderful, and I'm so grateful for all of you.

Thank you to Jay, my marvelous husband, my graphics exporter, my marketing eye-in-the-sky, my guy-who-can-make-cold-phone-calls-when-I-just-can't, and my occasional audio engineer. He also tolerates my agonizing over minor plot points when we're supposed to be having a nice date night or going to sleep.

Shortly after the publishing of *The Standard Book of Anything*, I realized that I had no idea how to market. Thus began the trial-and-error process of awkwardly approaching bookstores to ask if they'd consider stocking my book. I made some mistakes in those early days —some bookstores I made such a mess of my pitch that I'm still a little scared to go back and try again—but I also discovered a wonderful community of book lovers, book sellers, and other authors who were kind enough to give me free advice, connect me to others, stock my book, host events for me, and click the little heart on my social posts. To the following people and stores, I am eternally grateful: Keegan Prentice, Erin Olivia and her booksellers at Ink & Page Books, Kristin Helling of Parkville Coffee, Halley Vincent of Seven Stories, Bliss Books and Wine, Chase and Madeline at Cardboard Corner Cafe, Basement Books KC, Trailhead Books, Flint Hills Books, and Red Fern Booksellers. In addition, I'm grateful to KC Book Beat for the author community they're creating in the KC Metro Area. I'm also grateful for the many book/author events that have invited me so I can meet my readers face to face.

I'm sure I've missed someone important. But you know who you are. If the list above is any indication, I have not done this alone. My hope with *The Lost Ring of Destiny* is that I continue to connect with book people, who are the best kind of people.

ABOUT THE AUTHOR

Andrea H Rome lives in Overland Park, KS with her husband Jay, and her two cats, Marty and Jacob. When not writing, Andrea enjoys geocaching, reading, escape rooms, and acquiring craft projects faster than she can complete them. On weekdays, she works as a credentialed actuary. She is a member of the Kansas Author's Club, the Jane Austen Society of North America, and KC Book Beat.

There are many amazing books in the world; thank you for taking the time to read this one! If you enjoyed the story, please review it on the platform of your choice, or share it with a friend. Andrea's indie-author budget is small and precludes a massive marketing campaign, so she is eternally grateful for word-of-mouth.

You can find out more about Andrea's upcoming projects and join her email list at AndreaHRome.com. Or follow Andrea on social media for updates and the occasional cat photo.

AI STATEMENT

This book was written and edited by humans. The cover art was created by a human.

Our robot overlords may be rather exciting, and we like to see what they can do. But this author is of the opinion that robots should do menial, repetitive tasks and calculations that humans don't wish to do. Creating art is neither menial nor repetitive. Art is not an equation to be solved.

This book isn't perfectly calibrated to excite your senses or algorithmically aligned to ideal storytelling. It is admittedly flawed. The calculation stalls out from time to time. The right side doesn't always equal the left. Yet, the author is proud of it, because it's hers.